SHANDI MITCHELL

---◆---

UNDER THIS UNBROKEN SKY

Complete and Unabridged

CHARNWOOD
Leicester

First published in Great Britain in 2009 by
Weidenfeld & Nicolson
An imprint of
The Orion Publishing Group Ltd.
London

First Charnwood Edition
published 2010
by arrangement with
The Orion Publishing Group Ltd.
An Hachette UK Company
London

British Library CIP Data

Mitchell, Shandi.
   Under this unbroken sky.
   1. Ukranians- -Canada- -Fiction.
   2. Farm life- -Canada- -Fiction. 3. Large type books.
   I. Title
   813.6–dc22

   ISBN 978-1-44480-391-4

Published by
F. A. Thorpe (Publishing)
Anstey, Leicestershire

Set by Words & Graphics Ltd.
Anstey, Leicestershire
Printed and bound in Great Britain by
T. J. International Ltd., Padstow, Cornwall

This book is printed on acid-free paper

There a black and white photograph of a family: a man, woman, and five children. Scrawled on the back, in tight archaic script, are the words *Willow Creek, Alberta, 1933*. This will be their only photograph together.

They are posed in front of a hand-hewn log granary. The adults are seated on wooden chairs, centred to frame. They are dressed in their church best.

The man, his hair clipped short, wears a white, high-collared, pressed shirt, tightly knotted tie, a dark woollen suit, and broken-in workboots. He looks like a tall man. Large hands rest on his knees. His legs are crossed.

The woman wears a dark, modest knee-length dress and low-heeled shoes with sturdy ankle straps. No stockings. On her lap is a baby, a white blur squirming to escape the woman's strong hold. He is round and fat, in stark contrast to the other thin forms.

Three sisters ordered in ascending age are interspersed between their parents. On the far end stands the eldest boy. He is ramrod straight. Chin up. Though they all wear summer clothes, they are standing in four inches of snow.

They stare straight ahead, their eyes lost in shadows. Expressionless. Arms rigidly pressed against their sides. Holding their breath as the photographer counts: one hundred and one, one hundred and two, one hundred and three . . .

Within three years, this farm will be foreclosed. Two years later, one will die. Two others, of whom there is no photograph, will be murdered.

But this day, in the moment right after the shutter clicks shut, this family takes a deep breath and smiles.

Spring

—⚡—

1938

'We got some!' Ivan pokes his head out the hayloft and holds the bucket up victoriously to his cousin Petro.

A motley clan of barn cats mew and whine as they wrap themselves around Petro's skinny legs. Petro wheezes from the dust and hay. Ivan scrambles down the makeshift ladder with one hand, the bucket clanking at his side. He jumps the last rungs to the ground and with his free hand steadies the chipped crock plate that acts as a lid.

'How many?' Petro inquires, already on his hands and knees brushing aside a clearing in the hay for their loot. The cats crowd in close.

'More than one. It's heavy.' Ivan sets the bucket down and carefully slides the plate aside an inch. The boys peer into the dark crack.

'Do you see any?' Petro asks.

Ivan tilts the bucket and a scurry of claws against metal narrows the cats' eyes and straightens their tails. 'Three.' Ivan bats a cat out of the way and reaches into the bucket. He pulls out a fat mouse by the tail and holds it high above the cats. 'I'll betcha the yellow one gets him. I'll betcha my gopher skull.'

'For what?' Petro is always suspicious of his younger cousin's wagers, since Ivan usually wins.

'Your wool socks.'

Petro ponders the odds carefully. Summer is

coming and he won't need the wool socks. Besides, the heel and toe are worn out. 'Deal.'

An orange tabby pushes in, but a thin black female — its teats hanging to the ground, malnourished from feeding yet another litter — hisses back.

'I bet the black one gets it,' Petro challenges. Ivan drops the flailing mouse into the fray.

For a moment, the mouse stands still. Frozen. The cats hesitate. The mouse blinks. It spins around and races between Ivan's legs for the open field. Cats blur past, followed by the barefoot boys screaming, 'Get him, get him!'

The yellow tomcat reaches the mouse first and leaps. The mouse, sensing the airborne shadow, stops and careens off to the side. The cat lands with a heavy thud, its claws pierce the mouse's tail, ripping off the tip. A matted calico, missing one ear and blind in one eye, jumps with surprise as the mouse scurries under its belly.

The black cat cuts a wide swath and pounces directly on the mouse. Its incisors gnash to crush the neck. 'I win! I win!' Petro screams. The mouse twists and clambers up the cat, shakes itself loose, and hits the ground running, its leg injured. 'It's over here!' hollers Ivan. The boys crash through the stubble.

The yellow tom skids across the muddy ground and slides onto the mouse, trapping it between its paws. The cat flips it into its mouth and crunches once, then drops it to the ground. The cat bats it with its paw. The mouse lies still. The yellow cat growls a warning. The other cats slink back, except for the black one. It crouches on its belly, tail flicking.

'I win,' announces Ivan.

'It's not over till it's dead,' Petro states.

'It's dead,' says Ivan. The boys crouch down low.

'It's still breathing,' asserts Petro.

A heavy black leather boot crashes into the earth in front of them. The boys hear the mouse's bones crush, see blood trickle out from under a man's cracked sole.

Ivan and Petro look up against the noon sun, unable to discern the man's features. Ivan stands and takes a step back to assess his adversary. The man's eyes are sunken, a grizzle of grey whiskers shadow his face. His hair is long and oily. Filthy clothes hang off his skeletal frame.

Ivan runs for the barn, screaming, 'Mama!'

Petro remains frozen where he squats, gasping for air. The man licks his chapped lips and speaks with a voice caked with dust: 'Get up.'

But Petro doesn't get up. He turns to the sound of a .22 being cocked. As does the man. Ivan's five-year-old arms quiver from the weight of the gun: 'Get off our land.'

Maria appears from behind the makeshift shack attached to the cabin. Her hands are raw from scrubbing bedclothes with lye and ice water. She looks to her son, his finger on the trigger. She looks at Petro, gulping for air. She looks to the man. A railway tramp.

'Whad you want?' she asks in broken English. 'We no have nothing.' She repeats it in Ukrainian: 'Nichoho nema.' There's nothing left. The man looks to her and Maria sees his eyes.

9

She sees past the face, past the weathered lines, past the dirt and grime, and into his eyes. 'Teodor?' she asks. But she already knows the answer and starts to shake.

The man walks up to Ivan and takes hold of the barrel, waits for his son to unclench his grip. Teodor slips the rifle from the boy's hands, ejects the bullet, and hands him back the gun.

The metal bucket crashes to its side, shattering the crock plate. A blur of brown vanishes under the barn. The black cat with the swollen teats saunters away with the other mouse clenched between her jaws.

★ ★ ★

Somehow the children have fallen asleep. Maria drapes burlap bags over the ragged twine strung across the middle of the room, separating the sleeping quarters from the remaining few feet of living quarters. As always, she takes a moment to count them in their sleep. Five children snuggled together on one straw mattress. The girls and Ivan sleep curled into one another, while Myron lies lengthwise draped across their feet. At thirteen, he is getting too big to be sleeping with the girls. Five children, Maria counts, almost to assure herself that she hasn't lost one through the day. Their breath is quiet and even. Maria hangs the last burlap sack.

No one spoke all day. They ate their meal of borshch and flatbread in silence. All eyes watched their father. Watched him scrape the bowl with his fingers once the flatbread was gone. Watched him guiltily take a second bowl. Watched him shovel the broth past his cracked lips, unable to slow himself down. Watched him roll a smoke with the stash that Maria had saved for him almost two years earlier. Watched him inhale, eyes closed. Watched him exhale and open his eyes as if surprised to see them staring back at him. Watched him as they went to bed, as he sat outside staring into the night. No one said good night. The children are asleep now, certain that when they wake up the imposter will be gone.

Maria stokes the fire. A large pot of water boils.

★   ★   ★

Outside, Teodor is oblivious to the mosquitoes swarming his head. He exhales another long draw of smoke. He has forgotten to ask what day it is. Six hundred days and nights reduced to scratches on a wall. Four hundred and eighty thousand steps paced in an eight-foot-by-eight-foot cell. Five steps — wall, five steps — wall. One hundred and fifty steps shuffled down the corridor past the closed cell doors. Eyes to the floor. Eyes to the floor. The only sound the click of the guard's boots and the chattering of leg irons.

Shiny Boots's trouser cuffs were frayed at the back. The heels of his boots were rounded, more on the left than the right. Shiny Boots preferred the strap over the lash. He'd spread his feet apart for better stability. He had small feet. Teodor had to shorten his step not to overtake him and breach the mandatory six-foot distance.

Ten steps down the stone stairs. Eighty-five steps across the dirt yard to the iron gate groaning open. Six steps to the outside world. How many days ago was that? One hundred and eighty-six thousand steps. He takes another puff on the cigarette.

'I'm still here,' his voice rasps.

He hasn't seen his sister, Anna, yet. She hasn't come out, even though she's just eight inches away on the other side of the log wall. Teodor saw her watching him as he followed Maria to the shack. At least, he saw the torn slip that serves as her curtain fall back into place. Now he can see light through the chinks, obscured intermittently by movement inside. Maybe it's her children. Maybe it's her. She'll come to him in her own time. Teodor knows that she's ashamed of him, but he can forgive her that. She took his family in. He owes her his life.

It was my grain. The words roll dull and hollow in his head, worn from the constant repetition. Come to the land of wheat. A hundred and sixty acres. Ten dollars is all it will cost. Come, they said. Thirteen days in the steerage of a ship crouched in vomit, piss, and shit with his wife and four children. Come.

A year renting the land, waiting for a homestead entry. Working as a field hand in exchange for the loan of an axe, a saw, a team of horses, and a plow. He signed a contract he couldn't read. They said everything will be fine. You have three years to pay it back. Build a farm, clear the fields, dig a well, plant the seed. Learn English. The second year, lose the crop to hail. They give him more seed, add one dollar to the contract, shake his hand, and call him Ted.

Three weeks before harvest, they come for their money. Eleven dollars. They take it all — the house, the barn, the shed, the lumber, the fields ripe with grain — and say, 'Leave.' It was August. The grain in those fields was worth sixty, seventy dollars.

He took one wagonload of seed. From his field, his sweat, his pay. One wagonload to start again. And they arrest him. *It was my grain.*

The words collapse into dust. He swallows. His tongue licks at parched lips.

Above, a wash of northern lights pulse green and white across the prairie sky. Below, a chorus of frogs croaks. Their song swells across the fields, reverberates in Teodor's chest. Teodor listens, eyes almost shut. He leans against the shack, his smoke burning low between his fingers. He breathes in the space between him and the sky.

The frogs fall silent. The night has paused. Teodor is aware that he is holding his breath. He looks instinctively to the paddock. The scrawny cow chews compulsively on a fence pole, oblivious to the unsettling quiet. Teodor leans forward slightly, rooting his feet to the ground, ears straining, eyes squinting to penetrate the darkness. His muscles coiled, ready to fight or flee. Cautiously, a lone bullfrog picks up his refrain and soon a bevy of females answer.

Teodor breathes deep and flicks his smoke into

the night. Spring has arrived swollen and impregnated by the retreating frost. He can smell her sweet decay. He can almost hear the earth heaving and groaning beneath his feet, opening herself wide to push her seedlings into light.

Teodor crouches down and places his hand against the cool ground. For a moment, he thinks he can feel her heart beating, but realizes it is his own pulse. This surprises him because it means he is still alive. A movement catches his eye.

His sister's side of the cabin is shrouded in darkness. The oil lamps have been blown out. And then Teodor sees Anna standing at the window, a few feet to the left of him. She doesn't see him crouched in the shadows.

She is pale. Her face has lost its roundness. Her flesh clings to her bones. Dark circles heighten the sunken appearance of her eyes. Her hair, which she used to wear in braids coiled on either side, snaked with ribbons, is shorn and matted. She looks much older than the one year that separates them. Teodor remembers her eyes being icy blue. In the old country, boys had written poems about her eyes.

Anna stares straight ahead. Teodor wonders if she is looking for her useless husband. He hasn't seen Stefan since his arrival. But there is something about the closeness of her gaze that convinces him that she isn't looking into the night, or to the paddock, or at the sky. She is staring into her own reflection. Into her own eyes. Teodor wants to stand up and tell her that he is here. But Anna steps away from the window and disappears into the blackness.

14

★ ★ ★

Maria empties another pot of steaming water into the metal tub that serves as both bath and scalding tub for butchering chickens. She has no soap, no towels. She tears another strip of cloth from the remnants of a white linen skirt. Elaborate embroidery still adorns the hem.

She wore this skirt under her everyday skirt the night they escaped. The soldiers didn't take clothes. They took horses, cows, weapons, tools, even the shovels. They tore down holy icons and nailed up posters of Stalin. They took the land and the grain and said, You own nothing. Those who refused to meet the harvest quotas were marched to open pits and shot. After that, the quotas were met. The penalty for concealing even a handful of wheat was death. A bounty was offered. Houses and barns were searched and fields stripped until there was no more grain. Every day she had prayed to the Virgin Mother for Teodor not to fight back. To stay alive.

The soldiers would come, usually four at a time: two on horseback, two in the cart. They had a gramophone that they hand-cranked and Stalin's voice boomed the praises of collectivism. Then they would go door to door until the cart bulged with sacks of wheat. They carried pistols, but the starving don't fight back. Theirs was always the last house searched. Teodor had an arrangement with the soldiers, who had learned long ago that he made the best homebrew.

He was allowed to keep a pound of wheat, but if the liquor's quality ever degraded or the quantity diminished, the arrangement would be terminated. Maria hated Teodor for robbing her babies of even the smallest morsel of food. The soldiers would go through the motions of throwing their few belongings out the door and driving pitchforks into the thatched roof for contraband, while Teodor disappeared into the night and returned with half a jar of amber liquid.

But that night, he came back with a whole jug. They almost shot him on the spot, accused him of withholding grain. He assured them he had saved it up to make this batch. A gift for them. A token of respect for their difficult jobs. The liquid was clearer. He assured them it was purer. They were suspicious. Teodor had to drink first to prove that it wasn't poison. After that, they relaxed. The first drink made them feel like men, the second reminded them that they were powerful, and the fifth made them stupid.

Maria sat on the edge of the bed as Dania, Myron, Sofia, not yet five, and Katya, barely six months old, clung to her in their sleep. She could feel their bony arms; the swell of their bellies. She played over and over in her head what she would pack. And she prayed. She prayed for a miracle. They had to leave. She would not choose which child would eat and which one would die. They should have got out with Anna and Stefan, before Stalin, before it all happened. But then they still had hope. By the eighth drink, the men were unconscious.

They took the three horses and slipped away under the cover of dark. Teodor in the lead with

Sofia, followed by Dania and Myron, and Maria bringing up the rear with Katya. They travelled only at night, following the bush, avoiding the villages and blocked roads. If the horses' ears pricked west, Teodor went east before veering back. In daylight, they slept hidden under leaves and branches. They spoke only in whispers. She told the children it was a game to see how well they could hide. When they ran out of their few spoiled potatoes, they ate grass and berries. When one of the horses lay down, unable to go farther, Teodor whispered in its ear as he slit its throat and then they ate it.

When Maria wanted to stop, Teodor made them keep going. His belief never faltered. They would make it. He didn't allow for any other option. With every step, Maria expected the bay of tracking dogs; with every shadow, someone to betray them; with every bend, soldiers waiting; and with each crack of a snapping twig, a volley of shots. But no one came. She had her miracle. But it wasn't her conviction that had carried them; it was Teodor's. She would have lain down.

Five days later, they were safe in Halychyna, in Lviv. Teodor sold the horses for a few coins. Enough to pay for a forged exit document and third-class rail to the port in Hamburg. They told everyone they met what was happening to their country. People shook their heads and looked away. Some offered them bread.

Teodor found the government people who wanted Ukrainians to come to their country. The Canadian representatives smiled, gave them

17

food, and arranged their passage. One even spoke Ukrainian. The men wrote their names in logbooks and beside Teodor's name wrote *Farmer*.

They didn't want to talk about what was happening in Ukraïna either. They didn't want to hear about Stalin and that there was no drought; that soldiers were cutting down fields and confiscating seed; that people were eating horses until there were no more horses; eating dogs until there were no more dogs; eating rats, because there were always plenty of rats. They didn't want to hear that. They wanted to talk about Canada having the healthiest climate in the world and farms for everyone. They wanted to get them on the boat.

Maria was only to bring practical items but had managed to carry her wedding linen. She used it to bundle their other belongings: two pots and a pan, a few utensils, a goose-down quilt, her mother's hand-woven wool blanket, sewing supplies, tonics, medicine, seeds, two sets of clothes for each child, a hairbrush, six skeins of wool, and the family crucifix and Bible that she had retrieved from under the outhouse floorboards. The only other sentimental item she had smuggled in was a handkerchief filled with the rich, black earth of her homeland.

They were crammed into the lower deck of the ship with two hundred others. They pushed their way to a stack of crates beneath a hatch, which in the days to come would provide their only fresh air. They clung to their heap of possessions. The children — too weak, too overwhelmed — never wandered. She made them eat the foul-tasting stew ladled from the massive kettles into their dinner pails. She held the chamber pot for them to throw up in. She wiped their faces and sponged their bodies with her skirt. She held them up to the hatch until her arms went numb. She told them stories and sang lullabies, coaxing them to sleep, to forget.

When the ship arrived at the pier in Halifax, she had to open the handkerchief at customs. The officers laughed at her pile of dirt, but they let her pass. She carried it on the train across the country, two thousand miles. And when the tracks ended, she carried it on the wagon across the prairies and north into the bush. And when the wagon ran out of trail, she carried it on foot. Even when she had to leave behind clothes and a pot, she didn't put down the handkerchief. When the children were hanging from her waist and wrapped around her neck, she held on to that bundle. And when they finally staggered over the last hill and came to their squat of land, buried in trees and rocks, she fell to her knees, kissed the ground, and mingled her precious soil with this new land.

That was at their old home. Their first home in Canada. It's where they built their house, broke the land. Where Ivan was conceived on a still, warm April night. Teodor had led her to a patch where he had cleared the land of scrub and roots. This was where he would build their cabin. He had marked its frame with logs. He took her hand and guided her through the stick drawing. Here's the kitchen, here's the children's rooms, here's the pantry, here's the stove, here's the windows — see, they look out over the fields. In what was to be their bedroom he had laid out the wedding linen. Blue-white under the full moon. They made love there, immersed in stars. She had never been able to scrub the grass stains from the precious cloth. That was the last place her family had called home.

'Teodor, the water is ready,' Maria calls softly out the door.

The man who walks through the door is old. His body moves stiffly, his shoulders hunched over. His gait is almost a side-to-side shuffle. The feeble light of the kerosene lamp cloaks him in shadows. He seems hesitant to remove his clothes in front of her.

Maria pulls a chair up close to the steaming water. 'Sit,' she urges him, as if he is a small child. Teodor sits heavily on the rickety chair, exhausted by the effort. He leans over and tries to untie the broken string that acts as a shoelace. His fingers fumble with the knot, his hands tremble. Maria kneels down before him. 'Let me help.'

He doesn't protest. He is beyond dignity. He leans back and looks straight ahead, his hands limp in his lap. He looks past her, past the split boards of the wall, beyond the night. He doesn't blink. The binder twine snaps as Maria tugs at the knot. Gently, she loosens the stiff leather that sticks to his bare feet and ankles. Ever so carefully, she slips the workboots off. He doesn't flinch. Maria tries not to gag and refrains from covering her nose. His feet are caked in black. Sores ooze where the oversized leather tongues have rubbed mercilessly, and on the back of his heels the blisters have widened into a raw gash. His overgrown toenails are cracked and split.

Maria doesn't make a sound. She sets each foot, as if it were fine porcelain, on the makeshift towel. She fills a washbasin with the warm water and brings his feet to it. Not until Maria rolls up his ragged cuffs to keep them from getting wet does she gasp. The sound catches in her throat, like a wounded bird, before she swallows it down.

Teodor's bony ankles are a mottle of bruises — green, yellow, and brown. Each one branded by the chafing of iron shackles. Layers of rings, some recently scabbed over, others faded to deadened white scars. The constant wearing of steel on flesh.

Three feet away, one of the children coughs and rolls over in their sleep. As if caught in an act of transgression, Maria pulls the pant cuffs down before realizing what she has done. She looks up to Teodor's face, but he isn't looking at her. His eyes are fixed on the door. In the lamplight, she sees the creases that furrow his forehead and are etched around his eyes. He is listening to a lone coyote. Its plaintive howl echoes across the prairie, climbing higher and higher in pitch before trailing off. In the sustain, the coyote stops and listens. Calling for someone to answer him, someone to find him.

Maria lowers Teodor's feet into the basin.

21

Anna is awake. She hears the coyote calling her. Anna never sleeps at night. Not for the last twenty nights, anyway, not since Stefan came home drunk.

When she first came here, she wasn't afraid of the night. Anna wasn't afraid of anything. She wanted to come to this country. She wanted the adventure, wanted to start her life, build a new world. She was fearless and headstrong. Boys lined up to dance with her. Her father had received five proposals for her hand. But none of them had been good enough for his daughter.

And then along came Stefan. He was an officer, rumoured to be a friend of the tsar. People feared him. He brought presents. Pears and oranges. Once, a silver mirror and hairbrush. Another time, a sapphire necklace. He brought her father vodka, and her mother silk. He was handsome in his uniform; all the girls said so. Anna didn't know that Stefan's job was to chase down traitors and punish them. She didn't know that the silver mirror had come from a house where he had shot the owner in the head. She didn't know that the sapphire necklace was torn from the neck of a girl not much older than herself. She only knew that when Stefan danced with her, everybody watched. And so they married.

She should have known when he passed out at

his own wedding. She should have known when she wiped the vomit from his shirt. She should have known when he tried to kiss her, reeking of alcohol. By the time he threw her onto the bed and held her down, she did know. But by then it was too late.

Another war came, and this time Stefan was the traitor. He survived an assassination attempt, escaping with a bullet lodged in his thigh. He bought his way out of the country with the sapphire necklace. He sold all the spoils of his years in the service, except for the silver mirror and hairbrush. Anna refused to let them go. They were hers, the only things of beauty she still believed were given in love. Stefan loved her long chestnut hair that spiralled in curls to the small of her back. When they were courting, he would run his fingers through her tresses, brush the back of his hand against her cheek and neck, and breathe in its sweet lavender scent. The day after their wedding night, Stefan brushed her hair as he begged forgiveness. Tears streaming down his cheeks, he promised, promised as the brush twisted and pulled at her locks.

Stefan promised her that everything would be different in Canada. They would be treated with the respect and honour they deserved. They would be aristocracy. They would be rich. People would bow to them in the street.

Anna remembers her first night on the prairies. Stefan built a huge fire. He kept the pistol and rifle at his side. He said he was going to keep watch; she knew he was afraid. But Anna loved the darkness and the vastness. It made her feel like she belonged. Something woke her in the middle of the night. She looked to Stefan, who had fallen asleep wrapped tight in a blanket. Even his head was covered. Anna turned to the sound. Short, panting snorts. Feet padding back and forth. Then she saw the eyes, reflected yellow in the firelight.

A young coyote circled the edge of their fire. Head down, nose rising, sucking back their scent. Anna had never seen anything so beautiful, so wild. Slowly, she stood up. The animal retreated a few feet. Anna took another step away from the fire into the darkness. She spoke quietly in a singsong voice. She crouched down. The thin female, its tail between its legs, slouched warily toward her. Anna held out her hand. The animal sniffed the air.

Fingers outstretched, Anna sat still and quiet, her breathing even. She bowed her head and looked sideways into the animal's eyes. The coyote nudged its nose forward, inches from her hand. Anna could feel its hot breath condensing into moisture in the cool night air. She inched her fingers closer. The animal's lip curled, revealing an incisor. Anna stopped and lowered her head more. The coyote leaned forward and touched its cold nose to her warm fingers.

Off in the darkness, another coyote wailed. Startling the night, long and urgent. The female turned to its cry. A shot thundered and the female's side ripped open. Another explosion and the left side of its head erupted in blood and bone, spraying Anna's face. She stumbled to her feet and saw Stefan running toward her screaming, but Anna couldn't hear him. She could only hear the gunshot ricocheting in her head. She could only see the coyote's body convulsing at her feet.

That was the first night.

There were other nights. Night was when Anna braided Lesya's hair. Her baby girl had the same colour hair as she did. The same blue eyes. Lesya was ten now. When Anna looked into Lesya's eyes, she could almost see herself. But when she looked down at the child's thin body, to the deformed foot, she knew the child was nothing like her.

It was night when Lesya was born. Anna had been in labour since the morning, with the midwife chattering unrelentingly through it all. Soothing her, encouraging her, admonishing her to be quiet. Stefan had left the cabin when Anna first started to scream. He didn't return despite her pleas, even though she knew he was just on the other side of the door. When the baby slipped out, the midwife fell silent. She cut the umbilical cord, swaddled the newborn, and left her lying at the foot of the bed. The baby didn't make a sound. The midwife took Anna's hand, and Anna was sure that she was going to tell her the baby was stillborn. But instead she cautiously said, Sometimes babies aren't meant for this world. Sometimes it's better to let them return to God. She said that she could help. The newborn began to wail, its tiny lungs exploding with air, and Anna knew it wanted to live.

As soon as Anna wrapped her arms around the baby, its perfect face relaxed — a beautiful baby girl. Stefan was ushered back in, looking contrite. *Their* baby. She knew that she could love her. Love him. They could start again.

Her heart nearly broke when the child wrapped her tiny hand around Anna's finger. She unwrapped the sheet that was wound too tight around the child, freeing her fragile chest, the heart pounding visibly through the almost translucent skin. She freed the legs from the cloth binding and saw the left foot grotesquely twisted sideways, almost back onto itself. It looked blue, dead. Anna pushed the child away. The infant rolled over and lay splayed in the middle of the bed. Its deformed foot jutting out, pointing at Anna, accusingly.

Hysterical, Anna tried to get up from the bed, blood pouring between her legs. Stefan and the midwife pushed her back down. She tried to beat them away. She bit their arms, clawed at their clothes. They tied her wrists and legs to the bed, forced her to drink Stefan's bitter moonshine. Its heat seared her throat, as she choked on the salt of her own tears. She remembers Stefan stroking her forehead, his breath hot on her cheek, promising her everything would be all right.

When she woke, the baby was beside her, watching her. Not whimpering. Not crying to be fed. Just watching. She never gave her breast to that child. She milked herself like a cow and fed the baby like an orphaned calf. As Lesya got older, she followed her mother everywhere. Trailing a few feet behind. Watching, always watching her. Mimicking her mother's movements. Sometimes Anna wondered if Lesya was

26

mute, too. But the child could talk. She just knew when to keep quiet.

One day, when Lesya was two, Anna was making pyrohy, and as she rolled the dough and cut out the circle shapes, she absently sang the songs she remembered her own mother singing back home. Songs of soldiers going off to war, peasants wooing young girls, hymns for good harvests, songs of mothers teaching their girls to be good wives. When Lesya started to sing, she followed her mother's every note. That night, Anna let the child sit on her lap. She ran the silver brush through the girl's tangled hair and braided it. Stefan came home in high spirits and danced for them. They laughed. That was when the night was good.

Then she had Petro. Stefan was away on one of his trips to town again. Business. A day here and a day there. Returning home with expensive gifts they couldn't afford. Smelling of booze and faint, sweet soap. Anna was in the garden when her water broke. She took a few steps and a contraction forced her to her knees. She tried to stand, but was driven down again. Lesya was only three. She stood watching her mother crawling on all fours, writhing and wailing in pain. Petro was born right there in the August dust. It was Lesya who cleared the dirt from her newborn brother's mouth as Anna tried to crawl away, tethered to the umbilical cord.

It had been seven years since that day, and Anna had managed to protect herself. There were ways: vinegar douches; parsley tea; scalding baths; once, she rode a horse. And then she learned how to protect herself from him. The first time she pulled the knife on Stefan, it wasn't planned. She was chopping beets when he grabbed her from behind. She didn't think, she spun around, knife still in hand, and the blade sliced across his belly. His grimy white shirt split open and a fine red stain flowered outward. It was only a scratch, but Anna didn't drop the knife. She didn't feel remorse. Her hand didn't shake. From then on, Anna kept the knife under her pillow. Stefan stopped reaching for her. Now he spent weeks away from home. He didn't bother to bring back presents anymore or wash the perfume and women's scent from his body. But he left her alone.

Until that night. Twenty nights ago. That night, Anna was dreaming she was a young girl again. She was running toward something golden, something she couldn't see but knew was there, when she was plunged into darkness. Fighting for air, she opened her eyes to find Stefan on top of her. His hand pressed against her mouth, his forearm crushing her chest. His other hand tore back the covers, clawed at her legs, pried apart her knees. Anna groped under the pillow for the knife, knowing it was already gone.

That night, the moon was hidden behind clouds. Anna couldn't see the children, though they lay only a few feet away. Once, when the moon dared to peek out, she thought she saw Lesya's eyes watching her; an instant later they were gone. When he was done, Stefan tried to stroke Anna's hair from her forehead. He whispered how sorry he was, how much he loved her, how much he missed her . . . Anna spat in his face. She didn't cry when he walked out the door. She got up, found the knife, and cut off her long, tangled hair. That was twenty nights ago.

Tonight, as she sits in the dark, she can feel it growing in her belly. She listens to the coyote calling calling calling.

'I'm here,' she whispers back. 'I'm here.'

★   ★   ★

Teodor sleeps for three days and three nights, unaware that on the first day little Katya gathers wildflowers for him and sets them in a canning jar beside the bed. Or that on the second night, Ivan crawls in bed with him and falls asleep nestled against his belly until Maria carries him back to his own bed. He doesn't see Sofia place a spider on his hand and watch it crawl up his arm across his chest until it disappears into the bedding. He doesn't hear Dania, who is pressing his pants with a hot iron, burn her hand. He doesn't know that Myron stops at the bed and stares down at him each morning on his way to chores before turning his back on him. Or that his niece, Lesya, and nephew, Petro, touch his toes at Ivan's goading. Or that Maria's been sleeping in a chair the last two nights because she doesn't want to risk waking him.

The family becomes ghosts. They use sign language, hush one another, and tiptoe in socked feet. They are ever vigilant to catch a log before it crashes to the floor; carry the dishes one at a time so they don't clatter; wave away chattering magpies; stifle laughs and coughs; shoo the cats, moaning in heat, from the doorway. They take their food outside to eat. The smaller children — Ivan, Katya, Lesya, and Petro — head across the field, down the hill to the slough to discuss the stranger in the bed. Myron goes to the barn and oils all the machinery, cleans the tack and harnesses, and sharpens the plow. Sofia goes to school earlier and stays later, telling everyone she has a new English friend named Ruth. Dania scrubs and scrubs her father's filthy pants and mends the shirt he wore home.

Maria rubs balm on Teodor's feet, sponges him, burns sage around his head, covers him with a sheet through the warmth of the day, and pulls the quilt over him in the chill of night. She keeps the fire stoked, burning dead twigs that Ivan and Petro drag home in burlap bags. She takes count of all their stores, itemizes their belongings, sorts them for her trip to town. Once, she drops a spoon. Her fingers claw air, chasing, grabbing for its spinning handle — it lands with a thud. She and Dania stand still, not daring to breathe.

But Teodor doesn't twitch. He can't hear them. He is dreaming deep inside a dark abyss where even he does not exist.

★   ★   ★

When Teodor wakes, the shed is empty. A low fire burns in the stove. He smells soup simmering. Clean clothes are laid out on the chair beside him. Two neatly rolled cigarettes sit atop perfectly folded pants. Tentatively, he sits up. His insides drop, his head seems to float away; for a moment his vision blackens and then the room returns. A table, four mismatched chairs, two benches, an oil lamp, a wood stove, two beds, a curtain of feed bags acting as a divider, a crate with a wash basin, a shaving mirror, two shelves with dry goods, preserves, and dishes, and a framed picture of the Virgin Mary. Four walls confining a space not much larger than his prison cell.

He swings his legs over the edge of the bed, looks down at the feet dangling beneath him. They are scrubbed clean, pale white. The sores are drying up. He wraps the blanket around him. He touches his toes to the cool dirt floor and stands unsteadily. Using the wall for support, he sets one foot ahead of the other. Heel to toe, finding his balance, he opens the door of the shack.

Brilliant light pours in, illuminating sparkling specks of dust drifting in the air. Teodor smells cut grass, sweet alyssum, warm hay, and rotting wood. The sun washes over him. He closes his eyes and raises his face. Pulsing red orbs push through his eyelids. When he opens them again, sun halos are etched into his retinas. They dance between him and the unending fields speckled with tender green shoots. When he looks up into the blueness of sky, the sun halos float among the clouds. And when he looks down, they touch his bare feet before fading away.

The yellow cat lolling on the stoop stretches

on its side and decadently tips its head back to chew on a long blade of sweet grass dangling over its ear. A few feet away flies buzz over the desiccated remains of a mouse.

Teodor puts on the man's clothes. He opens the crisply starched cloth arms and slips his own inside. The shirt smells of lye and wind. He fumbles with the small buttons, fastening them one by one. He buttons the cuffs, which are slightly frayed. He pulls on the pants. The clothes, three sizes too large, hang loose on his thin body. He tightens the belt five extra notches. He looks at the arms, chest, stomach, and legs now clothed. He holds his arms slightly away from his body. His feet a few inches apart. He doesn't want to wrinkle this man.

He goes to the small mirror but doesn't approach directly. He steps sideways, peeking in. The man staring back at him has straggly, salt-and-pepper hair that hangs past his shoulders, a grizzled beard, cracked lips, and sunken grey eyes. He fills the basin with warm water and lathers up the soap. He runs his fingers along the razor blade, hanging from a nail beside the mirror. It is still sharp, untouched. He draws the blade across his neck. Globs of soap and whiskers fall.

It is another man who sits at the table to a white bowl full of beet-red borshch. He sits straight. His hair is short. It has been waxed and carefully combed to the contours of his head. His face is smooth. His sleeves are rolled up to the elbows. He holds a spoon in his right hand. The left hand rests against the side of the bowl.

He fills the spoon and lifts it to his mouth, holds it safely away so as not to stain his shirt. He blows. Brings his lips to its edge. Sips in the steaming broth. He holds it in his mouth, lets it spill against his cheeks. Cups it on his tongue. Vinegar. Beets. Cabbage. Potato. Dill. Pepper. It is the best food he has ever tasted. Teodor swallows and tears leak from his eyes.

★ ★ ★

It is almost supper when Maria returns home. The family enters the house in the order that has become customary over the last three days. Maria gives the children a harsh signal to be quiet and they line up, smallest to biggest, to file into the shack, then move stealthily to their bed on the other side of the room. But this time, when she slowly pushes open the door, she sees a flickering oil lamp and smoke drifting from a cigarette burning low in a man's hand. She sees a bare foot and cuffed pant and Teodor sitting at the table. He looks up and she sees the boy she married. He smiles. And she smiles back.

Ivan, who is first in line, pushes past his mother's skirt and sees the man who used to carry him on his shoulders and toss him in the air and never dropped him.

The three girls see him next. Dania sees how nice the clothes look on her father. How crisp the collar is and how straight the crease in his pants.

Sofia sees a man so handsome he could be a

33

movie star: Clark Gable, a banker, a tycoon — a hero.

Katya sees her daddy's face and remembers how she used to run her hands over his whiskers and he would rub his scratchy cheek against the nape of her neck and she would laugh so hard she thought she would throw up.

Myron sees that his father has shrunk. His shoulders are stooped, his muscles withered. He can't imagine him working in the fields or swinging the pickaxe or moving boulders twice as heavy as himself. He can't imagine this man knocking him to the ground for forgetting to water the horse because if anything happened to the horse then they would all die. Myron knows he can take this man with hardly any effort.

Teodor remains seated. They face one another, waiting. Him inside the room, them frozen in the doorway. It is Ivan who takes the first step forward. This small five-year-old boy, with his tousle of sun-bleached hair, missing tooth, chewed fingernails, walks up to his father and stands bravely before him. He takes the man's face in his hands and brings it close to his own. He stands on tiptoe and squints as he peers into the man's eyes. He looks past the bloodshot white, past the blue and grey flecks, and looks directly into the black centre.

'It's him,' he decrees and throws his arms around his father's neck as he climbs onto his lap and babbles about Petro, and the frog they found, and the cat that died, and the ice storm last year, and going to town, and Mama buying toffee, and still having some in his pocket, and his pants being too short, and the nail he stepped on, and the bird that got in the house, and can they get another dog . . . until Maria tells him hush.

Teodor holds out his hand to Katya, whom Dania gently pushes forward. Katya, now six — all skin and bones, knock-kneed with too-big shoes and hair that sticks out everywhere, who bruises at the slightest touch — trips over her feet and catches herself against Teodor's leg. She looks up at his face, disappointed that she can't see any whiskers. She touches his cheek for confirmation. Smooth. As she contemplates this, she frowns and chews her lower lip. Teodor bites at her hand and she pulls it back, shocked, before bursting into laughter.

He looks to Sofia next, her hair curled in tight ringlets held with a red ribbon. She wears a Sunday blouse the seams of which she has altered to give a better fit. Her skirt is hemmed just below the knee. She looks older than her eleven years. 'You've become a young lady,' he says, which makes Sofia very happy.

Dania, his eldest, lost in an oversized bland dress, her hair braided and coiled, loaded down with packages, stands beside her mother, hoping to be noticed. 'Aren't you going to say hello?' he asks. She sets down her bundle and approaches with her head down. She covers her chapped, lye-burned hands. 'You're all grown up,' and takes her hand even though she tries to pull it away. She breathes in his clean soap smell and notices how her arms now reach completely around him.

Maria places a bundle on the table in front of Teodor. 'This is for you.' She hopes that she hasn't changed that much. That she is still the woman he remembers. No more beautiful, no more common. The woman he wanted to come home to. The children huddle around for the big surprise.

'Open it,' they urge. And Ivan and Katya, who can't bear the suspense, tug on the strings, while Teodor looks at his wife. She is everything that he remembers: the small childhood scar under her left eyebrow, the lines that crinkle when she smiles, her lips — the top one twitches when she's angry, the bottom one pouts if she's sad — her nose that sneezes whenever she smells dillweed, and her eyes. Brown eyes that he would give his life never to see cry again. Teodor unfolds the paper, revealing a brand-new pair of black leather boots with brown shoelaces.

'How?' He breathes, not daring to touch them.

'Mama sold her fancy sheets,' blurts Ivan. Dania cuffs the back of his head.

Teodor stands and his children see that he is still tall. He kisses his wife. Hesitant. Their lips brush. An act of thanks. She wants to hold him and not let go, but instead she looks away. She knows the children are watching with eyes wide, mouths slightly open, imagining what such a kiss must feel like.

'I have to get supper ready.' She brusquely reaches for her apron. 'Go wash up.' She claps her hands together for emphasis. 'Get some wood,' she directs Myron, who is still standing in the doorway. 'Tonight we're having meat.'

Myron splits the few precious blocks of wood they've been saving. He takes one, halves it, quarters it, and tosses it onto the pile. He has enough chopped for several days, but still he lifts the axe high over his head and slams it into the eye of the wood. One clean crack and it cleaves open.

'You have a good swing.'

Myron looks to Teodor and sets another log on the chopping block. He lifts the axe again, stretches to show his father how tall and strong he has become. How he spreads his feet and allows the energy of his muscles to unleash through the handle into the blade like his father taught him and that the hardwood log is the size a man would split.

Teodor goes into the barn. It is cool and musty. The mud chink has dried and separated from the slats. The wind whistles through. It smells of urine, manure, and sweet decaying hay. He lays his hand on the cow's forelock and strokes the bridge of its nose.

'Hello,' he whispers. The cow greets his hand with a long, sandpapery lick. Teodor checks the tack. The bits shine, the leather reins and harnesses are supple, the tools have been oiled and scoured clean. He looks over the plow, runs his thumb along the freshly sharpened blade. The cow absently chews its cud, keeping an eye on Teodor. The stalls have been mucked out. There is fresh water in the buckets. The hay is dry. Rotten boards have been replaced and the walls shored up. There is nothing for him to do here.

Myron listens as his father inspects the barn, expecting his name to be called. He'll put down his axe and join him, maybe share a cigarette, talk about the weather and when the best time to seed might be. If they sit long enough and silent enough, maybe they'll talk about other things. About that night he helped fill the wagon. When he hid in the high stalks because it's what his father told him to do. His father, face down, a boot on the back of his head, his arms behind his back. They called him a thieving, filthy bohunk. Myron will nod and keep his eyes on the dirt floor as he listens. Listens to what can't be said anywhere else except between men.

But Teodor doesn't call his name. He shuts the barn door behind him and heads to the house. His boots squeak with their new stiffness. He nods to Myron as he passes.

'Good.'

★ ★ ★

Papa.

Teodor hears the word from inside a deep darkness. It echoes, then flits away like a whisper or a shadow.

Papa.

A child's voice. Desperate, urgent. Teodor pushes against the blackness. His heart quickens. He can see himself as if watching from a distance. There is nothing above him, nothing below. Just black.

Tato.

This time he understands the word, he feels a small hand around his arm, the fingers squeezed tight, shaking him awake. Teodor opens his eyes. Ivan stands inches from his face.

'I have to pee,' he whispers and dances from foot to foot. Maria lifts her head from her pillow and peers over Teodor. 'Use the pot.'

'I can't find it,' Ivan whines, the pressure building. He doesn't want to wet himself in front of his father. He says the only thing he can 'I have to pee,' knowing that using any more words might squeeze it out of him.

'I'll take him,' Teodor tells Maria. 'Go back to sleep.' He slips out from under the warmth of the feather quilt, his skin involuntarily erupting in goosebumps. The fire is out. His feet retreat from the cold ground. The room is dark, lit only by the moon hiding in corners.

'I gotta go *now*.' Ivan urgently pulls on his hand and Teodor stumbles after him out the door into the crisp spring night. Ivan pulls him toward the back of the house, a quick walk impeded by his knees knocking together as he struggles to keep his thighs pressed tight.

Ordinarily, if it was daylight, Ivan could go to the outhouse by himself. It was only a few hundred feet away at the back of the lot. But nighttime is different. Everything changes in the moon's shadows. Fence poles can be headless bodies. A horse can be a dragon. Bushes can be snakes. In this world that belongs to witches, ghosts, and demons, there are any number of creatures that will eat a small boy. Even the rustling wind can call his name and lure him into the woods, where he will be lost forever.

Ivan tightens his grip on his father's hand and presses closer to his leg. Another hundred feet and they'll be there. He can see the outhouse's faint outline silhouetted by the moon. It leans slightly to one side, tall and narrow, a coffin standing on end. Inside are two holes, a double-seater. Sometimes he and Petro look down the holes, daring each other to find the most disgusting sight. They hold pissing contests for accuracy, duration, and distance. They jump over the holes in death-defying hopscotch. It's easy to be brave when you aren't sitting on the hole.

Ivan hates having to poop. It means having to go alone. The hole is much bigger than he is. He has to lower his pants and back up to the seat, not looking in, then pull himself up, his feet no longer touching the ground, and slide carefully back, while he clings to the side of the wall closest to him, and grips the ledge with his other hand as he strains to hurry it up. Once he slipped, skinning his back, and was forced to grab the ledge of the other hole to pull himself up. As soon as he's finished, he jumps down and backs away from its gaping mouth, and spits once for good measure.

At dusk, it's his older sisters' job to take him to the outhouse for his last business of the day. All is fine if it's Dania; sometimes she even comes in with him and lets him hold on to her arm while she turns her back to give him privacy. But he hates going with Sofia. Once he's inside, she scratches at the walls and whispers his name. Ivan, Ivan . . . she tells him that monsters are going to reach up and grab him and suck him down and he'll never be seen again. He'll be just one more turd in a pile of turds. She cackles and pounds on the walls.

Sometimes she leans against the door as he throws himself desperately against it, kicking and clawing to get out before the night shadows take away all the light. She races away before he can pull his pants up, leaving him to struggle with the latch, until the heavy door swings open and he trips over his pant legs and slams into the ground and Sofia makes fun of him for letting it dangle out.

Ivan abruptly stops a hundred feet from the looming outhouse, unable to go any farther, his hand clutched between his legs. Teodor looks down and sees the fear in his son's eyes. 'We can go here,' he says.

Side by side, father and son aim their penises and stare straight ahead into the night. For a moment, neither can go. Both are too conscious of the other. They stand still listening to the frogs, the hoot of an owl. Both are acutely aware that the moon is much brighter than they first thought. They can see their shadows on the ground. See each other clearly lit, exposed beneath a canopy of stars. They wait.

Finally, Ivan lets go. It is a steady, relentless *pishhhh* that hits the ground and erupts into steam. He exhales deeply, his shoulders drop. And Teodor begins. They pee and pee and pee. It feels good to be breathing the night air, looking up at the stars, relieving themselves, knowing that soon they'll be back in bed. Finally, it slows to a trickle, a few more spurts, a drop, a shake, and done. Teodor slips his penis back in his pants. Ivan tries to imitate his father's action and slips his own in sideways under his nightshirt. 'Back to sleep,' and they head toward the shack walking taller and lighter.

Now that his eyes have adjusted to the night, Ivan can see the house, the fence posts, and the horse shining in the moonlight and is embarrassed that he was ever afraid. A coyote howls. Ivan looks over his shoulder and quickens his pace. The coyote calls again and this time is answered. Three short yelps followed by a long steady wail. The cries ricochet across the prairie seemingly from all directions. Ivan sidles against Teodor.

'They're just hungry for spring,' Teodor reassures him. 'It's probably a male and a female. They don't like people — they'll keep their distance.'

Ivan wants to believe him, but he's seen a carcass torn apart by coyotes. He and Petro found the dog in the middle of winter. Its belly and throat were ripped open, guts yanked out, mouth gaping, glossy eyes staring up at the sky. Red blood on white snow. Mama said the dog had gone into the coyote's territory. But Ivan knew better; the dog was on their side of the property line. It was a lot smaller than a coyote, a mutt, all white with a brown patch over its left eye. It used to spin around and around in circles to get a pat on its chest. Ivan loved that dog, even though he wasn't supposed to love him.

Animals were to be respected. Not mice and gophers and magpies. They were different. They were thieves. But farm animals had a job: to help humans survive, to work in the fields, to be food, to provide clothing, to be bred. But Ivan wasn't sure the animals were only meant to belong to humans. He knew they could think and feel, too. Ivan spent countless hours staring into the eye of their cow, regaling her with stories and questions, looking for a response, a blink, a tear, a flicker of understanding. He knew she was listening by the way she hung her head and nuzzled against him. He could tell whether she was happy, hungry, had an itch, or was lonely. He knew she was afraid when Josyp Petrenko's bull got loose. He knew she was sad when she lost her calf.

That was last spring. The calf's hind feet came out first, which was bad. Mama delivered it. Ivan was supposed to go inside the house, but with Dania running back and forth to the well for water and Myron trying to hold the cow's thrashing head, they forgot about him. Mama had to get the calf out before the umbilical cord broke and it tried to breathe. She wrapped ropes around the scrawny legs and pulled with all her weight. The cow bawled and writhed, slamming Myron against the stall. Its eyes rolled back in its head and the calf slipped out in a rush of blood and mucus. Splayed rigid and blue, its tongue hanging out. Maria hoisted the calf upside down to drain the fluids from its mouth and nose. After a long time, she cut the mangled cord and carried away the bundle in a bloodied burlap bag.

The next morning Ivan found the calf in the dumping ground. That's where everything went that died. Five birch trees grew there, nestled in a tangle of tamarack and spruce. In their shade were the remnants of their lives: broken bottles and plates, a bucket without a bottom, a cracked axe blade, one shoe, a rusted pan, twisted wire, heads of chickens, bones of cats and a dog, and now the calf. He knew it would be there. It was still wrapped in burlap with only its snout poking out.

Ivan stayed with the calf all afternoon. He found whatever objects he thought the calf might like and set them in a circle around it. The top of a blue bottle, a pile of fresh-picked spring grass, a prairie crocus, and a strip of white birchbark. He talked to it, sang it songs, and brushed away the flies. He didn't uncover it. He just wanted it to know that it wasn't alone.

The next day, when he returned to visit the calf, it was gone. He searched a quarter-mile, but all he found was the burlap ripped to shreds. He wanted to believe that the calf had got better and walked away, but even back then his four-year-old heart knew the truth was much darker. That night he stayed with the cow. He looked in her eyes and could see tears deep inside. He stroked her nose and sang her bedtime songs until Maria carried him to bed.

The coyote yips again and Ivan shivers. It's much closer now. Teodor protectively puts his hand on his son's head. 'Come on, let's get

44

inside.' They quicken their pace. They are only thirty feet from the shack when another howl rips through the night. It sounds as though it is directly in front of them. The fine hairs on Ivan's arms bristle. Teodor stops him, his arm across the boy's chest. He mouths the words Don't move. The cry climbs in exquisite pain before collapsing into a guttural groan.

Ivan's teeth chatter. His bare feet no longer feel the cold ground, his toes curl into the dirt. His nightdress clings to his suddenly damp body. Teodor circles around him, facing the night. In the distance, there is an answering call. A twig snaps. Teodor looks to the paddock. The horse is quiet. The night is calm. An owl *who-whos*. Ivan holds his breath.

'Let's go.' Teodor takes long strides as he herds Ivan ahead of him, poised to grab him and lift him above his head if the animal attacks. He wishes he had his .22. He knows it's loaded just inside the door, on the right-hand jamb, one bullet in the chamber. A box of ammo is in his coat pocket, if it's still there after all this time. They just have to get around the corner; it's only a few feet to the door. If he needs the gun, he can push Ivan into the house, grab the rifle, shut the door, and still get a shot off. The only time coyotes attack humans is if they are crazy. Teodor saw a dog go crazy.

It belonged to Old Man Kuryk, who worked the land adjacent to their old homestead. A big, lumbering jet-black dog that would lick you to death begging you to play. One day, Kuryk came by, said the devil had come to his house. The dog was skin and bone and frothing at the mouth. It was throwing itself at the locked granary door with such force the door was shuddering. The animal raged in frenzied bursts, barking hysterically, its claws shearing the wood. Then it would stop. In one of the lulls, Teodor opened the door. The animal lay on its belly, its head pressed to the ground, one leg broken, panting and moaning. It watched Teodor, its tail weakly thumping. It made a low plaintive whine and lunged. It took three bullets to put it down.

Two more steps and they'd be around the corner. Ivan is running now, trying not to trip, as he is pushed along by his father. He hears a sound and looks back expecting to see a coyote charge from the outhouse, its teeth gnashing. He is still looking back when they round the corner and he runs directly into Anna.

His throat constricts to stifle a scream. His arms want to fight, his feet want to run, his heart wants to burst, but his mind recognizes the lady-in-white and paralyzes his body. In that fraction of a second, Teodor yanks him backward, ready to slay whatever demon is ahead.

Anna stands still on the porch. Her white cotton nightgown reaches to her ankles and glows blue in the moon's light. She continues to stare straight ahead for another moment before turning her head toward the man and the boy gaping wide-eyed at her. She looks down at Ivan and then slowly up to Teodor. Her eyes blink as if waking up.

'Anna?' Teodor is shocked by his sister's

thinness, her empty eyes and shorn hair. She gives a small smile, and there is a brief glimmer of recognition.

'They're close tonight. Did you hear them, Teodor?'

'I heard it.' He tries to look past the night. 'Did you see it? Damn thing sounded like it was right here.'

'No, I didn't see them.' And she looks away.

Teodor feels the night's chill, or perhaps he shivers from the wistful tone in Anna's voice, or her deathly stillness. 'You'd better go inside,' he tells her, not knowing what else to say. 'It's not safe.'

Anna laughs a quiet, empty laugh. 'I'm not afraid of the night.' She touches his cheek with ice-cold fingers. 'I'm glad you're finally home. Now I can sleep.' She kisses his cheek and goes inside.

Teodor wonders if he should follow her inside and find out what's happened to her, but he doesn't know the questions and decides to wait until daylight when he can see how things really look.

He remembers Ivan and realizes that he has him in a bear hug, pulled hard against his legs, sheltered in the safety of his body. He eases his hold. 'Okay?'

Ivan nods unconvincingly.

'Let's go back to sleep.'

Far, far off the wild dogs yip and bark. 'You see, they're going away. One of them got lost, but now it's found its family. Everything's all right.'

Ivan wants to laugh and tell his father that he

47

wasn't scared and if that coyote tried to eat him, he'd tear off its head and use its hide for a saddle blanket. But he can't, because a droplet of pee is still dribbling down his leg.

★ ★ ★

Teodor wakes at dawn and gets dressed before even Maria has risen. The room is full of the soft sound of sleep as he shuts the door. The morning air is cool and damp, but the sky is clear. A blush of red announces the imminent arrival of the sun. Already the meadowlarks and sparrows are heralding the coming light. A hundred, maybe even a thousand songs vying to be heard. A hymn of thanks for having survived another day. In this vast land that goes on as far as the eye can see, Teodor is acutely aware that he is the only one witnessing this moment and he is grateful. He heads to the barn, careful to avoid the mud puddles that may sully his polished boots.

Inside he is greeted by the sweet smell of rotting hay and manure. The air is still and warm, filled with the cow's heat. A fresh cow pie steams on the dirt floor. The cow moos. Teodor rubs her forelock and she rubs her head appreciatively against the boards. The barn has always been one of Teodor's favourite retreats.

On the other farm, Teodor sometimes woke before dawn just to grab a few minutes alone to sit in the doorway of the barn to watch the sky slowly brighten. He'd strain to hear the first small birds begin to chirp, long before he could

48

see any light. He'd listen to the mice shuffling through the long grass, racing home with their night hauls. Sometimes he could hear cats slithering close to the edge of buildings. He'd see a flash of their reflective eyes and the cats would freeze, mid-stride, surprised that their invisibility had been compromised. Once, he saw an owl grab a rabbit that had ventured out too early in the morning. Another few minutes and the owl might have been asleep and the rabbit would have been filling its belly. Hunger made it careless.

Back then, Teodor thought that the barn, the house, the furrows in the earth, the wood he cut, the well he dug, the fences he drove, the wheat he sowed . . . he thought they were enough to keep him safe. He didn't know he was the rabbit.

Teodor heads to the tackroom and opens the side door that faces onto the paddock. He whistles sharply through his teeth and the horse's ears prick up. It looks curiously to the barn. Teodor lifts the halter to the sky and whistles again. The horse ambles over. It hesitates a few feet from Teodor and sniffs the air, turns its head slightly sideways so it can see the man with a full eye. Teodor offers his hand and the horse breathes in his scent. Teodor turns in to the barn and the horse follows at his elbow. It goes to the feed trough and snorts softly. It's thinner than Teodor remembers.

Teodor dips his hand in the feedbag and comes up with a meagre offering of poor-quality oats, husk, and dust. The horse nuzzles his hand, its soft nose brushing his palm as it hungrily chomps at the food. Teodor runs his other hand down its neck. The horse is old, but it's strong. Its legs are straight, its chest wide. Teodor takes hold of its fetlock and squeezes softly. The horse lifts its leg. The hoof is neatly clipped and clean. The shoe is in good shape. Teodor pats the horse on the haunches. 'Eat up, old boy, we have work to do.' The horse flicks its tail, revelling in the extra breakfast ration.

The iron plow weighs almost a hundred pounds. Ordinarily, Teodor would grasp the plow under the handles and cradle the support beams that connected the blade, then hoist it up onto the cart. But today, when he tries to lift it in place, he can barely raise it from the ground. He heaves, leans backward, his legs and back straining, and staggers closer to the cart. He manages to hook the front end of the plow. Still supporting its weight on his chest, he inches back to the handles. His arms tremble as he struggles to push it upward and forward. It scrapes ahead a few inches, precariously hooked on the edge of the wagon. It shifts backward.

Teodor struggles to keep his knees from buckling as his arms drop from the weight. He twists his body under the crossbeams and uses his back as a fulcrum. His new boots slide in the straw and dirt as he labours to push it up and in. Sweat beads on his forehead. Wet splotches appear on his clean shirt. His muscles scream. The wooden struts dig into his hands. Another foot to go. He gasps for air, unable to move forward, unable to retreat.

Myron buttons up his coat on the way to the

barn. His untied shoelaces trail after him in the mud. A few minutes ago, he got up to stoke the fire and saw that his father was already gone and that he had missed the dawn. A farmer always gets up at dawn. He refused Maria's admonishments to eat as he rushed out the door. He is combing his hair with his fingers as he enters the barn. He stops short at the sight of his father.

Teodor strains with his entire body; his face racked with pain, he heaves the plow the final few inches onto the cart. His hand pinned under the handle, it scrapes along the wooden slats. He yanks it back and the knuckles are already bleeding. His legs shake as he leans heavily on the side of the box.

Myron steps away from the door and tucks in against the wall. He waits a few moments, uncertain what to do, then quietly retraces his steps back ten feet. He counts another ten and then coughs, loudly, before slowly walking to the barn door. Teodor stands tall and straight, his injured hand hidden in his pocket. Myron lowers his head and stares at his father's boots, the toes now scuffed, bits of straw stick out from the heel caked in horse shit. 'I slept in.'

'You won't again.' Teodor ignores his throbbing hand. 'Harness up the horse, I'll get the pickaxe and shovel.' Teodor walks to the tackroom with slow, measured steps. When he is out of sight of his son, he leans against the wall and fights down the waves of nausea.

Myron slips the wooden collar around the horse's neck. He checks the fit, making sure there will be no chafing. He retrieves the harness from the wall, taking the sixty-pound weight easily onto his shoulder. The horse doesn't shy as the harness slides over his rump onto his back and shoulders. Myron checks and rechecks every strap and buckle. Then he gently inserts the iron bit into the horse's mouth and lifts the bridle over its ears. 'Good boy,' he whispers as he fastens the last straps.

'You can back him up.' Teodor enters as if he hasn't been watching his son's adeptness. 'I'll lift the shafts.' He heads for the cart, hoping his body won't betray him. Myron intercepts him and easily hoists up the long wooden poles, tilting back the cart and plow. Myron whistles softly. 'Back up.' The horse backs himself between the shafts. The boy and horse patiently wait, downplaying their new trick. Teodor nods slightly and hitches up the chains. It is enough of a nod for Myron to lower his head to hide his smile.

The animal seems to have grown a hand taller and has regained the brashness of a young stallion. It snorts and paws the earth, excited that something is about to happen. Teodor tosses the tools in the cart and hops on the front board. He takes the lines from Myron; they are soft and supple in his hands. *Tch-tch-tch*, he clicks his tongue, and the horse steps forward. The wooden wheels groan. The horse lowers its rump, digs in its hindquarters, and pulls. The cart lurches forward. Myron jumps on the back as it rolls out of the barn. 'Haw.' Teodor turns toward the fields. The horse prances as if on parade.

'Wait for me!' Ivan races out of the shack, hugging a gallon jug of water wrapped in sopped burlap. Myron grabs the jug. Ivan chases after the cart, his hand outstretched. 'Me!' he pleads.

Myron turns away.

★ ★ ★

Maria thrusts the shovel into the earth. It slices in smoothly. She turns the soil over, revealing a rich decay of loam, choking with worms. This year she will grow enough food for everyone to have seconds and even thirds. She will plant successively and harvest from early summer through late fall. The wheat will build their house, buy supplies, livestock, machinery, material for clothes, and pay their debt, but this garden will feed her family.

She broke the ground for the vegetable garden the previous spring, sixty feet long by forty feet wide. A portion had been Anna's original garden, but it had been abandoned to choke on weeds. Maria organized her children, and turned the dirt, one spade full at a time. They pulled what rocks and roots they could and planted late, knowing that the soil wasn't ready, knowing the season would be too short, but also knowing that without a harvest they would starve. Maria had vowed that when Teodor returned from prison, his family would be alive and well.

Last fall, no vegetable, however bruised, insect-ridden, or rotten, got discarded. The remains of the meagre crop were composted back into the soil. Twenty wheelbarrows of horse

53

and cow manure were forked into the soil. Six bundles of hay were strewn overtop. This year Maria will have a proper garden.

Seeds she carefully stored the previous fall are brought out from under her bed. An array of glass jars holding dried peas and beans; newspaper packets containing myriad tiny seeds alphabetized from beets to turnips; onions and garlic bulbs packed in wooden crates; potatoes in burlap bags, their blanched tendrils protruding — each is laid ceremoniously on the table. All her riches can be carried in the folds of her apron.

She plants them all. Row upon row, on her hands and knees, she gives each seed to the earth. She brushes the smaller seeds from her palm to her fingertips, carefully spacing them, trying not to lose any to the wind.

Now that school is out until after fall harvest, the children are all free to work. Dania follows behind her mother, brushing the dirt back up and over into supple mounds, gently closing the wound where the seeds are inserted. Onions, radishes, and parsley are planted beside cabbage and lettuce. Peas are followed by carrots and beets; tomatoes next to beans; cucumbers and squash next to potatoes.

Ivan and Petro erect a three-foot-high fence around the garden, a weaving of willow branches and spruce poles to protect from deer. Ivan has been entrusted with the axe and proudly walks around the two-inch saplings, picking the right spot to chop. Petro's talent is weaving the willows into fine arching trellises or bowing them in a delicate cross-hatch that lets in just the right amount of light.

Little Katya's job is making cardboard signs to identify the crop. She writes in delicate swirls first the Ukrainian name, followed by the English: *chasnyk* garlic, *kapusta* cabbage, *kartoplia* potato, *ohirok* cucumber. Maria doesn't like the English words, and when the children try to make her pronounce them, they laugh uproariously at her stumbling tongue. It is bad enough the children are forced to speak English in school, but at home she insists they speak their mother tongue. Even so, the languages have begun to cross-pollinate, creating hybrids she no longer recognizes, in which the English strain overpowers the beauty and nuance of the original. The youngest often mix the two languages together, and when Maria demands that Ivan speak properly, he becomes confused and has to search his mind for the right Ukrainian words, and he hasn't even started school yet.

Sofia tells Katya in English that their mother can't learn the words because she is too old and too Ukrainian. She'll never be a real Canadian. By their covert glances and Katya's guilty face, Maria knows they are talking about her, but when she asks they claim to be discussing how deep to plant the seeds.

Sofia practises her English pronunciations endlessly, trying to eradicate the last vestiges of a Slavic accent. She recites, 'A is for apple, B is for bed, C is for cat . . . ' and her favourite, saddest poem that she learned in school, 'Lucy' by

William Wordsworth, about a peasant girl 'fair as a star . . . whom there were none to praise and very few to love,' who lived and died unknown.

By the end of the poem, her eyes water, knowing that she could be Lucy, here with the dirt spoiling her skirt and sullying her hands, stooped over a row of parsnips. But unlike Lucy, there will be no one to mourn her, no one to write a poem for her . . . she will be forgotten. This tragic thought starts her reciting again, until Maria snaps, 'Speak properly!' and Sofia chooses silence instead.

Sometimes, when she is alone milking the cow, Maria tries to say the words her children teach her. Mil-ik, co-ow, milikingk co-ow. But even to her ear, the words sound harsh and awkward. *Korova* is a much prettier word. Teodor can speak English, and the rest of her family is rapidly adapting to its flat sounds and colourless rhythm. Only Dania seems to prefer using simple, garden-variety Ukrainian. Maria knows the children need to adapt in order to grow in this land, but she will never allow them to forget their roots. So Katya writes both words on the signs. Maria doesn't understand the heated discussions when Sofia points out misspellings such as *skwash* and *onyions*.

It is Sofia and Lesya's job to haul buckets of water from the well, which is downhill from the house. Despite Lesya's crooked foot, she always returns first with two buckets yoked across her shoulders while Sofia lags behind, arriving with only half a bucket, having slopped away the rest. She always has excuses: she tripped, a bee chased her, the bucket leaked, it was too heavy . . . Maria sends her back for another.

Sofia stomps off, hurling the bucket as soon as she is out of sight of her mother. Lesya hobbles after her in a vain attempt to alleviate her cousin's punishment, remaining silent while Sofia rants that she will never be a farmer's wife. She's going to live in the city in a proper house with an indoor toilet and electricity; she'll be a famous actress and people will shower her with chocolate and new dresses. Next summer, when she turns twelve, she'll get out of this goddamned place. She blends the two words together like her English friends, so they roll off her tongue as one, *goddamned*, the only English word in a tirade of Ukrainian.

Lesya is just happy to be with her aunt and cousins instead of inside the house with her mother. She doesn't think about her father. At night lying in bed wrapped in the sour smell of dirty sheets, scratching at bedbugs and lice, with Anna pacing the floor, Lesya wonders what it would be like to be Teodor and Maria's child. Maria never looks at Lesya like she is a cripple, she never gives her chores that are easier. She knows Lesya will figure out a way to do the work. They look at her like she is normal.

Lesya and Petro eat lunch and supper at their aunt's house, even though they can barely all fit into what used to be the storage shed; it still feels more like a house than their own. Crammed around the table, elbows and knees touching, laughing at Sofia's performances and Ivan's knock-knock jokes, it feels like a family. They

57

bathe with their cousins and sometimes Maria washes their clothes. They listen attentively to her stories from the old country. Sometimes while they work, Maria asks Lesya to sing. She starts shyly, the notes growing stronger, lifting skyward as she forgets her audience and sings for the dirt, the sun, the spider, and the curious magpie. At the end of each song, Maria thanks her. Diakuiu, she says in the same low voice that she says Amin'.

After lunch and supper, Lesya carries covert offerings of food from Maria to Anna. Her mother is still in bed in the middle of the day, staring at the wall. Lesya can hear the murmur of life seeping through the wall from the other side. She clears a space on the table, gathers up yesterday's dirty dishes to take back to Maria, swats away the flies, sets the plate of food on the table, and covers it with a clean cloth. Then just as quietly as she entered, she leaves, hoping her mother won't ask her to stay.

Anna wants to starve, but the longer she resists the food, the stronger the urge to eat grows. She finds herself seated in front of the plate. Her fingers inching toward the cold pyrohy, she tears off a mouse-sized piece and nibbles reluctantly. Then her hands grab the food, ignoring the utensils, and stuff it into her mouth, gorging down the last crumb. As if waking, she tries to understand where the food has gone, punching herself in the stomach, before crawling back into bed.

In bed, she tries to imagine being dead. Would it feel any different from being alive? Could she still see? Would she know who she was, would she remember anything, would she be free? She has held a knife to her wrist. But she couldn't. She can't. That's when the coyotes first started to cry for her. They cried all through the night, and they've come back every night since. She tells them everything and they howl her pain. She wants to grow teeth and run wild.

Lesya's singing wakes her. The sound is all around her, floating from the rafters, spilling through the chinks in the wall. Anna recognizes the fall and rise of the notes. It is a sad song. She follows its sweet sorrow outside, around the corner of the shack, to the garden.

Dania, Sofia, and Katya are watering the rows. Petro and Ivan are raising a panel of fencing. Maria is on her knees, squirrelling away seeds. Lesya sits cross-legged beside her aunt, passing her the seeds and singing about another land, a lost love, and a woman left behind. Lesya's soprano gives the song yearning tempered with hope. When she reaches the chorus, a call to return home, Anna joins in.

Her pure, smooth alto slips in under the high notes and wraps around them. Lesya stops singing and turns to her mother standing at the edge of the garden dressed in her nightgown, her hair bedraggled, her eyes fixed on the sky, singing as if hearing an entire choir, unaware that life around her has stopped. The last note sustains and flies into the wind. In the silence, not even a bird answers.

'Anna,' Maria says softly. Anna looks to her sister-in-law, suddenly aware of the staring eyes, her soiled nightgown hanging loose around her body, her bare feet rooted to the ground.

'Come help me plant.' Maria slowly rises and approaches her as she would a frightened animal. 'I'm planting peas.' She reaches into her apron pocket and extracts a handful of seeds, takes Anna's hand, and pours them into her open palm. They stand there a moment, searching each other's eyes. Anna's fingers curl around the seeds.

'You can take my row,' says Maria and heads back to the garden. Anna follows, kneels down in the dirt, opens her hand, and plants a shrivelled pea. All around her the sound of work resumes.

* * *

The following weeks are a constant vigil for the first green sprouts to poke their heads up. The peas are first, followed shortly by beans, then onions, lettuce, carrots . . . until the entire black earth is speckled with tender green. Mornings are for watering to fend against the drying sun. Daytime is for weeding and searching for insects hungrily intent on devouring the crop. Everyone participates, checking the rows for caterpillars, potato beetles, cutworms, aphids, spider mites . . . an endless barrage of invading armies.

Each person has their own killing style. Maria, Dania, and Lesya efficiently remove the offender and crush it between their nails without a second thought. Maria actually finds the sound of the bug's shell popping somewhat soothing. She starts debugging a row of potatoes, her mind spinning with the day's chores, but by the time she reaches the end of the row, having killed fifty or sixty bugs, her mind has calmed just to the sound of -pop-.

Sofia can't bear touching the bugs and makes Katya pull them from the plant. They have a killing block, a small piece of board they put the bug on and stomp. Once, Sofia was in such haste to annihilate a cutworm that she accidentally stomped Katya's retreating hand. A purple bruise bloomed like a cauliflower. Katya was assigned to another row, and Sofia was forced to pick the bugs from the plants herself.

Ivan and Petro prefer to race. Ivan in lettuce, Petro in cabbage, they count: ready-set-go. The first few games the victor was whoever finished first, but once Maria inspected their rows and found at least twenty bugs in the first ten feet, the rules were changed to the victor being the one who killed the most. The boys gather three or four bugs at a time, then rub their hands together, holding up the smeared remains to each other's delight. Large bugs, like cutworms, are gathered in jars so the final count can be verified, but also to act as execution chambers.

They experiment with myriad techniques: sometimes drowning, sometimes heat, suffocation, dehydration, dismemberment. The most dangerous method is frying them on the wood stove. The boys are certain the punishment will be severe if Maria discovers what the burned crisps are that she scrubs off the stovetop every night. The best method, by far, is leaving them on Sofia's side of the bed.

The garden is constantly under attack. The first tender shoots are prone to damping off — a soil infection that will rot the seedlings and decimate the crop.

If the infant plants manage to survive, they still need to overcome early blight, late blight, rust, and downy mildew. Any sign of a fungus is a call to arms. Infected leaves are pulled off, whole plants sacrificed, and their remains cremated in the wood stove. Maria concocts a sulphur mixture and pours the toxic tea over and around the plants.

If the plants survive the blights, they still face late frosts. Maria nervously steps in and out of the shack on the nights the temperature starts to drop. On more than one occasion, she sounds the alarm after the children have climbed into bed. Sofia and Dania follow their mother into the night, illuminated by the kerosene lamp, to cover the plants with burlap. Not until mid-morning, after the sun has warmed the soil, does she gently lift the burlap off, relieved to feel the escaping heat and find the plants still thriving.

There are so many enemies. The birds; the cats that dig at the furrows for a place to shit; their own clumsy feet; and the cow that got loose when Ivan left the barn door open because he said the cow told him it was afraid of the dark and didn't want to be alone.

Maria prays that there will be no hail, no drought, no frost, no swarming infestations, no floods, no fires, no rogue horses or cows, no birds, no mice, no gophers, and especially no rabbits — she prays every night for the safety of her vegetables. She asks Anna to make a scarecrow.

Anna selects two long spruce poles and uses the axe to sharpen one point into a stake. She lashes them together with binder twine, forming a cross or a man standing with stiff arms outstretched. She wraps the poles with willow, shaping a body, a curved body with breasts and a waist. She puts her ankle-length, hand-woven, elaborately embroidered wedding sorochka on the skeletal frame. She stands back and examines her work. Then she picks up a knife and slashes the skirt and sleeves and is pleased to see the wind grab at the tatters. Maybe Maria should have stopped her, but she knew this was an exorcism.

She had tried to talk to Anna about Stefan. She offered to make her a balm to heal her heart. Anna had laughed, laughed so hard that it frightened Maria. She was relieved when Anna joined them in the garden. Hard work, fresh air, sunlight, and, the most important, being surrounded by life would be the best cure for her sister-in-law. Sometimes it is better to forget.

Anna works obsessively, not stopping for water or food, refusing any help. She stuffs the arms with straw, ties strands of one-foot lengths of barbed wire to the hands, and fastens metal jar lids to the barbs. The scarecrow claps cacophonously, tambourines twirling and dancing grotesquely. Its head is a white sugar bag stuffed with hay, garroted at the throat with rope. Its eyes — metal washers stitched in place with red thread. It has no mouth.

She climbs a makeshift ladder, propped against the body, even though she is afraid of heights, to place the wreath upon its head. A crown Anna had worn when she was married. Back then it had been braided with Guelder rose and periwinkle. The dead petals crumble as she drapes the tail of ribbons — red, green, and blue — over the creature's shoulders.

Anna jumps down hard, letting the force of the landing jostle through her body. She steps back and for the first time in months smiles, her eyes blazing against the sun, looking up at herself.

Petro, Ivan, and Katya have nightmares for weeks.

★ ★ ★

Teodor chooses a site a half-mile northeast from his sister's house to cultivate, roughly at the property line that halves the two quarter-sections of land. Combined, their properties span three hundred and twenty acres. When Teodor was sent to prison, Anna applied for homestead entry of the quarter-section adjacent to hers on Teodor's behalf, knowing that when he got out he would be ineligible to own land. He would be responsible for making all the necessary improvements to earn patent as prescribed in the Homesteaders Agreement, including the breaking and planting of twenty-five acres over three years, building a house and outbuildings including granaries and a barn, digging a cribbed well, cutting timber, and erecting fences. It would be his land. He was her brother and Anna didn't hesitate to help him. Teodor insisted he would pay the ten-dollar entry fee on the first harvest.

Land up in these parts was untamed, choked by bush, rocks, and bogs. The flat, rich land, farther south went to the British and the gentrified. This part of the country was allocated for Ukrainians, Germans, Russians, Hungarians and shared with the decimated Blackfoot, who had been pushed farther and farther north by train tracks, towns, and fences. This was land set aside for labourers, non-whites, peasants with deep guttural languages and mysterious customs. It was a place of poor people, but the soil was rich.

Teodor could tell when he pushed his fingers gently into the dirt and found no resistance. Sliding his hand back out, he smelled the sweet scent. He rubbed the warm, moist soil between his fingers and let it fall loosely back to the earth. This land was fertile. If this quarter-section, all one hundred and sixty acres, was planted with wheat, Teodor would indeed be a wealthy man. 'This is where we begin,' he told Myron.

They clear-cut the first acre of brush and pile it in massive heaps. They coat themselves with mud and kerosene to stave off the blackflies and mosquitoes. Their hands and faces swell beyond recognition from the bites. After the first few days, they give up trying to swat away their attackers. The insects constant drone becomes a part of the daily sound swarming around their heads. One sweltering mid-afternoon, Teodor abruptly stops as he heaves up a root, acutely aware that he can hear nothing. He shakes his head, slaps at his ears. For a moment he thinks he has gone deaf, before realizing the bugs have been driven away by the heat.

When the trees are too large to be dug out, they are grubbed. Teodor chops and hacks through the roots around the base as Myron shimmies up twenty feet to fasten the rope around the trunk. The horse strains, its withers quivering, slathered in sweat, as Myron hollers and slaps its rump, until the tree finally groans and falls cracking to the ground. Then it is skidded to the growing woodpile.

Fuel for the wood stove is set aside to be gathered in the fall. The longest, straightest trunks are stacked for building material, and skinny poplars tagged for fence poles. Roots and branches are lit on fire. The smoke that stings their eyes and chokes their breath mercifully wards off the flies. Deep into the night, the glowing bonfires dot the horizon like so many rising suns.

They pry two tons of rocks from the ground, stack them one by one in the cart, and haul them to the property line that divides the two sections. There they unload and pile the stone to form a long, low wall. They hack, saw, rip, and curse at the roots that refuse to let go. They use picks, axes, shovels, and claw with their hands to reach the rich black soil. They clear an extra twenty feet around the entire perimeter to serve as a firebreak. And finally they plow — one agonizing foot at a time — coaxing this mistress to yield herself.

As Teodor tends the earth, he heals himself. In the field, he forgets about the past, forgets about the prison walls, and focuses only on the job at hand. His muscles grow taut and firm. He puts on weight. His chest fills out his baggy shirt and his pants stop slipping below his waist. His hands grow strong, the plow becomes lighter, his strides longer, and the land responds to his request to open. Deep furrows bloom upward, aching to be seeded.

But in those first days, he could barely lift the smallest rock. He had to carry it in both hands; his back stooped over, his knees bowed, he'd waddle to the cart where Myron was loading five stones to his one. His son would take the rock from him and toss it effortlessly to the front of the cart. Behind the plow, driving the horse, he reined the horse in hard, afraid to unleash its harnessed strength. Even holding the animal back, he was forced to run behind its lurching thrusts. The wide, leather plow strap cut into his shoulders, branding him black and blue. Once, he fell and was dragged through the twisted roots and jutting twigs.

Myron halted the horse, but Teodor screamed, 'Keep going!' And when Myron hesitated, he shouted louder, 'Go!' He struggled to his feet and slammed the full force of his remaining energy down into the wooden handles through the iron blade into the earth. He'd pushed what felt like a mile, only to find he'd made a twenty-foot run. His body dripping with sweat, his hands a bloody mash of blisters, his lungs bursting — he'd holler, *Whoa!*

And Myron, who was leading, rolling stones out of the way, and the horse that was just getting up to speed, would look back at him, wondering why they had stopped. Teodor would bend down on one knee, supporting his weight on an outstretched arm pressed against the ground, sucking back air, and curse his damn boots as he made a big show of retying a shoelace that he said had come undone.

Myron never says a word when he has to wait for his father. He stands silently a few feet away and busies himself looking at the horse's hooves or stares off, chewing on a blade of grass, as if assessing the time of day by the sun's position. Sometimes he has a sip of water, pretending to gulp back more, before passing the canteen to his father to drain. If he hurts, he never lets his father see it. To Teodor, Myron seems oblivious to the briars clawing his skin and impervious to the stings and bites welting his body. He tries to remember his own youth, when he, too, felt invincible and his body did his bidding without complaint, but that memory is lost.

Teodor feels every bump and bruise. He feels his hands dry and crack, not from the sun, but from the dirt leaching the water from his skin. Dust to dust. Blisters harden into thick calluses, robbing his fingers of sensation. He no longer feels how hot the soup is in a cup. He can't feel the softness of Maria's skin, only his own roughness against her body. He feels the sun blaze into his neck, face, and forearms, his skin on fire, shocking him with pain at the slightest touch. His skin bubbles, peels, and itches, then finally turns a deep, rich brown, as if he has taken on the colour of the earth.

At midday, Ivan and Petro can be seen running toward them. Two small dark flecks far in the distance. Dancing in the heat waves, growing into flailing arms and legs, until finally arriving with lunch in hand. Ivan always wins the race to his father. Myron unhitches the horse and lets it graze. The men eat cold pyrohy and flatbread with lard and the last of the chokecherry jam, while the boys walk up and down the fresh furrows collecting worms, round stones, the occasional bone, and, once, an Indian arrowhead.

Petro found the arrowhead. Ivan took it from him. Petro grabbed for it and then the boys were tumbling and rolling in the dust. When Petro started to cry and blood was dripping from Ivan's nose, Teodor separated them by the scruff of the neck, took the arrowhead from Ivan's clutched hand, and, in one smooth swift movement, hurled it far into the bush. He didn't say a word to the boys, just told Myron to hitch up the horse and slipped into the plow's harness.

The two boys watched the work start up again; his father didn't say Dopobachenia — until we see each other again. Ivan felt the urge to cry but punched Petro in the arm instead and raced home, not caring whether his cousin caught up.

The first day, Teodor plows eighty feet. An acre is roughly two hundred and eight feet by two hundred and eight feet. It takes him four days to reach the end of the first row. When he finally pulls the plow around and starts the next furrow, Myron is ten rows ahead of him, clearing the rocks and roots. Two hundred and seven more turns to make. Teodor counts his steps as he did in prison, measuring down the distance. Myron only counts the turns. At the eightieth turn, Teodor begins closing the gap. By the one hundred and tenth turn, Myron is once again scrambling to stay ahead of his father. By the one hundred and fiftieth turn, they are working in syncopated pace. Two men and a horse crossing back and forth with the precision of a pendulum.

When the day finally loses light, Teodor and Myron stumble home, unable to talk, their bodies one numb ache. They arrive blackened with the earth's body, her dirt ground so deep into their skin that only the whites of their eyes announce their arrival. They scrub her dust from their bodies outside at the metal tub that Maria fills with hot water as the sun sets. After the first plunge of their hands, the water mires into mud. It doesn't matter how much they scrub, the dirt never releases itself from their pores. It clings under their nails, obliterates their fingerprints, and burrows deep into their ears. It cries from their tear ducts. When they blow their noses, white handkerchiefs turn black.

Before Teodor collapses into bed, he pulls a chair outside for one last cigarette and to clean his boots. The boots have cracked and stretched from the sloughs of mud. Nicks and scuffs mar the surface. One shoelace has broken. The leather has moulded to the shape of his feet like an ancient skin. Despite the gruelling work, his boots have never inflicted any pain: not a blister, not a pinch, not even a chafe. They are good boots.

With his penknife, he scrapes off the chunks of caked dirt from the soles, then uses an old horse brush to vigorously scrub the edges and stitching before carefully fishing out the dirt plugging the eyelets. He rubs them down with a scrap of burlap, wiping away the residue of dust. Then he greases them with dubbin, rubbing the fat deep into the leather until the skin glows. He laces the boots back up, straightens out the tongues, and finally sets them beside the stove to dry. He always faces the toes toward the door. Only then can he let himself sleep.

That spring, Teodor and Myron break six acres.

Summer

Bilyi Borshch (White Borshch)

3–4 beets with tops
2 medium onions, chopped
I carrot, thinly sliced
I celery stalk, chopped
2 cups shredded cabbage
4 fresh mushrooms
2 tablespoons flour
2 tablespoons lard or chicken fat
7 cups chicken broth, vegetable stock, or water
I cup buttermilk
2 tablespoons fresh chopped dill
I tablespoon fresh parsley
2 cloves garlic (crushed)
I teaspoon salt
I cup sour cream
2 small new potatoes per person

Peel and shred vegetables. Wash beets and tops well, then shred beets and chop greens. Place beets, carrot, and celery in large pot with 4 cups broth. Boil until soft. Wipe mushrooms with a damp towel, slice thin and cook in lard. Add onion and garlic to mushrooms. Stir in flour to make a paste, add a little broth, bring to a boil, then add to soup. Add cabbage, parsley, dill, salt, and remaining stock. Simmer until vegetables are soft. Mix buttermilk and sour cream, add to soup. Do not boil; the borshch may curdle. Taste. Sprinkle with dill and garlic mashed with salt. Cook and serve potatoes separately.

★　★　★

The first meal from the garden is on Tuesday, June 14. Maria is up at five. The fire is stoked and hot before Teodor and Myron leave for the fields. The door of the shack is opened wide to vent the heat. Ivan, Petro, and Katya are told to stay outside and after their chores are free to play. They are given strict orders to be back at least an hour before supper so they can wash up and dress for the meal. The children are certain it isn't a holiday but feel they need to be on their best behaviour just in case. Once their chores are finished, they stay close to home, spying on the activities. Dania and Sofia are recruited for kitchen staff.

Anna and Lesya are next door preparing the house for guests. The house hasn't been cleaned in six months, but Anna insists that everyone sit at her table tonight. She now frenziedly attacks the corners, walls, and shelves. Bedding and clothing are hung outside to air. The straw mattresses are shoved through the doorway and beaten with a willow stick, fluffed and shaken, before being hauled back inside. The table, chairs, and stove are scrubbed. Every plate, mug, spoon, and knife washed. The window wiped. The floor swept.

Lesya, who can't remember her mama ever

cleaning, hops around the house feeling such joy she thinks her heart might burst. In the last few weeks, Anna hasn't been staying in bed all day. She gets up early and walks the properties, skirting the bush, her eyes scanning the ground as though she is looking for something. Sometimes she disappears into the bush and Lesya's stomach gets tight, but she always returns. Often her path takes her along the low stone wall where she sits watching the woods. When she returns from these walks, her eyes are bright and she seems happy.

Anna opens the pine trunk and extracts an embroidered tablecloth and the porcelain pitcher adorned with painted roses — Anna's own mother's pitcher — and entrusts Lesya to carry it to the table. Lesya clutches it to her chest as if holding her own beating heart and tries to walk tall and gracefully with hardly a limp so her mother will see there is nothing wrong with her after all.

Petro hides his excitement, plays the game, knowing the surprise. He knows what great event is upon them. He knows his father must be coming home.

⋆   ⋆   ⋆

Maria has planned the menu: white borshch, the last jar of jellied chicken, three potatoes per person, a pickled cabbage salad, and, for dessert, halushky with wild strawberries and syrup. By noon, the temperature outside is seventy-three degrees; inside the shack is at least ten degrees warmer.

The morning is set aside for making the dumplings. The flour is sifted with the last few precious grains of salt. Dania stirs as Maria adds milk and water to create a light dough. Maria forms the soft elastic mixture into a ball and covers it to rise. Sofia returns with a pail of wild strawberries. Taking her mother's warning seriously, she has guiltily eaten only half a dozen in the field. When she finishes hulling them, Maria sprinkles them with sugar. Sofia covertly dips her finger into the bowl, stealing a taste of the precious sweetness. The risen dough is placed on the floured table, cut in half and rolled into a rectangle. Then, using a small Mason jar as a cookie cutter, Maria carefully punches out round disks.

Dania heats the sugared strawberries on the stove, her fingertips light on the wooden spoon to sense the thickening sauce. Maria supervises the final consistency and pulls them just as they begin to boil. Once the fruit has cooled, she drops dollops of it in the centre of the cutouts and shapes them into balls. The girls plop the halushky into rolling water, ten at a time, and wait for them to float back to the top, perfectly cooked. Maria sets them on her best plate. She sacrifices one halushka to be sampled among the three, then sets the plate on the highest shelf to prevent temptation.

By midday, Maria is in the garden selecting vegetables. Sofia and Dania follow behind, ready to carry the prized bounty. Each vegetable has its own distinctive greenery, still pert and fresh from the early summer rains, vibrant from the rich feed, not yet battered and bruised by summer storms. The rows contain successive generations, each a few weeks older than the next. Small plants, just learning to stand, look up to the larger ones whose stems and leaves are already maturing. Some burst with blossoms while others fan luxuriantly; some climb trellises, twisting and spiralling around themselves, while others sprawl lazily, basking in the sun.

Maria pulls the carrot first. She feels along the base of the tops, gauging the thickness of the root below. Finding the right one, she wraps her fingers around the greens and gently tugs. The earth loosens its hold and out comes a straight, vivid orange root startling against the brown earth. Still young, it barely spans her palm. Not a single insect mark tarnishes its beauty. She brings the carrot to her nose and inhales the newborn scent. She fights the urge to take a bite, swallows down the saliva that fills her mouth. She hands the carrot to Dania and proceeds down the row. She checks the ingredients off in her head. As she plucks each one from the earth, she whispers, 'Diakuiu.'

Back in the kitchen, the girls are restricted to peeling and shredding duties. Maria is in charge of the borshch. She adds the vegetables to the simmering chicken stock, monitors them so they won't become too soft, lifts them from the heat if the fire is too hot. She fries the mushrooms Dania gathered down by the well, adds just enough flour to create a paste but not so much that it would mask their delicate taste. She spoons the mushrooms into the borshch. The most crucial part is adding the buttermilk and sour cream. The girls gather around as Maria drops in thick dollops. The fire, now a low glow, emits a gentle heat. The cream smoothes and blends beautifully into the stock.

Maria adds another clove of garlic and a last pinch of salt. Only then does she feel the wetness of her dress clinging to her body, her hair limp around her face, the crick in her back and the ache in her legs. She wonders if her face is as flushed as her daughters' faces. She fills the spoon with the rich broth, blows on it, and holds it out to Dania, who takes a sip, then to Sofia, who does the same, and then Maria brings it to her own lips. She holds the broth in her mouth, assessing the complexity of the flavours before swallowing. Her tongue runs across her lips. She looks to her girls and nods, and they nod back.

★　★　★

Just before her guests arrive, Anna dresses. Lesya tightens Anna's corset. 'Tighter,' she says. Lesya pulls the strings more but can see they are already cutting into her mother's flesh. 'Tighter.' Lesya wraps the strings around her fists and pulls. Anna exhales as the corset constricts around her belly and cuts into her ribs. 'Tighter,' she gasps and Lesya pulls harder. Anna presses her hand to her flattened belly. 'Enough.'

★　★　★

80

Anna meets her guests at the door, like a lady. She ushers the family to the table. Maria is relieved to see the room tidy and clean. Even the window has been washed. She notices that every trace of Stefan has been removed. Anna looks radiant as she caters to her brother, insisting that he sit at the head of the table. She keeps up a constant chatter, making everyone laugh, until they have eased into the comfortable role of guests.

The two families sit around Anna's table dressed in their best clothes, hair combed, fingernails scrubbed, blooming wolf willow in a Mason jar vase, the delicate porcelain pitcher glistening with condensation, and the table laden with glorious food — they could be mistaken for a well-to-do English family. Anna squeezes Teodor's hand: 'This is for you.'

Maria bows her head. The children follow, placing their hands together in prayer. 'Dorohyi Bozhe . . . ' Maria gives thanks and asks that her family, both her families, be watched over and protected, and given the strength and courage needed to build this new life. She asks for this food to be blessed, and for the garden to be blessed, and the cow and the horse and the fields and this house.

Teodor and Anna do not bow their heads. Teodor stares at the heaping bowl of steaming potatoes. Anna watches a fat housefly traverse the lip of her mother's pitcher. She leans into the corset rib digging into her side. Petro squeezes his eyes tight, expecting his father to be there when he opens them. The others give themselves

to the intoxicating aromas. Maria says, 'Amin'.'
The children echo, 'Amen.'

She looks at the faces hungrily turned to her
and says, 'Ïzhte.' A swarm of hands descend on
the offerings. She notices that Petro's eyes are
still closed.

The family wakes at six to ready themselves for their Sunday church pilgrimage. Freshly laundered clothes, laid out the night before, are donned. Shoes are polished and hair is washed. The youngest are given baths. The oldest sponge themselves behind the privacy of the burlap screen. A tentative knock at six-thirty announces the arrival of Lesya and Petro. Myron helps the smaller boys grease back their cowlicks. Katya's unruly curls are braided and coiled. Sofia covertly dabs wild rose petal water, a concoction she brewed in a liniment bottle, behind her ears.

Myron squeezes into his only dress shirt. It binds across his chest and shoulders, broadened from weeks of fieldwork. His fingers fumble with the tiny collar button and he grimaces as it tightens around his throat. If it wasn't for Irene, who sits in the second pew to the right of the altar, whose bare ankle Myron glimpsed when she knelt to pray six Sundays past, he would have found an excuse to stay home with his father. He squeezes the button through the hole and it snaps off. The curse that spits past his lips is greeted by a swipe across the ear by Maria, who blames Teodor for these new words. Dania offers to sew it back on and retreats to a corner, grateful for the reprieve from the eight other bodies tripping over one another in the shack's confines.

Ivan's rump is smacked once for kneeling in his clean pants on the dirt floor to retrieve a daddy-long-legs scurrying under the bed. Assigned to sit on the bed and not move, he sidles off when the spider reappears and grinds it into the floor with his recently polished shoes. When he insists that he is still hungry, Maria makes him remove his shirt and drapes a towel over his lap while he eats another half bowl of oatmeal. She makes Petro wash behind his ears again, though he claims he already did, and gives him a pair of Ivan's suspenders to hold up his droopy trousers. Noticing Lesya's bare legs, she orders Sofia to lend her a pair of her stockings. Sofia selects her oldest pair, not ever wanting them returned.

Dania wears one of Maria's dowry sorochky, a straight, cotton chemise with traditional embroidered red motifs on the sleeves, down the front, and along the bottom hem. She doesn't care that it is too large in the waist and bosom. Its shapeless form gives her comfort in its anonymity.

Despite the season, Sofia dons a black skirt and white sweater trimmed with a rabbit fur collar given to her by her classmate Ruth, whose father owns the bank. Her parents consider themselves tolerant Christians and they look for opportunities to teach their only child lessons of charity and compassion. They proudly watched as Ruth passed the bundle to Sofia, who was asked to wait on the back porch. Sofia darned the hole at the right shoulder as best she could, and if her hair hangs just right, no one can notice it. The stain on the skirt isn't obvious either, so long as she stretches the sweater past her hips.

When Sofia pulls back the burlap curtain and makes her entrance, Lesya gasps at her beauty. Maria gasps too, at the sight of the too-tight sweater hugging her daughter's budding breasts, and makes her change into something more respectable. Ignoring Sofia's sobs, Maria selects the blouse with roses embroidered down the arms, which she made for her three Christmases ago. It took seven weeks of hand-stitching, squinting beside the kerosene lamp after the children had gone to bed, to complete. The strain on her eyes gave her headaches and the precision of the stitches cramped her fingers. Sofia's protests that the blouse is too small and none of the other girls wear blouses like this are silenced when Maria questions the appropriateness of the skirt's length and whether the shoe's small heel, also a charitable present one size too large, is too high. Teodor intervenes and Sofia decides half a stylish wardrobe is better than none.

Katya's dress is one of Sofia's castoffs and hangs almost to her ankles. Maria tucks in the waist and adds a ribbon to cinch in the extra material, but the shoulders and collar still droop over her small frame. No matter how much she feeds this child, she doesn't gain weight. Maria pushes away the pang of guilt and promises to add more cream to Katya's oatmeal in the morning. As she takes in the seams, Katya refuses to put down the limp bouquet of daisies, milkweed, blazing prairie fire, brown-eyed

Susans, and wild oats she has collected for the baby Jesus.

Katya loves church. She loves the paintings on the wall, the fiery gold crosses, gleaming chalices, and the sickening sweet incense that makes her feel dizzy. Sometimes she imagines floating up to the ceiling and taking the crown of thorns from the Jesus on the Cross and pulling the nails from his hands so he can fly away. She hasn't made the connection that the baby and the man on the cross are the same person. She wonders if they keep the Christ body in a root cellar, or in a salt barrel, or frozen in the lake in the winter. She wonders how much of the body is left and how long everybody has been eating it and what will happen when it runs out. At communion, when she is on her knees, supposed to be praying into her hands, she spits out his body. She now has a large doughy ball of Christ she keeps hidden under the blanket chest in case the church eats all of him and doesn't save any for her family.

By ten to seven, the family is dressed and fidgeting in their uncomfortable clothes. Maria looks to Teodor, sitting at the table in his dirty workpants, bare feet, picking a poppy seed from his teeth, and frowns.

Since his return from prison, he has refused to attend church. At first Maria believed he needed time to recover and build up his strength, then once he started breaking the fields, he insisted he couldn't take the time or the planting would be late.

But he doesn't work the fields on Sundays. He

hitches up the horse, loads the cart with tools, and heads across the field. He rolls past the ground broken through the week, past the birch grove, around the bush, and northwest through the clearing to the top corner of his quarter-section, exactly one mile from his sister's house. There, on the crest of the hill, he is building his family's home. It overlooks all one hundred and sixty acres. From a distance, it seems to hover between the earth and the sky.

He hasn't made much progress. The frame is down and the first three rows of logs are laid. It will be a one-level house, ten times larger than the shack they are in now, with rooms for the children. He has planned for a window on the south side looking down over the fields, with wooden shutters that can be boarded up against high winds and bitter winters. This is his church.

Teodor releases the horse, free to feast on the tall grass or lounge under the shade of the trees, a day off from the fields, and heads to where the door will be. Here he feels calm. The sound of the crickets, the swish of the prairie grass, and the gophers watching him from a distance bring him solace. Here he can hear silence and that silence is holier than any words a priest could ever utter.

He no longer believes in promised lands. He rejects suffering for salvation later. He believes in life now. There was a time when he worshipped, bowed, and kneeled to a higher power. He believed if he lived a good life, he would be rewarded. But now he knows there is no God. A compassionate God wouldn't have tried to starve his family. A just God wouldn't have taken away everything that he had built. A merciful God wouldn't have abandoned him in prison.

Maria begged him for her sake, for his children's sake, for the sake of his soul, she begged him to tell her why. She tried to convince him that God was with them, that He had never left. How else did they survive? How else were they together again? She tried to make him see how much they'd been given. She showed him the garden, the fields, their children, each other . . . she begged him to come back. He always walked away, disappeared into the barn or headed to the fields. One night, she chased him.

The children were already asleep. She was in her nightgown and had just laid out the children's church clothes for the following morning. Teodor was working on the house plans by lamplight. She asked him again to come with her. She pleaded with him, her angry whispers heightened with his refusal to answer. One of the children groaned and shifted in the bed. Teodor pushed back his chair and stormed out. She followed him into the dark barn. Her voice now free, she demanded that he talk to her. He pushed deeper into the darkness, retreating to the empty stall beside the horse.

Inside the small pen, Teodor paced back and forth from wall to wall. He counted off the steps, *one two three four five*, and turned, *one two three four five*, stopping at the imagined stone wall that he had faced a thousand times a day in prison. Maria could see him moving side to side, his head down, his eyes fixed on the ground, slipping in and out of the moon's shadows. She couldn't see his hunched shoulders, his body coiled tight, his clenched fists. She couldn't know that the wooden boards of the stall had transformed into stone and iron bars, or that Teodor could smell the rank sweat of human decay that had gagged him for six hundred days. *Talk to me*, Maria cried, hurt by how far her husband had pulled away from her. *Talk to me!*

The horse snorted and banged against the stall, the cow rubbed its head up and down against the boards, unsettled by their intensity. Maria lifted the stall's latch and Teodor heard a metal lock rasp open. He tried to get past her, but she wouldn't step back. Leave me alone, he said over and over. He retreated to his right and tripped against a feed bucket. He smelled the stench of urine and feces from a jailhouse pisspot that hadn't been emptied in days. The horse jolted. He turned in the other direction, blinded not so much by the darkness but by the panic roaring in his head, and then he slammed into the wall.

Pressed against the boards, his heart pounding, he didn't feel the roughness of the wood. He felt the coldness of stone. He didn't hear Maria say his name or the concern in her voice. His erratic breathing merged with the animals' restless shuffling. His fingernails clawed into the wood, driving splinters under his nails, his shoulders heaved. *Leave me alone*, he said so low that she could barely hear.

She touched his shoulder. *Teodor?*

He felt a nightstick dig into the back of his

neck. Smelled his sour stench. Felt his fat gut pressed against his back.

Don't fucking touch me! He spun around and grabbed her arm and twisted it against her throat, driving her backward. His eyes wide, unseeing, his mouth distorted in a scream, inches from her face, he slammed her against the opposite wall. Maybe it was the lack of resistance, or her lightness, or the shock of hitting a wall that was more than eight feet away, or the softness of her skin, the thinness of her wrist in his grip, or the terrified eyes staring up at him — a woman's eyes — he saw her and let her go. He crumpled to his knees.

Maria stood, arms out to her sides, pressed against the wall as if she was holding it up. He looked to her, unable to speak, his eyes like those of a small child waking from a nightmare. Maria slid down the wall, her throat and wrist throbbing, kneeling in front of him. He lowered his head onto her lap and wrapped his arms around her waist. It took a long time for Maria to touch the back of his head. She never asked him to come to church again.

Maria dons her khustyna, tucks the loose strands of hair under the bandana and ties it severely back. She looks austere and proper in her crisp white blouse and long black skirt. She strings the crucifix around her neck. It is a simple wooden cross, carved from white birch.

She once owned an engraved silver cross, decorated with rubies. It had been in her family for five generations. The family story was that it had been a present from a Russian countess to her maid, Maria's great-great-grandmother, a thank-you for a lifetime of service. Maria had never seen anything so beautiful. As a child, she would sit in her mother's lap for hours, running her fingers over its swirls and patterns. She'd close her eyes and practise seeing it with her mind, until she no longer had to practise and could conjure it whenever she needed comfort. It was her family's only treasure. She thought it had been taken with everything else during The Hunger. She was pregnant with Katya then, the last to be born in Ukraïna. It's why her youngest daughter is so thin, why she's weaker than the others — it's Maria's fault for not having enough food.

The other children were mercifully too young to remember that time. That's what she wants to believe. Children see things differently. They don't know that Teodor went into the stripped fields at night to rummage for stalks of wheat that had been overlooked. Or that she made stews with mice and rats and pretended it was rabbit. If they saw someone lie down in the streets and not get back up, she told them they were tired and needed to sleep.

She made sure they didn't hear the rumours of graves being dug up and what was cooking in other people's soup pots. They didn't hear the stories of neighbours stealing from and betraying one another. She kept her children safe from all of that. Teodor travelled north. He had heard stories of others crossing the Russian border and returning with rations. He had heard many more stories about those who hadn't returned. He didn't tell Maria those stories. She wanted him to barter their wedding bands, but he wouldn't. He had another cache — an Austrian silver coin from the Great War and a gallon of whisky. He came back with potatoes and beets that he buried behind the house. She didn't ask where he got them or what he had seen. He didn't ask where she got the bags of flour.

Soldiers came to the village and selected peasants who looked fatted. The villagers pointed to Maria, whom they suspected of hoarding food, ignoring that she was pregnant. Her neighbours hid behind their doors when the soldiers came to her house. She was given new clothes and enough food for a week. They sat with her while she ate. She refused until they let her children eat, too. She was taken to the railway tracks, ten miles away, where there were a hundred others like her. Round, fat faces. Flesh on their bones. New clothes. New tools. Even a tractor. They had one job. When the train rolled past, they had to wave and smile. She waved; she smiled. They gave her two bags of flour in case they needed her again. That flour fed her family and her parents for six months. The neighbours were right. She did hoard her food.

The day of their escape, her mother gave her the jewelled crucifix, which she had hidden inside the hollow of a tree. She told her that its power had kept their family safe and Maria wanted to believe her. She had to believe her. Otherwise she would have hated her mother for letting them starve. When Teodor was sent to prison, Maria traded the crucifix for the wagonload of grain that the police had confiscated.

She had walked into the one-room prison with its three-foot-by-three-foot cell in the corner, the same cell that Teodor had been held in before being transferred to the penitentiary five days earlier, and startled the town's only officer, who was playing a game of solitaire. At the sight of a woman in the precinct, the officer hurriedly fastened his belt, tucked in his shirt, and brushed away the cards. He glanced out the window and saw a ragtag of children clustered around the cart. Their clothes were dirty and tattered. Their belongings huddled around them in gunny-sacks. Stove parts and pots and pans protruded from overstuffed bags. The smallest children sat on the bags, scuffing the dirt with their bare feet. A young girl held a toddler in her arms. The oldest boy held the reins of a sickly-looking horse. The officer put on his coat and made himself taller. Maria held out her family passport to prove who she was and pointed to the cart.

The grain that Teodor had cut still lay in the back. He had scythed only the heads for their seed. Confiscated property was usually sold to the highest bidder or distributed to gain other favours. In this case, there wasn't enough grain to sell, it wasn't worth the bother to husk, and the cart was so dilapidated no bidders had come forward. Maria pointed again to the cart and set a few kernels of wheat on the table. She pointed to herself and back to the wagon. The officer shook his head no. Maria opened the sack she was carrying and set out two jars of raspberry jam and a hand-woven tablecloth and pointed to the cart again.

The officer told her she had to leave. He could smell the garlic on her clothes. She didn't want to beg. She refused to let him see her cry. She tried to tell him that she needed the wagon for her children. They had taken everything else: the house, the barn, the land, the wheat . . . all she wanted was the cart and the seed. She was willing to pay.

He didn't understand a word she said. She was one more of a hundred like her that accosted him in the streets, fell to their knees, came begging at the door — they disgusted him. He moved to escort her from the building. Maria untied the strings around the collar of her blouse and the man's eyes sharpened. He watched as she reached into her shirt, saw a flash of skin and the shadow of a crease.

The officer looked out the window. The children were shuffling in the dirt, picking their noses, watching a stray dog take a shit. Only the oldest boy stared straight ahead at the police station, refusing to blink. The officer looked back to Maria. She pulled the silver cross from its hiding place nestled between her breasts. It was hot in her hand. She felt his eyes on her throat. She removed the necklace and pointed to the cart.

There was nothing beautiful about the woman who stood before him. She was coarse, with heavy hands, thick fingers, stout and overweight. Her features weathered and tanned like hide, her eyes almost black, her face chiselled expressionless, fierce. But her breasts were large and inviting. She stepped toward him and laid the cross on the desk. He picked it up and examined the jewels, felt the weight of the silver, and put it in his pocket. He pointed at the wagon and then he pointed to her.

That's when the Blessed Virgin appeared to Maria, her heart bleeding in her hands. A poor woman, in a coarse frock, her skin weathered from the fields. Maria looked into her eyes — eyes that had no colour, no centre, no pain. The Virgin smiled, lifted her heart to her mouth, and swallowed it whole.

Maria came out of the building, tying up her blouse with one hand and clutching the jam jars with the other. She hollered at the children to put their things in the cart and ordered Myron to hitch up the horse. The officer watched from the doorway, not bothering to buckle his pants. She threw their belongings on top of the grain. When the children didn't climb in fast enough, she roughly lifted them in. She yelled at Myron to go, even though he hadn't double-checked the harness. Maria walked behind the cart, her head held high, looking straight ahead, counting her children, praying that she would make the fifty-mile trek north to Teodor's sister's homestead, the contours of the cross still burning in her palm.

Maria checks herself in the mirror. Her hair, smoothed back in a bun and parted in the middle, frames her round face. Small lines show at the corners of her eyes and lips. A practical face. She makes the effort to soften her worry frown. She is surprised how much younger she looks even with a slight smile. She straightens the wooden cross so it falls just past the first button of her blouse. The first night they lay beside each other, after almost two years apart, Teodor asked about the crucifix. She told him that she traded it for the cart and grain. When he reached for her hand, she pulled away. She said it had to be done. Nothing comes from looking back.

The next day, he went to the grove of white birches and selected an unblemished limb. He carved the cross following the grain, revealing a perfect whorling heart at its centre. He sanded the edges round and smooth. Drilled a hole through the top and threaded a leather string. When he placed the cross over her bowed head and it touched her chest, she grabbed it away. He took her hand in his and kissed it. Gently, he placed the cross against her chest and covered it with his hand. In his eyes, she knew that her God had forgiven her.

Maria herds the children out the door. They fan across the prairies, a jumbling parade of quick steps and swinging arms, some running ahead, others lagging behind, veering to the right then to the left, before settling into a ragged line marching east into the rising sun. It is only seven. She is confident they will traverse the eight miles in time for the nine o'clock service.

★ ★ ★

96

One week later, Teodor breaks the last acre. He and Myron plow the final twenty feet by the waning moon's light. Walking home, they follow the dim beacon of the kerosene lamp Maria hung outside the shed, the only star anchored to land. After giving the horse extra hay, Teodor enters the shack, pulls off his muddy boots, and announces that soon it will be time to sow.

★ ★ ★

The next day, after church, Maria asks to see the field. She and Teodor head out alone, leaving Dania in charge. Maria still wears her black skirt and crisp white shirt from the service. Her hair is braided and coiled in a bun. She holds the skirt hem up to keep it from dragging in the mud and catching on nettles. Teodor guides her around marsh holes and puddles and takes her hand to help her over the stones.

Maria tells him the news from town and Teodor listens. Occasionally, she stops and pulls a long blade of sweet grass to chew on. They wander slowly, stealing glances at each other, reacquainting themselves with the oddness of being alone together. The sun is low by the time they reach the fieldstone wall marking the start of their property. Teodor helps Maria over the wall. She lifts her eyes across the tilled ground.

Long black furrows stretch ahead of them, not straight and rigid but rolling and soft. Maria takes Teodor's hand. They walk through the rows, a furrow between them. They walk from one end to the other. Teodor points out where the biggest stumps and rocks had been, where the horse had thrown a shoe, and where the pickaxe had shattered. When they reach the end of the furrow, they turn: Teodor from habit and Maria wanting to see again. The sun casts their shadows across the waiting ground. Maria asks to see the house. Teodor says it isn't ready. She asks again.

They walk the remaining half-mile not speaking. Maria keeps her eyes fixed on the building perched atop the hill, afraid that if she blinks it might disappear. They climb the path worn by the cart's wheels up to the front of the house. When they are a few feet away, Teodor stops and lets Maria continue alone.

The house is long and low. The logs, stripped of their bark, seep sap from their wounds. The six-foot walls are complete, the sides interlocked with notches. Soon the roof will be going on. A large hole for a window is set next to the door's opening. Maria reaches the door and runs her hand along the frame over the hand-hewn timber. She notices the slashes in the wood where it has been planed and carved into shape. Each mark, her husband's mark.

She steps inside a massive room tented by blue sky. On the back wall, the golden sun blazes against the wood. Her backlit shadow, framed by the door, looks back at her. A rectangle of light floats beside it. She turns and looks out the window's opening. Wild grass speckled with milkweed, clover, and starflowers unfolds from the threshold of the house to the black rectangular swatch of freshly turned earth. The horizon blushes pink and orange.

Teodor watches Maria burnished in the light. She looks at him, her eyes shining. Her hair has come loose. He brushes it from her eyes. It is the first time he has touched her since his return.

Maria leans against the wall between the door and the window and lifts her skirt.

Teodor wakes to a chickadee's song. He sees a robin facing south, choking back a big, fat worm. When he puts on his boots, he hesitates and empties them first, and a June bug falls onto the floor. All signs of luck indicating that today is a good day to plant.

The ground has absorbed the early summer rains, the sun has dried the puddles, and the earth is warm and swollen. The clouds are towering puffs with white bottoms. The birch leaves have flipped, showing their silvery-green underbellies to the sky, promising a soft rain in the next few days. A slight breeze blows from the south. The full moon has passed and the new moon is rising.

Teodor never plants under a full moon. He has heard the stories of seeds failing to germinate and seedlings shrivelling. The same stories caution against breeding livestock or birthing under a full moon or run the risk of lame colts, two-headed calves, and stillbirths. Something in the moon's light causes monstrosities caught between life and death to be born. But today everything is perfect.

Teodor is surprised by his good fortune of late. First, Josyp Petrenko, who holds the quarter-section northwest of theirs, lent Teodor his disc harrow and horses to help smooth the field, in appreciation for Teodor repairing a broken wagon axle and saving his family the shame of being late for church. Josyp's a respected man. He's paid off his homestead. He owns two horses, two oxen, three cows, a bull, and has just built a new barn. Now he is Teodor's friend.

And Maria managed to thresh and winnow almost three bushels of wheat from the confiscated stalks. Enough seed to bring in a good harvest so he can pay off his debts, provide for his family, maybe get ahead a little, and even repay Josyp Petrenko's generosity. They are planting three weeks late, but if the weather holds, if it is dry but not too dry, and the heat of summer spills into fall, there will be enough time.

The two families stand at the edge of the broken ground; even Anna has joined them for this occasion. Silhouetted against the sky, they look like a child's paper cutout stretched across the horizon, each person six rows apart. Strapped across their shoulders are bulging sacks cradled in their arms. The children tilt slightly backward, balancing the weight. They are watching Teodor.

It has been light for an hour. When they arrived, they lined up at the cart and Teodor dispensed the seed, adjusting the quantity to each child's size and weight. Ivan and Petro eyed each other's bags to make sure the amounts were the same. Anna insisted on carrying far more seed than Teodor thought she could handle. When she started swaying from the weight, he refused to give her any more. Her face red from the exertion, she carried the bundle high on her belly. Teodor filled his pouch last and brushed the remaining seeds from the cart floor, careful not to lose a single kernel.

He stands at the edge of the field, running his fingers through the loose seed, feeling its dryness slip through his fingers. The furrows glisten with the morning dew. The horse grazes, gently tearing at the tall grass on the other side of the stone wall. Its tail contentedly swishes back and forth.

'Ask,' insists Maria.

Teodor hesitates, but even he is unwilling to take such a risk. He asks. He asks for help from the sun, the souls of the ancestors, the spirits in the fields and woods to help make a good harvest; protect them from lightning, storms, floods, fires, and grasshoppers; and bless them with the sacred bread. The families cross themselves. Teodor reluctantly makes the sign. He does this for Maria.

Teodor fills his hand, takes a step forward, and strews the seed side to side in sweeping graceful arches. Like a priest, he anoints the ground: *Accept me, accept me.*

The family steps forward as one advancing line, scattering their offering in a silent, holy procession. The seeds catch the sun as they spin through the air, falling to life.

July brings the first vegetable harvest. Young green fruit, bitter and hard, nestles against swollen ripe vegetables that if not picked soon will fall and rot on the ground. Every morning the children free the overburdened plants from their offspring. They twist off the stems of beans, pickling cucumbers, and early tomatoes and toss them into overflowing buckets. They cut back lettuce, thin carrots, pull onion bunches, strip the vines of peas . . . only to discover the next morning the garden has birthed again.

They eat from the vine — shelling sun-warmed peas, one for the pail and one for their mouth, and no one tells them they can't. The first day, they gorged themselves so much, they had diarrhea and bellyaches for three days. The novelty of fresh food has worn off. They chew absently on celery and rhubarb stalks, not because they're hungry but because they can. They have settled into the daily chore of harvesting.

They sit heavily in the dirt as they root for the ripest vegetables to pluck. Their fingers automatically search out potato weevils and cabbage thrips and smush them as absently as brushing away crumbs. The heat keeps them pressed close to the earth's coolness. Maria fills the extra daylight hours with more chores: gather wild raspberries, sterilize jars, muck the barn, change the hay, repair the willow fence, stake unruly plants, fertilize, weed, water . . . a never-ending list of things to do.

Vegetables pile up on the table and on the floor, some for tonight's dinner, the rest to be washed and pickled. Braids of onion and garlic hang from the rafters. Dill dries in upside-down bunches. As Maria bottles the eighteenth jar of yellow beans and looks to the next three pails awaiting her, she decides that it is time to go to town.

She chooses Dania and Lesya to accompany her. Sofia is relieved that she won't have to carry the heavy baskets or be seen selling wares on the street, but is also dismayed that she won't see the new Sears Roebuck catalogue or be noticed by an English boy. The children sort the vegetables, scrub them, separate the bruised and damaged, then pack the flawless in baskets nestled with straw. They cover the bounty with crisp white linen cloths and line them up on the parched, dusty grass. They step back and admire the half-dozen baskets laden with treasure, a caravan of riches about to embark on a journey. Maria knocks on Anna's door and asks whether she would like to come.

Anna has put on weight. Her face is tanned from helping in the garden. Her shorn hair has grown a little and she even let Maria trim it once. She manages to help with the canning, smiling and nodding as if she is listening. Only when Maria looks directly at her while recounting a child's indiscretion or a day's funny event is she unsettled by the emptiness of her sister-in-law's eyes. Anna must notice, because invariably she contributes to the conversation, more of a query to keep Maria talking, or remembers something else she needs to do and turns away.

Every morning, Anna goes for a long walk. She follows the same path west toward the bush. She doesn't wipe away the sweat damping her face. She lets her skirt trail in the dust. She walks briskly, her breath laboured, until she reaches the shade of the trees. Then she slows and carefully searches for signs. A pawprint or a tuft of fur. She stops at a hollow beneath two twisted poplars. This is where the grass is trodden down and the dirt sometimes scratched away. This is where they sleep.

Initially, Anna would quickly leave her offering of a piece of bread, a half-eaten pyrih, or a cracked egg, a gift of thanks, and hurry away, not wanting to trespass. She would retreat to the stone wall and watch for their shadows darting between the trees. Rarely would she catch a glimpse. But every morning when she returned, the food would be gone. Lately, Anna lingers at the spot. She has started to leave her scent. She has sat on the grass. Touched the tree. Took a bite of the bread. Left a stocking. She wants to tell them, *I am one of you.*

The coyotes have moved farther away these last few weeks. Fatted and contented, they have retreated into the wilds to feast on gophers, rabbit, and fawns. But there is at least one that has stayed for her. She has seen its print in the mud. When she placed her hand over it, she was surprised that its track was smaller. She sits still, hoping she is being watched.

As the blistering sun climbs, Anna heads toward the stone wall. She knows the coyotes pass by it at night. She wonders what they must think of this strange thing that has cropped up in their fields. She wonders what they can smell. She runs her hands over the rough stones, then climbs over onto Teodor's side of the field.

Now that Teodor has been free of the field to work on the house full-time, he is pushing to complete it before the harvest. Anna can see him and Myron shingling the roof. She watches dispassionately. They are a part of the prairies like the gophers, the sky, or the fence posts.

She visited Teodor's new house once, in the early morning, before the world had woken. It rose grey and empty from the twilight. Gaping holes for the door and window. The rafters in place, but the roof not closed in. The framework of the house not yet marred by life. Full of promise and possibility. She wandered through its interior, absorbing the smell of fresh-cut timber, the dew clinging to her dress, the swallows and chickadees announcing the light. The sun rising orange, scalloping the clouds red, and she felt sad. Sad that this house would lose its innocence. The carefully hewn beams will crack, the chinking will crumble, the door and window will settle and twist. The roof will leak, the foundation will rot. The winds and rain and snow will strip away the facade. She ran her fingers over the logs, pondering a recess chiselled into the north wall, a small rectangle, eight inches wide and ten inches high. A strange anomaly in the straight, pure lines. She didn't hear Teodor approach or she probably would have fled. She has been avoiding her brother, unable to find words.

When they were young, they had no secrets between them. Now they've lost the ability to speak to each other. Afraid that through words, they will reveal too much. Afraid that each will see into the other and know what is being hidden.

'What's this?' she asked, running her hand along the carved-out niche. Teodor shuffled his feet and searched for an answer.

Anna answered for him. 'A secret?'

Teodor grinned and confirmed her guess. 'A secret.'

'What do you have to hide?'

But there were no more words. Teodor picked up his tools and set to work. Anna watched him strip bark from a log for a while. The green sweet skin peeled off in long strips, exposing alabaster flesh. She watched her brother crafting a new life, a new home for his family. Saw how much care he had put into every notch, noticed the tightness of the fits, and the pine trim he had framed around the window. She saw every cut of love and could have wept. But didn't. Neither of them would have known what to do with the tears. She has never gone back.

Anna's skirt skims against the foot-high blades of wheat, tender and green. The wheat bows and parts before her, closes behind her, veiling her path. She cuts across to the very centre until she reaches a small circular spot of flattened stalks. There she sits. She unbuttons her blouse and lays it neatly on the ground. Then she unstrings the corset, breathing in deep as it releases her. She opens her breasts and belly to the sun.

Her breasts are swollen. The nipples are larger and a deeper brown. Her belly protrudes round and low. This sensitive skin, usually kept hidden from the sun, is raw and red from a burn that has not been allowed to heal. Heat blisters weep and the imprint of the corset, like skeletal fingers, grip her belly. She slips off the corset and arches her belly toward the sky. It has been four months and it's still inside her.

She sits in the field, willing the sun's fire to sear its way inside her. She is unable to stop her hand, which claws fistfuls of cool black earth and shovels it into her mouth.

Anna tells Maria she thinks she'll stay home today.

★   ★   ★

'It's warm!' Ivan screeches with delight as he runs naked into the water, splashing torrents of spray in a shower of rainbow light. 'Come on!' He dives in headfirst and disappears from sight. Katya holds her dress high above her waist and wades into the water. Minnows flicker around her feet in the shallows. Her toes follow them slowly so as not to scare them away.

'Don't go out any farther and don't get your dress wet,' Sofia admonishes her, 'or I'll whip your behind.'

'No you won't,' Katya challenges, 'or I'll tell Mama.'

'She's not here,' Sofia reminds her, and Katya lifts her dress higher. Petro stands barefoot at the edge of Bug Lake, shyly gripping his shirt in his hands, acutely aware of Sofia staring at his thin, underdeveloped body. Ivan resurfaces, hooting and hollering, shaking his long hair from his eyes. 'Come on in, don't be a chickenshit!'

'Watch your tongue!' Sofia says with her hands on her hips, the self-appointed adult while the others are in town. Ivan ignores her and floats on his back.

'Chickenshit, chickenshit, chickenshit . . . '

The cool water embraces him as the burning sun evaporates the droplets on his belly. He tilts his head back, submersing his ears, enamoured by the deep bass sound of his voice echoing in his head. He stretches out the words, altering the pitch. 'Chic-ken-shit . . . '

Bug Lake is not much more than a watering hole skirting the west property line. By the end of August, it dries into a slimy green mire that's maybe four feet deep. The children can walk across it, if they keep their chins up. But at this time of year it's deep enough to swim to the bottom and almost run out of air before getting back up. At dawn and dusk, perch and pike jump, creating the illusion of raindrops hitting the water's surface.

'You don't have to go in,' Sofia dismisses Petro as she looks for a nice place in the shade, free of bugs and pokey roots. She has brought her mother's good woollen blanket that's kept tucked away in the blanket chest for safekeeping. It has never been used in Sofia's memory and she is certain her mother won't notice it has been borrowed. Besides, she'll have it back in with the camphor balls before Maria returns home. She also has a thin Hudson's Bay blanket to string in the branches for shade, her version of an umbrella she saw in a magazine that Ruth brought to school.

The black and white photograph showed a group of men and women dressed in white stretched out on a blanket, with a picnic basket, eating strawberries and drinking from tall glass goblets. It was titled 'Picnic in the Park.' The women, with their upswept hair, giggled at the camera. The young men, dashing in straw hats, lay on their bellies, looking up at the girls. One had his mouth open as a girl held a fat strawberry above him with a white-gloved hand. Sofia arranges herself on the good blanket, with her knees tucked coyly under her, like the girl in the photograph, and sets out a bowl of wild raspberries she has picked along the way. Their vibrant red contrasts beautifully with the blanket's muted blue, ivory, and salmon floral design, the green grass, and Sofia's yellow smock.

'Chickenshit!' Ivan bellows louder.

'Shut your trap or we're going home!' She snipes at Petro: 'Are you going in or not?' Irritated that his skinny shadow is falling on her blanket.

Petro wants to go in, but he doesn't want to take his pants off.

'Look away,' he says.

'I've seen a bare ass before.' She raises her voice to make sure Ivan hears: 'I saw his chicken ass last week running from the outhouse. Saw his little dangly too, bobbing up and down, like a hen peckin' seed.'

Ivan splays his arms low to create a tidal wave and drives it at Sofia. The wave peters out before reaching shore.

Sofia laughs. 'Sookie baby.'

'Cow.' Ivan fills his mouth with water. He squirts it at her in a long, high arch that almost reaches her toes.

'Don't get Mama's blanket wet!'

'You're scaring the fish,' Katya whines, trying to calm the rippling water.

Ivan fills his mouth again and aims for the blanket.

'Don't . . . I'm warning you, don't do it.'

Ivan spits the water high, a perfect stream cascading toward the blanket. Sofia steps in front of it, blocking the potential disaster. Water blooms across her chest, turning the fabric transparent, illuminating her small buds.

'I can see your teats,' crows Ivan. Petro can't help but look. Sofia whips off her smock and Ivan is surprised to see soft blond down on her crotch.

'I'm going to drown you.' Sofia races into the water after him, not caring about her recently curled hair. Water wheels wildly around her as she chases him down. Ivan swims for his life, screaming for help.

Petro slips off his pants and runs in to save his

cousin. From behind, his tiny butt is stark white against the deep brown of his back and shoulders. As he hops past Katya, shouting, 'I'm coming!' he forgets the long, thin black-and-purple bruises slashed across his backside, betraying the previous night's punishment.

If he was asked what he did wrong, he couldn't explain. She didn't say. He probably should have waited for Lesya, who was still in the outhouse, but the scarecrow kept watching him. He ran to the house, checking over his shoulder to make sure it hadn't followed him. Once inside, he headed straight to bed. Maybe his mistake was stealing a glance at his mother.

She was in her nightgown, sitting at the table with her back to the door. She had a willow switch in one hand. Her other hand clutched her belly. Her gown was hiked up to her waist. Her face was flush from exertion, her eyes red as if she'd been crying. As he passed by her, he saw whip marks on her upper thighs and belly. It was her stillness that scared him. 'Mama?' he said.

She looked at him as if he had called her a dirty name. She wrenched her gown down, bolted from the chair, grabbed him by the arm, and pulled down his pants. He was so shocked, he forgot to cry. With each strike, she hissed, 'You didn't see anything! You didn't see anything! You didn't see anything!'

Petro tried to cover his bum with his hand. 'I didn't see anything, Mama. I didn't see. I didn't . . .'

Maybe it was his small hand against his bony bum, or the welts already appearing, or his pleading voice, but it was more likely the baby kicking that made Anna drop the switch. It kicked hard, sending a shock of pain against her spine. It kicked again. Anna dropped to her knees.

That's when Lesya came in. She pulled Petro's pants up over his quivering legs and tucked him in bed. Then she picked up the willow stick and threw it out the door. She crawled in next to her brother and pulled the burlap curtain shut. She held him tight, whispering lullabies, to block out the sound of Anna rocking back and forth on the floor.

Exhausted by the pursuit, and cooled by the water, the hunt turns into a race before collapsing into a water fight. The boys gang up on Sofia, slapping the water, drenching her in wave after wave. When she gets too close, they lie on their backs and kick with their feet, spraying her with water, until she dives and yanks them under by their ankles. A tangle of arms and legs twists and wrenches away and breaks for the surface. One by one, the three heads bob up, gasping for air.

'Truce, truce, truce . . . ' They float on their backs, panting, catching their breath. The water sparkles and dances around their naked bodies. They no longer notice breasts or penises or pubic hair; they are once again children floating in the sun.

Near shore, Katya squats low to the water and pees. Yellow pools hot between her ankles. The back of her dress trails behind her, sopping up water. She wiggles her toes, 'Here fishy, fishies.'

***

Mr. Hardy examines the vegetables at the back entrance of his store, Hardy's General Shop & Meat Market. Dania and Lesya flank Maria; all three stand with their heads lowered as the shopkeeper goes from basket to basket, examining the wares. Occasionally, he extracts a tomato or cucumber and brings it up close to his nose, squints through his smudged glasses, and sniffs the produce. He squeezes the firm fruit, frowns, and discards it back in the basket. Once the inspection is complete, he stands with his back to them, rubbing his glasses on his apron, as he calculates his profit in his head.

'It's not the best I've seen,' he mulls. 'The tomatoes are small and the radishes have worm holes. I'm not interested in beans, I can't give them away. And the carrots, well, carrots are a dime a dozen.' Dania translates for her mother.

Lesya had packed the radishes herself and knows that not a single worm had got past her. Her ears blush pink with anger at the slight against her work and the fear that Maria will think she is incompetent.

'My mother wants to sell it all,' Dania responds. Maria stares hard at the shopkeeper, daring him to insult her. Mr. Hardy isn't a bad man, he gave her credit last winter for flour; of course it cost her five times the asking price, but he also gave Ivan a penny candy for free.

'I can give you seventy-five cents,' he offers magnanimously.

'For each basket?' inquires Dania.

114

'For the lot.' He holds Maria's eyes as Dania translates. The corners of Maria's eyes twitch ever so slightly. She holds her gaze on him as she replies.

'She wants four dollars for the lot.'

Hardy laughs, outraged. 'Four dollars! I might as well plant it myself for that and cook it up too.' The back of his head recalculates the profit margin. 'I'll give you a dollar fifty.' Maria looks to the girls and gives them an order. Hardy reaches in his pocket to count out the change.

'You can take them inside, set them by the counter.' Hardy pats himself on the back.

Dania and Lesya cover the baskets with the linen and hoist them up on the crooks of their arms.

'They're not for sale,' says Dania. 'Mama says we're going to La Corey. They pay a good price there.'

'That's ten miles away,' Hardy sputters, watching his profit preparing to leave. Lesya makes a big show of draping her cloth over the radishes. They had looked in Hardy's front window when they arrived in town. Jostled between the brooms and advertising signs for Gillette razors was a motley display of limp, dried-up carrots, overripe tomatoes, and generally paltry produce.

'She says, You're right. Ten miles is too far to go. We'll go to the hotel, sell directly to the restaurant. She says to thank you for the good idea, Mr. Hardy.'

And with that Maria makes three dollars and fifty cents for her wares.

Maria spends the first dollar and twenty cents on chicks. She lets Lesya help choose them. Shows her how to check their wings, feel their weight, see how attentive they are, and rejects the ones that are too listless or too aggressive, have weak chests or other abnormalities. One of the more obvious rejects is a chick whose foot is bent completely backward. It hobbles lopsided to the water dish. The other chicks crowd it from drinking, but it pushes its way through. As if to compensate for its physical inadequacy, this chick has been endowed with girth and size; it is even larger than the young rooster Maria selected. And it is fearless. It limps directly up to Maria and Lesya, dragging its foot behind, leaving a claw-mark trail in the saw dust, and pecks their toes.

Maria ignores it, but Lesya surreptitiously slips her deformed foot forward to kick it away and the chick jumps onto her shoe. Lesya pulls her foot back; the chick wobbles but holds its balance and surveys the world from its new perch. It looks up at Lesya, as if pondering, before sliding off. It looks up at her again, questioning or challenging. Lesya walks away. The chick follows, staying close to the left of her twisted foot. Lesya picks up her pace and so does the chick.

Maria plops the last of the chicks into the cardboard box and is about to tell the girls it is time to leave when she notices her niece. Lesya has squatted down in the dust and is holding the chick in the palm of her hand, stroking its head. The bird clucks and coos, bobbing its head back and forth, as if conversing. Lesya sets it on the ground and the chick jumps on her shoe again. 'Do you think it's a good one?' Maria asks.

Lesya knows it doesn't have much of a chance. It can't run from a predator; the other birds will ignore it or, worse, attack it; it will have to fight for food; it's no good as breed stock; it isn't even pretty. 'It's big and strong, it might make a good brood hen.' Knowing that answer isn't satisfactory, she adds, 'It hasn't given up.' And with that it is added to the cardboard box, for the reduced price of a nickel.

Whenever Lesya opens the cardboard flap, it is always her chick on top, stepping on the heads of the others, as dependable as a jack-in-the-box, and this pleases her. She opens it again, *peek-a-bird*, out pops its head. She taps it lightly on the beak and gently closes the top.

They return to Hardy's after making rounds to Lively's Feed Shop and the Willow Creek Post Office/Drugstore. As usual, there isn't any mail, but that doesn't deter Maria from buying a three-cent stamp, an envelope and sheet of paper, and sending yet another letter to Ukraïna: an update about the children, the farm, the weather . . . nothing that could be constructed as political. *We are well.* The same letter she has always written, regardless of their circumstances. *Hope you are, too.* She sends it, not knowing if it will ever get through or if there is anyone to receive it.

As they continue down Main Street, the

town's only street, Maria admires the colourful false storefronts masking squat square buildings: MERVIN BOARDING HOUSE — MEALS ALL HOURS, AP MACLEOD — SADDLER, MILBURN AND MILBURN FURNITURE. She crosses herself as they pass the church and stops to marvel at the new plank-wood house, two storeys high with a dozen windows, and wonders how many families are going to live in it. They hurry past the hotel and the ladies perched on the balcony railings lazily waving to the men passing by on horseback. When the train whistle blows heralding its imminent arrival, the ladies scurry back inside, straightening their dresses and preening their hair.

This time, when they reach Hardy's General Shop, Maria walks through the front door with her money in hand. She picks up an English newspaper for Teodor and a Ukrainian one for her. Mr. Hardy greets her as if he hasn't seen her in months and directs her and Dania to the new fabric arrivals from Edmonton. Maria takes note of her carrots neatly stacked in the front window and notices that the price has gone up.

Lesya chooses to wait outside. She peers into the cardboard box resting at her feet. The cheeps and chirps emanating from the dark confines make her smile. She opens the flap and ten chicks and the cockerel, still with patches of downy yellow amid the mottled brown feathers, gape up at her with beady eyes. Their stumpy, undeveloped wings flap and their awkward lanky legs scramble on top of one another to reach the light. Lesya quickly shuts the flap and feels their little heads bopbop against the cardboard.

'What's in the box?'

She sees his boots first. Polished to a shine, masking the cracks and scuffs. The flap of the sole has come undone at the toe. She looks up the frayed hems to the wrinkled but clean pants, follows the soiled cuffs along the too-short dress coat past the greying shirt to her father's face.

'Hi, Lesya.' Stefan smiles widely, too widely, and she can smell alcohol and cigar smoke. Protectively she puts her arms around the box and pulls it tighter to her legs.

'Is your mama here?' He looks nervously to the door. Lesya shakes her head no.

'Look how long your hair is,' and he runs his fingers through a strand, pulling the tangled ends. Lesya lowers her head and tries to disappear inside the cardboard box with her chick.

'Cat still got your tongue?' He grins, his teeth stained yellow. 'Don't you wanna know how your ol' man's doing? I got a job in the hotel. Got a room. Got lots of money to spend. Food and drink when I want it.' He puffs out his chest. 'I'm working on a land deal.' He leans in close as if someone might overhear. 'I'm gonna be ready when the spur line comes.' He swings his arm toward the elevator and the train station, which throws him off balance. 'I'm gonna own that land and then I'm gonna own the town at the end of it, you wait and see, Lesya. Your tato's gonna be a big man here.'

A police car slows to get around a horse and buggy. 'Gerry, Gerry,' hollers Stefan, 'this is my daughter.' The officer frowns and keeps on driving.

He confides to Lesya: 'I know him, he relies on me for information. He has to keep a low profile, all hush-hush. I beat the son of a bitch at cards last night.'

The bell on the door tinkles open and Maria and Dania step out.

'Maria!' Stefan stumbles up the bottom step, Lesya protectively leans over the box. Stefan removes his hat. 'You look beautiful, Maria. You always were a beautiful woman.'

'How are you, Stefan?' Maria responds neutrally.

'I'm good, I'm real good.'

The pause widens.

'I hear Teodor's back.'

'Yes,' she says.

He eyes the packages. 'Things are going well for you. It's good we could help you out in a time of need.'

'Anna's doing fine,' Maria states pointedly.

Stefan is about to reply, thinks better of it, and laughs. 'I'm workin' on things here, got a deal going.' He winks at Lesya. 'When I got it all sewed up, I'll be home to look after things. Tell Teodor to make sure he takes good care of my place.'

'We have to go.' Maria takes a step down. These words release Lesya and she picks up the box, ready to run.

'Sure, sure, me too, I gotta get back to work . . . at the hotel.'

'Goodbye, Stefan.' Maria descends the stairs,

the girls huddle close to her skirt.

'Maria?' He grabs her arm but promptly lets go when her eyes pierce him. 'You got anything you can spare?' He tries to smile charmingly. 'I'm between paydays.'

'Go on ahead.' The girls hesitantly obey. Maria reaches in the pouch around her neck and fishes out twenty-five cents, careful not to let him see the other dollar. 'That's all I have left.' His trembling hand clutches it thirstily.

'I'll pay you back.' He laughs, and says half jokingly, 'Or we can call it rent payment for the land.'

Maria's eyes turn cold. 'Take care of yourself, Stefan.'

'Lesya!' Stefan hollers. 'Aren't you going to say goodbye?'

'Goodbye,' she says weakly. She quickens her step and trips over her crippled foot.

★ ★ ★

The boys construct a henhouse fenced with willow, designed more to keep the chicks contained than to keep danger out. Ivan and Petro, tired and hungry, race to complete the job. In the middle of the night, the families wake to hysterical cackling. Lesya arrives first, ignoring Teodor's shouts to stay back as he loads his gun. She rips open the makeshift fence gate and the yellow tomcat glares back at her. Its shoulders hunched, its claws extended, its eyes reflecting green and empty in the moon's light, its mouth stuffed with feathers, it flees into the night.

The young cock and eight chicks scurry frantically in circles, ricocheting off the fence, screeching, *The sky is falling! The sky is falling!* And this time they are right.

'Here chick, chick, chick,' she calls, trying to sound calm, her voice wavering. Her twisted foot throbs from the impact of running across the yard. 'Here chick, chick, chick,' ignoring the ones colliding into her ankles, looking for only one. She walks toward the chicken coop, a hastily slapped together shelter of pallets and crates. Her bare feet follow the trail of feathers. Flecks of white, softly glowing, tremble in the breeze. She falls to her knees, not caring about the hot chickenshit smearing her hands, and crawls into its darkness.

Her fingers grope the straw and search the corners, finding nothing but splinters and mouse droppings. She holds her breath and listens with her entire heart, until the blood pumping in her ears deafens her. She falls back in the dirt, a small feather stuck to her big toe, and looks out to her family.

Maria gathers the other chicks safely in her nightgown. Anna stands at the gate, her arms impassively crossed. Teodor brandishes the .22 like a soldier pacing the perimeter, looking for the enemy. Behind them the sleepy faces of her cousins peer over the thatched fence, an odd display of floating heads barely visible in the night. Petro keeps his head down, knowing he is the one who left a hole in the fence. He had asked Lesya if she had seen Tato in town. She said, *No, he's gone and he's never coming back.* Like she didn't care.

Inside the roost, apart from everyone else, Lesya wishes she had never been born. She imagines herself inside an egg, getting smaller and smaller, until she is nothing more than a fleck, floating in a thick sea of yolk, upside down, surrounded by warmth. Outside the voices recede, muffled by the walls of her shell. She could disappear if it wasn't for the *peck-peck-peck* intruding on her silence.

She opens her eyes and sees a loose floorboard flopping up and down and a yellow head pushing through the space between. The chick squirms its way out, sprawls onto the floor, shakes its ruffled wings, and then hops onto her foot. That very instant, Lesya names the chick Happiness, a word she had never understood before, and in the next breath she vows never to tell anyone. She carries the chick to Maria and passes it to her waiting hands.

Ivan and Petro, with Teodor supervising, spend the rest of the night reinforcing the fence. It isn't until the morning sun peeks out that he releases them back to bed. A few hours later, Ivan wakes with a start and runs to check the fence, a pattern he will repeat every night for a week. Over the next month, the boys add briars and another layer of willow. Whenever Ivan sees the yellow cat, he throws a rock at it.

★   ★   ★

The hens are each laying an egg a day now. The families gorge themselves on fried eggs and boiled eggs, ladled with hand-churned butter. Maria makes thick, fluffy pancakes. She bakes poppyseed cakes that require eight whipped egg whites and scrambles the yolks for breakfast and dinner. She pickles dozens more. Those that go bad or break are given to the cats, the eggshells are scattered in the garden, and the boys smuggle a few for their stink-bomb arsenal. The family takes on the roundness of a soft-boiled egg.

The girls' hips widen, their breasts grow heavier, the boys' muscles swell and their bellies soften. The girls wash their hair in egg yolks to make it shine. Every Sunday, they sell two dozen to the hotel for twenty-five cents. Maria keeps the money in a tin can under her bed, a savings account for the purchase of a window for their new house.

It is Lesya and Katya's job to tend the chickens. Lesya is in charge of collecting the eggs and overseeing the feeding and watering. Katya is poop patrol and the clean straw brigade. Every morning, Lesya's chicken greets her by hopping on her foot, then following her as she does her chores, keeping up a constant chatter, as if relaying the previous nights events. Lesya sings to the bird and it cocks its head back and forth as if trying to catch the notes, tapping its crooked foot like it is dancing, all the while clucking off key. Ivan says she should sell it to a travelling circus or better yet let him take it to town and hold a show, *Ivan's Singing Dancing*

Chicken. He even volunteers Dania to make the hen a dress. They'd be rich. But no matter how much Ivan coaxes the bird to perform, the only one who can make it dance is Lesya, and she has no intention of ever taking it back to town.

Each night, Lesya locks Happiness safely in its roost, slipping an extra handful of fresh straw in the nest, before kissing the top of its head good night. Some mornings, she sits in the corner, lulled by the soft clucking and warmth, and watches as hen after hen pushes out an egg. Only her chicken allows her to slide her hand under it to feel the contractions and final push before shoving out a perfect, warm egg, still wet and sticky, into the palm of her hand.

Katya is also fascinated by the hens laying. She once held a poor bird suspended in the air for more than an hour, squeezing its sides, hoping to see one come out, wanting to know how something so large could come from something so small. But the hen wouldn't reveal its magic. It pecked her arms and hands, piercing through the wool socks she wore for protection, until she dropped it and it ran squawking to the rooster, *Kill her, kill her, kill her.*

Katya's other job is helping to crack the eggs for her mama's cakes. Once, a bloody clump plopped out, mingled with the yellow yolk. It looked like a minnow curled up on itself. Maria scooped it out and threw it away. Later, Katya fished it out of the slop bucket and buried it under a wild rose bush with a small chunk of the doughy ball of Christ. She recited Our Father twice for good measure and covered the spot with a pebble.

★ ★ ★

When Dania takes to bed complaining of a bellyache, no fever, just aches deep inside, Maria touches her swollen belly and pushes down. *Does it hurt?* Dania moans no. Maria recommends sleep and prescribes a drink of three raw yolks to be swallowed in one gulp. The children snuggle into bed around Dania, trying their best not to jostle her.

It scares them that their big sister is sick. Dania is never sick. She's the one who takes care of them. Katya tells her a story about angels and cows and is just introducing Lesya's hen as one of the characters when Dania hushes her. Ivan snuggles against her as he does every night, but knows not to play cold feet tonight. Sofia lies still and imagines the worst. Last winter, three of her classmates were sick and never returned to school.

★ ★ ★

Ivan wakes in the middle of the night with the bedsheets soaked beneath him. He kicks off the covers and reaches between his legs and finds his nightgown soaked. He hasn't wet the bed in months, not since his tato came home. In tears, he shakes Dania awake. She immediately feels the wetness.

'Shhh, everything's gonna be all right. I'll get a

cloth and some water. Don't wake the others.' She slips out of bed. Ivan fights to stifle his sobs as he holds the gown away from his skin and pulls his knees up tight to his chest.

As Dania moves quietly to the washbasin, she feels the wetness of her own gown between her legs and along her backside. She feels it running down the insides of her thighs. She lights a match and sees blood on her hands. Ivan screams and doesn't stop. The house bolts awake. Dania stands frozen, holding the match, looking down at her gown stained red between her legs as Ivan kicks and fights to escape the tangle of his own bloody nightgown.

Teodor helps scrub Ivan clean, the others change the bedclothes. Maria takes the kerosene lamp and goes with Dania to the outhouse to show her how to use the rags. Teodor stammers an explanation about girls becoming women and eggs and monthly cycles and cows and horses and dogs and chickens before sputtering to a stop. Katya and Sofia listen wide-eyed and Myron tries not to hear. When Dania returns, they all pretend to be asleep and leave her extra room. Ivan hugs the edge of the bed, even though the covers lift up and the cool air chills his legs.

Maria stays behind to use the outhouse. As she pees, she ponders her eldest daughter's rite of passage and suddenly feels old. She remembers her first period. She was fourteen and at church. She thought God was punishing her for thinking impure thoughts about the handsome young boy standing at the back of the church. She didn't know his name then or that she would marry him two years later. Her mother and the other village women gathered around her and walked her past the congregation, past him as he held the door open.

Maria tears off a piece of newspaper and wipes. She checks the paper, looking for blood, and wipes between her legs again. The liquid is clear and yellow-tinged. She checks her breasts; the nipples are hard and large. Her abdomen is swollen. It's been three weeks since her period was due.

She knew the moment he came inside her. She knew. She almost heard it whisper its name. Teodor thought the tears in her eyes were because it had been so long, or that he hadn't satisfied her, or that he had hurt her. She couldn't explain the feeling that at that moment something had entered her and opened up, filling her with a love so intense she could hardly bear it.

She returns to bed with a final look at her children. A fleeting thought enters her head: *Where will this one sleep?* She pushes it away. Teodor holds up the quilt for her to slip back in. He puts his arm around her and she nestles against his chest. They lie in the dark, listening to each other's breathing, smooth and regular. The bed smells of straw and sun and wind. Maria takes Teodor's hand and lays it on her belly. His hand is hot and he rubs her belly in small circles. She stops his hand and presses it against her roundness. She looks into his eyes and sees the question. She nods and he pulls her close, buries his head in her neck and breathes her in. 'Yes,' he whispers. 'Tak,' she replies.

He burrows under the covers and kisses her belly. She suppresses a giggle and joins him under the covers. 'Shhhh,' she cautions. He pushes her nightgown up and kisses her belly again. He traces his finger around her belly button; inside is their baby. He presses his cheek to her stomach as a fleeting thought enters his head: *Where will this one sleep?* But it is pushed away by Maria's fingers running through his hair. He pulls himself over her and kisses her ever so gently. His penis hardens between her legs and she opens. The children fall asleep to their gentle rocking.

★ ★ ★

The next morning, Maria takes a basket of eggs next door. Anna answers; she looks healthy and robust. Her colour is flush and her skin glows. Her hair is growing out fast and is almost to her shoulders. It shines in the sun. Maria congratulates herself for knowing that a diet of eggs would help restore her sister-in-law's balance.

'I have good news.' Maria beams. 'I'm pregnant.'

Anna's upper lip twitches and her eyes crack for just a flash, as if the sun has momentarily blinded her, but she blinks it away. She puts on a smile.

'I'm happy for you.' She takes the basket and shuts the door.

Teodor wades through the field of hip-deep, swaying wheat. He inhales its sweet, musty smell baking in the sun. Buzzing grasshoppers erupt in his wake. His hands, palm down, brush the tops of the full, ripe heads. Their spiky crowns tickle his fingers. He spins slowly around, taking in the golden field framed by the firebreak of black earth, set in an endless emerald green. A breeze ripples through the grain, creating an illusion of a herd of golden beasts stampeding all around him. Its beauty makes his chest hurt.

He selects a single perfect stalk and plucks it from the earth. He feels the fullness of its head, admires the perfectly symmetrical kernels, and snaps it from the stalk. He rolls the head between his palms, rubbing its warmth into his skin. The grain crackles and snaps. He cups his hands, loosening his fingers, and gently blows. The chaff scatters to the wind. He opens his hands, revealing a life map of calluses and scars, etched by deep lines stained with dirt. A dozen pale seeds, almost translucent, shine.

He tucks them into his shirt pocket and looks over his riches. This year will be a good harvest. This year will be the year that he dreams again. He looks across the shimmering grain, undulating against the prairie sky, up to his nearly completed house perched on the hill. He feels the blood coursing through his body, tingling from his toes to his fingertips, the oxygen filling his lungs, his heart pumping against his chest, against the seeds — and he knows he will survive.

He wends his way back through the field, stepping softly, not wanting to crush a single stalk.

'Don't forget to check the chicken fence,' Ivan cautions.

'I won't.' Petro is offended by the lack of confidence.

'I'll come by every morning to clean the poop,' Katya promises Lesya as she carries out a bundle of blankets.

'I know.' Lesya stands taller since Maria entrusted her with the sole care of the chickens. It doesn't bother her if she has to water, feed, and clean up after them by herself; they are now hers to love.

'And I'll have to still come for the eggs and to help pick tomatoes.' Katya struggles to make her contributions invaluable, though she has to hand off her load to Lesya because she can't reach over the side of the cart.

'I'll meet you at the stone wall every day,' Lesya reassures her and sets the blankets on top of the quilts.

Myron struggles through the door with a bedroll and flops it on the overstuffed cart. Teodor rearranges the dismantled stove to the front of the load to make extra room. The children march back and forth between the shack and the cart, loading the last of the supplies, utensils, household goods, and pre-serves. Maria and Dania scrub the log walls. Sofia sweeps the dirt floor. Behind the blanket chest she finds a wad of hardened dough and swats it out the door. A black cat pounces and bats it under the shack. When Katya sees Myron hauling out the blanket chest, she charges into the house.

'Where's Christ?' she shrieks. Through her inconsolable sobs, Katya blubbers in half Ukrainian, half English, about starving and a Christ ball and hiding the body and none left for them, which doesn't quell Maria's confusion at all. Sometimes she worries Katya will never outgrow her imagination.

Dania notices the black cat swiping its paw under the shack, its tail twitching, and shoos it away to see a roundish ball, which she fishes out with a stick. Gingerly, she picks up the yellow-tinged glob smeared with dirt. 'Is this it?'

Katya scoops it to her heart and Maria, who has had enough, swats her with the broom: 'Back to work.'

The cart is fully loaded by noon. Maria takes one last look at the room and is struck by its darkness. Even empty, it's too small for a granary. She almost forgot how low the rafters were. How cold the nights. How many times she wanted to run screaming from its confines. Maria gives thanks and shuts the door. She props a fieldstone at the foot to keep it closed.

Teodor scoops up the yellow tomcat and tosses it on the pile. The cat disappears under the blankets. The children stand alongside with their bundles in hand, waiting for the order to move out. Maria knocks on Anna's door. Lesya makes circles in the dirt with her foot and tells herself over and over not to cry. Maria knocks again. Anna slowly opens the door.

'We're going now.'

The two women look at the ground rather than each other.

Teodor urges them on. 'For God's sakes, woman, we're just goin' to the next quarter; we'll see them every day. Besides, you have the garden here,' refusing to make this a goodbye.

Maria ignores him. 'Send Petro if you need anything.'

'We'll be fine,' Anna insists.

'I'll never be able to thank you.' And before Anna can retreat, Maria puts her arms around her and hugs her. She feels Anna's body stiffen as she tries to pull back, her arms still at her sides. Belly pressed to belly, Maria feels the roundness and firmness. She feels the engorged breasts, the soft baby fat padding her arms, the long loose dress covering her from neck to toe. She looks at her face and sees the plumpness, the glow of her skin, and her eyes pleading Maria not to say anything.

Anna throws her arms around her and pulls her close, suffocating her with fear. She whispers, 'Please, don't.'

'Maria, we still have to unload.' Teodor shifts, embarrassed by the women's display of affection.

'Please,' Anna's fingers dig into Maria's arms, her forehead bows against her shoulder. 'I'm not going to have it.'

Maria pulls back, fighting the urge to throw up. 'I'm coming.' She refuses Teodor's hand to help her into the cart. 'Go.'

Teodor leads the horse. 'We'll see you tomorrow.' The cart rolls forward, the children fall in line behind it. A cloud of dust trails after them.

'Bye,' Ivan shouts.

'Bye,' Katya chimes.

'Bye.' Petro waves.

Maria looks back at Anna framed in the doorway. Maria raises her hand, but Anna disappears in the dust.

'Bye!' Petro hollers, though he can no longer see them. 'Bye!'

The white cloud plumes upward, drifting across the skyline. 'Bye!'

Lesya says, 'They can't hear you.' She heads to the sanctuary of her chicken coop.

Petro watches the cloud spilling across the field. The day is perfectly quiet. Not a breath of air. Petro's heart quickens. Then his feet begin to run. They run as fast as they can through the dust, over gopher holes, jumping cow patties. They fly across the prairie grass, through foxtails and burrs . . .

Late that night, Teodor brings Petro home, curled up asleep on the floor of the cart.

★ ★ ★

The children climb the hill in silence, awed by the size of the house and the glass window reflecting the sun. They enter with the same reverence reserved for church and stand huddled in the doorway as Maria unpacks the food and Teodor assembles the wood stove.

'Put your things in your rooms,' Maria directs, but the children don't respond, unable to grasp the idea of rooms. Dania takes the lead.

'Sofia, Katya . . . ' and shepherds them to the back of the log house through a door opening into a room nearly as big as their previous shack. Lined up against the wall are three small crates, roughly the same size, stamped DR. GIBSON'S LINIMENTS, GREAT WEST IMPLEMENT CO., and ROBSON'S SOAP. All have carved pine tops.

Dania runs her fingers over the letters of her name, entwined with wild roses. Katya places her ball of dough in the back left hand corner of her box, then closes the butterfly lid and sits on its wings. Sofia's chest is adorned with a fawn. She imagines it lined with scented paper overflowing with beautiful dresses. Her three smocks, two sweaters, two blouses, Sunday skirt, and two pairs of stockings snugly fill the box.

Ivan follows Myron through the adjacent doorway. A new bedframe, long enough to hold Myron's lankiness, fill the room.

'I get the side closest to the door,' Myron declares as he runs his hand over the rail of coat pegs that span the length of his wall. On the other wall, Ivan hangs his coat on a peg mounted at exactly his height. 'This side's mine.'

They go to bed early, feigning sleepiness, so they can lie in their beds and feel the new space. Without Ivan in the bed, the three girls can lie on their backs and not touch one another. In the boys' room, Myron can stretch his legs long. Out of habit, Ivan curls against Myron's back and is promptly kicked over to his own side. He spreads his arms and legs wide, amazed that all this is his.

Teodor and Maria's bed is in the living and kitchen area, nestled against the back wall, with the foot of the bed facing the wood stove and the head tucked against the boys' wall. Teodor sleeps against the wall so Maria can have a clear view of the stars.

★   ★   ★

Lesya half wakes before dawn with a cramp in her foot and Petro's legs sprawled over hers. She tries to pull her foot out, but it is deadened to her will. She grabs the shin and drags it out. She wiggles her toes and winces as the blood surges back in.

An ache in her arm rouses her again. Sleepily, she rolls over but is blocked. She looks over her shoulder and Anna is pressed against her, fast asleep with her arm draped heavily over hers, cutting off the circulation. Lesya lays her head back down. She wills herself to sleep, but the tingling in her arm won't relent.

She feels Anna's warm, rhythmic breath on her neck, the rise and fall of her chest. She examines her mother's hand hanging loosely over her shoulder, across her chest. Her fingers are long and tapered, tanned a deep brown, the knuckles chapped. There is black dirt under her nails. On the thumb and index finger, alongside the nail, small ragged strips of skin have been chewed away, a nervous habit since childhood. Lesya brings her fingers close to their tips but doesn't quite touch.

The sun is poking through the chinks in the wall when Anna stirs. Lesya shuts her eyes. Ever so carefully, Anna extracts herself from the bed. Even after she is gone, Lesya doesn't move. She holds on to the warmth of Anna's impression against her body until her arm, throbbing for blood, falls limply across her stomach, demanding to be resuscitated.

★　★　★

Teodor slips quietly out of bed, careful not to disturb Maria. His eyes half shut, he stretches in front of the window, a recent morning ritual. The last few weeks in his new house, he has found sleep again. Deep, undisturbed, dreamless nights. He rubs the sleep from his eyes and yawns. A smile crosses his lips as he savours the sun's warmth. He opens his eyes to the glory of his field. Not bothering to put a shirt on, he steps outside and smells acrid smoke. His stomach knots. To the north, he can see a yellow haze. He licks his finger and checks the direction of the wind.

By noon, a thick grey plume clings to the skyline. The wind is still true from the north. He knows there are farms in that direction and miles of tinder-dry bush. He looks nervously to his field and walks down to check the firebreak. He pulls the weeds that have sprouted up over the summer and examines the perimeter for any dried roots or branches and drags them farther to the side. Off in the distance, Teodor notices a low trail of dust. He watches until he can make out two horses, an appaloosa and a palomino. The speckled grey appaloosa is saddled. They stampede to the south.

At three o'clock, the wind shifts and blows from the northwest. Teodor orders every bucket, pot, washbasin, barrel, and kettle filled with water. The children form a brigade from the recently dug well to the cart, shuffling up full buckets to Myron, who empties them into barrels tethered in the back of the cart before passing them back down the line.

Teodor and Myron drive the wagon to the east firebreak and with difficulty off-load the heavy barrels twenty feet apart along the field's edge. They return for another load. Along with four more bulging barrels, they cram the wagon with wet burlap, soaked blankets, shovels, and rakes. Teodor tells Maria to pack supplies, just in case. After they unload, he gives Myron the reins and tells him to get Anna and the children.

He guesses the fire is maybe fifty miles away now, though the prairies play tricks and a storm cloud that appears on the other side of the world can suddenly be on top of you. If the wind stays this direction, it should pass them by. It'll come close, but should run east and drive below them to the south or better yet burn itself out.

Anna's property and the barn are set well back, and a slough on the east side should divert the fire. His house should be safe on the hill, unless the windbreak of spruce that wends up the north side catches; he orders the children to douse the cabin with water. There's nothing to protect the field though, except twenty feet of dirt. He should have made it forty. At least there's the lake on the west side to keep them safe.

At six o'clock the horizon is a wall of white smoke punctured by bursts of flame darkening the evening sky. He sits on the stoop of the house, lights a cigarette, and waits.

Myron returns with Anna and the children. Perched in the back of the wagon is the chicken coop. Lesya sits at its doorway, cooing at the clucking hens locked inside. The rooster ran off and was left behind. The black cat and her kittens hid under the barn and refused to come out, even with an offering of a fresh mouse. The cow tied to the back jogs behind, pulling at the halter, its eyes and nostrils wide, smelling the danger. The horse stomps and snorts, protesting Myron's command to stop.

Maria greets them when they arrive and offers supper. Anna, wrapped in a full-length cloak, declines. Lesya and Petro swallow down their hunger and Maria insists. She threads her arm through Anna's reassuringly. 'You have to eat.' Anna suddenly craves dill pickles and wild blueberries.

As the hours tick by, the children join Teodor on the stoop. They curl up against his legs and spread their blankets on the ground beneath his feet. They silently watch the night sky. Half of the stars are obliterated by the unnatural darkness. A pulsing red glow looms in the east. Lesya and Katya snuggle together in a blanket, their heads covered. Katya furtively rolls the doughy ball of Christ between her fingers. Sofia coughs sporadically. Dania licks away the taste of smoke on her lips. The boys sit stoically, mimicking their father's posture. Elbows on their knees, leaning forward, hands clasped, watching. Ivan struggles to keep his eyes open. It's well past his bedtime. They all feel the low thump of danger in their chests and the need to stay close.

Teodor estimates that it's ten or fifteen miles away and the wind is picking up. When a sprinkling of white ash showers down, Ivan takes his father's hand. Teodor looks to Maria. 'We have to go now.'

Maria claps the sleepy children awake. 'You heard your tato, grab your things.'

She doesn't look back when she shuts the door, afraid that she will run in and barricade herself inside.

Teodor leads the caravan of children and animals by the light of the kerosene lamp, down the hill, over the field; he skirts the rough ground of the firebreak and sets up camp in the clearing a few hundred feet from Bug Lake. The coop is hauled off the wagon and the cow tethered to a tree. Three more barrels are filled and strapped down in the back of the wagon. He chooses Dania and Myron to go to the east border with him. He needs two more and scans the faces of the children. They're all too small.

'Sofia.' Her head is down and her shoulders drop when he calls her name. Lesya steps forward, standing as straight as she can. 'And Lesya.'

'And me!' Ivan takes his place beside Myron.

Maria signals Teodor, No.

'You stay with Mama. I need you to protect the cow.'

'I'll go.' Anna climbs aboard the cart, pulling herself up heavily.

'You can't.' Maria looks to the bulge poorly concealed by the ill-fitting cloak. 'I need you here.'

'We'll be okay,' Teodor promises. 'If it reaches the firebreak, get everyone to the water. Cut the animals loose. Don't wait.' And he is off.

'Don't you wait!' Maria hollers after him, but Teodor doesn't hear.

★ ★ ★

Sparks ignite the sky not two miles away. The wheat bows in the breeze as if in retreat. The horse, tethered to a stake in the ground, yanks at its restraint. The cart rocks back and forth, jostling the water. Teodor stands in the middle of the firebreak, surrounded by buckets, barrels, and soaked blankets. He is flanked on his left by Myron and Sofia, to his right, Dania and Lesya, and at the far end, Anna. Water barrels dot the east perimeter every twenty feet.

Myron surveys the hundred feet they barely cover and glances back at the six acres stretching behind them. He plants his feet deeper in the earth. Billowing black smoke rolls toward them, searing their eyes. They hear its crackle first, like a splintering of trees.

'Hold your ground,' Teodor calmly directs, but Sofia has already taken a step back. They can see

142

the fire now, running on a southeast course. The flames seem to jump and leapfrog, fanning themselves wider. It looks like it's going to pass by with maybe two hundred feet to spare.

They feel its devouring heat. Partridges explode from the bush; flames lick up the branches. The fire converges in a muskeg knoll and ignites the tops of the trees. A burst of wind drives the sparks toward the firebreak. They watch them float to the ground like fireworks, a gentle rain extinguishing itself. The few that make it to the earth alive pulse red on the ground. Teodor stomps them dead.

'Myron, water!' Myron grabs a bucket and drenches the throbbing embers.

'Over there, there's more,' Lesya shouts.

'Stay in the firebreak,' Teodor hollers as he rushes to the next threat. It is the southeast corner that might get hit.

'Water it down!' Teodor yells to Anna. She pushes against the barrel, a sharp pain stabs her side. She pushes harder and the barrel slowly tips and topples over, drenching the ground. The fire catches in the thick underbrush and smothers low. A rabbit bursts from the trees, zigzags madly across the firebreak, and charges past Anna into the wheat. The flames roll across the spruce trees and wrap away from the field.

'Keep going, keep going . . . ' Teodor wills it onward.

A snake of flame shoots up the trunk of a hollow, dead tamarack. It flares alive, writhing to the upper limbs. The wood pops and snaps, a burning torch illuminating the upturned faces.

143

The trunk cracks and branches crash to the ground, shattering into fire. Teodor grabs a bucket and races toward the tongue flickering through the weeds. He hurls water on the beast, cutting off its head. Around him dry grass erupts into halos of flame. He jumps on one, crushing it back. Another erupts to his right. A gust of wind swirls around him and a trail like spilled gasoline whooshes past. The wind slams Teodor in the face, directly from the east.

'Get back!' he screams to Myron. 'Get back!' The fire rears its head behind him. They scramble for the firebreak with flames biting at their heels.

'Drop the water!' Teodor orders.

Lesya and Dania push their barrel over and run for the next. Anna strains to topple the third. The barrel groans over and slams against the earth. The ground is so dry that the water skims the surface and spills into the cracks, disappearing instantly. Sofia struggles to overturn her barrel, but she can barely jostle the water. She leans against it. The fire rolls toward her, floating low across the prairie, a cascade of iridescent orange. Myron slams against her barrel. Water splashes over her shoes, soaking her stockings. 'Get more water!' Myron yells at her as he runs to the next barrel.

The horse tugs and snorts against its restraints as Sofia climbs aboard the cart, tossing her onto the floor. She struggles to fill the bucket, slipping on the boards, as she is jostled by the horse's fear. 'Hurry!' Myron screams. She is running back with the bucket clanging against her knees, water slopping down her legs, when the flames reach the firebreak. The fire roars upward, screaming against the impasse. It climbs straight up, twenty feet, howling its rage. She can see its eyes, looking straight at her. Sofia falls to her knees, unable to move. Teodor hurls water at the demon; it sputters and groans, before opening its mouth wider. Dania tears the bucket from Sofia: 'Get up!' Sofia buries her face into the dirt and covers her head.

A deer, its coat singed, leaps through a hoop of flames, its hooves crash into the ground beside Sofia. Its eyes wide, its sides heaving, it bolts sideways and plunges through the wheat.

Lesya passes a full bucket to Anna and runs back for another. Sparks spit across the dirt barrier, igniting half buried, tangled, dried roots. Anna's cloak trails through sparks. They grab the fabric and flare up her leg. She watches mesmerized as a blue-yellow flame circles her. 'Mama!' Lesya screams, the word sounding foreign to her ears. Teodor reacts instantaneously, smothering the flames with a blanket.

'It's cold,' Anna marvels. But he doesn't have time to ponder her words.

'Take her to the cart,' and Lesya leads her through the wheat, not understanding the smile on her mother's lips.

The fire licks along the firebreak, rushes to the southeast corner, and surges around the rock wall. Dozens of snakes slither from their hiding place. They writhe across the ground, coiling over Teodor's boots. Wild daisies curl and shrivel in the heat. The ground steams and hisses, grows

145

hot underfoot. The fire twists upward and slams down, stretching across the barren ground, its fingers groping for the wheat. Teodor beats it back with wet blankets. With each waft of the cloth, sparks rage upward. His face wears the fire's reflection, red and twisted, filled with hate, two demons dancing in the screaming light. Teodor pummels back the flames.

The children rush to his aid, hurling buckets of water, tripping and falling, sparks raining down on their arms and hair, stinging them. They stumble over one another. Myron grabs a bundle of soaking burlap and unfurls it over the southeast corner. The wheat collapses under the weight. The smoke blinds them. They choke on the heat.

'More water!' Teodor yells, losing ground, his back pressed up against the wheat.

Lesya and Dania reach the cart simultaneously. They jump onboard. Lesya rams her knees against the sidewall but doesn't feel the pain. They force their buckets into the barrels and yank them out full.

'More water!' he screams as the fire rears up behind him. Dania jumps over the side, her foot rolls in a gopher hole, and she crashes to the ground. The bucket slops over, emptying its contents. She looks to her father, knowing she has failed. The fire howls and spirals downward, a crashing wave of flame. It barely licks the tips of the grain . . . and the wheat ignites. With blinding white intensity, the stalks explode.

'Go to the lake!' Teodor tramps down the

wheat to intercept the flames. 'Now, goddamn it! Now!'

And they run. Dania grabs Sofia and hoists her into the cart. Lesya drags Anna, who is riveted by the fire's wild beauty. As far as the night reaches, the flames rage. The entire world is on fire.

'Cut the barrels,' Teodor yells as he unrolls wet burlap behind him. Myron rushes in with another wet blanket to carpet the wheat.

Teodor tears the blanket from his hands. 'Go with your sisters!'

'I'm staying here.' Teodor shoves him, knocking him to the ground. 'Get the hell out of here!' He kicks him in the ass. 'Go!' In that moment, Myron hopes his father fucking burns to death. He runs blindly to the wagon and wrenches the reins from Dania. The horse bolts even before Myron whips it. Lesya and Dania throw themselves on the barrels to keep them upright.

'Let them go!' Teodor calls after them. 'Drop them!' Dania pushes over the first barrel. Water floods the cart and pours off the back, soaking the crushed wheat flattened by the horse and wheels. The cart cuts a swath through the grain. Fire crashes against the firebreak. Only the southeast corner has been breached. Dania looks back at her father, beating down the grain, shrinking against the backdrop of flames.

The water trickles to a drizzle. The empty barrel bangs and rolls against the cart. Dania clings to the side as the horse gallops madly through the night. 'Drop it!' she yells. Lesya squeezes between the barrel and the side and heaves. The wagon slams into a hole and jolts upward, driving the loose, empty barrel against her crippled leg. The pain explodes white in her head.

'Drop it!' Dania screams.

Lesya strains against the weight pinning her leg, throws her body against the full barrel. Again and again she slams into it, until slowly it teeters and falls, releasing a stream of wetness that slicks a glistening trail behind them through the flattened grain.

★ ★ ★

'Get up!' Maria shakes Katya, curled up asleep in a blanket on the ground, and pulls her to her feet. Katya groggily looks up at the night sky turning into day and the stars falling from the sky like angels. She feels the ball of Christ warm and sticky in her clenched hand.

'Go to the water, wait for me there.' Maria throws a cold wet blanket over her shoulders. 'Go!' Katya stumbles a few steps toward the lake, then turns back looking for her mother. She sees the fires of Hell bursting from the earth. 'Go!' Katya runs.

Ivan and Petro fumble to untie the knot that the cow has pulled tight, anchoring itself to the tree. Their small fingers tear against the twine. 'Cut it,' Petro wheezes. Ivan scrambles for the axe. Maria reaches the chicken coop and pries open the door. She grabs a squawking hen and stuffs it into a gunnysack.

The horse and cart burst from the darkness. The horse's head pulled back, its teeth grimacing, as Myron reins it in hard. It fights to keep running, but Myron holds on and the cart rumbles to a stop. Water drips through the floorboards.

Maria scans the sooty faces and wild hair. 'Where's your father?'

'He wouldn't come.' He spits the words.

Behind them the horizon flares white and they feel its hot breath. Maria tosses the gunny sacks into the wagon. Lesya jumps off and her foot gives way under her. She crumples to the ground but slaps away Dania's proffered hand and scrambles to her feet. Sofia, huddled in a corner of the wagon, doesn't budge. She grips the sides, her arms shaking from the exertion, her eyes fixed on the fire chasing them.

Maria and Dania throw utensils, shovels, pots, and blankets wildly into the back of the cart. Myron warily gauges the speed of the fire. 'We have to go, soon,' his voice cracks. Mice scamper wildly around them. Birds scattershot into the sky, screeching their warnings. Grasshoppers catapult and ricochet.

'Get that cow out of here!'

Ivan chops through the rope. 'Let's go!' Petro grabs the halter and pulls. The cow plants its feet and refuses to budge. Ivan slaps its rump as Petro hauls on the rope. 'We have to go,' Ivan pleads with the cow. He talks to its eye, trying to make it understand. 'You're going to die here.' He can see that it can't hear past its fear. He grabs its tail and twists with all his might. The cow jumps, kicking its heels, and lurches ahead. Ivan and Petro chase it, clapping and whooping, herding it forward.

From the wagon, Anna calmly watches the chaos. A blur in the bush catches her attention. The rustling branches part and a coyote steps out. It freezes at the sight of the humans and the noise and commotion. It looks back to the bush, its ears and nose twitching, and back at the humans blocking its path to the water. Anna stands and slowly steps down from the cart. She walks toward the wild dog. The coyote growls, it lowers its head and snarls. 'It's me. Don't be afraid.' She holds out her hand, but the coyote bolts back into the bush. She hears it crashing through the undergrowth, skirting the water, and she follows.

*　*　*

Katya stands at the water's edge, waiting for her mama. The smoke hangs low, obscuring her view. The sky throbs red and orange. She holds Christ cupped in her hands, wishing she had more of him and if he was going to wake up and save them, now would be a good time. She hears a whishing sound. 'Mama?' The long grass sways. A stick falls onto the shoreline, and then another, and another. They wriggle alive and glide across the bog toward her. It is not until they are a few feet away that she realizes they are snakes.

She backs into the water, up to her ankles, then her knees . . . still they come. Slithering toward her, thin golden streaks, curling and uncurling. A tightening in her lungs reminds her that she can't swim. Her dress hem touches the water and she instinctively lifts it up. The snakes reach the water and keep coming. Katya stumbles backward to her waist, her chest. The snakes float on the surface, their heads arched up, their tails and bodies propelling them forward. The water ripples behind them. Katya stops when the water reaches her neck. The snakes' heads level with hers, she raises her hand and holds up the doughy ball of Christ. A white paste oozes between her fingers, drips down her arm, and spills into the water. Jesus dissolving all around her. The brigade of snakes part and dart past her ears, their tiny wake lapping against her chin.

★　★　★

Myron struggles to hold back the rearing horse. 'We have to go *now!*' The fire surges toward them in long strides, smelling its prey.

Maria throws on the last of the load. 'Where's Lesya?'

Lesya fights to shove another chicken into the sack. It kicks free and the birds tumble out. 'Leave them!' Maria screams at her. The hens careen in all directions. She drops to her knees and crawls into the coop to retrieve Happiness. The bird pecks at her hands.

'Leave it!' Dania pulls on her legs. Lesya grabs the hen by its feathers as Dania drags her out. She tucks it under her arm and they run. Myron

151

snaps the reins and the cart hurtles past them. Maria glances back to see the flames bleed across the clearing, searching for the woods. She runs faster, her arms laden with pots and pans clanging wildly.

From the safety of her holy water, Katya sees her family emerge from the smoke and flames. The horse charges for the lake. The wooden wheels slog through the mud. The horse lunges against the harness, driving it forward. A few feet from the water's edge the wheels mire down completely in the bog. Myron jumps off and pushes. The cart rocks an inch and rolls back. He sees Sofia still crouched inside.

'Get off.' And when Sofia doesn't respond, he drags her out. She lands hard on the dirt. 'Push!' Myron yells and his fury shatters her paralysis. Dania, Ivan, and Petro join them. The fire funnels toward them. Maria sees her children, feet away from safety. 'Leave it, get in the water!'

Myron jumps into the cart and hurls the empty barrels, shovels, and supplies into the water. 'Push!' Maria drops her pots and pans and throws her weight against the back. The wagon breaks free and rolls a few feet into the water, before bogging down again. The horse's hind legs sink in the slimy bottom. It loses its footing and falls on its side, flailing in the water. The cart slowly tips over, twisting the horse's head underwater. Myron splashes to the front of the cart, knife in hand, he gropes underwater for the harness. He saws at the wet leather. The wagon slams down. The horse rises from the water in a spray of moon and flames. It spins around and swims to the opposite shore. The fire roars behind them.

'Go deeper.' Maria herds her brood. She counts her children's heads, momentarily panicked that she has forgotten one.

Myron refuses to go. 'I have to keep it wet,' and ladles water over the wooden sides, jutting high past the waterline. Dania plows through the water to help him. Her feet sink in the murky slime. She loses her shoe. Ivan, Petro, and Katya climb onto the cart's shafts and take refuge behind the front board. Lesya wades in with her hen held high over her head. Sofia hugs her body as she forces herself into the cold water, imagining eels and leeches clinging to her skin.

Maria sees the fire creeping through the bush and Anna still on the shore, as if waiting its arrival. She splashes toward her. But Anna doesn't hear her. She is listening for the coyote. The baby kicks and writhes. Her knees buckle and she sinks to the ground as Maria reaches her. 'Do you hear it?' Anna asks. Maria hears the fire ripping through the muskeg.

'Yes. We have to go.' She tries to pull her to her feet.

Anna fights her off. 'I have to stay. It's come back for me.'

'Get up!' Maria screams and drags her into the lake. She feels her own body cringe in pain. The fire swings wildly around, the flames race along the south shore, up the trees, swinging from branch to branch. The water glows red, and in its light, Maria sees a deer, a cow, and a horse standing in the shallows. Mice, rabbits, and chickens veer up and down the shore, throwing themselves into the lake. The children scream as the fire flares toward them. Anna shakes herself loose from Maria, falls, and sits motionless in the water. 'Stay here,' Maria warns her and wades back to the wagon.

Anna stares up at the flaming treetops. The cold water soothes the baby inside her. Her wet cloak weighs her down. At the shoreline, the coyote emerges from the undergrowth, its back smoking. The deer doesn't even notice, but Anna does. The coyote paces frantically, its tail tucked between its legs.

'Come,' she calls it. 'Come.' The animal looks uncertainly at her and back at the fire. 'Come.' She stands up, hands outstretched, water dripping from her sleeves. Branches plummet to the ground behind the coyote. It yelps and leaps into the lake. Anna wades toward it. The animal's back is black; raw red flesh scars its coat. She smells its torched hair. She fills her hands with water and spills it over the animal's burns. The coyote trembles. Anna gently runs her hand over its back. It flinches from her touch, then swims away from her and climbs onto a rock shared by the yellow tomcat.

★   ★   ★

The animals and humans huddle in the water. Maria clings to her children burrowed against her, repeating the only words she can think of to keep them safe: 'Keep your eyes closed. Don't look, don't look.' But she watches.

She watches treetop torches crash to the ground and the fire claw at the shoreline. She watches to brush the sparks from her children's hair and submerge their heads when the heat threatens to choke them. 'Don't look, don't look.' She watches when Myron can no longer lift the pail to douse the wagon and tears of frustration blind his eyes. She watches when he rips off his shirt to slap at sparks that aren't there. 'Don't look.' She keeps watching to prevent them from slipping underwater when they can no longer hold themselves up.

She clutches them until after the fire has passed, leaving behind only the moon that has slid high across the sky. She holds them until only faint embers pulse. Blackened tree limbs steam. Twigs crackle. White smoke drifts low between the trunks and she is certain that it is gone. 'Open your eyes.'

The children rouse. Their heads nod up. Their eyes blink open. They loosen their stiff limbs from the cart and from her. Ivan and Petro, leaning against the wheel, are nudged awake. Maria unwraps Katya's grip around her neck and waist and lowers her into the water. Katya groans, reaching to be picked up again and carried back to bed.

Maria leads her family out of the lake. Chilled and exhausted, they stumble on shore to the charred remains of the chicken coop, barrels, buckets, and pots. Water drips from their sodden clothes, cools the baked earth beneath their feet. Myron picks up an axe head. Drops it as it sears his palm. Lesya's foot drags behind her. She hugs Happiness close to her chest. Not until she is on dry land does she uncover the hen's eyes.

'Teodor!' Maria calls. Her voice booms across the silent expanse. 'Teodor!' She walks into the smouldering night. Her feet follow the glistening trail of drenched, trampled stalks. To her right, barren ground smokes. All around her the acrid smell of burned sweet wheat. Up ahead, she senses a faint impression, a petrified shadow. He sits on the ground, his face and clothes blackened, staring at his scorched boots.

'Teodor?'

He looks up at her, his eyes hollow. 'I couldn't stop it.'

She takes his chin in her hands and turns his face toward her, wondering how he can be so blind. She steps aside, revealing the surviving ragged swatch of wheat glowing white in the pale moonlight.

'Let's go home.' She helps him to his feet but crumbles under his weight.

Myron races to his mother's assistance. 'I have him.' He drapes his father's arm over his shoulder and guides him up the hill. The others follow in a slow funeral procession. Ivan leads the horse. The cow ambles after them. Only Anna, pulled along in their wake, looks back.

The lake is calm and empty, holding only the moon and the outline of the cart.

In the south, the sky glows red.

★   ★   ★

The fire cut a swath through the centre of the properties, its path impeded by the stone wall. The two houses were spared. The back wall and roof of the barn were scorched. The chicken pen and paddock torched. Of the six acres of wheat, three were lost. Also lost or damaged were seven barrels, two pots, three blankets, a harness, two rakes, one shovel, one axe, one chicken coop, six chickens, one rooster, and a child's shoe.

A half-mile northwest, Josyp Petrenko's farm was untouched.

⋆ ⋆ ⋆

By ten in the morning, it is eighty degrees. They've been in the smouldering field since daybreak. No one speaks. There is only the sound of Teodor's scythe cutting through the grain, and the grunt of his exhale with each wide swipe. Each cut is so quick that the stalks hang erect for a moment before collapsing to the ground. The sweat that soaked Teodor's shirt and pants earlier has dried, and he is no longer sweating. He ignores the thirst and thickness in his throat. One step, one cut, one step, swing back, one step — his eyes only on the golden sea he is parting. With each stride, he widens the gap between himself and his children.

Myron wraps a sheaf of wheat with binder twine and stands it in a stook. He glances to Dania, keeping pace beside him. She deftly wraps her bundle, completes another stook, and moves ahead. Myron waits empty-handed.

'Hurry up!' he hollers up ahead to Sofia, who is gathering the felled grain. 'You have to keep up with him!' She is a hundred feet behind her father.

'I'm working as fast as I can!' She no longer feels her fingertips, numb from scraping the fallen stalks into armfuls and passing them off to Ivan and Petro like overstuffed batons to race back to their older siblings.

'Don't you cry!' Myron warns, forcing tears to well unwillingly in Sofia's eyes. She pushes the kerchief back from her forehead, smearing her face with dirt and soot. Her cotton dress hangs limp, its hem tucked under her knees to give some relief from the prickly stalks. The dust sticks to her body, knots in her hair, and makes her skin itch. She must look like a peasant here on her knees, rooting in the dirt like a pig.

'Don't cry,' Ivan whispers and takes the bundle from her hands.

He scampers back to Myron. His heart beats wildly in his chest; his lungs suck in the dry heat, searing his already parched throat. His head floats from the sudden acceleration. *Run run fast as the wind run run fast as the wind*, he chants in his head.

He plugs his nose to the smoky smell that reminds him of burned bread and scraps of bone tossed in a wood stove, and breathes through his mouth. When they walked across the charred stubble this morning, he could feel its heat bleeding through his leather soles. The children stepped slowly, careful not to desecrate the remains. Only Tato forged ahead, not looking right or left, but straight ahead to the remaining crop. Ivan wondered whether he would be forgotten as quickly by Tato if he had burned up. Myron snatches the grain from his hand. 'Go!' Ivan laps Petro on the way back.

Petro has fallen twice, and his skinny knees are smeared with dirt and streaks of dried blood. He stumbles again and the wheat scatters. He sweeps it up.

'Leave it!' Myron barks. 'Help Sofia.'

Petro joins Sofia scooping up the loose grain. The chaff tickles his nose and scratches his throat. The dried stalks splinter in his palms like a thousand pinpricks. He tells himself, *You're not my brother*. And looks to Teodor to see whether he notices how hard he is working.

'They need to rest. They need water,' Dania admonishes Myron.

'We stop when he stops,' and he doubles his efforts.

Dania wipes the sweat from her eyes. 'We have to stop.'

'Then stop!' Myron screams at her and grabs the sheaf from her blistered hands. And to his surprise, she does and walks away.

The children look uncertainly from her to Myron and back to Teodor, whose step hasn't faltered.

'It's time to rest, come get a drink.' Dania lifts the blanket shielding the bucket of water and scoops up a ladleful. Her parched, numb lips open to receive the tepid liquid. It trickles to the back of her throat. Pours through her insides. A hot breeze blows on the back of her neck and goosebumps shiver up her arms. Sofia abandons her post.

'Girls,' Ivan sneers to Petro and turns his back on them. He picks up the slack by filling his arms with a double load. When he bends over, black dots jumble behind his eyes, the ground sways, and he seems to float up. He breathes in, braces his feet, and pulls himself back down. He hears his own rapid panting, feels the rise and fall of his chest. When he turns around, Petro is with his sisters.

His head is tilted back, the too-large ladle suspended over him. The water splashes against his mouth, spills down his sunburned chest. His throat hiccups up and down, guzzling down the water. Dania draws the ladle back but Petro pulls it forward again, like a nursing calf not ready to let go of the teat.

Ivan wants to knock the ladle from his hand and choke the water from his throat. He wants to grab the bucket and pour it over his own head, feel it shower over his body. He'll open his mouth wide until it sloshes in his belly, pools at his feet, and floods to his waist. Then he'll lie back and float in his own golden pond. He licks the salt from his lips and looks to Myron.

Myron strangles another armload of wheat with twine. Sweat burns his eyes, blurring his vision, and for a moment the grain turns to liquid dripping through his fingers. He wants to drink its paper dryness. Up ahead, his father in his white shirt and black pants looks like a magpie dancing in the heat waves. Black and white. Its silver beak slashing at the light. Its wings beating the air. *He should have stopped by now.* Myron feels a flash of fire ignite in his belly. *He's supposed to stop.* In his hands, the liquid thickens into molten gold and hardens into shimmering sheaves. He places the bundle on the golden altar along with all the others. He blinks, and the stook of wheat leans heavily to the left. 'Get me more!' he shouts.

Ivan finds his feet and rushes to him, arms full, showering wheat . . . *Run run fast as the wind . . .*

$$\star \quad \star \quad \star$$

In the shade of Anna's cabin, Katya lies naked on the stoop, her legs splayed, her dress crumpled beside her. Her toes wiggle in and out of the hot dirt. She breathes shallowly. The soft breeze whispers, *Go to sleep go to sleep go to sleep.* Katya's eyes open and shut, afraid to surrender in case the fire tries to get her again. She can taste it on her tongue. It seeps from the corners of her eyes — black, gritty gobs that stick to her fingers and taste like fear.

The fire was stronger than Jesus. She held Jesus up to protect her and he disappeared. Or maybe she used him all up for herself and that's why the fire ate their wheat. She failed the test. She killed Jesus to save herself.

But Mama made them give thanks to God and Jesus and the Blessed Mary before tucking them into bed. Mama says Jesus did protect them. The fire didn't take their house, didn't take them, didn't take all their wheat. Maybe Mama doesn't know that Jesus is gone.

But Tato knows. Tato refused to pray. He wouldn't wash the ashes from his face and hair, even though he smelled like fire. She was afraid to kiss him good night.

If she has killed Jesus, then that means God won't want her now. Only the fire will want her. *Go to sleep go to sleep.* She didn't sleep last night or this morning. She kept herself awake by pinching her arms and legs and poking at Sofia until she punched her. Mama thinks the bruises were from the Night of Fire. She kissed each one and rubbed a yellow flower salve on them. *Go to sleep.*

Mama doesn't know the fire is coming back for her.

This hot is different. This hot wraps around her from head to toe like a cat's purr. *Sleep.* This hot isn't angry. This hot is day . . .

★　★　★

Lesya spends the morning salvaging boards and crates for a new chicken coop. She borrows from the barn, scavenges behind the house, and then heads to the dump. There she finds an old board peppered with almost straight nails and a crate with a faded, crinkled picture of a smiling lady holding a bar of soap. She is missing the top of her head and one eye, where the label has torn away.

Lesya sits in the shade of the birch trees. Their leaves are dusty and muted but otherwise unperturbed by last night's event. She looks

162

down across the fields. A bird's-eye view. She can see the new house on the hill, its timbers green and one window blinking in the sun, calling to her own dull grey house below. She can see the stone wall separating the worlds. A child's line scratched in the dirt. She can just make out her uncle and her cousins, mere specks bobbing after him. Like a hen with her chicks. She smiles, forgetting that she is mad at them for not letting her come along.

From her perch she sees what remains of the field. It is no longer straight and rectangular. Ordered. Its edges are ragged and frayed, shaped like a hardboiled egg that someone has taken a bite out of with the shell still on. Cracked and broken. She looks to the black gashes that split open the prairies north to south, widening and narrowing, blooming outward, as far as she can see. A snake that slithered around hills and trees, jumped gullies, dodged right then left before spotting its prey.

She spies a perfect magpie's tail feather, long and glistening black with a white tip, and picks it up. The spine is translucent and hollow. She runs her finger down its edge. It softly parts to her touch. She lifts her long skirt, too heavy in this sweltering heat, exposing her pallid leg and twisted foot, hanging limp.

'You did good,' she tells it. 'You did your very best.'

She runs the feather down the blood-dried scrape extending below her knee, down her shin to her bruised and swollen ankle. Three times she asks the feather to carry away the pain. The third time she releases the feather to the day's hot breath. It tumbles lifeless to her feet. She works the kink from her aching foot, gathers up her spoils, and heads home.

★ ★ ★

In Anna's house, not a breath of air stirs.

'You'll feel better once you're cleaned up,' Maria coaxes. 'Lift your arms.'

Anna protectively grips the filthy fabric of her dress. Maria suppresses the urge to slap her. There are so many other things she should be doing: helping Teodor in the field, preparing lunch, mending her children's ravaged clothes, or any other number of tasks. She shouldn't be babysitting a grown woman. Once she gets her cleaned up, she'll prepare her sister-in-law a poppyseed tonic to calm her nerves. It's time this stopped.

'It's only me here. You don't have to hide.'

Anna looks into her eyes, questioning whether to trust her. Maria hopes her face is empty, non-judgmental. 'Let me help you.'

Anna loosens her hold and obediently raises her arms. Maria pulls the dress over her head. The cloth reeks of smoke and the sour smell of mildew. The fabric is damp; Anna refused to take it off last night. She also refused Myron's bed and instead sat up all night staring out the window.

'I don't think it can be saved.' Maria examines the tattered hem, mud stains, and scorch marks. 'Maybe this piece — I'll take it home with me.'

Even with the door open, there is no breeze. Only suffocating heat.

'This too.' Maria stands behind her and unknots the grimy string clenching the corset. The soiled fabric strains at the eyelets. The crisscrossed string burrows into the soft folds of Anna's flesh where the material should meet, and bulges around her spine. She loosens the string and the corset springs free. She pulls it open, uncasing the body, revealing bruises and welts where the wire ribs have branded her caged flesh. She pries it away, gently now, skin peels away, heat blisters weep around her nipples.

'What have you done?'

Maria touches her distended belly, feels for the head. Her fingers expertly push past the fat and muscle, lift under the ribs . . . and the baby kicks.

'It's still alive.'

Tears break through Anna's heart and flood her eyes, searing her cheeks. She chokes on her own spit, drowns in her own gulping wail. The tears fall on her belly and splash on her hands — she cries because she didn't know she still could.

★   ★   ★

The new chicken coop is a jigsaw of planks and boards of varying lengths. Nothing is straight or square. When Lesya kneels inside, her head brushes the bottom of the lopsided roof. She has used the crate with the lady's face to make the roosts. She hasn't figured out how to fasten the door yet, so a palette proclaiming NO SAG GATE leans against the opening. She has scattered fresh hay on the ground, plumped up the nests, filled a tin with water. Now she sits in the back, quietly clucking.

'*Tch-tch-tch*, here, Happiness, *tch-tch-tch* . . .'

The other two surviving hens have already wandered in and claimed their spots, leaving the smiling chin and hand holding soap as the last vacant roost. Lesya sprinkles water on their backs to keep them cool. None of them have laid yet today. She can hear her mother's wailing. Lesya focuses on the sound of the hen's soft cooings, grateful that her aunt is visiting.

'*Tch-tch-tch*.' She tosses out another handful of feed as bait. The two sitting hens cluck their indignation. Lesya pours a small mound in front of each of them. No sign of her hen. Lesya sings her name. Happiness peeks in. She keeps on singing, making up the words as she goes, exhorting her to come in and lay her egg, everything is fine, look at the pretty house I made you . . . the chorus is composed only of her name, *Happiness, Happiness* . . .

The hen hops onto Lesya's bad foot, gingerly resting on its own lame claw.

'That's a good girl. Are you hungry?'

The bird frantically pecks the seed, scattering more than it takes in. Lesya lifts it onto its roost. The hen squawks and flails its wings, kicks to jump off. Its twisted foot claws her hand. The other birds squawk an anxious chorus.

Lesya sets Happiness back on the ground.

166

Immediately calm, it jumps back on her foot. The hen cocks its head, looking at her through one eye and then the other.

'Maybe later.' Lesya lies down and forms a circle with her arms. Happiness nestles into the human nest.

★ ★ ★

Runrunfastasthewind, the words blur in Ivan's head. His legs are no longer connected to his body; his hands fill magically with wheat that flies from his hands to theirs. A hot gust wraps around his ankles and breathes into his face. The loose grain lifts and swirls between his fingers. One playful stalk skitters up, tickles his arm, and twirls around his ear. He brushes it away and turns to see if the others have noticed the dancing wheat. But their eyes are fixed on the earth, their minds fixed on their thirst.

Ivan turns his face into the breeze. Coming over the hill, looming behind their new house, a black crest swells skyward. Rolling and widening, the top ballooning, it arches forward. A pheasant breaks from under the stone wall in a whir of feathers. Two ducks, flying low, *honk honk honk* and pass directly overhead. He can see the white of their bellies and orange feet tucked up tight.

'The clouds are upside down.'

Dania gives a sigh of relief as the sun disappears and the temperature drops a welcome degree. But there are no clouds. A blast of hot air billows her skirt. She looks over her shoulder and sees a mountain of dust obliterating the sky. It avalanches down the fire's path, growing as it feeds on the exposed dirt and ash, sucking the hot air into itself. She has never seen a dust storm before.

'Get down!' Her shriek wakens the others to the swell of dirt storming toward them. She races to cover the water bucket with the blanket.

'Lie flat! Cover your heads,' Teodor yells.

Sofia and Petro drop to their bellies and bury their heads in their arms, creating a cocoon of air. Their noses are inches from the ground. They smell worms.

Dust sprinkles Ivan like a fine shower. It stings his eyes. Dirt peppers his cheeks, sprays into his mouth; the earth rears in front of him and he is inside black.

Myron slams him to the ground.

*　*　*

Maria lays a damp cloth on Anna's forehead. She has rubbed her belly with honey and butter. Stroked her hair until she fell asleep. She has prayed every prayer she knows. Now she sits beside her, watching her breathe, as unguarded as a child, wondering what she should tell Teodor. She looks up to the sound of ducks passing close overhead, honking their alarm. She wonders what's chasing them.

She hears a soft sprinkling and is relieved that the rain has come to smother the heat, wash away the smoke and ash. She forgets the sun is still shining. The room darkens and the sound grows sharper, more insistent. She doesn't smell the sweet release of a summer shower. A plume of black earth sprays through the open door. She looks out as a wall of dust hits the barn.

* * *

Katya can't breathe and it feels as though ants are biting her all over. Wake up, her head screams. *Wake up!* She tries to open her eyes, but a gust of heat blasts her face, grabs at her hair. Her skin is burning. She stands, trying to cover her bare chest and bum. She feels flames all around her, licking at her legs. She wants to tell God she's sorry. She didn't mean to kill his only son. But he is roaring in her ears. She prays the first prayer that enters her head: *Now I lay me down to sleep, I pray Thee Lord my soul to keep; glad and well may I awake. This I ask for Jesus' sake.* The heat swirls around her, the fire scorching her skin. Her body trembles as she dares to shout the words. *I pray Thee Lord my soul to keep; this I ask for Jesus' sake! This I ask for Jesus' sake!*

The Lord picks her up and she is flying through the air.

* * *

Dust gushes through the chicken coop, whipping the straw into the air. Happiness pushes under Lesya's skirt. Lesya gropes for the other hens. Her fingers brush the warmth of a fresh egg. She grabs one bird by the foot, the other by the neck, and shoves them under her hem. She pulls her blouse up over her face. They sit tented, breathing one another's air. Lesya softly sings: *Everything will be okay. Everything will be okay.* Dirt rattles against the boards; she doesn't hear Maria calling her name.

★ ★ ★

Maria slams the door shut. She gasps for air, her nose clogged; she coughs and spits up dirt. In her arms, Katya is quiet. She sets her on her feet, wipes the dirt from her eyes. Her thin, naked body is a mess of red splotches already turning purple.

Katya stands still, listening carefully, wondering if she has been taken to heaven or hell. 'Katya.' The voice is soft. She opens her eyes. God looks like Mama.

The earth hammers against the doors and walls. It spills under the door frame. It sprays through the log chinks, showering Anna, who doesn't stir, in fine black dust.

★ ★ ★

Ivan, his head tented under his arms, his belly pressed to the stubble, peeks up once. He plugs his nose, breathes into his hand, and squints through the driving dust blasting his face. He's never been inside a cloud before. He peers through the blinding sheets and sees a ghost in a white shirt and black pants. The wind whips at his sleeves and pant legs. The blackness swirls around him. His feet planted, scythe in hand,

170

eyes closed. His face turned upward. His tato's face. A look he's never seen before. A look that scares him. Ivan lowers his head and breathes.

And then it's gone. The sun is back. The heat blazes. The stooks are still standing, anchored in drifts of dirt. The loose wheat that hasn't blown away gleams like golden threads poking through a shroud of black earth. The children rise from their dusty graves, their mouths thick with the taste of being buried alive, as sparrows drop from the sky, their beaks crammed with dirt.

THE WILLOW CREEK WEEKLY

FIRE DESTROYS 90 HECTARES
5 FARMS LOST, 7 PEOPLE DIE
By Joffre M. Dechene

The farm home of Mr. and Mrs. Philip Normand, forty miles north and west of Willow Creek, burned this Thursday morning.

The fire started while Mr. and Mrs. Normand were milking. Noticing the smoke, Mr. Normand rushed into the burning building to get the two children, who had left the house and were sitting in the automobile. Mr. Normand, who did not know this and who looked for them until convinced they were safe, suffered severe burns about the face, arms and hands. He received treatment at the General Hospital, but tragically later died.

The fire spread quickly to nearby bush and fields and was driven south by unusually high winds. Exceptionally dry weather is partly blamed for the fast moving fire. Smoke could be seen as far away as Vermilion. The town of Willow Creek escaped tragedy, likely due to the railroad tracks that diverted the fire south.

John Chubey was not so lucky. Despite his neighbour, Albert Limoges, warning him to pack up and leave as quickly as possible, Mr. Chubey and his family stayed to fight the fire. Three children, aged six to twelve; Mr. Chubey; his wife, Mrs. Margeret Chubey; and her brother Gunther Mann all perished when they became trapped near the barn, possibly trying to save the horses. The horses, an appaloosa and a palamino, were found sixty miles south, near St. Paul, on Friday.

Willow Creek, Alberta, Canada, Saturday, September 8, 1938

Fall

The first snow falls October 12, while everyone is sleeping.

Teodor sees it when he wakes up at four to throw another log on the fire. Large wet flakes drifting softly down, blanketing the grey-brown remnants of fall. He steps outside for a smoke. At least he got the field up in time.

He was expecting the six acres would average thirty bushels an acre, giving him one hundred and eighty bushels. After the fire, he harvested seventy-eight. Hold back fifteen bushels for seed crop and four for flour, that leaves fifty-nine. At ninety-three cents for grade one, that's $54.87. If the prices hold. On the safe side, it's eighty cents. That's $47.20. Less ten dollars for Anna to pay the homestead fee, that's $37.20. Less feed, nails, and hardware for a new barn, barbed wire. He'll have to build a granary next summer; he can't expect to store the wheat at his sister's again. He was hoping to get a pig or another horse, but that'll have to wait. He'll have to buy a side of beef to get through the winter. He could use another shovel, a couple of barrels, the harness can't wait, he needs to get the horse shod, the children need winter boots, none of their coats are warm enough for a bad winter, there's the baby coming . . . and Anna's baby. He has to calculate the upkeep for her place, their food, and her children don't have proper boots either.

He takes a deep inhale of the smoke until the heater burns his fingers. He flicks the butt into the snow.

And tobacco . . . he exhales.

* * *

After his father's measured bootprints heading across the field to Anna's to check on the animals and Myron's shoeprints crisscrossing back and forth to the woodpile, Ivan's feet are the next to run through the new-fallen snow. He zigzags back and forth, kicking up curves, sliding on his toes until his heels catch, and he barrels forward spraying black earth on white. He finds an alder switch and drags it behind him, drawing looping circles and squiggly bits. Then he closes his eyes and takes two steps forward, listening to the scratch of the stick against the fresh new snow. He takes two more steps.

* * *

Maria looks out her window at the thin whiteness blanketing the prairies. It flattens the hills, gullies, wagon ruts, and furrows into smoothness, swallows up the shadows and illuminates the smallness of their lives. She shivers, even though the fire is roaring. Perhaps it's the draft from the window. She watches Teodor, black against the white, disappear just the other side of the stone wall. She knows it is

178

an optical illusion, that he's in the dip, but her heart tightens.

This is just a dusting, she scolds herself, this isn't even winter. A moment later, he reappears. She chastises herself for her silliness. Soon she won't be able to see him at all. He'll turn right at the round boulder and come up on the paddock from behind trying to surprise the horse, but it will be waiting for him. It always knows when he's coming. Teodor would be disappointed if it didn't. He'll feed it and brush it. Talk to it.

Maria often saw him running his hand down its mane, across its neck. Its head nuzzled into his chest. His mouth close to its ear. Telling it what? All his secrets? Everything he can't say to her? Using up all the words, so by the time he gets home, he is silent again, shoulders stooped into himself. He pretends — smiling, joking with the children, listening to their stories, talking but saying nothing. The fire burned a part of him away. He will heal. Come the spring, once the scorched field yields life again, he'll forget what was lost and see what he has.

She looks up at the black smear of smoke suspended off in the distance. Anna's keeping the wood stove burning. That's a good sign. She hasn't hurt herself since the summer. She's not hiding the pregnancy any more; granted, that would be difficult at seven and a half months. All Maria told Teodor was that his sister was pregnant. That was enough. He wanted to go to town to find that good-for-nothing son of a bitch Stefan and beat some responsibility into him.

179

Maria pleaded with him not to go, but it was Anna who told him she didn't want Stefan back. Things were better now.

Maria feels the baby turn in her belly, a flutter of butterflies. She rubs her belly reassuringly. *It's okay, little boy, it's only snow*. He must be close to four months now. He'll be a March baby.

She knows it's a boy; he came to her in her dreams. She asked him: *Are you all right?* He said, Yes, I'm fine. She asked him if there was anything wrong with him. He said no. She asked, *Are you sure?* He said, *Yes. I have a birthmark*. She told him: *That's what will make you special*. And right then she knew everything would be fine.

Teodor reappears. He walks straight, never veering, his trail cutting the prairies in half. In a few hours, she'll walk the same path to take lunch to Anna. Since the dust storm, it's been a daily trek. She tells Teodor that his sister needs company, that it's hard for a woman to be alone when she's expecting. She doesn't really mind going, though lately she's been feeling the strain of carrying an extra ten pounds. Her lower back aches and by nightfall she can barely keep her eyes open. But it's a chance to walk with her thoughts, check in on her sister-in-law and the children, milk the cow, and still get home in time to make supper. It's a way to make sure nothing happens.

Every trip is the same. First Anna eats. She eats and eats and eats. Maria doesn't eat with her. She keeps count of how many eggs, how many potatoes, how many jars of preserves, how much bread, how much milk . . . and calculates the impact on their winter stores. Sometimes she intervenes and covers a jar of dill pickles or pickled eggs — and puts it on the shelf, suggesting that maybe she should save some for tomorrow. But when Maria returns the next day, the jars are empty and more have been opened.

After she's finished eating, Anna allows Maria to examine her belly and tells her of any physical complaints. Maria prepares a tonic. This one for back pain, this one for constipation, this one for nightmares. She rubs honey and butter onto her stretch marks, massaging the baby. At this point, Anna always looks away. Once Maria has finished the exam, she wipes down the table, cleans the dishes, throws a log in the fire, and sits in the chair closest to the stove. Once enough silence has passed, Anna tells her stories.

She talks about her life before she came here. Stories that Maria has heard hundreds of times. Stories about childhood, stories about boys, stolen kisses, and dances. Maria listens patiently, never interrupting. If Anna's having a bad day, Maria prompts her — Tell me about the time you rode the white horse; danced in the field; found a gold coin . . . Anna's eyes come alive and the stories start again.

Maria's eyes follow Teodor to the round boulder. *Anna's baby will be here soon and then we can get on with life. I should dig up the last of the carrots and beets before the snow buries them. Ivan's socks need darning. He looks so small . . .*

And then Teodor's gone, leaving only white.

Ivan marches past the window, eyes closed, dragging a stick behind him.

★ ★ ★

Katya lies on her back in the snow. It makes her legs and neck tingle. She feels it melting through her coat, her skirt, even her stockings. She knows Mama will be mad and her boots probably won't dry until tomorrow. But she doesn't care. Her mouth is full of its coldness, dissolving on her tongue.

She is safe for another day. She has started a new doughy ball of Christ, a mix of the body from church and pyrohy dough that she takes when Mama's not looking. The fire is kept inside the stove now. It is small and can't get out. She's not sure which one is more powerful. Every morning she opens the door and feeds it a small taste of Christ.

It has burned her only twice.

★ ★ ★

When Ivan opens his eyes, he is almost at the stone wall. He is surprised how far he has got. Behind him, a staggering path carved in the snow winds its way back to the house. He steps to the side and leaves two perfect footprints. He puts his feet together heel to heel and waddles. He hops on one foot, then the other. He takes big steps and small. He admires his handiwork. He takes a run and hops to a clean, fresh patch. But the snow here isn't untouched. It is

182

flecked with tracks. They skitter beside the rock wall, then cross over here, stop, then hop over there, a widening circle, then back toward the wall. Farther and farther apart, and then short and close together. Ivan follows the trail, dragging his fingers over the scorched, cracked rocks where the wall pressed up against the fire. Ivan looks up ahead to see how far the tracks go. A mottled brown rabbit sits perfectly still against the white snow. *You can't see me. I'm invisible.*

Ivan stands perfectly still too. *I see you.*

He remembers the rabbits Myron brought home last winter. How they tasted in Mama's stew. How happy they made her. He blinks. The rabbit twitches its nose. Ivan leaps and the rabbit bursts away, zigzagging through the powder, its feet bounding side to side, it disappears in a cloud of snow. Ivan comes to a panting stop. *Stupid rabbit.*

Ivan realizes he is at the far eastern line of the property. He's never been this far by himself. From here he can see his house and Petro's. One up and one down. And the ragged grey line of stone capped with white. It looks small from here. He must be close to the dump. He sees his tracks jumbling across the field and is sorry that he ruined the perfect whiteness. To the south, far away, he sees a person approaching. Black against white. He wonders how his father got way down there without leaving any tracks.

★   ★   ★

183

Teodor slows his step as he rounds the back of the barn. He softens his footfall to deaden the crunch of the snow. He pokes his head around the corner. The horse greets him with a whinny and a headshake. Teodor swears it is laughing at him. He rubs its forelock; the horse presses its nose into his chest. He reaches in his pocket and extracts a carrot. He leans into its ear as the horse nuzzles his palm.

'I don't know what I'm going to do,' he confesses.

After strewing fresh hay, breaking the ice in the water bucket, and filling the feed pail, he gives the horse a snow bath. He brushes the dirt from its coat, until the old boy shines. He gives it a pat on the rump and heads to the barn to check the cow.

He hears Lesya singing. It is a long-ago song about a shepherd having to leave his true love but promising to return home before the first snow falls, *Wait for me, wait . . .*

Milk squirts in the pail. The cow chews its cud, eyes half asleep. Lesya massages its teats like a harp, her cheek resting on the cow's flank. Her voice resonates high up in the rafters, filling the space with its melody. A black cat sits behind her, tail twitching slowly, its ears pricked skyward. Head slightly tilted, listening.

The smell of the hay, the warmth of the animals, and that voice — Teodor closes his eyes and listens, feeling as if he has walked into a church. A church for men like him. It makes his heart ache for something lost. *Talk to me*, this place says to him. *Talk to me.*

The singing stops, as does the milking. Teodor opens his eyes. Lesya stares at him. Her cheeks blush and she bows her head.

'You shouldn't be afraid to let people hear you.'

She focuses on the milking — *phish, phish, phish*.

Teodor checks the cow. Its coat is thick. The teats a healthy pink. The milk is pure.

'How are the chickens?'

'Good.'

'How are they laying?'

'Fine.'

'They're all laying?'

Lesya stops milking. 'One's not.'

Teodor looks down at his niece, her face hidden behind her long hair. Her twisted foot, splayed beside the bucket. She never looks him in the eye, yet he always feels she's watching him. She's like a skittish colt he expects would bolt if he held out his hand. She's not like any of his daughters. Her face never betrays what she's thinking. Her eyes are always guarded.

'She's looking good,' he says and heads for the door. The cat follows, its tail hooked high. Lesya resumes milking.

Teodor hesitates at the door. 'What size shoes do you wear?'

* * *

Petro isn't allowed out today, because he couldn't find his wool socks. He didn't tell his mother that he lost his socks on a bet with Ivan.

185

She is knitting him a new pair, but they're not ready yet. He watches her stitch: purl and knit, purl and knit. There is a cuff and a heel. Tomorrow he should be able to go out. He is kneeling on a chair, looking out the window, waiting for Teodor to come out of the barn so he can wave to him. The soles of his bare feet are toasty facing the wood stove.

'Come try this,' Anna calls him.

He goes to her and holds up his foot. She slips the opened-toed sock over his foot. He wobbles on one leg as she nudges it over his heel. Off-balance, he rests his hand on her shoulder. She is surprised by the contact.

'It's not too big?'

The sock slumps down his skinny leg.

'No, Mama.'

He can smell her hair. He is looking at her belly. Round and wide. It looks bouncy and soft. Not thinking, he touches it. Realizing what he has done, he quickly pulls back.

'You can touch it.'

She slips the sock off his foot. He's not sure whether this is a test and he's not supposed to touch.

'Go ahead.'

She lays his hand on top of her belly. He feels a thump. His eyes widen.

'Can I hear it?'

She nods.

He rests his ear to the side. He feels the thump on his hand. He crawls up onto her lap and drapes himself over her belly. His ear pressed tight.

He is so light. His arms so thin. Anna looks

down on her son, not sure if she should touch him. It's so much easier with the coyotes. They ask nothing of her.

The first time she saw the coyote, she was bringing two hardboiled eggs. She wasn't paying attention as she approached the twisted poplars. She was looking at the charred trunks to her left, wondering why the hollow had escaped the flames. When she was thirty feet away, she saw it. It jumped back from the treat of pyrohy she had left the night before, ready to flee. She lowered her head, averted her eyes, and crouched down slowly. She sat still, tried to calm her breathing. The coyote finished its meal and ran off.

Each morning, it has let her approach another foot. She is now only eight feet away. She can hear it sniffing the air. Hear the gnash of its teeth as it gobbles the food. She can steal sideway glances at it. It is the coyote from the fire. The singed hair on its back has grown in short and ragged. Over its left haunch, a patch of scar tissue remains bald. Anna tried to speak to it once, softly, but the coyote bolted and watched her from a distance, abandoning its morning meal. Anna didn't speak again. She had to start another ten feet back to make amends.

Petro taps her belly lightly with his fingertips.

* * *

The cat races ahead of Teodor to the shack that now serves as the granary. Mewing in anticipation, it weaves through his legs. Teodor lifts the latch and opens the door. The cat rushes in.

187

Again he is surprised by the smallness and darkness that greets him. He can't believe they lived here. The grain is piled high; the mound heaps up to the roof and spills into the corners. It is dusted in a light powdery snow, blown in through the cracks. He'll have to get bags to haul it to the mill. Twenty cents a bag. He sighs. He dips his hand into the wheat. It pours like sand through his fingers. It's good grain.

He ponders the quantity and decides he can sacrifice a quarter of a bushel for some homebrew. Just enough for one Mason jar, a little warmth to get him through the winter. It's dangerous to be caught with moonshine. An automatic one-year sentence. But this is more medicinal than recreational. He's not going to sell it. He'll just brew one pot, keep it tucked away. For a free country, they have some strange laws. He dips a pail into the wheat and fills it half full. He pours out a quarter, decides it will be enough. He takes one last look around to make sure everything is safe and steps out.

'Come on, cat.'

He sees it lurking in the corner, its back hunched, its tail waving, eyes narrow . . . its ears scanning the mound.

'You hear something in there? Do you have a mouse? Get the bastard.'

The cat's back end quivers. It crouches low. Front legs tucked tight. It leaps.

So precise, so focused, Teodor marvels at its beauty. Claws outstretched, calculating the exact distance, speed, and timing. Adjusting its curve, mid-air, its head swings around as if sighting its unseen target, hidden beneath the grain. It dives into the wheat, paws already reaching, even before the head and shoulders plow their way in.

'Looks like we did good this year.'

Teodor spins around, dropping the pail, his muscles tense, ready to defend or attack.

Stefan laughs. 'Jumpy these days, aren't you? It's been a long time. I heard you were back.' He holds out his hand to shake. 'It's good to see you again, Teodor.'

Teodor looks hard at his brother-in-law. His rheumy eyes, sagging cheeks, drunkard's nose. His smile bares tobacco-stained teeth. A wolf's grin. He wants to smash him in the face. He kneels down, rights the toppled pail, and scoops the grain back in.

'The old place looks good. I saw the house up on the hill miles back. Didn't know what it was at first. Hadn't heard you were building.'

The toes of Stefan's boots curl up from the soles. The shoelaces are missing. If Teodor swung the bucket up now, he would catch him under the jaw, snap his neck in two. In prison, he saw a man die like that for taking a bite of another man's piece of bread.

'I read about the fire; it was the talk all over town. It must have come close by here, eh? We're lucky it missed us.'

Teodor slowly gets up. Stefan's hands are in his pockets now. The bottom two buttons on his coat are missing. His collar is stained. His mouth is stretched into a smile, the corners tight and practised.

'I don't know if Anna told you, but I've been

working on a deal. I've got my eye on some land — it's going to be worth a fortune when the railway goes through. I was this close to signing the papers, needed a bit more money . . . so now it's on hold until the spring. You almost get there, you know, and it all falls apart.' His eyes narrow. 'We've been through a lot, haven't we, Teodor?'

One jab to the nose, drive the bone up into his brain. Instant. Like the guard did to his cellmate. He was dead with his mouth still open, screaming for water. There wasn't any surprise or pain in his eyes, just the indignation of a thirsty man who can see the water barrel ten feet away.

'How long are you staying?'

Stefan's eyes harden into an officer's eyes, a traitor's eyes, a guard's eyes. His smile thins. 'As long as I want.'

Teodor picks up the pail. Reminds himself that Petro is just on the other side of the wall and that Lesya could step out any moment. He's still their father. He's still their father. He's still their father . . .

'Making a little liquid gold?' Stefan's mouth involuntarily salivates.

The cat explodes through the door; a thin pink tail hangs out of its stuffed mouth.

Teodor shuts the granary door and latches it tight.

★　★　★

At first Petro thinks he is hearing the baby talking. A low, deep voice. He presses his ear

190

tighter to his mother's belly. But there are two voices. Men's voices. One is Teodor's. He lifts his head. Anna's hand clenches the knitting needles. Her body is rigid. She stares at the wall. Petro looks to her, but she is no longer aware of his presence. He slides off her lap and goes to the window.

'Tato!'

He throws open the door and runs barefoot into the snow.

'Tato! Tato!'

He throws himself into Stefan's arms.

'Look at you! Look how big you are.' Petro clings to his neck. His nose crinkles at the smell of body odour and sourness. 'Tato.' He looks to Teodor and sees that he is sad. Petro thinks he wishes it was him being hugged instead. He holds on tighter to Stefan.

'Okay, okay. You're choking me, get down. Get down.' He sets him in the snow, not noticing the boy's feet turning pink. 'I brought you something.'

He reaches in his pocket and pulls out an apple. One red apple, slightly bruised. Petro takes it, holy, in his hands.

'Share it with your sister.'

He looks up to Lesya, who has come out of the barn, the milk pail in her hand.

'Hi, baby girl.'

Her hand trembles. The milk sloshes in the pail.

'Do you have a hug for your tato?'

She looks to Teodor, who looks at the ground and focuses on its whiteness. She drags her foot toward her father and lets him hug her. He runs his fingers through her hair. 'Look how beautiful you are.'

She hides her face behind her hair.

'Where's your mama?'

Stefan goes to the open door and steps inside. Anna sits in the chair, the knitting needles digging into her left palm. The sock unravelled on the floor. A knife by her side.

★ ★ ★

Maria is putting on her coat and boots when Teodor returns. He takes off his coat, removes his boots, shakes off the snow, and sets them in front of the stove. He throws a log in the fire, sits down, rolls a cigarette, lights it, and takes a deep puff.

'Stefan is back.'

★ ★ ★

The moon hangs low and swollen over the incandescent, pale blue fields. The night sky is pricked with light. There are so many stars. Maria loses count again. She stretches her aching back and lifts her stiff joints from the chair. The fire crackles reassuringly. Quietly, she makes the rounds. Myron is snoring. He is splayed on his side, his head hidden under the covers. Ivan's feet dangle over the edge of the bed. She tucks them in. He groans and pokes them back out. Katya is snuggled into Dania. Sofia lies rigid on her back, her hair coiled in rag strips, her mouth gaping, the sheets tucked tight on both sides. Only Teodor tosses and turns.

She returns to her post at the window. She has been up for hours watching the stars slowly circle overhead. The baby hasn't let her sleep.

She has an urge to put on her coat and boots and walk. Just follow the moonlight to wherever it leads. She imagines the crisp sound of the snow underfoot. The chill of the air on her cheeks. The sharp cold sucking at her breath. The sensation of walking in blackness, not knowing what's behind or ahead . . .

She leans close to the window. Her warm breath condenses on the glass. She draws her finger through the moisture. *We have to sleep now, baby. It's time to sleep.*

Lately, even when she closes her eyes and opens them to find that dawn has arrived, she's certain that she hasn't slept. She has been suspended between awake and dreaming. But tonight she remembers a dream. Someplace warm and safe. She hears the fire. She sees colour. Transparent red. She floats in a sea of sound. She hears muffled laughter, fragments of song, the deep, low pulse of a man's voice, the clang of the wood-stove door shutting. She is sucking her thumb. She is inside a poppy flower swaying in the breeze, the light bleeding through its petals, rocking her to sleep. The petals close around her, tight and heavy. She pushes against them, but their weight crushes down, constricting her ribs. She woke up in bed, pinned. She lifted Teodor's sleeping arm from her belly and got up. That was hours ago.

She traces the frost in the corners of the windowpane. She wishes she could make some bread or mend Teodor's pants, but she's afraid she'll wake the others. She wants to shake Teodor awake: 'I can't sleep.' Make him sit with her or take her for that walk. She wants to clap her hands and announce, 'Breakfast is ready.' Hear the clamour of her children, crawling out of bed, squealing as their bare feet touch the frozen dirt floor. Answer their groggy questions: 'No, the sun's not coming up today. Today we're going to live at night.' She scratches the frost from the glass; it curls under her nails and melts.

She wonders if Anna is awake and remembers her nocturnal walks. She looks hopefully across the field, wanting to see her cloaked figure. It used to frighten her when her sister-in-law wandered off into the night. Now she yearns to join her. How could she have not told anyone? Why didn't she come to her? If she had come earlier, she could have helped. She could have made her parsley tea and a vinegar bath the very next day, before there was a baby. God forgive her, but she would have helped. She would have prayed to the child's soul and asked it not to come. She would have explained that this mother had two children already and no one to help take care of them. She would have asked for mercy.

But Anna didn't tell her, even though they were only separated by a wooden wall. If she had told her, she would have said, 'I understand what it feels like to be alone.'

She would have told her about the night last winter, when she couldn't sleep. A blizzard had come in and the wind was wailing. Snow was ferreting through the cracks. The children were huddled on the straw mattress, shivering. She had piled every spare piece of clothing on top of them to fend off the bitter cold. Ivan had cried himself to sleep after Maria caught him eating a raw potato he had stolen from their precious stores. She had whipped him with the wooden spoon until it broke.

She was shoving one of the last sticks of wood into the stove, realizing that she would have to burn one of the chairs next, when she saw herself pulling it back out of the fire, its end flaming. Its warmth scorched her cheeks and hand. She thought, *If I set this place on fire, we'll be warm.* It was so simple.

Then she remembered Teodor's promise that he would come back for her. That she wouldn't be alone forever. She thought about what would happen to him if he came back and they were gone. He wouldn't understand how cold they were. She put the kindling into the stove, fell on her knees, and prayed for forgiveness.

She would have understood. But now it's too late. Now there is a baby. Now there can be no forgiveness. She prays for Anna's mistakes, tries to make Him understand why Anna can't ask for her own forgiveness. Asks Him to see the loneliness in her soul and guide her back from the wilderness. Make her love this child. Make this child her salvation.

Her fingers rub the wooden cross around her neck. She looks up to the stars, wanting a sign.

Maybe Stefan will stay this time.

Teodor told her not to bother going to Anna's this afternoon, but she did anyway. He answered the door, crowing like a rooster. His chest puffed out, he welcomed her in like she was a guest. Invited her to sit down and have some lunch; she declined. Lesya was serving him eggs, pyrohy, bread and raspberry jam. He asked for bacon or ham — a proper meal for a man. Lesya told him they didn't have any. Feigning shock, he announced that now that he was home he would get them a pig. He pulled a flask from his pocket and topped up his coffee. He winked at Petro and told the boy to get more wood. He rubbed his old war injury and told Maria how much it hurt in the cold weather.

He regaled them with stories from town, the latest gossip of politics and intrigue. He told Petro about a toy train that ran on steam. He told them about the rich people who drove through town in a Model T, wearing goggles and fur coats. He told Maria about a washing machine that ran on electricity and could wash ten bedsheets in one load. He told them about a hip-of-beef dinner at the hotel, which cost five dollars a plate, and a windup piano that played music all by itself. He told Lesya about a dance where the women wore dresses that shone like silver, their hair held up in swirling buns with feathers and tortoiseshell combs.

Petro sat beside his father, clutching a mottled apple, hanging on to every word. Lesya busied herself at the stove. Anna never said a word. She sat at the other end of the table, eating a jar of jam with her fingers, ignoring the bread. Her

196

belly engorged beneath her smock, her breasts low and full, she stared at her husband. He said none of the women could dance as good as his Anna.

When Maria tried to help with the cleanup, he insisted that Lesya would take care of things. When she offered to stay the night and keep an eye on Anna, because the baby was unusually active and her pulse was high, he assured her that he would look after his wife. When she got up to go, he walked her outside. The last thing he said was: You don't have to come by any more. I'm home now.

Out of the corner of her eye, she sees a star streak across the sky. But when she turns to look, it is already gone. *We have to sleep, baby. It will be morning soon.*

Teodor whimpers in his sleep. Maria creeps quietly to the bed. He lies on his stomach. His right leg twitches. His face is anguished, his hair slick with sweat. She rests her hand on his feverish forehead.

He bolts upright, grabbing her wrist. His eyes seethe with hate, his teeth are clenched, his breathing laboured.

'Teodor.'

He blinks.

'It's only a dream. A very bad dream.'

He looks past her shoulder, as if searching for the voice.

'You're home, safe in bed.'

He looks at her, unconvinced.

'Go back to sleep.'

His eyes follow the touch of her hand on his as

she lifts his fingers from her arm. She guides him back to the warmth of the quilt and tucks it high around his neck. He curls tight into her pillow. He breathes, 'Maria . . . '

'Yes?' She leans in close, but his breath is once again soft and even.

She rubs the bruises on her wrist and pulls down the sleeve of her nightgown.

★ ★ ★

Petro has been asleep for hours. His hand cups the apple now pressed against his cheek. He had hidden it under his pillow and fell asleep breathing in its sweet scent, dreaming of its redness against his white sheet.

Before he fell asleep, his fingers rubbed the smoothness of its skin, outlining its one soft brown spot. He poked a fingernail into its flesh, and juice squirted onto his finger. It smelled like summer. He licked its sweetness. He touched his tongue to the open wound and suckled its tartness.

His father had given it to him. A special present that he said had grown far away in the mountains and journeyed by train, wrapped in straw. It had been polished and displayed in a window. A ruby jewel destined for him.

He wanted to bite it. Cut into its whiteness. Devour it — seeds and core, suck up every last drop, hide it inside him. But then it would be gone.

Lesya already told him she didn't want any of it. But if he ate it by himself, there would be nobody to share in its memory. Nobody to remind him what the first bite tasted like or the last. So he has decided that Ivan will be his witness, so when he forgets that the juice was sticky, that a peel got stuck between his teeth, that its soft pulp lingered on his tongue, someone else will remember.

He is dreaming. There is a big smile on his face. He sees an apple as big as a house and he is chewing his way through it bite by bite.

Lesya promised herself that she wouldn't fall asleep. She sang every song she knew twice in her head. When her eyes fell shut, she lifted the covers and let the cold draft freeze her toes. She imagined monsters under her bed and coyotes circling the house. She ordered herself to stay awake. She dug her nails into the palms of her hands. When her breathing began to match Petro's even inhale, exhale, she poked him in the ribs. But the bed is warm, and the blanket cocooning her head reminds her of the closeness of the chicken coop.

Through heavy eyes she watches her mother and father at the table, silhouetted by the flickering light of the kerosene lamp. Their voices low. His voice low. A soft murmur, soothing rhythm — low bass caressing . . . muted light waltzing on the walls. She needs to stay awake. She needs to keep watch.

Last time, it was her fault. She just watched when her mother looked straight at her, her eyes begging for her help. But she was too scared of his grunts and her silence. She was only ten, now she's almost eleven. This time she won't be afraid. This time she has a plan. This time she won't cover her head. She'll get out of bed, with her good foot first, and walk up behind him. She won't be afraid. She'll tell him stop. Stop hurting her.

Her eyes shut again as his voice drones on, like a bedtime story. Warm and safe, drawing her in, making her forget that it isn't a dream. Stay awake, she tells herself, as the world dims dark. Stay awake, she pleads, as she floats away on a bed of feathers.

Stefan has been talking for hours. Explaining where he has been, what he has been doing. Anna watches him talk. His face indistinct at first. A stranger who doesn't know it is time to leave. She doesn't nod or encourage him, just watches, lets the words pour over her. Her fathomless blue eyes look into his. Who is this old man in front of her, with his blotchy skin and yellow teeth? His hair too long and stringy. Thinning on the top. He has been confessing his indiscretions for hours. The other women, the alcohol, the loneliness — his failings as a husband and a father. He looks familiar. Someone she once knew. Why is he telling her these things?

The more she looks at him, empty and non-responsive, the more Stefan opens his heart, needing her to understand. He tells her things he's never admitted even to himself. He tells her how afraid he is of dying poor and forgotten. He tells her how sickening it is to wait on rich English men as they discuss their next financial scheme while he holds out a pan ashtray to catch their cigar ashes and empty their spittoons.

He tried to talk to the owners about his ideas, but they didn't want to hear. The customers liked him because he made them feel important. They bought him drinks and let him sit in on card games. He entertained them, catered to them, stroked them. He played whatever role made them feel better about themselves. That's how he heard about the land for sale and the railway. He just had to bring the players together. Move the money in a slow play, until the big showdown, when he'd be the one holding all the cards. Aces, king high. Then they would bring him drinks and ask his opinion and hope they would be invited to sit beside him.

He tells her: 'I'm doing this for us.'

He tells her about the house he saw that he is going to buy for her. A beautiful two-storey house, painted white, with eight rooms, a pantry, and an indoor toilet. A bedroom for each of them. At the very top a turret with a single window facing south. And electricity.

He cries when he describes the view from the bedroom looking down on the railway tracks where he can oversee his business. He'll check his gold pocket watch to confirm the train's arrivals and departures. He'll wave to the engineer and count the boxcars filled with commerce, adventure, and riches — his riches. People will tip their hats to him. Offer to light his cigar. Admire and envy him.

He tells her there is a carriage house for a buggy or an automobile. He says the grocery is just around the corner. And the women's auxiliary holds socials once a month where people dress in their fineries and eat finger cakes on silver plates and drink from fine china. He tells her: 'This is what I want for us. This is what I'm working for.' He has tears in his eyes. He actually believes himself.

As he talks about who he is going to become, his back straightens and his eyes light up. His hands stop shaking and command the air with authority and style. He laughs, a young man's laugh. And for the first time since Anna was a young girl, she sees Stefan as he was when his eyes were a clear blue and his blond hair was cropped close to his ears. When he stood above everyone else. His uniform immaculate, a silk handkerchief tucked cavalierly in his belt. His boots polished black. A proud man. A man with dreams. A man who rode stallions and drank cognac, and wore a sash and a tapered sword slung low on his hip. She sees the man who walked across the dance floor, took her hand, and said, 'You're mine.'

'Forgive me,' he says and bends low and kisses her hand as though she is a lady and he is a gentleman.

Anna yawns, deep and long. 'I'm so tired,' she says.

★ ★ ★

She wakes once through the night. She is hot and sweaty, tangled in the bedclothes. He is pressed tight against her. His whiskers scratching her shoulder. His hot breath on her neck. His arm draped around her swollen breasts. His leg entwined with hers. She puts her hand in his. A man's hand. It has been so long since she has been touched. A quiver shudders between her legs.

She takes his finger in her mouth; it tastes of salt and nicotine. He stirs in his sleep. She presses his hand to her breast and squeezes. His groin, already hard and swollen, pushes against her backside.

She has been so lonely. She is thirty-eight years old. Who else will ever touch her? Who else will ever want her? She wants to be desired. She wants to be that girl again who made boys beg.

She wants to be loved.

The ache between her legs surges to her heart. She can forgive him. She can forget.

'Maybe this time . . . ' she wants to pretend.

'Maybe this time . . . ' as he lifts her nightgown.

'Maybe this time . . . ' as the darkness disguises their bloated bodies and decaying faces. He is young and she is beautiful.

'Maybe this time . . . ' as he lifts her nightgown and she lets him enter her from behind.

'Maybe this time . . . ' knowing they haven't much time. The morning light is coming.

⋆   ⋆   ⋆

Petro balances on the stone wall, willing Ivan to look outside. He stomps his feet to warm his toes. His boots are wet from the trudge through the snow. His new socks, sticky with dampness, are balled around his toes. The left one, which is two sizes too large, has slipped beneath his heel, but he barely feels the cold; in his right pocket, his hand cherishes the perfect roundness of his apple.

Up on the hill, Ivan waves as he barrels out of the house, only to be called back by Maria. Her voice reaches Petro, soft and chastising. She adjusts his cousin's coat or maybe wraps a scarf around his neck. It's too far away to see. They are close together and Petro pretends that he is watching himself with his mama. She is tucking in his sweater, brushing the hair out of his eyes, worrying if he will be warm enough and did he have enough for breakfast. She smells of the wood stove, fried eggs, and warm bread. She is laughing. She sends him on his way, thinking, *My, he's getting big.*

Petro sits on the wall; his bum sinks into the pillow of snow. He wiggles his toes. They feel clunky and wooden. He burrows his nose into the collar of his thin jacket. He exhales. The hot air swirls against his chest and warms his cheeks. His ears are cold. He forgot his hat . . . and his mittens.

When he woke up, the fire was out. The walls of the house were coated in sparkling frost. He poked his head out from under the covers and saw his breath. Lesya was at the stove, lighting the kindling. It was just beginning to crackle. She was wearing her coat, but her bare legs shivered beneath her nightdress. Mama and Tato were still in bed, lost under a pile of quilts and blankets. His father's snore gurgled and then hiccupped;

Petro couldn't help but laugh. Lesya glared at him. *Get some wood.*

On the table were four empty jars of jam. The bread and butter had been left out. The bread was hard. The butter frozen. His father's flask sat open next to a tin cup that was a quarter full of golden liquid. Petro's nose crinkled at its sour smell. He ran his finger around the cup's edge and hesitantly licked. It burned his tongue and lips. He tried to spit it out. Lesya cuffed him on the back of the head and told him never to touch it again. She hissed at him again when he left the door open too long on his way out.

He stood before the woodpile, uncertain what to do next. Teodor hadn't come by last night to split the wood. He had watched his uncle swing the axe, up and over, striking the heart with a solid whack driving a crack that splintered down the middle into two perfect halves. Surely he could do it.

He brushed away the snow and selected a squat, fat length of poplar. He strained to lift it, but it barely budged. Using his feet, he pried it from the pile and rolled it to the chopping block. Teodor had left the axe embedded in the wood. He grabbed the handle and yanked back, surprised when it didn't move. He grasped it with both hands and finally pried it loose. Grunting, he heaved the firewood up on end onto the block.

He picked up the axe, not expecting it to be so heavy, and swung. It bounced off the side. He swung again. *Thwack*, it sank an inch off-centre. He pulled it out and swung again and again. He

205

was hot in his coat, and with each swing the axe became heavier. Panting, he whacked at the log, not taking aim, his anger rising. Bark chipped off the edges. Dents gouged the wood. Twice he missed altogether. *See how weak you are*, the wood taunted. Petro swung with all his might, and crashed down sideways. The impact ricocheted up the handle, shuddered through his hands, and the axe head splintered from the handle.

He hurled it across the yard and headed to the bush to gather broken branches. When he returned with an armful of sticks, the fire was almost out again. Stefan was up, growling about the cold and that breakfast wasn't ready. Lesya shoved the kindling in the stove and snarled that the sticks were green. Stefan barked and sent him out for another armload. Anna stayed curled up warm under the covers.

Breakfast was better. The boiled eggs and oatmeal with the last of the strawberry jam lifted everyone's spirits. Lesya limped back and forth, filling the plates. Anna had dressed in her loosest-fitting smock, the one that best masked her girth. She had brushed her shoulder-length hair and pinned it back to softly frame her face. She laughed and conversed about the weather and made sure Lesya topped up Stefan's cup of coffee. After his third egg, Stefan emptied his tin cup, sat back in his chair, and rubbed his belly. He spoke brusquely to Petro only once, when he told him to sit up straight and keep his elbows off the table, only farmers sit like that.

Ivan reaches the edge of the field. Petro

watches him hop through the furrows, kicking up snow. Maybe he shouldn't tell him about the apple. Maybe he should save it for another day. Eat it all by himself. One bite a day. Keep it his secret. Maybe if he shares it, it will lose some of its magic. What if it's sour? What if it's rotten inside? What if Ivan wants to bet him and he loses like he always loses. Would Ivan share it with him? Would he have even told him? Or would he have wolfed it down in front of him, taunting him, keeping it just out of reach? It's his apple. It doesn't belong to anyone else. He doesn't have to share.

Huffing and panting, Ivan plows into the stone wall. His cheeks are red, his eyes shining. A brown scarf is wrapped around his neck, hoary with frost just below his mouth. He wears oversized mittens and on his feet are two pairs of socks.

'You wanna go to the dump?' he blurts, ready to run again.

Petro extracts the apple from his pocket. He holds it in the palm of his hand. It is red and shiny, perfect in this white world. He sets it gingerly on the snow capping the stone wall. Ivan's mouth drops open. Petro sits straighter, taking in this newfound awe and respect. For the first time he feels that he is older and he has won.

'Do you want some?'

Ivan nods, unable to speak. His tongue licks his lips.

'We need to clear a spot,' Petro declares ceremoniously. 'There.' He points.

Tight against the stone wall, Ivan scoops out a snow bed. On his knees, he pushes the snow away in a widening circle.

'Bigger,' Petro commands as he holds the apple to his heart, no longer able to feel his chilled fingers.

Ivan stomps the white down, flat and smooth. Petro enters the circle. The boys squat down. Petro sets the apple reverentially in the centre.

'My tato got it for me. He went far, far away and picked it from a tree. He carried it across the ocean, through the woods. People tried to steal it from him, but he fought them off so he could bring it home to me.'

They breathe little white clouds.

He wasn't planning to say it, but he did. 'Whatcha got to trade?'

Ivan looked at him, searching his mind's pockets. A rock shaped like a heart. A shard from a busted crock. A gopher's skull. A twig that looks like a snake. Nothing on him. Nothing good enough. Petro reads the disappointment in his eyes.

'Your mittens look warm,' he says.

Ivan's hands curl into their woollen warmth. They were Myron's. They've been darned a hundred times and bear the scars of blue, grey, and brown wool stitches. A loose red thread hangs from the thumb where he snagged it on a branch. At night, Maria hangs these mittens on the back of the chair beside the stove. Ivan's favourite moment of the day is slipping his hands into their warmth. Good morning, they say.

'Deal.' He yanks them off and hands them

208

over. Petro pulls them over his numb fingers and is instantly immersed in their heat. His fingers throb, the tips burn icily. He picks up the apple, two pawed, and takes the first bite.

The cold juice sprays his tongue, trickles down his throat. He closes his eyes and chews. He memorizes the first crunch, that cold sweet, the pulp softening to a mash, floating across his tongue. He swallows and opens his eyes. Ivan is memorizing the rapture on his face, the wetness of his lips, the radiance in his eyes. He is remembering the look of profound goodness. Petro holds out the apple, Ivan reaches.

Petro stops him: 'I'll hold it.'

Ivan leans forward and bites.

They chew slowly. Matching bite for bite until the red is gone, and then the white, until all that is left are three seeds and a stem. It's too awful to contemplate that it's all gone. That they'll never get it back. That they ate it and in doing so they destroyed it.

'We should plant them,' Ivan offers. Petro nods in agreement, knowing that if he speaks, he will cry.

'We need to plant facing south so it gets lots of sun.' Ivan clambers over the wall. 'It has to be someplace we'll remember.'

Petro follows him, mitts clasped together carrying the precious seeds.

'Here, where the two white rocks touch.'

Ivan gets down on his knees and scratches at the snow with his bare hands until his fingers claw the frozen ground. He finds a stick and gouges a shallow hole.

'Deeper,' Petro whispers.

Ivan scrapes the dirt with his fingernails. His hands flush red from the cold. His fingertips blanch white. The nerves scream cold. He shoves his hands under his armpits.

'Enough?'

Petro nods his approval and crouches over the hole. He opens his hands. The seeds cling to the woollen mittens. Ivan scrapes them free. Together they cover them with the frozen dirt and pack them in. They kick at the snow with their boots, tramping down the spot. They stand back and half expect a green shoot to pop out of the ground.

'How long?'

Ivan shrugs. 'Maybe when you're nine and I'm seven.' They ponder that eternity as their tongues search the inside of their mouths for one last taste.

'They should be watered,' Ivan says, like a seasoned farmer.

They look up from the wall that divides their properties. They're just as far from the well as they are from the lake. They'll need a bucket. If they go to the well, Lesya will catch them and they'll have to share their secret. If they go to the lake, by the time they break through the ice and haul it back, they'll be late for dinner; besides, they're not allowed at the lake by themselves.

Ivan's numb fingers fumble to unbutton his pants. 'It'll be hot. Apples like hot.'

Petro removes his newly acquired mittens and unfastens his trousers.

With careful aim they melt away the snow and imagine the seeds already sprouting.

★ ★ ★

Teodor notices that the wood hasn't been split and the cow hasn't been milked yet. Even the smoke coming from the chimney is weak and thin. He heads to the chicken coop, following his niece's irregular bootprints, and pulls aside the NO-SAG-GATE palette propped against the entrance. Two squawking hens explode from their roosts. He squints into the darkness and sees Lesya jumping up, brushing straw from her dress. The lame hen flaps its wings, keeping balance on her boot.

'I was just getting the eggs,' she stammers.

Teodor glances at the bed of straw betraying her indentation. It reminds him of an oversized nest. 'The cow needs milking.'

Embarrassed, Lesya grabs the two eggs left by the laying hens and rushes past him with a feather stuck in her hair.

Odd child, he thinks. The crippled bird stares at him accusingly. He makes a mental note to build a proper door for the coop. He heads to the shack to check the grain.

From under the house, the skittish black female cat slinks alongside. Two of her grown litter, a calico and a blond, rush ahead to the granary door.

As he passes the chopping block, he glances at the log waiting to be split. Small bootprints circle around. He shakes his head at the poor attempt.

A boy doing a man's job. He looks for the axe and sees the head four feet away. He digs it out of the snow and brushes the blade clean. The handle is severed at the neck.

He considers dragging Stefan's lazy ass to the woodpile, but the son of a bitch would probably take it out on the boy later. He's only been home for a day and already the cow isn't milked, the wood's not split, and the axe is broken. What's it going to be like in a week? In a month? In the middle of February? He's prepared to help his sister and her children, but he'll be damned if he's going to feed that poor excuse for a man. He pockets the axe head and adds another seventy-five cents to the things he needs to buy.

He finds the broken handle a few feet from the granary. He shakes the snow from the ragged end. A crack runs down its spine. Maybe if he wraps it with wire he can salvage it. The cats weave excitedly at his feet, mewing insistently. They rub against the door frame, with their backs arched, their tails high and eyes sharp. He boots them aside and unlatches the door.

In that first instant, in the dim light, he thinks the mound of wheat is moving. Then he sees the mice. Dozens of them. Their cheeks stuffed full, their pink tails dragging, their eyes alert — danger, danger. They run from the light. Their nails skitter across the wood, creating an avalanche of seed. They scurry under floorboards, race for corners, burrow into the hill of seed.

The cats spring, talons knifing the air. In the

chaos, a small mouse careens blindly for the door. Teodor crushes it with one stomp. He wipes its smeared remains from his heel.

⋆ ⋆ ⋆

'We have to get the grain out.'

Myron pauses mid-strike with the axe high, a pile of split wood at his feet.

'Now!' Teodor barks. 'Get the shovels and whatever bags you can find.'

He doesn't stop to stomp the snow from his boots as he barges into the house, startling the women in the midst of dinner preparations.

Katya beams. 'Look, Tato, I made a pyrih.' She holds up her lopsided creation.

'What's wrong?' Maria's heart tightens.

'We need blankets and sheets. We're taking the grain in.'

'But it's almost lunch.' She looks up from folding her fiftieth pyrohy. Her hands are covered in flour; a pot of mashed potatoes and onions steams on the table. Dania, sweating over the stove, hesitates boiling the next batch.

'It'll be dark before you get back,' but she is already moving toward the chest. 'Pack some food for your father.'

Sofia gratefully pulls her hands out of the sticky dough glomming her fingers.

'And for Myron.' Teodor retrieves the news-paper, a hand-me-down from Josyp Petrenko, and searches the pages for last week's market prices. He tears the column from the page and folds it into his pocket.

213

'Can I come?' Katya pipes up hopefully.

'No.' Maria slaps flour from her hands. 'You have work to do.' She opens the chest and is repulsed by the rank, mildewy smell.

'Anything will do, I just need something to cover it.' He is already impatient to leave. Maria grabs a cotton sheet, grey with age and torn at the hems, and a faded wool blanket.

'Wait.' She hands him an extra sweater and two dry pairs of socks. He grumbles about having too much to carry. 'Take them,' she says. The discussion is over.

★ ★ ★

The horse neighs, tossing its head up and down, as Myron harnesses it to the cart. 'Not yet,' Myron soothes.

He has jury-rigged a harness by knotting together braided binder twine to the remains of the leather hitches damaged in the fire. Despite Myron's having dried, rubbed, and oiled the tack, the leather has shrunk and hardened. All the hours that he spent caring for it have been lost. He consoles himself that soon they'll buy a new harness.

'Next time we go to town, you'll be the finest-dressed horse they've ever seen.' Myron rubs its forelock. The horse whinnies appreciatively.

'Myron!'

'Coming!' He grabs the halter and leads the horse out of the barn. The cart shimmies and groans as the wheels plow through the snow.

'Back him up.' Teodor guides them to within

inches of the shack's narrow door.

'Good.' He has already filled the six half-decent burlap bags he could find. He hoists them up on the cart.

'Pile them down the sides, keep three for the back. And spread the blanket out.' He grabs the shovel and digs into the loose seed. 'Goddamned mice,' he says with every heave.

Myron wrestles the bags into place, keeping his back turned to the constant shower of seed. A few grains trickle down his collar. He props up the last bag and hops down to join his father. He waits at the door, timing the rhythm of the shovel's swing like a skipping game; seeing the opening, he slips inside as the shovel blade whishes past his head.

The dust is thick. Teodor wipes the sweat from his brow and removes his leather jacket. He's had this jacket since he was eighteen. It's lined with sheepskin. It holds the heat and keeps out the wind. This jacket has kept him alive in many worlds. The supple leather has burnished into a deep brown. It has shaped itself to his skin. It is his skin now. He folds it neatly and sets it in the corner. He picks up the shovel again.

'Goddamned mice.'

He digs in and throws the seed toward the narrow doorway. His shovel clangs into Myron's. Seed ricochets off the walls. Myron takes a step back and Teodor swings again. Myron watches, waits for the moment, digs as his father throws. Soon, they are alternating shovel loads. Myron, panting, struggles to keep pace. Once, he falters and the shovels slam together again. Sweat trickles into Myron's eyes. He wishes he had taken off his coat too.

The grain flies through the air, sprays across the cart floor. It fills the grooves and cracks. The thick golden layer builds higher, mounding upward. Myron jumps onboard and spreads it level under a constant hail of seed, grateful for the break. They don't stop for lunch. His stomach growls as he fights his way back through the torrent of seed and resumes shovelling. Goddamned mice.

Their shovels scrape the floor. Teodor glances up at the sun. It must be almost two o'clock. They have to get going if they're going to get there before closing. He checks the remaining pile. They'll keep loading for another fifteen minutes. The rest they'll keep for seed. He'll need to buy more bags today. He can't leave the seed loose in the granary, there'll be nothing left come the spring. Goddamned mice.

Maybe he should build crates and put the bags inside. It'd be safer. Tar them with pine sap or line them with tin. But he's seen the bastards chew through wood and tin. And if there's not enough ventilation, the grain will get mouldy. He should get some poison, but then the cats . . . maybe he should lock the cats inside for a few weeks.

'That's enough.' He leans on his shovel. 'Let's tarp it.'

They are fastening the last corner of the bedsheet when Stefan steps out of the house. He hasn't bothered to put on a coat. Petro follows close behind, also coatless, but wearing a pair of oversized mittens.

'Taking it to town?' Stefan inquires.

Teodor doesn't bother to answer. 'Loop it twice around that rail.'

'It's a good load.' Stefan pats the horse's withers. It flinches and kicks. He sidesteps out of the way.

Teodor grabs the calico around its pudgy midriff and tosses it inside the shack and shuts the door. 'Are you done back there?'

'Almost.' Myron struggles to stretch the sheet to hitch the knot. Petro scoops up a mittful of clean snow and absently licks it as he watches Myron work.

Myron glances over his shoulder. 'Where'd you get my mittens?'

'Ivan give 'em to me.' He drops the snow and hides his hands behind his back.

Teodor makes a round, checking the cart's wheels and harnesses. Stefan follows him like a supervisor, his arms looped behind his back, nodding as if he knows what he's looking at.

'What's wheat goin' for these days? I hear the markets been all over the place.' He tries to sound knowledgeable. 'They say the farther east you go, the fields are dust. The grain's so poor, the yield's three bushels and they can't get fifteen cents for it. We're the lucky ones.'

Teodor throws his leather jacket back on; his body retreats from the cold skin. 'C'mon, Myron, let's go.'

Stefan rubs the horse's nose too hard. It tries to bite him. He grabs the bridle and yanks it down, hard. 'Remember whose barn you're staying in.'

Teodor takes the rein, catching the strain of the bridle. 'He doesn't like his nose touched.'

Stefan releases his hold. 'We all have our weaknesses.' He eyes the grain. 'How much d'you think we'll get?'

Teodor checks the tie-down in the front corner. He snaps too brusquely at Myron, 'You've got too much at this end, pull it back.' He unties the knot and readjusts the sheet.

Stefan sidles up close to Teodor; he slips his fingers into the seed. 'Maybe I should come with you. I'm a pretty good negotiator.'

'I'll be fine.'

Stefan measures the weight of the seed in his hand. 'Maybe I should come and protect my investment.'

Teodor glares at him. 'What investment?'

Stefan glances at the grain and shrugs. 'My land, my granary, my wheat.'

Teodor answers in measured words. 'I did the work.' He feels the back of his neck flush hot, feels his body tighten. Eyes to the ground. Eyes to the ground.

'I know, I know.' Stefan feigns sympathy. 'But the claims office only looks at the papers.' He brushes the seed from his hands. 'If I remember, you can't own land . . . ' He chooses his words carefully. ' . . . After that incident.'

Myron looks up from his task and sees his father's cheek twitch. Teodor knots the sheet and pulls it tight. 'Anna and I made an arrangement.'

'Did you?' Stefan smiles cordially, but his eyes

glint. 'Have you paid her yet? You don't want to get to town and be mistaken for a thief.'

Teodor grips the side of the cart. His back to Stefan. It is a stance he knows. Hands on the wall. Feet planted. Ten swipes of the belt. His stomach constricts.

'I'm not a thief.'

Stefan leans in close. 'That's not what the papers said.' His lips curl, baring his teeth into a smile.

Teodor grabs him by the collar. If he twists the fabric it will tighten like a noose.

The smile is still on Stefan's face. His eyes are mocking. 'Think about what you're doing, Teodor.'

Petro, who is rolling a snowball on the ground, rounds the cart. He stops, startled by the closeness of his father and uncle.

Teodor speaks low and hard. 'You're not in the old country now, Stefan. You don't have an army backing you up here. You're nobody here.'

Stefan leans into Teodor's grip. 'I'm the nobody who married your sister. So, I'm the nobody who owns this land.' He almost growls the words. 'What's that make you, Teodor? My farmhand?'

Teodor's grip tightens.

'What are you going to do?' Stefan challenges. 'Kill his father?'

Teodor looks to the small boy with the oversized mittens. His skinny arms, covered in goosebumps, shiver. Teodor releases Stefan with a sharp push.

'You'll get your goddamned money.'

'I know I will.' Stefan adjusts his collar. 'Family looks after family.'

'You want to help your family?' Teodor snarls. 'Split the wood, fix the axe, milk the cow, put clothes on your children's backs!' Petro runs to his father's side.

Teodor grabs the leads. 'Get on the shaft and weigh down the load.' Myron immediately obeys. Teodor slaps the horse's flank too hard. The cart lurches ahead. Teodor keeps pace beside it.

Stefan hollers after them: 'If anybody asks you where you got the grain, Myron, you tell them your uncle gave you permission to bring it in. Say my name — everybody knows me in town.' Myron looks back at Stefan. 'Never take the first offer, boy.'

Petro doesn't understand why his father is grinning as if he's just won a game.

Stefan cuffs him on the ear. 'Stop gawking and get some wood.' He saunters back into the house.

Petro grabs a mittful of snow and throws it as hard as he can at the retreating cart.

★ ★ ★

They only stop twice to knock the sticky snow from the wheels. Once they get onto the main road, the ride is smooth. They don't talk, they just let the prairies roll past. They give themselves over to the *clip-clop* of the horse's hooves and its occasional snort. Myron wiggles his toes every few miles as the cold seeps

220

through the thin leather. He is grateful for the extra sweater. For the first few miles, he steals sidelong glances at his father, hoping to catch a glimpse of what he is thinking or maybe to tell him in a man's way, *I'm here if you want to talk.*

But Teodor doesn't accept the invitation. He stares at the horse's hooves, his hands loose on the reins, his face frozen in its imperviousness. After a while, Myron looks for magpies, rabbits, and deer instead — any other sign of life. He sees only fence posts.

The low sun bounces off the white fields and both men squint through its blindness. Miles ahead, the grain elevator rises on the horizon, proclaiming the town in bold blue letters UNITED GRAIN GROWERS — WILLOW CREEK. The road veers right and cozies up to the train track leading straight to the elevator on the edge of town. Their little cart passes through the long shadows of the boxcars, each one loaded with tons of wheat waiting to be shipped to countries Myron never expects to see.

They arrive half an hour before closing. 'Stay with the horse,' Teodor tells Myron.

Inside, the grain elevator smells of wood and dust. Two men sit close to a pot-belly stove, playing cards on a crate. One is large; his stomach hangs over his pants. His eyes are close together, sunken in the fleshy folds of his cheeks. The other is thin and hard. His coveralls and hands are black with grease. A home-rolled cigarette hangs from his lip. They don't look up when the cowbell tinkles Teodor's arrival. They

221

finish out their play. Full house beats two of a kind.

'Goddamn.' The skinny man pulls another cigarette from behind his ear and tosses it on the table.

The fat man gathers up the cards and shuffles again.

Teodor clears his throat. 'I have wheat.'

The fat man looks at the clock. It's twenty-five to four. 'It's almost closing. Come back tomorrow.' He deals out the cards.

'I have wheat. Today.'

The man checks his hand. Nothing. He looks at the thin man, whose eyes betray the two aces in his hand. The fat man folds his cards and heavily gets up. He looks out the flyspecked window at the paltry load.

'Shit. Why do they even bother?'

'Sell wheat.'

'Yeah, yeah, bring it around the side.' The man waddles away, his knees stiff from carrying the extra weight. He points and speaks louder. 'The side door.'

Teodor heads back out. The fat man puffs, 'They oughta make 'em have to learn English before they let 'em in.'

'They shouldn't let 'em in,' the thin man counters.

Teodor leads the horse and wagon to the side entrance, up the low plank ramp and into the cavernous belly of the elevator. Myron ducks as the cart rolls through the doorway. The wheels rattle over the iron grid that covers the hopper below. The fat man rolls the heavy door shut behind them. It groans across the rusted rollers.

'Shovel it off and make it quick. I ain't stayin' past four.'

Myron jumps off and starts untying the bedsheet knots. The fat man grabs his clipboard. Teodor doesn't hurry.

'What's your name? Name.'

'Teodor Mykolayenko.'

'Christ, how do you spell that?' Teodor looks at him blankly. 'Spell, do you understand?'

Myron answers, 'M-y-k-o-l-a-y-e-n-k-o.'

'What kind of name is that? Communist?'

'Ukrainian,' Myron answers calmly.

'What quarter-section?'

Teodor nods his permission for Myron to continue. 'Northwest Section 2, Township 64, Range 6, West of 4 Meridian.' He struggles to free the knot his father tied.

Teodor pulls back the bedsheet and hops up into the back of the cart. He rights a bag, and balancing it on the edge of the cart, cuts the binder twine to open the sack. He proceeds to the next bag.

The fat man goes to his land claim maps and checks the lot numbers. Myron pulls on the knot with his teeth. It tastes like mildew and sawdust. He tries to pry it apart with his fingernails.

'We got a problem, bud. I don't see your name here. Are you sure you gave me the right numbers?'

'It's my land,' Teodor replies.

'Here it says it's registered to Anna Sev — Shev-chik.'

'Shevchuk, my sister.'

'You got any documentation, a permission letter, something giving you rights to bring in this grain?' Teodor cuts open another bag. 'Does he understand what I'm saying?'

Myron looks to his father.

'My grain,' Teodor answers.

'I can't take this if it ain't yours. Get it out of here.' The fat man slams the clipboard shut.

'You buy.' Teodor stands knee deep in his wheat.

'I told you — no buy. No!'

'You buy.'

The fat man yanks on the door. It rumbles open. 'Get him out of here.'

Myron looks to his father. Teodor holds his ground. 'You buy.'

The fat man plants his feet and picks up a bat he keeps near the door for emphasis. 'You want to argue with me?'

Myron sees his father's eyes empty and his hand tighten around the knife. He steps between the man and Teodor. 'My father didn't understand what you were asking. We have permission. My uncle said to tell you he gives his permission. He said you'd know him. He said everyone in town knows him. His name is Stefan. Stefan Shevchuk. He's my uncle, we're bringing in the wheat from his land. He said you would treat us fair. He said you were a fair man.'

'You're the guy working Stefan's land?' The fat man directs the question to Teodor, but Myron answers, 'Yes.'

In Ukrainian, Myron pleads with his father:

224

'You have to say yes, Tato. We need to sell it, right? It doesn't matter what he says.'

Teodor looks at the mound burying his feet. He knows what he has to answer. He bows his head like he's done a hundred times before to the guards.

In English, he answers, 'Yes.'

'Why didn't you say that when you come in?' The fat man sets aside the bat. 'We heard he had someone working up there.' He looks at Teodor, his head bowed, the ratty jacket with holes in the elbows, frayed cuffs, and tattered sheepskin collar. He almost feels sorry for the poor bastard. His stomach growls, reminding him he hasn't eaten since noon. 'Off-load it.'

The fat man pulls a knife from his hip sheath and with one swipe slices off the stubborn knot. 'You ain't got all day.' Myron bundles up the bedsheet with the missing corner and wonders what his mother will say. He jumps up and joins his father.

With sausagelike fingers, the man sets the weights and counterbalances. From the bowels of the elevator the auger groans and churns, ready to carry the grain to the bins. Dust blooms through the grid. 'Empty it!' the fat man shouts over the din. Myron picks up the first bag and prepares to spill its contents. Teodor stops him.

'How much?'

'What?' the fat man hollers.

'How much?' Teodor asks.

'Sixty-three cents.'

'No,' says Teodor. 'Ninety-three.'

'What'd he say?' the fat man wheezes.

'He thinks it should be more.'

'Tell him that's the price.'

Teodor pulls the crumpled newspaper from his pocket. He points to the market column. 'Wheat Number One, ninety-three cents.'

'You think I'm cheating you?' The man puffs out his chest.

Teodor points again at the paper. 'Ninety-three cents.'

The fat man waves him away. 'Those were last month's prices. That's for grade one. This is grade four. Sixty-three cents a bushel.'

Teodor grabs a handful of wheat. 'Good grain. Number one.'

'That's the price. Tell him he can take it to Bonnyville, what's that — fifty miles away? But the price ain't going to be any better. He's lucky I'm offering this much. But if he thinks he can get a better deal . . . '

'Seventy cents,' Myron blurts. 'He wants seventy cents.'

'No!' Teodor sputters in Ukrainian, 'I want full price!'

Myron tries to reason: 'He's gonna give us nothing. We can't take it back! You know we can't.'

Teodor crouches down and picks up a handful of wheat. It's good wheat. Grade one. 'Tie up the bags,' he calmly tells Myron.

'Tato . . . '

'Do it.' Teodor twists a sack closed and wraps it with twine. Myron looks helplessly to the fat man.

'Crazy bohunk.' The fat man shakes his head. 'Seventy cents.'

Teodor doesn't look up. 'Eighty.'

'Seventy-five and that's it.' The fat man recalculates his profit. 'Make up your mind, it's almost dinnertime.'

'Seventy-five cents.' Teodor recalculates his losses. He pulls the string off and tips the bag. The wheat spills through the grid. Myron is surprised how quickly it is gone.

★   ★   ★

After Teodor leaves, Maria finds the source of the mildew. Balled up and stuffed in the corner of her chest — her mother's blanket. Its ivory-and-salmon flowers obscured by splotches of grey-green mould.

Months and months, hand spinning and dyeing the wool; over a year weaving the intricate patterns; all done by her mother's arthritic hands.

Her mother said she wouldn't leave her beloved Ukraïna; that she was too old to start again. But with her gnarled hands, she would have been denied entry. No defects allowed in Canada. They had agreed not to say goodbye. No tears, no chance to raise suspicions. Maria didn't even tell her father they were leaving. He might have told. The night they were to run, her mother came to the door. She held up a warning finger — no words — and thrust a bundle into Maria's arms. It was the blanket.

Maria opens another layer of the woollen

fabric, revealing the grass stains and red smears.

'What's this?' escapes her lips.

It is Katya who chimes, 'Raspberries.'

Sofia, who is rolling dough for the pyrohy, stops mid-roll. Her heart begins to pound, her mouth grows parched as she remembers that hot, sunny summer day picnicking at the lake. Katya rambles on about fish and bubbles and holding up her dress and catching a minnow in her hand . . . not once does she mention Sofia's name. Not even when Maria asks through clenched teeth: 'Who else was with you?'

Katya answers, 'Just me.'

Maria drags her to the bedroom, screaming about taking something that didn't belong to her and that her father would deal with her when he got home, because she is afraid of what she might do to her. Her hand tight around her daughter's arm, she worries that she will bruise her, but God forgive her, she doesn't let go. When Katya starts to whimper, Maria yells at her to stop, that she has nothing to cry about, she isn't the one who is hurt, and that she best get on her knees and beg for forgiveness. And Katya does, even though she doesn't know what she's done wrong.

Dania offers to wash the blanket. Maria tells her to burn it, get it out of the house. But Dania scrubs it with snow and hangs it between two pine trees to air, with plans to wash it properly tomorrow.

Sofia keeps rolling the dough. She tells herself, *Katya's little. They won't punish her hard. Not like they would with me.* She's older, she's supposed to be like Dania and take care of the smaller ones. Sofia rolls harder to block her mother's sobs.

It is dark when Teodor and Myron get back. Ivan sees them first from his perch at the window. Maria can barely contain him long enough to wrap the scarf around his neck and pull the hat down over his ears, but when it comes time for his mittens, they are nowhere to be found. When he is warned that he can't go outside to greet his father unless he finds his mittens, he breaks down and confesses that he lost them. He is promptly stripped of his winter clothes and sent to stand in the corner.

When Teodor and Myron return home, the women set the dinner plates in silence. Each of them senses the tension that will shatter, injuring them all, if anyone dare ask, 'How was your day?'

Myron eats quickly so he can finish chopping the wood. He can't bear his father's silence any more. Ivan has fallen asleep in the corner and Dania carries him to bed. She then excuses herself. Sofia, who wants more than anything to see the money and ask her papa for a new dress from the Sears Roebuck catalogue, hides the advertisement under her pillow, thinking it best to wait.

All the children are in bed early, but only the smallest are asleep. The others' ears are straining to hear the sound of money. Maria lights the oil lamp and sets it on the table. She sits across from Teodor, who is finishing a lingering smoke. He butts the cigarette and reaches in his pocket.

He lays the money on the table. Forty-two dollars and seventy-five cents. He sets ten dollars aside.

'This is already spoken for.' He doesn't meet her eyes.

Thirty-two dollars and seventy-five cents. That's it. She wants to cry. She feels it climb up her throat and push at the back of her eyes. Her cheeks flush. *Don't*, she reprimands herself. *Don't*. She takes a deep breath. 'What do we have to get?'

Teodor's fingers rub the rough tabletop. 'We need a harness.'

Maria counts out the money.

★ ★ ★

It is three in the morning when the final penny is divvied among the piles. Teodor and Maria sit exhausted from their negotiations. Teodor will have to wait for a new shovel, hardware for the granary, and getting the horse shod. Everyone will have to make do with the boots they have, save for Ivan and Petro, who can't get through the winter with what they have now. Lesya won't get new shoes. Only the eldest will get new long underwear and winter stockings. Their old winter underwear will be passed down. Myron won't get his fur-lined hat. Maria will knit Ivan new mittens and socks for the men. She will try to stretch the fabric to make three heavy skirts for her daughters.

She will need to patch the men's pants again.

There won't be enough meat to get through the winter, but hopefully the potatoes and rice will carry them through. Maria has already evaluated the preserves and vegetables, and noted the ones she will try to trade in February for more meat. She picks up the remaining thirteen cents and squirrels it away in the tobacco can on the highest shelf. She calculates the pennies, nickels, and dimes. They have a dollar and eighteen cents for emergencies.

Teodor checks in on the girls. They sleep blissfully unaware. Katya and Dania are snuggled back to back. Little Katya's legs are stretched out against Sofia, who is pushed to the edge of the bed. *Where will the baby sleep if it's a girl?* he wonders. He should build a cradle. He has a birch log. He was saving it to make Maria a cupboard, but that will have to wait. Dania rolls over and wraps her arm around her little sister. Her long blond hair is loose around her face. She is almost a woman. Soon she'll marry and have her own farm. She'll be like her mother. Practical and sensible. She'll make do with what she has.

I'll keep you safe, he wants to tell them. He tucks Sofia's arm back in. As he pulls the quilt up, he notices the piece of paper protruding from under her pillow. He slides it out and unfolds the catalogue page, *Girls and Misses' Cloth Dresses*. Circled, in the bottom corner, is an illustration of a young girl, her arms tucked behind her back, her head tilted demurely, her hair short and curled. Teodor reads slowly, stumbling over the odd words. *Girls' Dress made*

231

of all-wool flannel, bolero effect, shoulder flaps, high-standing collar and band in front are made of black velvet, trimmed with white cord. We can furnish this dress in royal blue and red. Price $3.75.

He doesn't know the words bolero, velvet, or royal. But he understands the price. He folds the page back up and slides it farther under the pillow. Of all his children, she is the one he worries about the most. She wants to be someone else. Katya groans and stretches, digging her feet into Sofia's side. Gently, Teodor reaches under the covers and lifts her legs. Katya squirms, her eyes open blearily.

'Tato?'

'Shhh,' Teodor soothes her.

Tears spring to her eyes. 'I stole Mama's blanket.'

He thinks she's had a bad dream and is about to say so when Katya breaks his heart.

'Do I have to go to jail now too, Tato?'

Hardy's General Shop & Meat Market
October 14, 1938

12 bushel Oats	3.48
Harness	11.75
3 lbs Nails	1.00
Axe handle	.75
1 barrel	1.00
1 box Bullets	.73
8 boxes of matches	.16
Kerosene	.50
6 Grain bags	1.80
2 med chickens	.40
3 lbs Sausage @ .20 lb	.60
3 lbs Bacon @ .20 lb	.60
5 lbs Pigs feet @ .10 lb	.50
9 lbs Chuckroast @ .12 lb	1.08
15 lbs Sugar @ .12/ lb	1.80
1/2 lb coffee @ .19 lb	.10
10 lbs Salt	.80
10 lbs Rice	1.00
Yeast	.10
Soap	.15
Children's winter boots size 6	1.00
Children's winter boots size 7	1.00
1 young ladies winter underwear	.65
Yarn	.70
6 yards fabric	.60
1 tin of tobacco	.32
Penny candy	.10
	$ 32.67

PAID CASH

Maria neatly folds Dania's old winter stockings for Lesya. The legs might be a little long, and the wool is picked, but they're clean and darned. Dania washed them herself yesterday, while she and Teodor were in town getting supplies. She built the fire, cut through the ice, hauled water up from the lake, filled the washtub, and topped it up with snow. It was ten below yesterday.

When they arrived home before dinner, she was still outside. Her hands were raw and cracked, and the front of her coat and sleeves had frozen. She was churning Maria's blanket for the third time through the steaming water. She had scrubbed the mouldy patches and raspberry stains with a horse brush. She was down to the last thumb-sized cake of soap. The dyes in the wool had leached where she had rubbed. The grass stains were impenetrable, but still she scrubbed. Maria told her, *That's enough*.

From the window Maria can see it hanging on the line, frozen stiff, the sun bleaching its pastel colours to bone white. Tonight she'll hang it by the stove, let it thaw, and see if the smell is gone. She plans to nail it to the back wall to keep out the wind's chill. Put it to some good use. She lays the folded underwear in the bottom of the basket. The clothes smell like winter.

She tucks in one bar of soap, two skeins of

yarn, and Petro's new boots, size 7. She hopes they're large enough. His toes were poking through the old ones. Ivan hasn't taken his new boots off all day. Last night, he tried to sleep with them on. His feet were jutting out from under the covers so he could admire their shine. When she insisted he remove them, he set the boots in front of the wood stove, beside his father's, carefully lining them up to face the door. This morning he slipped them on, in unison with Teodor. Left foot first, then the right. He laced them across, giving a final tug, mimicking his father. But he still needed help tying the bow: *The rabbit comes out of the hole, goes around the tree, and back down the hole again.* He has been clopping in and out of the house all morning. She caught him twice bending down to wipe snow from the toes.

If there had been a middle boy, Ivan would be wearing hand-me-downs, like his sisters. But Myron's old clothes have long been reused as rags and patches and his old leather boots have been cut up to repair harnesses and saddles. Ivan has always been the roughest on his clothes. No matter how many times she tells him to stay out of the mud and not to drag his toes, he doesn't remember. He's worn a hole through the toe on his left boot, and the leather has cracked and split at the seams from the constant soakings. She had to get him new boots this year. She tried not to make it an event — she just casually passed them to him.

He let Katya touch them. Sofia pouted and kicked her boots against the table leg until Maria swatted her still. Sensing that it wasn't fair that his boots hadn't lasted another year, he did his best to hide his feet under the chair. When Dania unwrapped her new winter underwear, Sofia ran to her room and didn't come out for the rest of the afternoon. Later, Maria found a pile of shredded paper under the bed; all she could piece together was the head of a young girl with ribbons in her hair. She is thankful school is back in and the house is quiet today.

Maria folds a little bag of candy and hides it in the layers of linen. Lesya will make sure Petro doesn't eat it all at once. Dania divided up their stash: two blackballs, three peppermints, four butterscotches, and one lemon drop apiece. None of them took a bite, instead they squirrelled their treasures away in their trunks, hiding them in socks, under skirts, and in pant pockets. Even Myron, who initially said to give his share to the little ones, was relieved when Maria refused his charitable act. He tucked the lemon drop in his shirt pocket.

Maria sucks on the butterscotch candy she pilfered last night. There are five more stored in the tobacco can. She prefers to bite down on these hard candies, feel them shatter between her teeth, but then it would dissolve too quickly. Instead, she holds it in her cheek, her tongue gauging the halfway mark, when she will wrap it in wax paper and hide it back in the tin.

It's been harder dividing the food. The way Anna has been eating, she'll empty the pantry in a month. And she's not convinced that Anna will salt the meat or that Stefan will freeze it properly. Maria decides to ration the supplies: half a pound of sausage, a pound of chuckroast, a pound of sugar, two pounds of salt, and a pound of rice. She adds four jars of preserves to fill out the basket. She ponders including a chicken, but knows Stefan will want it roasted and then will eat it in one meal, whereas she can stretch it for weeks by turning it into jellied chicken, making a broth, and using the feet, gizzards, and heart in stews. She reassures herself that it is best that she administers the food. She can send over a basket once a week to replenish their supplies.

'It's ready,' she tells Teodor, who is repairing the axe.

★　★　★

Ivan holds Teodor's hand as he tries to match his father's stride through the snow. His leather boots squeak. He looks back at their tracks. Big and small, marching side by side, *we were here, we were here, we were here*. He stumbles and scuffs his toe. He wears a pair of Myron's oversized mitts. Mama has promised to start knitting him a new pair tonight with the grey wool, and he's asked for a red stripe.

He breathes into his scarf and it condenses wet against his throat. Overhead, dark clouds hang low and heavy. Tato says it's going to snow. He can't wait to show Petro his new boots; they'll have matching pairs. He wonders whose will be faster.

Tato carries the basket. The axe handle sticks

out from under the linen handkerchief that Mama used to cover the presents. Teodor lets go of Ivan's hand and shifts the weight to his other arm. He pulls his glove off with his teeth and reaches into his pant pocket. Reassured, he puts the glove back on. Ivan races around him and takes his other hand.

They sneak up on the horse first. Its head is cocked and ears pricked when they round the corner. It neighs and tosses its head, like a good joke. Teodor reaches in his coat pocket and brings out a palm full of sugar. He winks. 'Don't tell your mother.' The horse licks appreciatively.

They cut through the barn and Teodor is pleased to see that the cow has been milked. He unties the sack and pours a handful of oats into the feed bucket. Ivan fetches an extra armload of hay and stacks it where it can be easily reached. The cow chews on it like it's nothing special.

On the way to the house, Teodor assesses the snow-covered pile of wood and makes a note to split a week's supply before he leaves. He can't let his sister freeze.

He bangs on the door. He hears Stefan's muffled voice. The door opens slowly. Petro pokes his head out.

'I got new boots,' Ivan beams and sticks out his foot as proof. 'And so do you.'

But Petro doesn't respond, doesn't even seem to care. Ivan notices that Petro is wearing his mittens indoors.

'Where's your mama?' Teodor asks the boy. His sweater has unravelled at the bottom; the front is soiled. He has no socks on in his ragged boots. And he's not at school.

'In bed.'

Teodor scowls — it's almost noon. 'Tell her to get up.'

Petro shuts the door. The sound of voices, a man's grumbling, followed by heavy footsteps. The door swings open. Stefan looks grey and shaky. Teodor looks past him for Lesya. He finds her at the stove, trying to restart the fire. The house is freezing.

'I'm here to see Anna.'

Stefan squints into the bright light as if it's burning his eyes. He heads to the table. 'Shut the door.' Teodor follows him in.

Stefan pushes aside the tin cup and the empty flask tipped on its side. He ignores the dirty dishes and empty jars. 'Anna, get up, your brother's here.' Teodor glances to the mound of covers that shift and groan. A layer of ice has formed in the pail of water.

Stefan sits down heavily. 'My head's killing me. It's been throbbing since yesterday. Need something for my nerves. Do you have that fire going yet?'

Lesya nervously squeaks, 'No.'

'What's taking so long?' He rubs his forehead, his own voice jarring the pain. 'She let it go out.'

'I was milking the cow,' Lesya protests feebly.

'I don't give a goddamn, it's freezing in here.'

Teodor watches Stefan's shaking hands sift through the remnants of cigarette butts. 'Do you have a smoke?'

Teodor's first reaction is to say no, but Stefan's eyes are desperate. He retrieves his one hand-rolled from his pocket. Stefan lights it from the oil lamp. He breathes in deep.

'Thank Christ.' His body relaxes into the nicotine. 'I'm going crazy cooped up in here.'

'It's going!' Lesya blows on the crackling fire.

'Get some wood,' Stefan orders, and Petro, who is standing behind him in the shadows, flinches, startled that his father can see him through the back of his head.

Petro reaches for the axe, but Teodor stops him. 'He's too small.'

'No, I'm not!' Petro stands as tall as he can.

'Mind your manners,' Stefan snaps. Petro lowers his head. 'You think you're strong enough to chop the wood? You think your uncle is wrong?'

'Yes,' Petro answers, staring at the holes in the toes of his boots.

'Pick up the axe, hold it over your head. Higher.' Stefan leans back in his chair and blows a smoke ring. 'Hold it there. Show us how strong you are.'

The axe wobbles for balance. Petro spreads his legs farther to brace himself. The axe pulls him to the right. He straightens, his arms tremble, his face flushes pink.

'Look at those arms, there's no meat on them at all. Do they look like a man's arms?'

Petro sways backward. The axe tilts and Teodor grabs the handle before its weight pulls him over. Petro drops his tingling arms, his ears flush with shame.

'Your uncle's right. You're not strong enough.'

Teodor sets the axe on the table. 'You get

some branches. Your father will split the wood later. He's strong.' Stefan glares at Teodor as if he's just been trumped.

'I'll help,' Ivan offers, eager to escape the danger he senses but can't identify.

'I don't need any help.' Petro storms past.

Ivan wishes Petro would put on his shiny new boots and then he'd be happy too. But Petro slams the door in his face and he has to run to catch up. His new boots squeak with every step.

'Maria sent some things over.' Teodor sets the basket on the table and speaks to Lesya: 'There's something for you in there.'

'Don't be shy, take a look.' Stefan waves her forward.

Lesya lifts the linen cloth covering the basket, sees Dania's stockings neatly folded, with a lovely new soap perched on top. Stefan's eyes brighten.

'Is that sausage?' He sniffs. 'Mmm . . . smell the garlic. And beef. You're cooking that tonight. No more eggs and stale bread.'

'Maria thought you might want to salt it.'

'And ruin a good cut of meat? Tonight we eat like kings. Anna, come see this, get up.' Anna grunts and heaves herself up. Her hair is dishevelled. As she swings her legs over the bed, Teodor sees a purple bruise across her shin. Anna modestly pulls her hem down and looks to see if Teodor noticed. He has. 'I ran into the table last night,' she murmurs.

'She's up all night pacing. Bumping into things. Drive a man right out the door. Stoke that fire, girl, we need the oven hot.'

Lesya, who wants to touch the winter underwear and feel its softness against her skin, limps back to the stove.

Anna swings her bloated belly off the bed and gingerly puts weight on her leg. It was her fault he threw the log. He didn't mean to hit her. He just wanted her to stop rattling the dishes so loudly. When he gets his headaches, he can't take the noise. She knows that. She knows the pounding in his head only goes away with a shot of whisky. He felt terrible afterward. She calmed him with a warm towel on his forehead and promised to be quieter from now on. She pads across the icy floor in bare feet. 'Make yourself look presentable, woman, we have company.'

She brushes the hair from her eyes, which are outlined with dark circles, and investigates the basket of goodies.

'Is that jam?' She helps herself to the strawberry preserve. 'Can you open it?' She hands it to Stefan, whose spirits have lifted with the prospect of food. He twists the lid firmly and it pops off. He hands it back like he's a champion.

'What time is it?' she asks, absently dipping her finger in the sugary concoction.

'Time for lunch.' Stefan pats his belly. 'Looks like you made a killing, Teodor.' He fishes for a dollar figure as he rifles through the basket. 'Candy! Any lemon drops?'

Teodor can't help but notice his sister's size. 'Maria might come by tomorrow. She wants to see how you're doing.'

'Tell her I'm fine.' Teodor searches Anna's eyes

for the truth, but a smile is pasted on her face.

'Stefan, I need to talk to Anna alone. I'm hoping you'll understand.' He lowers his eyes to avoid a confrontation.

'There's nothing you can say to her you can't say to me.'

'I know that. It's between us. Brother and sister. I know it's your house — I'm just asking for a few words.'

Stefan, confident that Anna will report back everything to him and not wanting to spoil the moment of gracious host or jeopardize his newfound riches, acquiesces. 'I'll step outside. A gesture of my goodwill.' He pushes back the chair. 'I don't want any bad feelings between us, Teodor.'

'Neither do I.'

Stefan nods regally, one gentleman to another, and stands to leave.

Anna panics as the familiar sense of him leaving rears in her stomach. 'Whatever you say to me, you say to him. He's my husband.'

'It's okay.' Stefan pats her on the behind. 'I'll go see how the boy's doing. Maybe split some wood.' He takes the axe. 'You wouldn't have another cigarette?'

'No.'

Stefan hides his disappointment poorly.

'Can you send Ivan back in?'

Stefan suppresses a pang of servitude. 'Of course.' He smiles graciously. 'Ivan, your father wants you.' He leans on the door frame and smiles thinly. 'Back home, I would think you were planning a rebellion.'

Teodor doesn't blink. 'I'm just talking to my sister.'

Ivan rushes in with twigs in hand. His cheeks glow; he smells of cold and snow and spruce. Stefan nods his best officer's nod and shuts the door.

'Petro and I are having a contest, to see who can get the most wood fastest.' Ivan wipes his nose with his mittens. He has to get back or he's going to lose again and he likes his hat.

'Come here,' Teodor orders abruptly. 'You too,' he addresses Lesya. They gather around the table. 'You two are witnesses.' Ivan doesn't know what the word means but hopes it means he can leave soon.

'I want to settle between us.' Teodor retrieves the ten dollars from his pocket.

'You don't have to do that now.'

'Yes, I do.' He unfolds each bill and lays it flat on the table. 'I'm paying for the land tomorrow.' He counts it out. 'Ten dollars. The full amount.'

Anna touches the flimsy paper. 'It's not due until the spring.'

'I need to pay now. I need us to settle.'

'Stefan should be here.' She's worried that he'll walk in and see the money. Last time there was money in the house, two dollars she had hidden in the flour tin, he took it and didn't come home for three weeks.

'He's got nothing to do with it. You took the claim out for me.'

Ivan shuffles through the bills. He's never seen paper money before.

'Pay attention,' his father warns. The adults

244

keep talking above his head. He can see the bag of candy from here. He thinks his favourite will be the white ones with the red stripes, like an apple.

'I need it in writing, that you received ten dollars from me to purchase this land. It's my land, Anna.'

'I know it is.' She looks hard at her baby brother and wonders when he became so old.

He sets a pencil nub on the table and smoothes out a piece of brown wrapping paper saved from the sausage. 'Write it, so everybody knows.'

Anna picks up the pencil.

'Watch this,' he orders Ivan and Lesya. Anna scrawls the words in a cryptic, flowery script: *Teodor Mykolayenko has payed me ten dollars for the land.* She signs her name. Teodor picks up the paper.

'What does it say?' he asks Anna.

'It says it's your land.'

He nods. He looks to Lesya. He knows she is listening.

'Did you hear that?' he asks Ivan.

'Yes, Tato.'

'What did she say?'

'She said it's your land.'

'Why?'

'It's on the paper.'

'Why?'

Ivan hesitates. It feels like a test, but he doesn't know what will happen if he gets the answer wrong.

'Why?' Teodor asks gruffly.

'Because of the money.'

'So tell me why it's my land.'

'Because you gave her money and the paper says so.' He looks to his father, hoping he's done good.

'That's right.'

Ivan grins. Teodor slaps him hard across the face. 'Don't ever forget this.'

★ ★ ★

On the way home, Ivan doesn't hold his father's hand. He lags ten feet behind. The sting of his handprint still on his cheek . . . he tries to forget about the land, the money, and the paper . . . but he can't.

He wishes there was never any land. He wishes his father never came back. He wishes he still had his hat, so his ears wouldn't be freezing right now. He wishes he hadn't got the answer right.

★ ★ ★

Stefan laughs when Anna tells him what she had to sign. He tells her that doesn't mean a thing, the land is registered in her name and that's all that will ever matter. He basks in the aroma of the roast and wishes he had a glass of whisky to wash it down, and a big cigar. Anna fights waves of nausea from the smell of the cooking meat. When she tells him he didn't give her the money, that he paid the office himself, Stefan hurls the tin cup across the room.

★ ★ ★

The next day, it snows large, fluffy flakes. Their heavy wetness quilts the land a foot deep. To the children's delight, Maria has kept them home. It is the perfect snow for making snowballs and snowmen. Katya and Ivan throw themselves into its softness, chase each other through the drifts. They let themselves fall backward to be caught by the earth. They stick their tongues out. The flurry of flakes misses their mouths, hits their cheeks, and clings to their eyelashes. They spread their arms and legs wide and fly. They roll away, leaving a chain of snow angels strung across the field. The snow falls so thick and straight, with not a breath of wind, that it curtains the prairies and they can't see fifty feet ahead.

Teodor went to town early this morning, despite Maria's protestations that he could lose his way. The snow would obliterate his prints, landmarks would be hidden, the road would be covered . . . he told her he would be back soon. He slipped his hand in his pocket to check again that the money was still there, and left.

Maria knits compulsively. She has finished one mitten and is already adding the red band to its mate. He should have been back by now. Another couple of hours and it will be dark, and no sign of the snow letting up. What if he's not home by dinner? Is she supposed to wait until dark? If she waits until dark, how will they find him then?

Her anger mounts. She knits faster. She'll have to go to Stefan. How is she supposed to wade through this snow four months pregnant? What if she falls? She could send Myron, but then she's left waiting and wondering. They'll need a search party. They'll probably go to Josyp Petrenko's and get his dog, try to retrace Teodor's steps, so long as he hasn't wandered too far off trail or went too far east and crossed one of the ponds. If he broke through the ice . . .

She drops a stitch. He doesn't think about the consequences of his actions. What would happen to her and the children if he . . . she stops herself from thinking the word, afraid that she will conjure the reality.

He could have waited until next week to pay. He could have waited until the spring. He could have waited until next season, after the next crop. They could have used that money this year. Sometimes, she wants to scream at him: *Think of us! Forget your pride, forget being right. Being right sent you to jail. Being right forced us to leave everything we knew. Being right brought us here. Being right sends you out in the middle of a snow storm and gets you lost and we find your body next spring in a gully or under a spruce tree curled up like you went to sleep!*

She gasps, terrified that she might have just conjured a curse. She spits over her left shoulder three times. She clutches her cross and gets down on her knees. She prays with all her might that Teodor is a good man, a good husband, a good father, and that she's the one who should be punished for her sinful thoughts. She prays to the Blessed Virgin to keep her family safe; she opens her heart so that God can see how much love she has inside her and not to listen to her momentary weakness. She prays to bring him home safe.

She stays on her knees, even though the baby in her belly digs against her ribs and presses against her bladder. She stays on her knees when Dania kneels beside her and prays that her mama will tell her what's wrong. She stays on her knees when Sofia pulls on Lesya's hand-me-down long underwear, with the bulging worn-out ankle, dons her winter coat with the burlap patches, and clomps outside in her cracked boots to sit in the snow, refusing to pray. She stays on her knees as a pot full of snow turns to water and boils on the stove. She is still on her knees when she hears Katya and Ivan screeching with delight and Teodor's laugh as he hammers them with snowballs.

★ ★ ★

Myron tramples a path through the snow alongside the stone wall. The trail reaches all the way back to the lake. This is the best snow for trapping. When there's just a dusting, the rabbits wander all over — willy-nilly. They're almost impossible to catch; you can't predict their route. But when it's deep like this, they tend to follow the easiest route.

Myron sharpens the end of a willow branch and drives it into the snow. Rabbits love to eat willows. He pulls off his mittens and untangles the coiled wire. The cold metal sears into his warm palms. He straightens the wire, loops it

249

once, threads it through a washer, then ties the end to a poplar stump. He bends the snare so that the noose is camouflaged among the willow twigs, adjusts the height until it skims the snow, then pulls it tight so the loop is six inches across. Wide enough for the rabbit to enter, but narrow enough to catch its haunches. He could rig a spring pole that yanks the animal up and strangles it. Some swear that method's quicker and the meat doesn't taste as strong, because the rabbit struggles less. Fear has a taste. But he's never seen a difference in the killing method. Nothing makes dying easier.

He prefers to check the snares more frequently so they don't suffer long. He goes out at dawn and dusk, the most likely time they'll be feeding. He always carries his father's .22, a little club made from white ash that he keeps in his back pocket, and his hunting knife. His father made him carry the rifle as a safety measure, in case he ever met coyotes on the hunt for easy food. Last year, Myron saw plenty of tracks but never a coyote. They got half a dozen of his rabbits. Sometimes he'd find the snare, sometimes he wouldn't. There'd be tufts of fur, spatters of blood, some entrails, but nothing else. Just tracks leading away.

His dog used to come with him. He could smell rabbits a hundred feet away. He'd tense up and point one leg, his whole body shaking with anticipation. Myron would crouch down low and scope the horizon. He'd see only white snow. He'd look harder where the dog was fixated and finally see a black nose and eyes, and then the shape of the rabbit would separate clearly from its white camouflage. Myron would give the signal and the dog would chase it down, until the rabbit veered in the wrong direction and the dog would snap its neck. He'd carry it back and lay it gently at Myron's feet. He was a good dog. Then the coyotes got him.

Myron dusts the snow with his mitten, obliterating his tracks. He wishes that when the rabbits got caught, they would sit still and wait for him to come. But they always fought. Twisting and kicking, wrapping the wire tighter. He's found them with their paws cut off; or with their bellies cinched so tight he's had to cut them open to get his fingers around the wire. One was almost decapitated. The wire caught around its throat.

He doesn't understand why they just don't give up. Realize that there's no escape. Sit peacefully and he'll come by shortly. He'll speak gently and make them feel that everything's going to be okay. Then with one quick rap on the back of the head, hold them until their feet stop twitching. But it's never like that.

He hears them crying before he reaches them. A sickening squeal that shivers through his bones. He finds them throttling their bodies, flailing and twisting. Their eyes bulging with fear, bubbles of blood dripping from their noses. They look him straight in the eye as he holds them down: *You did this to me.* He cracks their heads until their eyes empty. Sometimes it takes three or four blows, because his own eyes are closed. If he was rich and didn't care how much a bullet cost, he'd shoot them, one shot behind the ears. Then he wouldn't have to see their eyes.

Myron sits on the stone wall. The world darkens grey with the approach of night. It is so quiet, he can hear the silence. It has a sound this quiet. A low, hollow pulse. Empty, yet all-embracing. Snowflakes flutter down, coating him white. He pops the lemon drop in his mouth and holds it on his tongue. Tart and sweet, it dissolves.

★ ★ ★

It is dark by six o'clock. Ivan and Katya have been given permission to stay outside but aren't allowed past the third spruce tree with the crooked top, about twenty feet from the house. They stand on twin boulders. Ivan's rock is slightly higher and rounder. At the top of their lungs they singsong *Myron, Myron,* pausing only to hear if he is answering. They call high and sweet. *Myron.*

It was a game they started last winter, when Myron was only twelve and the .22 was still too large for his hands. Maria started the chant one night, when he didn't come home at the expected time. It was February. There was three feet of snow. It had been bitterly cold for weeks. Rabbits were scarce. All that week, the coyotes had been close. Howling through the nights. In the morning, their tracks passed by Anna's. The snow was stained yellow where they had marked the corners of the house and shack.

That night, the children were already in bed,

fully clothed. The stove was burning, but there was no warmth. The lamp had been blown out to conserve kerosene, but the shack was bright from the full moon stealing through the cracks. Maria was sitting beside the door, wrapped in a blanket, bundled in her coat and boots, listening for Myron when she heard the coyotes. One near, one far. A short, yelping howl answered by a long, plaintive wail. *I'm here*, they moaned.

She waited breathlessly for the crack of the .22, and when it didn't come she stepped out into the night. Her heart pounding in her chest, her ears straining to hear, she willed her eldest son to come home. The night was frozen. The horse and cow, safe inside the barn, were quiet. Her little boy's tracks led into the darkness.

Myron? she quietly called, as if she could make him emerge from the night's veil. He would appear dressed in his father's wool pants rolled up at the hems and wearing his father's leather jacket that had been left behind for safekeeping. The shoulders too wide, the cuffs hanging past his mittened hands. The .22 slung over his shoulder. A little boy pretending to be a man.

The coyote wailed again, closer this time. With all her maternal senses electrified, her entire being strained to feel her child; to feel any sense of him being ripped from her heart.

Myron. Maria called as if he was on the other side of the barn and late for dinner. In the distance, a second coyote answered, and to the east, a third. Rage filled her belly. *He's mine*, she screamed inside.

Myron! she hollered, reaching for him across the field, not caring who she woke. *Myron!* She screamed until her throat hurt. His name stretched into a long howl. *Myron!* Her call filled the night.

The children shuffled outside. Scared at first by the night, by the cold, and their mother's cry. *Myron!* They peered into the dark, afraid to see what was on the other side, knowing that it could be one of them out there alone. Ivan was the first to join in, followed by Katya and then the others. Their voices swelled, a repeating chorus — spilling over one another: *Myron . . . Myron . . . Myron . . .*

He appeared like a ghost with two rabbits in hand. He scowled at them, embarrassed. Grumbled about them waking the dead. Kicked the snow off his boots and went inside to skin the rabbits. That was the first time they called him home.

Myron . . . Katya sings. *Myron . . .* Ivan bellows. Myron walks out of the night. He is taller now and stronger. His father's pants no longer need to be hitched up. In his own tightly fitting wool coat he could be mistaken for a young man. The gun sits comfortably in the crutch of his arm. Ivan and Katya run to greet him.

'Did you hear us?' Katya grabs his hand.

'Hear what?' Myron gruffs.

Katya falls for it every time. 'We were calling.'

'Was that you?' Myron feigns astonishment.

'Did you see a coyote?' Ivan jostles his sister.

'I think I did.' He casually slings the .22 over his shoulder.

Their eyes widen. 'Really? What'd it do?'

Myron crouches down to share a secret. 'It was as big as you, walked right up to me, looked me in the eyes. It had yellow eyes and teeth as long as your fingers. It spoke to me.' He waits for them to lean in close and hunger for the words.

'What did it say?' Ivan can barely speak.

'It said' — Myron pauses between each word, stretching out the delicious terror — 'I . . . want . . . ' He looks over his shoulder. 'Did you hear that?' He stares into the night. The children huddle closer.

Ivan whispers, 'What did it say?' His mitten rubs the gun's stock.

'It said' — Myron bares his teeth — 'I want to eat you!' He grabs their bellies. Roaring, he chases them screaming all the way to the house.

★　★　★

It has been six days since Anna has been to the coyote. It has been six days since Stefan returned. She pushes through the fresh snow, her belly weighing her down. She pants from the exertion. The morning is just turning grey. She had to sneak out while it was still dark.

Up ahead, she can see the twisted poplars against the tamarack. Beside her, the burned trees are dotted with puffs of soft snow that drop sporadically in clumps. Their charred limbs and trunks, rimed with frost, remind her of bones, vertebrae standing upright.

Inside the bush, it is darker. She sees tracks circling the hollow. One smaller than the other set. She is pleased that there is more than one. She sees where the snow has been trampled and the curved indent where one has slept or rested. Not ten feet away, she sees the coyote. She wants to wave, she has missed it so much. Its fur is getting thicker.

She holds up her hand, as if to say, *It's me.* The coyote sniffs the air, backs away, its lips curling. Anna hesitates, then steps forward, keeping her eyes low, knowing that she is moving too fast. She opens her cloak. *It's me.* She reaches in and pulls out a handkerchief. *I've brought you something special.* She kneels. Opens the package; inside is a chunk of beef. She sets it on the snow. Moves four feet away and waits.

The animal paces uncertainly back and forth. Anna is disappointed that it doesn't seem to remember her. She can't start all over again. She's brought real meat this time. It's her. Nothing has changed, except Stefan is back.

The coyote moves closer. Ducking its head. Sniffing the air. *It's meat that you smell.* But the animal seems to be catching the air in its nostrils, inhaling her. It approaches the meat. *It's me.* She inhales deeply, breathes in crisp air, musky earth. She focuses her smell. Smells wood stove, musty clothes, sweat, garlic, morning breath, and something else. She breathes in again — sour, pungent, nicotine, whisky — him.

She holds her breath. The coyote is four feet

away. Its nose reaching toward her. She offers her hand: *It's still me.* But now, even she can only smell the stench of him.

The coyote lunges in a sharp, explosive bark. It snaps up the meat and runs.

★ ★ ★

Anna bursts through the door. Lesya drops the log she is about to put in the wood stove. Petro, still in bed, ducks under the covers. Stefan roars awake: 'Shut the goddamn door.'

Anna rushes around the room, picking up Stefan's things, his cup, his coat, his boots; she piles them on their bed. 'You have to go,' she says.

'What the hell are you yapping about?'

Anna gathers up a jar of raspberry preserves, the new soap, the bacon, a pot, his razor, and drops it on the table. 'You can't stay here.' She ignores the baby's kicks.

Stefan sits up in bed, still in his undershirt and trousers. He watches her. She grabs the tin on the shelf. Empties it on the table and fans out the coins.

'Look.' She counts. 'Fifty-eight cents. You take it.'

Stefan walks to the table and looks at the coins.

'It's yours.' Anna is relieved.

'You want me to go?' Stefan stands straighter.

'Yes.'

Stefan smiles at Lesya and Petro as if he's heard a joke. 'Your mama wants me to go. Isn't that the silliest thing?' Petro smiles back at his tato because he doesn't know what else to do.

'You don't want me to go, do you?' Petro shakes his head, unsure if they are playing. Lesya hides behind her hair.

'They don't want me to go.' He holds up his hands and shrugs. 'But you want me to go?' Anna considers telling him about the coyote, but he would shoot it like he did the other one. He would never understand that it is her only friend.

'Yes.'

Stefan punches Anna under the ribs. He doesn't leave marks on the face. She falls to the ground on her hands and knees.

'This is my house! MY HOUSE! And you want me to go? Get up!'

He kicks her in the ass.

'I go away, I work hard, and you and your brother think you can take what's mine behind my back. You want to go? Get out.' He kicks her toward the door. 'Go on.' She stops, her belly cramping. 'Get out!' He grabs her by the hair and drags her to the door, shoves her into the snow. 'You have nothing, you own nothing, you're not worth as much as the cow. And you want me to go?'

Anna can't answer. The baby kicks against her ribs.

'I can't hear you!' He wrenches her head back and rubs a handful of snow in her face. She chokes on its frozen pain.

'Do you want me to go?' he screams in her face. The snow melts on her cheeks. Her stomach churns.

'No . . . ' If he stays, he will do what she can't. 'What did you say?'

She can taste blood on her lips. 'Yes,' not wanting him to stop.

He shoves her face in the snow.

★　★　★

Dania and Sofia wash the supper dishes. The taste of sausage and fried potatoes is still on their tongues. A fire roars in the stove, draping everyone in its warmth. Since Maria put the soiled blanket on the north wall, the heat hibernates in the front room. Two oil lamps cast an orange light that from outside looks welcoming and safe and inside makes everyone younger and happier.

Katya sits on Teodor's lap; he bounces her high and sideways, a bucking bronco. He grips the back of her dress and makes her dip and bow. She is giddy with hiccups.

'My turn,' Ivan insists.

Teodor slows to a trotting horse. 'This old horse is tired.'

'That's enough, give your father a rest.' Maria slips off the final stitches of Ivan's new mittens. 'Come try these on.' Ivan tucks his hands into their perfect fit.

'And you' — she points her needles at her husband — 'it's almost their bedtime.'

'Uh-oh, Mama Bear is growling,' Teodor goads. 'Don't want to get big bad Mama Bear riled up.' He whinnies and rears his leg; Katya tips off, and he lowers her gently to the ground.

'Stop your foolishness, old man,' Maria warns.

Myron, grinning despite his seriousness, looks up from oiling the bolt of the .22. He remembers this game from when he was little.

'Who are you calling foolish, old woman?' He pours another shot of homebrew from the quart jug. 'Would you like a little sip to warm you up, missus?'

Maria shoots a chastising look toward the children. Teodor dismisses her. 'Ahhh, a little medicine will do you good. Besides, we're celebrating. You can't say no to a little taste of honey.' He pours a splash of whisky in a tin cup.

'I like honey.' Ivan wants to celebrate too.

'No, no, this is wheat honey,' Teodor warns. 'It's only for mamas and tatos on very special occasions.' He winks at Maria. 'Like tonight.'

Ivan ponders what he has missed. 'What's special tonight?'

Maria glares at Teodor. It has been hard enough keeping the crock of fermenting brew a secret from the children. She told them it was cabbage heads souring. And late last night when Teodor distilled it, she was terrified one of them would wake and catch him.

Teodor stands, glass high in hand. 'Tonight we have this place, we have one another, we have everything that matters.' He parades around the room. 'Tonight we drink to . . . ' He searches for the right blessing. 'Tonight we drink to tomorrow.' He offers Maria the cup.

'You are a foolish man.'

'So kiss me and keep me quiet.'

Maria swats him away.

'One kiss.' Teodor leans in close. His eyes dance in the candlelight, shining with freedom and 180 proof.

In the glow of the lamps, he is that young, fearless man with an idealist's swagger and a heart full of righteous dreams. He is that man who held their firstborn child before the midwife had swaddled her in a blanket and laughed back tears. He is that man who chased her through the wildflower fields and always let her reach the apple tree first. She kisses him.

The children giggle and cover their eyes. Dania wishes that when she finds a young man, he will kiss her like that.

Myron flushes, remembering how Irene had looked up at him behind the church last Sunday, her eyes brown and nervous. The warmth of her breath. Her lips red and chapped from the cold. How they angled their heads to dodge their noses. How their teeth clanked together and his lips brushed her chin. He pushes the cold rifle hard against his lap.

Sofia pretends not to care, thinking it common to show such affections in public. A real lady would never allow a man to be so forthright. Yet each night after the others have fallen asleep, she practises kissing the back of her hand so she will be ready when her time comes to impress a young English man.

Teodor holds up his cup. 'Tomorrow.'

Maria raises her cup and drinks. She gags. The whisky sears her throat, races through her veins, and pickles her toes.

Teodor roars with delight. 'It's good, no?'

She nods, her eyes bulging. The baby rolls slowly in her belly.

'Come.' Teodor motions for the children to gather round. 'We need a song. Clap your hands.' He sets the rhythm. 'Everybody.' One by one the children join in. The driving beat grows stronger until the whisky on the table trembles with their enthusiasm.

'This is a song about where we come from.' He prances inside the circle his children have formed around him. He looks each one in the eye. 'A song about a strong people, a proud people, a song you must never forget.'

He spins around, wobbling only slightly. His boot slaps out time. He places his hands on his hips and sings. Low and flat.

'Now the chorus . . . ' He shouts the words in advance so the children can join in. He downs his cup of spirits. Their clapping drives harder.

'This is the part where the tsambaly and fiddle dare each other.' He commands his orchestra to drum: 'Faster. Let the horses gallop.' He hums the part of the instruments, high and low, weaving in and out, until the music is throbbing in each one's chest. 'Can you hear them?'

The children listen and they can hear the instruments in their blood reaching back hundreds of years, calling up the songs of their past.

He pulls Maria up. 'Dance with me.'

'The baby . . . ' Maria protests. He kisses her belly. 'The baby is already dancing.' She allows herself to be led. Myron pushes back the table.

'This part goes like this.' And he claps with

vigour in 2/4 time, one-two-one-two, as he dances with Maria. At the end of each refrain he shouts a jubilant 'Hey!' He puts his hands on his hips and leaps. Landing on his heels, he twirls and in one continuous movement squats. Kicking out his feet, he claps his hands behind his back. 'Hey Hey Hey!' He manages three before he crashes to the floor. The house stomps and cheers.

'I'm too old,' he pants. 'Myron, show them how.'

The family cheers and applauds. Myron steps back, embarrassed by the attention. 'Come on,' Teodor goads. 'Are you a boy or a man?' Myron steps into the centre of the circle. He enters tall, with his shoulders back. Teodor bellows the tune. The children's voices swell. Myron twists through the air — a whirling dervish, he drops to the ground. Balancing on his heels, he kicks high. His arms crossed over his chest, elbows thrust out, defying gravity. He pivots onto one hand and swings his legs around and under him, until he is a spinning top.

'Watch, Ivan, watch how it's done.' Teodor counts the rotations: 'One-two-three-four-five-six . . . ' When Teodor was just a little older than his elder son, he once did seventeen gyrations in a row to impress a young Maria. Myron's heel drags across the floor; he wobbles off balance.

'Ten!' Teodor shouts, triumphant. Myron jumps away, dizzy with adrenalin, disappointed that he still hasn't beat his father's record. Teodor bows to the women and waves them in. 'Your turn, my ladies.'

Maria takes Dania and Sofia by the hand and leads them to the centre. They form a ring that pulses open and closed. They let go of one another's hands and spin, their skirts flailing wide. Maria's bun comes loose and her hair spills around her face. Their hands high above their heads, their feet *tap-tapping* the dirt floor. They lift their faces to the imagined sun and bow to the mythical wheat. Their hands weave through the air like butterflies, calling the men forth. Teodor enters the circle and spins Maria into his arms. They two-step, skimming past clapping hands. Their feet magically land in syncopated pace. Maria looks at Teodor's face and marvels at the joy.

They don't hear the knock on the door. They don't hear Stefan call Teodor's name. It is Myron who hears the first out-of-rhythm beat. He stops clapping and listens above the din. He turns toward the door, unsure. Sofia, who is closest to the door, stomping and singing unabashedly, feels the discordant note next. She steps away from the door. Maria, her cheeks flushed, the weight of the baby slowing her down, sees Myron stiffen, suddenly alert. She stops mid-step. Teodor crashes into the table, laughing like a mad fool. It is then he hears the pounding on the door. They all hear it.

Maria looks to Teodor, who slides the jug behind his back.

'Teodor?' Stefan's voice intrudes.

The children look to their father. Huffing for breath, he staggers for his footing.

'Goddamn it,' he snarls and the man from a

moment ago is lost. This man leans crookedly, his jaw clenched, his eyes sharpened to approaching danger.

'Sit,' Maria orders him. Surprised by the authority in her voice and the swaying of the floor, he complies, but only on the edge of the chair. Maria tucks her hair up, straightens her blouse, and opens the door.

Stefan stands in the knee-deep snow, his hands thrust in his pockets, his collar pulled high. His face is red from the walk, his eyes water. Behind him, Petro stands in his father's footprints. His shoulders are hunched, the cold cuts through his thin jacket. She notices he is wearing Ivan's hat and mittens. A flush of guilt assails her for having punished her son for giving to someone less fortunate. She glances down at Petro's feet and is relieved to see he is wearing the new boots.

'Is everything all right?' She feels the familiar tightening of her heart. 'Is Anna all right?'

'She's fine.' Stefan avoids her eyes. In his mind's plan, it was always Teodor who answered the door.

'What are you doing here?' Maria bars the entrance, aware that she should be inviting them in. She rubs her belly, trying to calm the churning baby.

Stefan had a plan when he stormed out of the house, yanking the boy with him. He was going to show his son how a man deals with a thief. He had already shown him how to deal with a sobbing woman pleading with him not to go. A woman who cared more about offending her brother than the fact that he had stolen money from her own family's mouths. He was going to show his boy why men feared and respected him in the old country.

But he lost most of his anger before they reached the stone wall, his energy depleted from pushing his way through the deep snow. His leg was throbbing. He couldn't feel his cheeks and his head was pounding again. He would have turned back if he was alone, but the boy was shadowing him. The last half-mile, all uphill, took the rest of his will. He concentrated only on making it to the light shining through the window. He never looked back at the boy tripping behind him, unable to match his stride but refusing to fall behind. Determined to prove to his father that he was a man.

When Maria opened the door and the heat and smell of food embraced Stefan, he could have cried with relief. When he looked beyond her shoulder and saw on the table a tin cup and a jug of whisky, his entire being shouted hallelujah.

Stefan clears his throat and tries to sound calm. 'It was such a beautiful night, the boy and I were out walking and we saw the light and thought we'd come up and look at the place.' Maria doesn't budge. 'Then when we heard you singing, I thought, Well, everybody's awake. I should say hello.' He straightens his back to appear more like a nobleman out surveying his estate.

Maria looks to Teodor, who shakes his head no. She looks at Petro, his head hanging low and his lower lip trembling, which she mistakes for the cold, but in truth is the confusion of a child who no longer knows why they are here.

'Come in and get warmed up.' She opens the door and a blast of icy air makes the lamps flicker.

'Thank you.' Stefan removes his cap, kicks the snow from his boots, and nudges Petro to do the same.

'Have a seat.' Maria glares at Teodor to be on his best behaviour. 'Go warm yourself by the stove, Petro.'

'I'm not cold,' he chatters and holds fast by the door.

'Don't argue with your aunt,' Stefan warns. Petro clomps to the wood stove, leaving a trail of already melting snow. Ivan grins widely, happy to see the new boots on his cousin's feet, finally knowing what others see when they look at his own new boots. Ivan pulls his boots from under the stove and plops down on his bum to slip them on. He hopes that Petro is admiring them as much as he admires his.

'Teodor,' Stefan acknowledges cordially and settles into the chair across from him. His eyes slide down to the half-full cup. 'You've built a fine place.'

Teodor watches him like a dog watches a stray that has wandered into his yard. He sizes him up, confused by the wagging tail.

'It's bigger inside than it looks.' His eyes scan the shelves of preserves, the neatly ordered supplies, the full stack of wood, the socks strung over the stove, Maria and Teodor's bed nestled beneath a down quilt. He thinly smiles and says the words he knows they want to hear. 'It feels like home.'

'Are you hungry?' Maria asks. 'We still have some sausage and potatoes.'

'No, no . . . ' Stefan demurs. 'Don't go to any bother. It's more the cold that's got in my bones.' He eyes the jug and rubs his hands together to warm them, hoping Teodor will take the hint. 'I heard the singing halfway up the hill. I remember that song, haven't heard it in years. Anna used to dance to it. She was like watching fire, the way she moved . . . '

Teodor knows he should be on guard, but his full belly, the whisky glowing in his veins, and the crackling fire lull his senses. He rolls a cigarette, spilling half the tobacco on the table. He licks the paper and rolls it loose. He doesn't know why he is grinning.

'I see you brewed up a batch.' Stefan plays it casual.

'Josyp Petrenko gave it to Tato for helping him,' Ivan corrects. Teodor's laughing eyes give away the white lie.

'Is that right?' Stefan picks up the jug and breathes in. He swallows back the urge to tip it to his lips. 'How is it?' He sets the jug back down.

'Warm and smooth like a good piss,' Teodor slurs the last word and he hears himself laughing, inviting in the camaraderie of another man. A free man, in his own home, sharing his good fortune. He knows now what he is feeling. He is feeling safe.

'Maria, get us another cup.'

'No, no,' Stefan feigns disinterest. 'I know how hard it is to come by.' His mouth can barely shape the lie, his body flushes hot. His mouth salivates.

'I insist,' Teodor responds magnanimously. 'One shot.'

'Girls, get ready for bed.' Maria stiffens, but Teodor ignores her protest.

'I'm not tired,' Katya argues. Her mother's sharp look silences her.

Dania takes Katya's hand and leads her to the bedroom. 'Come on, I'll tell you a bedtime story.'

'Good night, Tato.' Katya wraps her arms around her father's neck and kisses him on the lips. He smells funny, sour and bitter. Her lips burn from touching his.

Sofia follows suit. ''Night.' She pecks him on the cheek. He throws his arms around her and bundles her on his knee, giving her a whisker rub.

'Good night, grumpy-dump.' He swats her behind and she is delighted, even as she pouts and straightens her skirt.

''Night, Tato.' He looks up at his eldest daughter.

'Good night, Dania.' He speaks to her as an adult, which makes her proud. She leads her sisters to the room, eager to escape Stefan's burning eyes.

'They're getting big, aren't they? How old is Dania now?'

'Fourteen.' Teodor pours a splash of liquor into Stefan's cup. Dania pulls the blanket modestly across the door frame.

''Night.' Stefan nods, mesmerized by her long blond hair and piercing blue eyes. 'She looks like you, Maria. A beauty.'

Myron pushes back his chair and stands too abruptly, the .22 in his hand. He slams the bolt in. 'I'm going to check the snares.' He is out the door before he has pulled on his jacket.

'Why don't you boys go play in your room,' Maria suggests. 'Keep it quiet, though.' Ivan, who is struggling to tie his laces, unable to remember if the rabbit goes into the hole or around the tree, gladly gives up. Tripping over his bootlaces, he leads the way.

'Why don't you take off your hat and mitts, Petro, you'll get too hot. I'll hang them up, then they'll be warm for you later.' Maria holds out her hand.

Petro protectively grabs his hat. 'I want to keep them.' He hurriedly follows Ivan into his room.

Teodor lifts his cup. 'Daî Bozhe.'

Stefan takes hold of the mug as though shaking hands with an old friend. His trembling fingers steady themselves against the tin.

'God give you health,' Stefan concurs and raises his cup. He breathes in the earthy, bittersweet fragrance. He kisses his lips to the cup and drinks. The amber fire spreads through his body. A warm, golden light bathes his brain and numbs the pain. He is filled with pure liquid joy. His shoulders relax. He leans back in the chair, his eyes soft. 'It's good whisky, Teodor. Fine whisky.'

He holds up his cup for more. The men smile

at each other, willing, in this moment, to pretend to be friends. Teodor fills his cup. Stefan helps himself to tobacco and unbuttons the top button of his too-tight collar to let the golden liquid pass more freely. Maria warily watches, fighting the irrational urge to gather up her family and run.

★ ★ ★

Ivan and Petro sit on the bed, dangling their feet over the edge. Ivan tries to hold his feet in the same position as his cousin's. Toes slightly pointed inward. He pretends he has four legs. He lifts his left foot up, hoping Petro's leg will do the same. It doesn't. He swings his right foot, coaxing Petro's to follow. Nothing. Their feet hang lifelessly.

'What d'you wanna do?' Ivan prods, eager to please. 'Wanna see my gopher skull?'

Petro shrugs, but Ivan has already clambered onto the floor. On his belly, he sidles under the bed and retrieves a dog-eared cardboard box labelled WINCHESTER .22 SINGLE SHOT. He sets it on the bed and ceremoniously flips open the top. The gopher's skull, gleaming white, crowns the treasures.

'You can hold it if you want.' He sets it in Petro's hand. 'It's light, ain't it?'

Petro examines the empty eye sockets and gaping mouth. 'It's got more teeth than I thought. They're sharp.' He runs his finger across an incisor. Then sticks his finger through the gaping eye hole, feeling inside for bits of brain.

271

From the next room, a loud burst of men's laughter, punctuated by fragments of boisterous stories — names of Ukrainian people and places Ivan's never heard of before — distract the boys. His father is talking loud and fast, tripping over his words, laughing mid-sentence. Stefan speaks even louder, as if making sure that everyone hears him. Ivan wonders why they are hollering at each other when they are sitting so close together. Petro tosses the skull on the bed and rifles through the box.

'What else you got?'

He throws aside the blue crockery shard. Ivan doesn't bother to show him that it's the exact same blue as the sky just before it gets pitch-black. He shuffles past the twig shaped like a snake that if you hold sideways, you can see a sliver of forked bark curled up like a tongue. Instead, he extracts a silver pocket watch. The cover is dented and twisted, the glass smashed, and one hand is missing. He shakes it to his ear, a tinkle of metal shards.

'Does it work?'

'No.' Ivan knows his cousin will be disappointed. 'But it's got a name on the back. You gotta open it.' He pushes on the clasp 'I found it where we used to live before. See . . . ' He points to the engraving. 'F. P. Williams.'

'It ain't worth nothing.' Petro tosses it aside. Ivan frowns. He wants to tell him that *F. P. Williams* is engraved slanted, like someone important. That makes it worth something. Maybe F. P. Williams lost the watch because he had a hole in his pocket, because he didn't have

272

a mama to sew it up. Or maybe he was robbed and he fought with the robbers and was killed right there with his watch. Or maybe . . .

'What's this?' Petro holds up a grey heart-shaped stone.

'A lucky rock.' Ivan yawns, his body reminding him that he's up way past his bedtime.

'You make it?' Petro runs his fingers over its smooth curves.

'Found it in the lake.' Ivan wants to lie down and nestle against his pillow, but that would be rude. In the next room, Maria shushes the two men. Their voices drop, then rise again, low and booming.

Petro sets the rock aside. He finds a peppermint candy and pops it in his mouth. The red-and-white one.

'I was saving that one,' Ivan protests, suddenly wide awake.

'You got another one. Besides, I shared my apple.' Petro digs to the bottom of the box and finds a penny. 'You got money.'

Ivan shrugs. He doesn't care about money. He likes the picture of the leaf, and the coppery colour and the date that is the same as the year he was born, 1933. He likes to think it was made just for him.

'You could buy anything you want,' Petro exclaims.

'I don't want to buy anything, I want to keep it.'

'That's stupid.'

'No, it's not.' Ivan reaches for his penny, but Petro pulls it back. 'You don't keep money. You

273

spend money to get other things. That's how you get rich. You're such a baby.'

Ivan snatches for the penny. 'Give it back.'

'Babies shouldn't have money.' Petro jumps up on the bed, holding the coin high above his head. 'Let's play a game; if you can take it from me, it's yours. If not, it's mine. Deal?' He spits in his hand and offers to shake.

'I'm not playing.' Ivan pushes aside his cousin's hand. 'Give it back.'

'No.' Petro makes his stand.

'It's mine.' Ivan's heart swells with rage and frustration, confused that his best friend in the whole world is being mean to him. 'You can have the other candy.'

'I don't want your candy. I've got my own.' He spits the peppermint onto the floor. It rolls in the dirt, picking up specks of black, bleeding red and white. 'Get your father to give you more money, he's got lots of it. He took ours.'

Ivan slams Petro's chest with his hands, driving him into the wall. Petro laughs and holds the penny higher. Ivan swipes the wool cap from Petro's head and growls, 'That's mine too.'

Before Petro can snatch it back, Ivan throws himself into his soft belly, fists swinging.

* * *

Teodor wipes tears from his eyes, only half aware that Stefan is filling his cup again. He hasn't laughed in such a long time, his ribs are aching. He almost feels sick.

'Maria.' He waves to her. 'Come sit with me.' He slaps his knee.

Maria ignores him as she dices the leftover meat and potatoes for a stew. 'I have work to do.'

'She's a stubborn woman,' Teodor teases. He tries to stand. 'Come show Stefan how we were dancing.' He holds out his arms and falls back in his chair. The men laugh uproariously.

Stefan stands. His body leans too far back to be balanced. He bows sloppily to Maria. 'If you'll excuse me, I must step outside and water a horse.' He winks at Teodor.

Teodor waves farewell. 'Watch out the coyotes don't bite it off.'

'It'd take more than one,' Stefan brags. He steps into the crisp night. As the door shuts behind him, Teodor takes another sip and looks lovingly to Maria, who is burning a hole in his heart.

'What?' His head bobs indignantly.

'That's it.' Maria grabs the jug of whisky. 'I want him out of here.'

'We're having a good time.' He brings the cup of cheer to his lips. Maria stops his hand and takes away the cup.

'You're drunk and he should be home with his pregnant wife, not here drinking this poison.'

She drains the cup back into the jug.

'What kind of man brings a child out at this time of night? And you . . . ' she spits, 'what kind of man keeps pouring it into him? You know what he's like.'

'You're spilling it.' The whisky dribbles down the jug and pools on the table. Maria slams the empty tin cup onto the table.

'You're lucky I don't pour it out.'

She drives the cork into the jug. She goes to the back wall and pushes aside the framed picture of the Virgin Mary holding her beating heart in hand. Behind the frame is the carved-out niche in the log wall.

'We were just havin' a drink,' Teodor slurs, the golden glow starting to dim.

'And what's he going to do when he goes home? What's he going to do when he wakes up and there isn't any more? What's he going to do to those children and your sister? That man has the devil in him. I want him out of here.'

She shoves the jug into the hole and covers it back up with the guardian Virgin, hidden in plain view. She turns to see Petro standing in the doorway watching her. The wool cap is in his hand. Blood drips from his nose and trickles into the corner of his mouth. It's his eyes, though, that pierce Maria's heart.

'Petro . . . ' She wants to explain, she wants to pick him up in her arms, she wants to kiss away the hurt, but she can't find the words and her body won't do her bidding.

'Colder than a witch's teat out there.' Stefan throws open the door, still buttoning up the front of his pants. He staggers against the door frame as he pulls the door shut behind him, a lopsided grin on his face. He stops, feeling the sudden freeze in the house. He notices the absence of the jug on the table; and Maria, her cheeks flushed and her eyes ashamed; and Petro, scrawny and pathetic. His nose bleeding.

'What happened?' His voice cracks.

Petro breaks for the door. Stefan grabs him by the collar and wrenches him back.

'What did you do?' The boy's blood drips onto his hands. 'What did you do?' The taste of hatred for this child, who has ruined everything, biles in his throat.

'Nothing,' Petro stammers.

'Ivan!' Teodor bellows, the fire turning hot in his veins. Angry that he has lost something again, something that he can't even identify, something that was good.

Ivan skulks into the room, his chin thrust up, his lower lip pouting. His fist clenches his penny.

'What happened?' Teodor barks.

Ivan searches for the right answer. He searches through a jumble of images: a penny; a peppermint candy he tried to wipe the dirt off that stained his hand red; a crushed gopher's skull. One eye caved in, where his new boot stomped it. The bruise under his ribs, where his cousin kicked him; the throbbing of his knuckles when he punched Petro in the face; the red, red blood . . .

'Answer me!' Teodor slams the table with his open hand. Surprised by the loudness of the swat.

'He stole my hat.' He glares at Petro, knowing that it isn't the right answer, but it's the only way he can explain everything.

'I did not!' Petro screams back.

They look at Petro, the hat clutched tight to his chest, blazing his guilt.

'This?' Stefan pulls at the ragged wool cap,

with its red darned patches and unravelled threads. For a moment, he thinks he can salvage the night, they'll laugh at the children's pettiness and pour another drink. 'Give it back to him.'

'It's mine.' Petro clings tighter, protecting it with both arms.

'Give it to him.'

Petro shakes his head. 'It's mine,' he says to the floor.

Stefan wrenches it from his hands, but Petro holds on, his head yanks backward as his father drags him forward and lifts him off the ground. 'Let go.' He shakes him.

'It's mine.' Petro tastes the blood in his mouth, salty and metallic. He closes his eyes and hangs on. The wool hat stretches between his fingers. Stefan slams him toward the ground and Petro's knees buckle, but still he holds on. His new boots drag little trenches across the dirt floor. His arms stretch in their sockets.

Ivan covers his ears. Teodor is standing. His face twisted and angry. Everyone is screaming. His sisters cower behind the thin blanket shielding their doorway. Sofia and Katya cling to Dania. Their cheeks are wet with tears, their voices screech high and frantic. Ivan looks to his mother. Her mouth wails as she runs toward Stefan. He looks to Petro twisting in the air like his sister's rag doll. He doesn't want the hat any more. He never wanted it back. He only wanted Petro to say he was sorry for being mean. All he wanted was for them to have the same boots so they could be brothers.

Maria grabs Stefan's arm, but he doesn't even

see her. He sees only the hat and the pitiful defiance of something so weak it doesn't deserve to live. He yanks viciously back, his elbow slams into Maria's belly, the hat tears from Petro's fingers. Stefan lifts it, victorious, high above his head and, as he turns to toss it to Ivan, sees Maria slumped on the floor, gasping for air. Before he can make sense of this image, Teodor is driving him back against the door frame.

He slams into the wood jamb, the door wrenches open, sucking in the bitter cold. A lightning bolt of pain rips up his spine. Teodor's hand is around his throat. Choking. Stefan's tongue rolls back, lungs gulping, as the room reels and blackens. He gropes for the knife in his pocket. His fingers curl around the handle and his thumb pries open the blade. He can't get a proper grip and drives it upward, blade down, through the jumble of arms and elbows. The dull knife drags across the back of Teodor's hand.

Teodor's hand recoils. The wound welts red, filling with blood thinned from the alcohol. Stefan rasps for air. The two men stare each other down. Eyes wild. Lips parted, teeth bared. They size each other up for the kill. Stefan nimbly flips the knife around, the blade becoming a natural extension of his hand. His fingers tighten around the handle.

'Come on,' Stefan snarls. 'Finish it.'

A shot cracks their eardrums. Wood splinters from the door frame, inches from Stefan's head. The world goes deaf and all eyes look past the door into the night. In a split second, Myron reloads and aims the .22 at his uncle's chest.

'Get out of our house.' Myron's voice is low and steady, so contained it might explode. The gun doesn't quiver.

'Now,' he says. His lips dry.

Teodor steps back, his mind sober. He sees his wife holding her belly, tears streaking her flushed cheeks. He sees his children's terrified eyes. Blood drips from his hand onto his boots. At his feet, Petro kneels before the wool cap splayed on the floor. The boy's eyes are locked on the end of the barrel pointing at his father. Teodor feels the pulsing pain in his hand.

'Get off my property.' He chokes down the white hot rage. 'It's over between us. Don't ever come back here.'

Stefan calculates the odds of his knife against Myron's aim. He wants to drive it into Teodor's smug, righteous belly and twist it. Make him beg him to slit his throat. Mercy. A technique he honed well in the army. But it would take a step and a thrust to reach Teodor, and his back would be to the boy. He looks at the gun's sights, fixed on his chest, steady. Myron cocks the firing pin. Stefan pockets the knife, straightens his coat, and slicks back his hair.

'Now I remember why I came by in the first place, Teodor. I wanted to thank you for paying off our land. Not many brothers would do that for their sister.'

Teodor restrains himself. 'It's my land.'

'We'll have to see what the courts say.' Stefan buttons up his collar. 'Thank you for the fine whisky. You're a brave man, Teodor. I wouldn't want to get caught with it. What's the penalty now? A year in jail? Another year. No worries, I'm sure you have it well hidden.' He looks at Petro, who is still on his knees. 'Get up.'

Petro reaches for the wool cap. Stefan steps on it.

'It's mine,' Petro tries one last time. 'I won it, fair and square.'

Stefan looks to Ivan. 'Is that true?'

Ivan looks to his new boots. His bare feet are stuck to the insoles. The tongue digs into the top of his foot. A blister chafes his right heel.

'Well,' Stefan considers. 'Like father, like son.' He slides his foot off the cap. 'Pick up your hat, boy. We're going home.' Petro pulls the misshapen cap over his ears. Stefan bends over to dust the dirt from his son's knees and offers some fatherly advice. 'Some people don't know what's theirs and what isn't.' He taps him on the behind. 'Let's go.'

Petro scrambles out the door. Stefan straightens his back into his best soldier's posture and tipsily heads for the door, as if he is the one who has chosen to leave.

Teodor blocks his exit with his arm and leans in close. 'If you touch him again, if you hurt any of my family . . . ' he whispers, 'I will kill you.' He lowers his arm to let him pass.

Stefan whispers back with a smile: 'You're already dead.' He turns and bows to Maria. 'My apologies for my son's behaviour. I've brought him up to fight for what's his.' And with that he leaves.

Myron keeps the gun trained on his uncle's

back until he is swallowed by the night. Only then does the barrel begin to shake uncontrollably.

★ ★ ★

Curled up under the feather quilt, the box of treasures safely back under his bed, Ivan breathes in the green scent of his straw mattress. His boots and long underwear are warming by the fire. His mind is already washing away the night. He plays his father's song in his head, making up the words he didn't catch, drowning out the gunshot, the crushed gopher skull, the blood-red candy, the howling voices. He is spinning, his arms crossed, his legs kicking high. He is dancing in a twilight sky. He falls asleep, wondering what time tomorrow Petro will come out to play, not even caring that his heart-shaped rock has disappeared.

★ ★ ★

Katya pads quietly through the kitchen, past her sleeping mama and tato to the orange flickering glow escaping around the wood-stove door. Its light licks at the walls. The stove roars and the pipe tinkles from the heat. Its belly is full of wood. She wraps her hand in her nightie and slides the flue open. She opens the door. Heat blasts her face. The flames twist and reach for her. She tosses in an extra large piece of the doughy Christ. *Amen.*

It bubbles and shrivels into a blackened lump

282

and bursts into flames. The fire is angry, like her tato and her uncle. It wants more. She feeds it the last bits of newspaper lying nearby. It grabs hungrily at the paper. Katya looks around the room to see what else it wants. The shelf of preserves glows in its light. She sees another piece of paper.

Katya stretches on her tiptoes and grabs it with her fingertips. Brown paper for wrapping meat. She gives it to the fire. The edges curl and the fire licks at the pencilled words on the other side.

★   ★   ★

Two days later, the police arrive to search the premises. They look under the beds, the mattresses, the pillows, and inside the children's blanket boxes. They rifle through the tin cans, preserves, bags of flour, sugar, and salt. The tall officer with the walrus moustache and a bandoleer strung across his crimson chest pulls the straw mattresses from the beds.

Teodor sits at the kitchen table rolling cigarettes, licking the papers with slow measure and winding the tobacco tight. He sets the finished smokes on the table in a careful, straight row. Maria kneads bread dough, sprinkling in extra handfuls of freshly ground wheat flour. She mistakenly adds an extra cup of water.

Outside, the children sit crowded on the stoop. The cold seeps through their long underwear; their bums mould the snow. Their leather soles freeze to the ground. They don't brush away the light snow dusting their shoulders.

Only when the door opens and the two officers step outside empty-handed do the children part. All except Myron, who remains seated and makes them walk around him.

They watch the officers slip and slide down the hill to their car, mired in snow on the far side of the stone wall. The engine sputters and growls. Black smoke belches from its tail. The tires spin. The passenger gets out and makes his way to the rear of the car and pushes. The tires whir, the vehicle rocks. The officer waves to the children to come and help. No one moves. He pushes again. The car jitters forward and fishtails down the hill. The officer chases after it; scarlet arms and black-trousered legs windmilling against the white expanse, he jumps inside. The children watch until the car is a black speck.

As does Maria. She waits until she is certain they are not coming back. Then she goes to the Virgin, which has been bumped crooked by the man with the thick moustache when he brushed past her to look in the pots. She slides away the frame to retrieve the jug.

'What are you doing?' Teodor watches her fumbling to uncork the jug. 'Maria . . . '

'I won't have this in my house.' She grabs a knife and pries into the cork. He stops her hand. Maria wrenches the jug away.

'Give it to me.' Teodor holds out his hand.

'No.'

Teodor squeezes her hand that clutches the knife tight. 'Let it go.'

Maria lifts the jug above her head with her free arm. 'I'll drop it.'

Teodor easily reaches over her and grabs it. 'Let go.' He presses her hand against the table, forcing her to release the knife. She struggles to smash the jug against the table. Teodor holds it steady. They stand locked in a twisted dance.

'Is this what you need to prove that you're as good as them? That you're not a peasant who can be kicked and ordered to bow?' She pleads, 'Are you willing to risk us?'

Maria sees his eyes cloud with disappointment. He speaks gently, as if to a child he doesn't expect to understand. 'A man should be able to have a drink in his own house.'

'I won't wait for you.'

Teodor coaxes the jug from her hand. He sets it back in the niche and straightens the picture.

* * *

The children gather around Teodor at the kitchen table. He lights a cigarette from the oil lamp. The smoke curls around them. He speaks to his hands, the nicotine-stained fingers, the greyed linen bandage that dresses his wound. He forbids them to have any contact with the people in the house on the other side of the stone wall.

Maria kneels before the Blessed Virgin and prays.

Wheat Wine

Cook two pounds of well-washed wheat until soft. Drain. In earthen crock, pour five gallons of boiling water over wheat, then add ten pounds of white sugar and one yeast cake broken.

Drop this in when mixture is lukewarm.

Cover with cloth. Let sit behind stove or in warm place for 3-4 weeks.

Strain through pillowcase into creamery can.

Pillowcase with solids can be placed in can and tied off, so long as it doesn't touch the bottom.

Fit creamery can with wooden block for lid. Drill 1½" hole in bottom of block and ½" hole in side of block.

Insert copper pipe through hole on side. Make sure fit is tight. Coil pipe through tub of ice, snow, or cold water. Heat can on stove for 1–2 hours.

Use half-gallon jugs or jars. First jars nice and strong.

Keep pouring until just water. Test by throwing some on the fire. If it flashes, keep pouring.

Makes 1 gallon. Adjust recipe for quantity needed.

Winter

The temperature drops to twenty below in the days and forty below at night. Night steals away the day by suppertime. A hoary frost coats the exterior of the log cabin. Inside the house, even with the fire burning, the family wears long underwear, sweaters, socks, and boots.

The four-mile walk to school has been deemed too dangerous. The children aren't allowed out for more than ten minutes before Maria herds them back inside to check their raw cheeks for frostbite. The crusted snow groans beneath their feet. The dry, cold air sucks their breath from their lungs. Tears freeze on eyelashes. Scarves and mitts grow stiff from condensation and sweat.

Each day Myron chops through the lake's two-foot-thick ice to fetch water, only to find the hole frozen again the next morning. There have been stories in the newspaper about people losing their toes and fingers. Cows and horses have been found frozen solid, still standing in their paddocks. Bodies are piling up in the shed behind the church, waiting for the ground to thaw so they can be buried.

In some places the snow has drifted four feet. The mice and rabbits are scarce, already starved or frozen, unable to reach the prairie grass. Coyotes have been spotted in the town streets. It is the worst winter on record and it's only November.

Teodor planes a long strip of bark down a ten-foot log. For the last two weeks, he has been building a barn with two stalls, a small room for the tack and one for the grain. He has to get the horse out of Anna's barn before Stefan claims it as his own or worse. Teodor knows he's capable of hurting the animal to get back at him.

The walls are up. The rafters are in. He is hewing the boards for the roof now. He brushes away the ice clinging to his scarf, obscuring his vision. It is wrapped twice around his head, leaving only a gash for his eyes. He wears two pairs of mittens. The palms are bound in burlap. Once, he removed the mitts to better control the plane and his hands stuck to the metal handle. He had to breathe on the steel to thaw it with his breath, but it still ripped away a layer of skin. He knows now how long he can push after losing feeling in his fingers and toes before he is forced to hobble into the house and let the fire warm his blood.

Maria unwraps his scarf, pulls off the mittens, removes his coat, and hangs them over the stove to gather heat. She unlaces his boots and slips them off his feet. His feet are so numb, he can't feel the floor through his socks. They are like stumps, the toes fused together. Maria sets hot rocks in his boots and wraps him in a blanket. She rubs his feet as he sips hot water. The blood starts to melt and the nerves scream on fire. He tries to rock away the pain. His face contorts in agony; he stuffs the blanket in his mouth and bites down to suppress the moans. The children retreat into their rooms. They sit, wiggling their fingers and toes, unable to imagine not having ten of each.

After twenty minutes, Teodor gets dressed again and returns to his work. In another week, he should be finished.

★ ★ ★

It's been two weeks and the families haven't spoken. Each night Maria prays for them all. *God bless Anna, God bless Lesya, God bless Petro, God bless the unborn child.* She has to reach deep in her heart for *God bless Stefan.* No one utters their names out loud. In the first few days, Ivan cried himself to sleep, demanding to be told why he couldn't play with Petro. After the third night of Maria's whispers and empty consolations, Teodor barged into the room and threatened him with a strapping. After that, Ivan covered his head with his pillow and learned to cry without sobbing.

Maria tried to reason with Teodor that he was punishing his sister and her children for her husband's betrayal. He rolled over in bed and slept with his back to her. She pleaded with him that he couldn't let them starve. Think of Lesya, think of the boy.

He screamed back at her: 'He didn't think of my children! Who'll feed them if I'm not here?' He stormed out and didn't return until after dark.

Maria didn't worry, she knew he was in the

barn. Every hour she could see the end of his cigarette glowing hot just outside the barn door. In bed, she put her arms around him, her round belly pressed against the small of his back, her legs spooned against his. She breathed into his neck: 'Do it because you are a good man.' He didn't answer.

Before morning broke, Maria slid quietly out of bed and replaced her sleeping form with a pillow. She kept her feet bare, despite the chilled ground. She didn't stoke the fire for fear of waking the household. Quietly, she navigated the room, her hands groping the darkness, her eyes adjusting to the faint moon shadows. At one point she closed her eyes and searched the shelves with her fingers. She was amazed to discover that she could sense the objects at the end of her fingertips before they touched. When Teodor woke, Maria had finished packing the basket full of food supplies.

'You take it or I will,' she said calmly. Teodor cursed, and Maria slipped her feet into his oversized boots. She clunked over to the coat hook and pulled his coat over her nightdress and five-months-pregnant belly. She wrapped his scarf around her neck and pulled on his mittens.

'I'll take it.' Teodor got out of bed.

Now every morning he walks down the hill to the forbidden place on the other side of the wall. He approaches the back of the barn. Some days the horse is waiting for him; other days it is mercifully inside. He doesn't go around front, he enters through the tackroom. He checks that the cow is being milked and fed; that the teats are clean and healthy; and that the stall has been mucked out. He brushes down the horse. If it is an especially cold day, he feeds it extra oats. Occasionally, he drapes the saddle blanket over its bowed back. He rubs its head and promises that soon he'll take it to its new home.

He peeks out the barn to see if smoke is rising from the stack and that wood is chopped. He is surprised how the pile has grown. He can see the footprints are small. The axe is stuck in the chopping block. The first few days, it was mostly small branches, then a few small logs, but with each day the stack has grown and now the logs are fat and thick, split perfectly down the centre. He wishes he could see his nephew swing the axe.

He sets the basket a few feet from the cow's stall and picks up the two eggs or the jug of milk offered in return.

Only once did he encounter Lesya, when he arrived an hour earlier to get a jump on the day. Her back was to him as she set the two eggs on a cushion of hay inside the empty basket. The horse's whinny made her look around. Teodor stood awkwardly with the other basket in hand, self-conscious of the pink embroidered linen cloth covering it. Lesya scrambled to her feet and bolted for the door.

'Lesya . . . '

She stopped at the door but kept her hand on the latch.

'Is there anything else you need?'

Lesya shook her head and hid behind her long hair.

'Is your mama okay?'

Lesya hesitated and nodded.

'If you need anything, if anything happens, you come get me. Do you understand?'

Lesya nodded again. Teodor set the basket on the ground and pocketed the eggs. 'I won't come by before seven from now on.'

That was the last morning he saw her there.

★　★　★

Ivan trudges after Myron, having successfully badgered Maria to let him help check the snares. She acquiesced, hoping he would expend some pent-up energy and stop tormenting his sisters.

His trouser legs rub together, padded by the extra pair of long johns. He walks stiffly; his arms hang away from his sides, propped out by two sweaters. He feels thick and heavy, swaddled by his mother's worry. The scarf tourniquets his forehead and winds over his nose and mouth, chokes around his throat, obstructing his peripheral view. Twice he fell in the deep snow, floundering on his back until Myron grabbed him by the scruff and hoisted him up.

'Myron . . . ' His voice sounds muffled and far away. He shouts louder: 'Myron.'

'What?' Myron grouches, expecting to find him flailing in the snowdrifts again.

'Can I hold the gun?'

'No.' Myron slings the rifle over his shoulder and pushes forward. The steel light of morning is already greying the clouds. He's late. He's usually at the wall before first light, but this morning he had to wait for Ivan to get dressed and now he has to wait for him to catch up. He quickens his pace, forcing his little brother to run.

Checking the snares is his job. It's the only time he can be alone, away from the family. Away from the confines of the house. Away from the unspoken tension between his mother and father. It's the only time he can breathe.

He has a routine. He wakes up long before the others stir, even his father. He always puts his right foot out first, then his left. He retrieves the pants and shirt he laid out on the end of his bed. He always starts with his right leg in his trousers. He doesn't tuck in his shirt until the quilt is straightened. That night when everything went bad, Myron had unthinkingly tucked in his shirt before he had straightened the bed covers. He has been much more careful ever since. Before he leaves the room, he glances over to Ivan and counts him breathing three times, then enters the day. He knows the rituals are childish, but it's all that he can control.

No matter how stealthily he moves or how early he wakes, Maria always gets up to set out a slice of bread with lard or jam and a cup of hot water coloured with a few grains of coffee. Before climbing back in bed, she tousles his hair as she did when he was a little boy. His morning hug. They don't exchange words. Enough has been said. He stacks his dirty dishes. Then swallows the last mouthful of lukewarm water just before he steps outside.

In the twilight of dawn, when his ears are still

fresh to the day's first sounds, he can hear clearer than at any other time of day. He turns his head back and forth, cocking his ears to each direction. Sometimes, he closes his eyes to listen better. He hears the branches cracking from the frost, the groan of the snow beneath his feet, the rumbling of the lake ice, the timber in the house shrinking and shifting, sometimes he thinks he can even hear the clouds sliding across the sky. This morning, though, when he opened his eyes, his brother's face was inches from his own. 'Can I come with you?'

Myron scans the snow for fresh tracks, but he and Ivan are the only animals foolish enough to traverse snow this deep. He's only trapped a dozen rabbits this winter and the last two were skin and bone. Maria never complains about the meagre catch, but he feels the shame of failing his family.

The first rabbit he skinned, he tore the pelt and nicked the stomach. The rancid contents and stool poured onto the floor and contaminated the meat. He had said he knew how to do it. His father skinned the next rabbit. He set up a truss in the corner and strung the rabbit up by its rear legs. He began by sharpening the knife, polishing the blade against the grinding stone in smooth circular movements. He showed Myron how to test its sharpness by running his thumb along the razor-sharp edge.

With a surgeon's precision, he made the first incision, cutting cuffs around the paws, under the tail, over the backside. Then, grabbing the skin, he pulled it down over the belly, carving through the fat, until the entire skin was turned inside out, draped over the rabbit's head. Its entire musculature exposed, bloody and raw. He opened the chest and stomach cavity next, dissecting the heart and liver for Maria's stew pot. Then, with one final pull, he yanked away the pelt hooding the head. The animal no longer resembled a rabbit. It had become meat. Teodor handed the knife to Myron and stepped back. Only once did he take his son's hand and adjust the angle of the blade. Myron didn't make any more mistakes.

Whenever Myron skinned a rabbit, Ivan watched intently over his shoulders, mimicking every move. Maria lined Myron's and Teodor's boots with the pelts for insulation and stitched together a baby blanket for Anna. Ivan added a rabbit skull to his treasure box.

'Can I take it from the snare?' Ivan hollers, the words punctuated by his breathless gasps.

'There might not be any rabbits.' Myron, impatient, stops to let him catch up. Ivan pushes through the snow, lifting his boots high, clouds of white puffing from his mouth like a steam engine. His body is overheated in the extra clothes, each leg weighs ten extra pounds; he kneels in the snow pausing for air. He blinks his eyes, his eyelashes sticky with ice. Myron notices his brother's smallness and remembers that he's still just a kid.

'Why don't you wait here?' Myron suggests.

Ivan struggles to his feet. 'I'm comin'.' He trudges past his big brother, determined to get to the rabbit first. Angry that Myron would think

297

that he would give up. He concentrates on putting one foot in front of the other. He sinks to his waist; he heaves the other leg over, and sinks to his knee. He pushes his upper body up, his hands disappear to his wrists; icy snow crams under the cuffs. He hits a crusted drift; the snow holds his weight and he scrambles across. He doesn't notice the tracks leading up from the lake, loping toward the stone wall, but Myron does.

Myron veers off the path to check their freshness. They are large prints, dog tracks. The gait is long and bounding. Coyote. It came through a few hours ago at the most. Myron scans the horizon. There's no sign that the animal returned the same way. He drops the gun to the crook of his elbow. 'Ivan, wait up.'

But Ivan doesn't hear him through the scarf and hat muffling his ears. He is running now. He's only thirty feet from the wall. He scans the whiteness for any sign of a rabbit. He shoves the scarf away from his eyes. The cold numbs his forehead and he pulls it back down too far, covering one eye. Myron chases after him. The snow grabs at his legs and ankles, slowing him down. 'Ivan!'

Ivan hears the crying first. He thinks it is a baby. He turns his head, peering through the slit, trying to locate the source. Stone/wall/grey/snow/white — *Help, help, help*, it cries.

'I can't see you.' Ivan runs blindly toward the wall. *Help. Help!* He looks to the east and to the west. White on white. Suddenly he is afraid that he is all alone. He turns, searching for Myron, terrified he won't be right behind him. Myron rushes past, gun in hand, nearly knocking him over.

The rabbit twists and lurches; the snare is caught around its hip, tightening with each frantic lunge. It throws itself at the end of the line, flops back spinning, wrapping the wire around its torso. It wails. Myron lunges for the rabbit's head and presses it into the snow. The flailing animal kicks and writhes. Its back feet claw Myron's arms, and it breaks free. It runs, until the wire tether slams it to the ground. Myron grabs it by the waist and wrestles it down. He tears off his mitten and fumbles for the club. He hits it once behind the ears.

The rabbit thrashes and leaps away, dragging the wire around Myron's ankle. It circles around and slams against his leg. Again and again. Myron tries to free his foot from the tangle of wire, but the rabbit's frenzy cinches the snare tighter. The cold metal strangles his leg, cuts off his circulation. With his other foot, he steps on the rabbit. Its head wrenches backward, its eyes roll back looking up at him. *Guilty*, they say, *guilty*. He takes aim and fires.

Ivan wishes he could have closed his eyes. White on white. Red on white. Red on red. The rabbit's feet twitch, its body convulses, but Ivan knows it is dead. It has stopped crying.

Myron untangles the snare from his leg and kicks away the rabbit. He can still feel its feet thumping against his shin. He still sees its eyes accusing him. He keeps the rifle trained on the animal in case he needs to use another bullet. He hears the soft, whistling exhalation of its lungs. He hears the gurgle of blood. When he finally stops hearing the swish, swish of its paws against the snow, he turns his back to Ivan and staggers to the next snare twenty feet away. With each step he fights to control his breathing. Inhale. Exhale. Grateful that the cold is numbing his insides.

He approaches the snare warily. Empty. But he sees signs of a struggle. The log pole that anchors the snare is yanked sideways. Flecks of blood speckle the snow. It sprays across the stone wall. The snow has been trampled by something larger than a rabbit. Coyote. Its chaotic prints obliterate the path. A coyote got this one. He is relieved there won't be another rabbit. He digs the wire out of the snow and follows the line.

He yanks the snare free of the ice and snow. A paw dangles from the noose. The wire has cut deep into the flesh, sawed into the bone. Above it, the limb has been chewed through. Torn flesh, encrusted with ice, haloes the crushed bone. Myron gently loosens the wire and gingerly holds the coyote's foot. The tendons are taut, the hair coarse. The pads are rough and hard, criss-crossed with scars, the nails are long and splintered. Tufts of fur curl between the toes, caked with snow and ice. The end of the savaged limb has already frozen, congealing the blood.

Myron follows the bloody trail to the end of the wall. Three paw tracks groping forward. Drops of red. A front paw missing. He looks across the vast expanse of field toward the bush surrounding the lake. He half expects to see the coyote crumpled in the snow. But it's not. It's hiding somewhere, licking its wound, dull to the pain. Slowly dying. He considers leaving the paw there or burying it, but instead he pockets it, disregarding the fleeting unease of possessing something so fierce.

He feels the cold nails pressing against his leg as he walks back to Ivan. His baby brother squats beside the rabbit, stroking its back with a mittened hand. The other hand he has over its face, where there were once eyes. He speaks quietly into its long ears. He looks up at Myron.

'He's okay now,' Ivan reassures him. 'He was scared because he was all alone.'

Myron doesn't try to understand. 'You can carry it back,' he offers.

Ivan declines. 'He wants you.'

Myron picks the carcass up by its hind legs and heads home.

'Aren't you going to set the snares?'

Myron doesn't look back. 'Not today.' He's had his fill of killing today.

Ivan remembers the reason he came, the reason he got up so early, why he lied to his mother, why he couldn't sleep last night, why he kept it secret all these days, why he's disobeying his father. He runs to the stone wall and finds the two white rocks. He pulls down the layers of pants and long johns, pulls off his mitten, and pees. He pees in a widening circle, not wanting to miss the spot. The white snow bleeds yellow and dissolves away.

He pulls up his pants, his exposed skin already tingling from the cold, and looks over his shoulder, but Myron has forgotten him. He unballs two wool socks from his pockets, the socks he won last spring. He leans over the stone wall and stuffs them in a crevice. The socks unfurl like flags, proclaiming their newly darned red heels. Ivan waves to the house at the bottom of the hill and imagines Petro waving back.

★　★　★

Petro is yanked from an uneasy sleep by the crack of a rifle firing. He wipes the sleep from his eyes and blinks at the dim grey light. Beside him, Lesya breathes soft and even. He lies rigid on his back, straining to hear. It sounded far away. His heart beats rapidly, he licks his dry lips. It sounded like the shot he heard that night.

He pushes aside the blanket curtain separating his bed from the kitchen and searches the murky light, uncertain whether to be afraid. Across from him, he sees the lump of his parents buried under the quilts. His father is snoring, loud and gurgling. His mother is on her side, her legs curled toward her belly. He can't see her face. She is hiding behind her pillow. Her arm covers her mountainous belly. Perhaps he dreamed it again.

He reaches under his pillow and finds the heart stone. It is cool to his touch. He curls up with it warming in his hands. Soon Lesya will wake, stoke the fire, prepare breakfast, and head to the barn. She doesn't sing him lullabies any more. She barely talks, unless spoken to directly. Even then she almost coos her answer, and you find yourself leaning in to hear her. The louder Tato shouts, the quieter she gets. She bows her head like she's willing herself to disappear. *You can't see me. I'm not here.*

Since Mama went to bed two weeks ago, Lesya is the mama. She serves Tato his food. Washes his clothes. Warms his water for baths. He likes to watch her brush her hair with Mama's silver brush. He makes her brush it a hundred times, until it gleams. When she reaches one hundred, she sits perfectly still as he touches her hair. He twirls a tress around his fingers, slowly slips down its length.

His breath is always deep and laboured. After a moment, he pulls back as if she has burned his fingertips. His face is flushed. His eyes shift around the room not wanting to see her. His confusion quickly fires into anger. He snaps at her to go to bed, as though she's done something wrong, and he stomps off into the bitter night. Petro tries to console his sister, but she yells at him: 'Stop looking at me!' Then lifts her crooked foot into bed and cloaks herself with blankets.

Once Petro followed his father, with the excuse of needing to use the outhouse. He found him at the back of the house, scouring his bare arms and chest with snow like he was washing off lice. He knew not to ask what he was doing.

Lesya comes to bed fully dressed now in her stockings, undershirt, skirt, and blouse. She sleeps like a corpse, with her arms over her chest and her ankles crossed. She makes Petro sleep on the edge of the bed, exposed to the room. She prefers to be sandwiched up against the freezing wall.

Petro presses the heart stone against his chest. It is already warm. He glides it across his skin. Undulating along his ribs, up his shoulder bone, down his forearm over the bump of muscle hardened from the weeks of chopping wood, down the skinny wrist to his palm, callused and cracked. He wraps his hand around the stone. Mama's dreaming again. Her foot jerks, she whimpers.

Mama has filled up with water. Her legs and ankles have swollen like she drank the lake. Her cheeks are stretched smooth. Her breasts hang on her belly. She had to take her ring off. The flesh swallowed up the gold band. Her finger bruised blue. Lesya rubbed Mama's finger with soap and oil, then pulled. It cut into her flesh, refused to budge. Finally, Tato twisted it off, leaving behind a permanent dent.

Mama hardly ever gets out of bed any more. Lesya feeds and bathes her and brushes her hair. She rubs her belly. She places a cool rag on her forehead for her aching head. Mama complains of blurred vision and black spots behind her eyes. She doesn't bother getting up to go to the outhouse any more. Lesya keeps a pot by the bed and helps her squat over it, a dozen times through the day. Twice, when Lesya was outside doing chores, Mama didn't make it to the pot. Lesya had to restraw the mattress, wash the sheets, and air the quilt. Tato calls Mama names and kicks at her to get out of bed, but she and the baby are too tired. Lesya says that soon they'll have a baby brother or sister. Petro already hates the baby and doesn't want it sleeping in their bed.

Anna moans and covers her belly; the pillow slips away from her face. She is talking in her sleep, but he can't make out the words. Once Petro tried to snuggle up to her, laid his head on her belly, so she would talk to him, but she pushed him away. She said he was too big to be crawling in bed with his mother. Petro dug his hands into the deep folds of fat and told her she was fatter than a sow, which made his father laugh. He made pig sounds, which made his father join in. They grunted and snorted. Petro got down on his hands and knees and waggled his behind. He stuck his nose close to the floor and rooted for crumbs. He lifted the hem of Lesya's skirt with his snout and she dropped a jar beside his head. She said it was an accident.

Petro rolls the heart stone between his thumb and forefinger, following the smooth curves. A thin white quartz vein runs through the centre of the rock. He licks the stone and it shines awake. The grey glistens brown and pink with undertones of blue. The white sparkles like glass. The wet spot evaporates, drying dull and flat. He tucks the stone beneath his chin and lets it draw upon his heat. He carries the stone everywhere, tucked in his front trouser pocket. When he is with his father, his fingers worry against its smoothness. He has trained himself not to jump when his father calls his name. He feels his muscles twitch, but it materializes only as a small tick in his left eye that nobody else notices.

Since the night of the hat, he has worked hard not to displease his tato. He spit-polishes his boots, splits at least two armloads of wood a day, remembers to fill the buckets on the stove with snow, stays out of the way, anticipates good days or bad days, talks only when he's spoken to, sits straighter, doesn't kick his boots against the chair. He always lets his father finish eating first, so that if he complains that he didn't get enough food, Petro can offer his remaining portion.

Occasionally he is rewarded.

Like the time his father noticed the muscles in his arms and made a fuss about how big his little man was getting. Or the time his father showed him the tintype taken in the old country of him in full uniform. A sword at his hip, tall leather riding boots, medals on his chest, a blurred half-smile. On the small side table: a plumed helmet and a pair of gloves draped casually over the edge, a half-full decanter.

In the picture, the floor was dirt, but behind his father was the corner of a room, with wallpaper, wainscotting, pictures, even a window with curtains. A rich man's house. But the walls and window looked wrinkled. And there was an odd line where the dirt met the wood floor of the house. Petro realized the house was a painting that rolled up from the bottom. But he let his father regale him with the story about the night he dined at the general's mansion. Petro even asked what was inside the decanter. Cognac.

Sometimes they sit outside together when the women need privacy. He nods his head knowingly when his father says, 'This life ain't fit for an animal.' And he leans back and crosses his legs like his father.

Lately Stefan has taken to long walks to the town road and back. Petro covertly follows him, hiding behind the house, then darting through the bush, keeping low across the clearing, then spying from the last stand of spruce, just before the road sprawls into the prairies.

Stefan always does the same thing. He steps onto the road and stands there as if he's waiting for someone to come along. He stomps his feet and blows on his hands to keep warm. He looks toward town as if he can see something in the distance. Most days, nothing comes. He walks a few steps, then stops. His shoulders stoop, he shakes his head and curses. He spits twice on the road and turns back home. He looks older and tired on the walk back.

Sometimes, though, the police drive through and Stefan waves them down. They slow to a stop and roll down the window. His father acts as if it's a casual meeting of old friends, as if he just happened to be walking by as they were driving through. He laughs and calls them by name, asks about their families and the news in town, gripes about the godawful weather. Begs a cigarette. The officers don't laugh or engage in Stefan's small talk. They nod, playing the game, until one of the officers gets tired of playing and gruffly asks, 'What's new?'

Stefan leans into the window and lowers his voice. The talk is serious. Petro catches the names of neighbours, his uncle, people he doesn't know. Talk about timber, squirrels, stolen property, and stills. It reminds Petro of a confession. The officers looking straight ahead, Stefan's head bowed toward them. When he finishes, there is a moment of silence, then the officer slips Stefan a quarter. His father stands up straight, once again the gentleman. He demurely pockets the coin, glad that he could be of assistance. He slaps the car as it pulls away, as if he's sending it on its way. He waves, but they never wave back. Once they are far enough away, Stefan deflates. His shoulders drop, his head hangs. He spits twice, kicks the snow, and turns back home.

After these walks, it is always a bad day. Tato rails at Mama about her thieving brother and how much money that land is worth. He tosses the contents of Maria's care packages around the room as evidence of them being treated like charity cases. Turnips from their garden, a rabbit-fur baby blanket poached from their land, salt beef bought from their seed.

He demands that Mama write letters to the land office and report that squatters are on their property. He composes the letters himself: offering proof about how much work he's done on the land, clearing the fields, erecting buildings, cultivating and sowing; he cites all the legal facts of the case, that the land is in his wife's name, and that they just need to check the homestead entry records. He tells them that Teodor is a convicted criminal and by their law he has no right to own land. He asks with all due respect that the trespassers be evicted.

Initially, Petro was confused by his father's

stories about doing all the work. Petro couldn't remember him there. He remembered Teodor being dragged through the mud behind the plow, sitting in the cart's shade eating cold pyrohy, the mosquitoes, and the Indian arrowhead. He remembered the fire, the smoke, the smell of burning grain and singed hair, his uncle standing up against a wall of flames. He remembered stooking the wheat with his cousins, sunburned shoulders, and dust in his eyes and up his nose. He remembered his uncle felling trees and the horse dragging logs to the top of the hill. He remembered them moving and Teodor bringing him back to his own house. He remembered holding his hand and not wanting to let go.

But after a while, he made himself remember that his father was there too. And soon his father was doing all the things that Teodor had done. He practised these memories until Teodor disappeared and only his father remained. Occasionally, Stefan would appear wearing Teodor's clothes or speaking in that calm, low voice his uncle used when he spoke to horses and children. When that happened, Petro knew the memories were lies and wiped them away.

At first Mama wouldn't sign the letters, no matter how loud his tato yelled. She covered her ears. She burrowed under the covers. She chanted, *I can't, I can't, I can't.* Tato stroked her hair, gave her a drink of water, spoke softly in her ear, put the pen in her hand. *Sign it.*

Finally, he walked away from her. Didn't say another word. He gathered up his clothes, his comb, his tin cup, his flask, and stuffed them in a burlap bag.

'Where are you going?' she asked, her voice trembling.

He put on his hat and coat and walked out the door. Petro clung to his legs, and when his father flung him aside, he got right back up and grabbed his sleeve. He promised to be better, he promised never to cry ever again, though he couldn't stop then. He pleaded, *Don't go*, and then he begged, *Take me with you*. He promised to work hard and make lots of money. His father hollered at him to get back in the house. Lesya pulled him inside. He kicked at his mother as she rushed out the door after Stefan. He screamed, *This is your fault!* Lesya slapped his face.

He watched his mother chase after his father. Her bulbous body floundered through the snow. Her cape spread out behind her like crow's wings. He made her chase him almost to the road. She wrapped herself around his ankles. He stood like a king. He helped her back up to her feet. Petro could see her head nodding. His father put his arm around his mother and brought her back home.

She signed the letters. Stefan kissed her on the forehead and told her that soon he'd get her that big white house. He'd cut wild roses for her every day. He'd run her a hot bath in the cast-iron tub and the water would never get cold. She'd sleep in a brass bed and at night they'd turn on the electric lights and stay up way past dark. Soon they wouldn't have to remember any of this.

Petro slides the stone heart over his own heart. He breathes in deep, watching it rise and fall. Now he remembers where he found the stone. It fell out of his chest the day he was born.

★　★　★

Lesya nails a blanket to the inside walls of the chicken coop. She stuffs the cavity with straw and chinks the holes with cow manure. The grey wool diffuses the light, casting a warm glow. The hens cluck appreciatively.

She fluffs the straw covering the floor, shaping it into a knee-high mound. She steps into the middle, compacting it with her feet. She sits, draping her skirt around her. She pulls the straw close. Kneading it into place. She curls up in its roundness. Makes herself small.

Department of Lands and Mines
Nov. 3, 1938

Dear Sir,

I was farming in the Northern district until 1935. In 1936, I went broke, had to vacate the land, but had no other place to move to and therefore had to go on a homestead. My sister advised me to file a homestead in her name, with the understanding that she would abandon the same in my favour when the necessary improvements to earn patent had been done by me. Having no other choice but to do so, I secured a quarter-section in my sister's name and have settled there with my family.

After I broke 6 acres on the said land, erected a house, barn, granary and fencing, my sister's husband, as well as my sister, are asking me to vacate this quarter-section. Please advise me whether or not my sister is in the right to take this land from me that I have paid my own entry fee. There was a paper signed and my son can say what it said.

Yours truly,
Teodor Mykolayenko

November 7, 1938

Madam,

I am in receipt of your letter, having reference to your Homestead entry and note your statements concerning the occupation of this quarter-section.

This office has already been advised by the said party that he is your brother and he went into occupation of this land with your permission and has completed all the improvements which are at present on the land.

If this is a fact it would appear that you have not been completing the required duties in connection with this entry and the entry is liable to cancellation.

You might be good enough to furnish me with a statutory declaration as to the actual improvements completed by you at your own expense on this quarter-section.

Until this matter is resolved the $10 entry fee will be held in trust.

Your obedient servant,
John Bosford
Agent

Deputy Minister of Lands and Mines
November 12, 1938

Dear Sir,
  I would like to know what I can do from
the Deputy Minister. There is a man that he
is living on my wife homestead. He told me I
could charge him to live on your wife homestead and then when another homestead
opened then I will find some kind of a homestead and I will pay. So now he doesn't want
to go from it. And I don't know what I have
to do. I made improvements on the land and
plowed 2 acres. I gave him notice to pull out
but he doesn't want to. I am pleasing you
will give me the information what I have to
do.

Anna Shevchuck

The man on the land is Teodor Mykolayenko

TRANSLATION JE/ 20/11/38
Department of Lands and MinesNovember
14, 1938

Dear Sir,
   I am writing in my own language, as I am
unable to write in English and have no
money to pay someone else 25 cents for
doing it for me. I received your letter in
which you ask me to make a settlement with
my sister.
   First, I cannot come to any agreement
with my sister because I cannot vacate this
land where I have been working.
   Second, she is unable to pay me for my
work. She asks me to move from this land,
but where shall I go?
   Third, I did all improvements. I cleared,
broke and cultivated 6 acres on the land. I
built all the buildings: the house, barn 12 x
16, and well 15 feet deep.
   In view of the above I am of the opinion
that the Department alone can settle this
matter between us, because I will not move
from here. If I should vacate this land I
would be forced to go on relief and become
a public charge.

Yours truly,
Teodor Mykolayenko

From: D. H. Burns
Director of Lands
November 19, 1938

To: Agent of Provincial Lands
Edmonton, Alberta

RE: N.E.2-64-6-W, 4th Meridian

I understand from your communication and the letter from Teodor Mykolayenko that Mrs. Shevchuk was granted homestead entry of the above land; that prior to having acquired the land, she entered into an arrangement with her brother; whereby the brother, who was not eligible to make entry for land under homestead regulations, was to make certain improvements necessary in order to earn patent; and that the entrant was then to abandon the land in favour of her brother. It is further noted that the entrant refuses to carry out her part of the supposed arrangement.

Mykolayenko claims to be in residence on the land. From his communication he claims he is in residence for the reason that he has no other place to go because this is his land.

This would appear to be a case where there was a collusion between the two parties and now that they have disagreed it is desired that the Department arrange a settlement.

Mykolayenko should be informed that his representations cannot be given consideration by the Department, that the land is a homestead entry in the name of Anna Shevchuk.

If there was any work performed by him for his sister, the entrant, and for which he has not received payment, it would appear to be necessary to take action in the civil courts and is not a matter which the Department can in any way enter into.

Homestead Inspectors Report
No of Report 3419 (taken in field)
RE: N.E.2-64-6-W, 4th Meridian

November 24, 1938

While engaged in inspection work, I was accosted by one Teodor Mykolayenko, brother of entrant on above land, and who is now occupying the land entered by Anna Shevchuk, and gave the following information. He gave his sister the sum of ten dollars and asked to (and she agreed) to enter the land in her own name for him. He said she signed a paper, which he could not produce.

He has built a house, barn, dug a well, broken 6 acres of land, cleared 4 acres ready for plow and cut 3 acres back. He is married, 5 children, and his wife is pregnant. He claims he is resident and doing the improvement work by reason that the homestead is his, as his sister got it for him and not for herself. Now the husband of Anna Shevchuk orders Mykolayenko off the homestead and threatens to take court action to have him evicted.

Mykolayenko says he will move off if his sister will give him not less than $500 for the work he has done. He says she refuses to even pay back the $10 filing fee. Anna Shevchuk has no labour or money in the place whatsoever, according to her brother. I warned Mykolayenko to be careful what statements he made, but he boldly admitted that he and his sister had conspired to procure the homestead for him.

No action of any kind was taken by me in the matter. This is for your information.

P. Lamond
Inspector Dominion Land

Sworn Statement of Anna Shevchuk
November 25, 1938

Improvements

6 acres cleared and broke, work done by my husband and Mr. Mykolayenko and a borrowed plow. Mr. Mykolayenko being at the time hired by my husband.

In July, Mr. Mykolayenko started living on the above land. My husband spending two weeks with his horse and wagon to help Mrs. Mykolayenko move her goods and family a distance of 50 miles. Mr. Mykolayenko agreeing to pay for this in work.

House erected by my husband and Mykolayenko. The logs being cut by Mr. Mykolayenko who was hired by my husband.

4 additional acres broke by my husband with his own plow.

I hereby state that at no time did I instruct or ask Mr. Mykolayenko to do any particular work or improvements — any work or improvements done by him were of his own free will.

A. Shevchuk
Witnessed by Stefan Shevchuk

Government of the Province of Alberta

From: F. W. Nelson
Chief Timber Inspector

To: J. Hall, Esq.
Deputy Minister

RE:N.E.2-64-6-W, 4th Meridian

November 30, 1938

Complying with your request, I inspected the above land and interviewed the entrant and Mykolayenko who is in residence on the land.

I have attached affidavits from both parties concerned. It will be noted that the information contained in these affidavits is very contradictory.

I also interviewed several neighbors (Petrenko/Olynik) concerning the representations made by both parties. The impression held by the neighbours is that an understanding had existed between Mrs. Shevchuk and her brother, Teodor, that he was to get the homestead. I found nobody, however, who was willing to take an affidavit regarding this and none of them would say that they ever heard Mrs. Shevchuk allude to any such agreement. Their impressions on the matter were apparently received from statements made by Mykolayenko and words dropped by Stefan Shevchuk who is Mrs. Shevchuk's husband.

While I feel that some such agreement probably existed, both she and her husband denied knowledge of such agreement.

I might add that the neighbours whom I interviewed all expressed the opinion that both parties were crooked.

While in my opinion, there has undoubtedly been sufficient land brought under cultivation, as well as other improvements made to earn patent, it would appear under Section 17 of the Provincial Lands Act the entry is liable to cancellation and neither party should hold claim.

December 6, 1938

Innacuracy about improvements
I build a house and I did pay for the work that is done on that farm and I have witness for what I done on Teodor farm.

Your truly
A. Shevchuk

December 10, 1938

Sirs:
RE: N.E.2-64-6-W, 4th Meridian

Referring to your letter I beg to advise that Mrs. A. Shevchuk obtained homestead entry for above described land. Teodor Mykolayenko, brother of the entrant, claims that he has resided on the land, performed the improvements, and that when Mrs. Shevchuk filed, the understanding existed whereby he was to get the homestead.

The whole matter is being investigated and when a decision is arrived at you will be further advised.

For your information, I may say that all homestead entries are at present under winter protection and although an application to cancel may be accepted, no action would be taken until the first of March next.

Yours very truly,
D. H. Burns
Director of Lands

Anna heard the coyotes again last night. They were crying for her while she slept. She hasn't been able to go to them. She can hardly move. She sleeps all the time now. It is easier to sleep than be awake. When she sleeps, she feels nothing. Floats between here and there. She doesn't have to think about who she is and what she has done. She is separate from her life. Not a mother, not a wife, not a sister — she is something outside of time, waiting to be reborn.

How far back would she have to go to change her life? What if she hadn't got on the boat that brought her here? What if she hadn't gone to the dance where she had met Stefan? What if she had kissed the boy with the brown eyes and crooked teeth instead? What if she hadn't signed the letters? Who would she be now?

Anna's legs cramp. She rolls onto her back, straightens her legs. The baby turns inside her, its feet push against her insides. She rubs her belly, moves her fingers along the soft flesh until she finds a hard lump. She presses around the shape. A foot. The baby kicks. She drapes her arm around her belly, pulls the quilt tight across her, wanting to feel constricted.

She dreams of faces looking down on her. Lesya's worried blue eyes. She dreams of floating in a lake below the surface. She is breathing underwater. Suspended. The water is cool against her forehead, like a damp cloth. She hums.

The baby relaxes and curls up. Anna shifts onto her side, pulls her knees to her belly, her thumb near her mouth. The fragments of melodies vibrate in her throat, spill down her chest, pulse through her uterus. Sometimes she repeats one note — low, low, low, then high, high, high. Her eyelids grow heavy, her breathing slows, and life falls away again.

Asleep, the sounds are muffled and far away. Mysterious and disconnected. She finds herself identifying them. That's the door opening. That's fire crackling. A man's cough. Footsteps. Pots being stirred. Hair being brushed.

What's that?

'A bird.'

What's that?

'Wind.'

What's that?

'My heart.'

She doesn't know that she says the words out loud. The voice is small, a little girl's voice. It sounds like Anna's voice. Sometimes it sounds like it's inside her head. Sometimes it sounds like it's whispered in her ear. It's not really a voice. It's more like a feeling. A question she's compelled to answer.

Light flickers through her closed eyelids. 'That's the sun. Cloud. Night. Candles. Fire.' She turns her face away from the light, and blackness seeps in. Sometimes Anna feels as if she is encased in someone else's skin.

She opens her eyes. 'Lesya.' She is flooded

with warmth, even love. *Safe.*

Lesya tips a glass of water to her mother's cracked lips. 'Drink.' Anna's eyes shut.

Open your eyes. 'Petro.' Uncertain. Wary.

'Come closer,' she tells him. 'Let me see your eyes.' A stranger. *Be careful.*

She pushes him away.

The man?

Anna blearily opens her eyes. 'Stefan. Your father.' She feels nothing. Not curiosity. Not disappointment. Not apprehension. Nothing. Just exhaustion. Her eyes shut.

Where?

'Home.'

Feeling more questions, she tries to explain. 'House, land.'

Land?

'Forever. Empty. Flat. Alone.'

Alone?

'Nobody. Life. Sadness.'

Anna's pillow is wet beneath her cheek. She is crying. She burrows deeper into the covers and pulls the quilt over her head. A cocoon of warmth. 'Sleep,' she tells herself.

Soon?

'No.' Anna doesn't want to be born yet.

Soon, the voice persists.

'No,' Anna commands.

The voice curls up, small and tight, and Anna floats away again.

At first she thinks the coyotes have come to her in her dream. Their voices circle around her. Their wild cries grow louder, more insistent. Distressed. She rushes toward the sound, not wanting to be left behind. She wakes.

It is dark. She is alone in bed. The blankets stick to her wet skin. Her mouth is dry. She rolls heavily on her side. She strains to hear through the silence of the night. Is that a dog panting? The rustle of paws on snow? Is it pressing its nose against the cracks of the shack? Breathing in? Anna presses her hand against the log wall, feels a cold draft on her palm.

Somewhere up toward the field a coyote calls. Its beautiful, mournful cry wails down the hill. Anna hoists herself up to a sitting position. She wants to see it. Tell it that she hasn't forgotten. It yelps three short barks that open into a sustained sorrow.

She heaves up onto her feet and wobbles unsteadily. Pain grabs her lower back and spreads across her lower abdomen to her legs and cinches her tight.

Don't go.

Her heart races. She is flushed with heat. Her thighs tremble. Another contraction seizes her belly, makes her bowels constrict.

Don't go.

She breathes erratically. The coyote wails again. Anna breaks into a sweat. The baby twists, kicks up under her ribs. Anna clutches her stomach, tries to calm it.

'Coyotes. Friends.'

Adrenalin floods her body. Her muscles tighten. Her heart pounds. Fear crackles under her skin.

'Coyote. Friend.'

Her muscles release. The baby lies still. Anna

breathes deep. She straightens her back and soothingly pats her belly. The coyote calls her again. Anna takes a step forward.

Liar.

Pain sheers through her body. White light explodes behind her eyes. She fights to hold on to consciousness. The world reels away, and when she can no longer bear it, it subsides.

She is standing in the dark. The ice-cold dirt floor numbing her toes. The weight of her flesh pulling her down. She breathes in her sweat-soaked nightdress. She listens to the silence. It's gone.

She looks at her belly. The baby is quiet now.

'This one will betray you too,' a voice says. This voice is louder and stronger than the other one. Anna collapses onto the bed and pulls herself tight in the covers. Her breathing slows. Her body goes cold. She draws the quilt over her head, a fragment of a dream slips past her eyes of Stefan in the dark, standing perfectly still, his hands behind his back, his coat on, holding his breath.

★   ★   ★

Stefan has always hated the sound of coyotes. It reminds him how far from civilization they are. He was never meant to be a farmer. He is awake again, sitting at the table, staring at the empty flask. Tremors rip through his body, crawling under his skin, erupting in his hands. He is sweating, he feels nauseated. He came back this time to be a gentleman farmer, hire hands to do the work, get enough money from the fields to get back to town. Instead he's worse off than before. At least in town, he could always find a drink. There was always someone to talk to about the old country.

If he had a good night at cards, he could get a bed, a bath, and a woman. The girls knew him by name; they teased him and called him The Tsar. And he liked that. Even if he couldn't afford the full night, he could often scrape enough together for fifteen minutes. Enough to release the ache between his legs. He looks at the lump of Anna in the bed. He hasn't touched her in weeks. How could that be the woman he married? Her breasts fold into her belly. She lies there like a sack. Even the whores pretend. His groin tingles awake. He places both hands on the table and presses down hard.

It's all Teodor's fault. He thought he would be off the land by now. He would sell the homestead for two hundred dollars. A steal for the right buyer. There's at least five hundred dollars of improvements and then there's the fields. Two hundred dollars would give him a new life. New clothes. A house in town. Access to the poker tables and the girls. His groin tilts upward, brushes against his trousers. He's sick of the letters. It should have been so easy. One letter and have him removed. He didn't count on Teodor fighting back. He can't keep all the stories straight, and now the government bastards don't believe that he did the work. He knows a bad hand when he sees one. He thought if he put everything in, the others would fold.

But they've called his bluff. If somehow they give him the land, he won't be able to sell it. They'll be watching him. They'll want another six acres next year. He didn't start this to become a farmer.

The coyotes are wailing tonight. He wonders how much a pelt would bring. But being out there alone in the night with them quashes that idea. He could sell the horse and wagon and the tack. Maybe he could get fifty dollars. That's a good idea. First thing tomorrow he'll talk to Petrenko or maybe he should go directly to town. Town would be better; then he could ride instead of walk. His hand rubs his groin. His hips yearn upward. He puts his hand back on the table. He could go outside and relieve himself. Stand in the snow like an animal, but even an animal doesn't have to relieve itself. He looks to Anna. He deflates.

How has it all gone so wrong? He sits at the table with his back to Lesya and Petro asleep in their bed. He doesn't want to look at his daughter. She reminds him that he is old. She reminds him of the girls back home, with their long, shiny hair. Hair that doesn't feel like a woman's. He surges awake and presses his knees together. The way she looks at him through her hair. The attention she gives him. Serving him his meals. Heating his water for the bath. Putting her hand in the washtub to make sure it's not too hot. How she never talks. He's not a bad man. It's this place that is driving him crazy. Imprisoned in these four walls. Unable to move. Unable to breathe. Unable to be a man.

A coyote yelps madly, closer now. He should check on the children. Make sure they're covered up. Like a good father. Make sure the coyotes aren't disturbing them in their sleep. He is an officer, a man of discipline. A man in control. He's not a bad man. He's a father. He's a good father. Good fathers check on their children.

★ ★ ★

Lesya hears the coyote first. Lately, she doesn't really sleep. Even with her eyes closed, she is always conscious of her mother's needs and her father's movements. Tonight, her eyes opened at the coyote's first faint note.

She has named them. That's Kozma. He lives in the north. She imagines Kozma to be a big, grizzled male, protective and sullen like her uncle Teodor.

Luka should answer next. She smiles at the sound of his faint, high whine. Luka is younger, maybe a son of Kozma. He always stays south of the wall. His territory is east. His bark doesn't have Kozma's strength or authority. She imagines he's smaller and slinks, whereas Kozma lopes.

They come through at the same time every night. There are three of them. Every night, they call out to one another. Lesya counts between their calls. One thousand one — one thousand two — they answer like thunder.

At first, she was afraid when the coyotes returned. Afraid that they would breach the coop and slaughter her hens. She boobytrapped the perimeter with sharpened sticks that she skewered into the snow. She strung tin cans to the willow fence so she could hear any sudden, unusual movement. For added protection, she barricaded the henhouse door with a log pole that she can barely lift. The coyotes have never bothered her chickens.

Lesya listens for Yvonne. She named the third coyote after one of the Quints. Everybody in town talks about them. Five baby girls born at once. Each one the same. Coming from one egg. Each one perfect. They live in a glass house, where nurses take care of their every need. She imagines that their beds are little nests and that they have wings, but they can't quite fly. That's why people need to take care of them and keep them safe. She can't imagine a happier life.

Lesya doesn't really know whether the coyote is a female. But she didn't want Kozma to be lonely. She wanted him to have someone, even if they couldn't be together. Yvonne has a lonelier cry; it starts low, rises high, and holds. Yvonne comes from the west, toward the lake. But tonight she isn't answering. She hasn't answered in weeks.

Kozma still calls her, but now he doesn't wait for her answer. His yelps and bays spill over each other like alarms. Frantic. His howls bleed east and then west and back again, like he is running back and forth along the stone wall. Lesya looks over to Petro, but he is sound asleep.

Answer him, she thinks. *Don't leave him all alone.* She worries that Yvonne might be gone. Maybe she starved, maybe someone shot her, or maybe she just moved on. A flicker of anger responds to Kozma's hysteria: *Then let her go. Get on with your life. She's not coming back.* Immediately, she regrets belittling Kozma's grief. She's the one who wanted them to be in love. *Poor Kozma.*

She is so focused on listening to the coyotes that she doesn't hear her father get up from the table. He is almost beside them when Lesya feels his presence. She shuts her eyes tight and quells her breathing. *I'm asleep*, she pretends. Her arms are pressed tight to her chest, her legs crossed.

This is the fourth time he's watched her sleep. She wishes she was closer to the wall. She could have been two inches farther. Petro is on his side, his back to her. Her elbow nearly touches him. She can feel his heat. It reassures her that something is between her and her father.

She doesn't know why she feels afraid when he looks at her. She knows that somehow he is dangerous, and when he is too close, she can hardly breathe. Her heart beats as fast as the baby sparrow's she held in her hands last summer. She held it as gently as she could. But its chest kept heaving and its heart pounded on her fingertips. Uncle Teodor said it fell from the nest and that its mother wouldn't take it back now that it had been touched. He was telling her how to take care of it when its head dropped down and its heart stopped. Teodor said it died of fright. Her tato makes her feel as though she's that baby bird and she's fallen out of the nest. And he's a cat watching, waiting . . .

He's moving. Usually he stands still, then leaves after a few minutes. She hears the door open and shut. Hears his footsteps come back. He's still again. She wants to open her eyes. She takes a deep-sleep breath. He feels closer.

Then she feels it. Lightly on her hip. A light fluttering. There it is again. His fingers on the blanket, barely touching. He's reaching over Petro. She feels the goosebumps rise on her leg. His fingers travel down her leg, tracing her outline. They slide slowly across, inch toward her inner thigh. They stop. Pull back. She can sense his hand hovering over her body.

She wishes that he had never come back. That Teodor and Maria were right next door. That her cousins were calling her to come out and play. That it is summer and she is working in the garden, the taste of a sun-warmed pea in her mouth, Happiness perched on her foot, bobbing its head for a song, and she is completely unafraid. She hears his breathing, deep and shaky.

She stretches in her sleep, groans, and rolls over on her belly, wrapping herself tighter in the blanket. Her eyes clenched tight, her face to the wall. She forces herself to breathe as if she is in a deep sleep. She thinks of Happiness, the smell of the chicken coop, the warmth of the straw. She puts herself back inside a hard white shell. Happiness is smothering her with her warmth. Her muffled heart echoes through the shell. It thumps, *I'll protect you.*

She hears him step back, his breath catching

in his throat. Choking for air. He bumps into the table. Stops. He breathes short, shallow breaths, like he is afraid. He stumbles to the other side of the room. She hears him pull his coat down from the hook. She hears the door crack open, then quickly shut. He is still inside. He is at the door. She hears him gulping for breath. Maybe he's afraid to go outside because of the coyotes. Because of Kozma. Something thuds against the door. His hand? His head? He catches his breath. She hears him step forward.

Lesya braces herself. Her shell cracks. She tells herself, *Don't scream, don't cry, don't let him know you're here.*

She hears the clink of the tin flask, scraping across the table. He's at the cupboards. She hears the tinkle of coins. Fifty-eight cents she earned selling vegetables. She hears the hollow clunk of the canister. Now he's near the washstand, picking up something. Searching. He moves to the middle of the room and stops again. Mama is talking in her sleep. *Don't wake up*, Lesya prays.

The bed groans under her mama's weight. She must be rolling to the other side. Lesya can't make out what she is saying. *Go back to sleep*, she wills her. Outside, Kozma wails. His howl is going to wake everyone. Petro stirs and curls his knees up to his chest. Is she standing? What is she doing? *Go back to bed, Mama. Go back to playing dead.*

Lesya has opened her eyes, but all she can see is the grain of the log and a crumbling chink of cracked mud and dry straw. Kozma rages, howls his anguish in one long wail. He doesn't call again.

Lesya forces herself not to hold her breath. She listens for the smallest noise. She hears her mother's breathing, the creak of her knees, and her settling heavily back onto the bed. She whimpers as if she is already asleep. Her breathing quiets, soft and regular. Lesya listens for her father. She hears him exhale. Hears one boot scuff the ground. He walks lightly to the door. The latch lifts, the hinge creaks open. Cold rushes in. The door shuts quietly. Lesya hears the squeak of his boots receding.

* * *

Mama!

Maria bolts awake. The house is dark. She throws back the bed covers, her feet hit the floor; Teodor grumbles in his sleep. She pauses, suddenly unsure whether she has dreamed her child's voice.

Katya shrieks again, 'Mama!' Followed immediately by Dania's sharp 'Hush.' And Sofia's protesting groan. Teodor sits up, groggy but alert to danger.

'It's Katya,' Maria reassures him, 'she's dreaming again.' Teodor falls heavily back to his pillow. Maria hurries to her daughter, whose sobs now threaten to wake the boys.

'Shhhhh,' Maria calms as she enters the room. Katya, her hair a tousled mess, her cheeks flushed, leaps out of the bed, pulling the covers off her sisters, and throws herself in her mother's arms.

Sofia wrenches the quilt back up. 'It's cold!' she whines.

'Shhh, don't wake your brothers.'

'I saw the coyote,' Katya whimpers. 'It was at the foot of the bed.'

'There's no coyote here.' Maria scans the room for Katya's benefit. 'See, just coats and dresses.' She sits on the bed and loosens Katya's stranglehold around her neck. 'The coyotes are all outside where they belong.'

Katya doesn't believe her. 'I saw it.' She looks around the dark room to see where it is hiding.

'I came right in,' Maria reassures. 'I didn't see anything.'

Katya has been having nightmares ever since Teodor couldn't find that piece of paper. Usually she dreams of fires chasing her. It's no wonder, how he scared them. Ranting like a madman, pulling jars off the shelves. He broke two jars of beets. He shouldn't have left it on a shelf if it was so important.

'Maybe it's under the bed?' Katya lifts her toes up higher.

'You crawl back in bed. I'll check.' Katya hesitates, assessing the distance from her mother's arms to her sisters. 'Quick, like a bunny,' Maria taps her bottom. 'Nothing will hurt you. I won't let it,' she promises. Dania holds up the corner of the bed covers. Katya scurries under the quilt's safety, jostling Sofia, who shoves her back toward Dania. 'It was here, I heard it.' Katya senses everyone's disbelief.

'The coyotes were crying earlier; you must have heard them in your sleep,' Dania explains. Dania, who tried to help find the paper, only to have Teodor push her aside.

'I saw it,' Katya insists. 'It was looking for something.'

Sofia grouches, 'Too bad it didn't take you.'

'It would've ate you first.' Katya elbows her. Sofia retaliates with a kick.

'That's enough,' Maria commands. 'All of you, back to sleep.'

'What about under the bed?' Katya reminds her.

Maria checks. 'No coyote. Coyotes won't come into our house, they have their own place to live.'

'Maybe this one doesn't,' Katya considers, unwilling to believe that it was just a dream. She could smell the coyote. She heard it panting.

'Don't you remember the story about the mitten?' Katya shakes her head no. She doesn't want Mama to leave just yet.

Maria plays into her game. 'One story and then to sleep.' Sofia quickly makes room for her mother, an automatic response from when she was little. She knows she's too old for these stories, but she still feels a tingle of excitement.

Maria snuggles in next to Sofia, who inches over more to make room for her mother's round belly. It's been a long time since she's crawled into bed with her children. They smell sweet, like fresh-baked bread. When they were small, she used to love bedtimes — they would tumble around her, their limbs tangled, their bodies pressed against hers, willing to follow her voice into dreams. Ivan appears at the doorway.

'I heard them too,' he sheepishly explains, wanting permission to enter.

'Come.' Maria waves him in. He bounces onto the foot of the bed and squishes between Dania and Katya. It's a wonder he's not having nightmares too. Teodor slapped him across the face. *What did it say?* Ivan could barely stutter the words through the snot and tears. *You gave money and it's your land.* And Teodor hugged him. *That's right, that's right.* Myron pulled Ivan away and stood between him and his father. She thought Myron was going to hit him. The girls tussle for space, clinging to one another so as not to fall off.

They all know this story; it has been passed down for hundreds of years all the way from Ukraïna. Mother to child. Dania memorizes her mother's cadence, knowing that someday she, too, will be telling it.

'Once, a child was walking through the woods and he lost his mitten.' Sofia points an accusing finger at Ivan, who responds by touching his freezing toes to her shin.

Maria continues with her best folktale voice: 'When along came a little mouse. It climbed into the mitten. The mitten was large and warm and soft. And the little mouse announced, 'This is where I'm going to live.' He'd just settled in when along came a frog, who asked, 'Who lives in this mitten?'

' 'Squeaky Mouse. Who are you?' replied the mouse.'

' 'Croaky Frog. Can I come in?' '

'Squeaky Mouse says, 'No, there's no room, this is where I live.' But Croaky Frog pushed his way in anyway. Now there were two of them, when along came a rabbit, who asked, 'Who lives in this mitten?' '

' 'Squeaky Mouse and Croaky Frog. Who are you?' '

' 'Hoppity Rabbit,' ' Sofia interjects. ' 'Can I come in?' '

Maria nods her approval. 'Squeaky Mouse and Croaky Frog say, 'No, no, there's no room.' But Hoppity Rabbit squishes in.' The children nestle closer. 'When along comes . . . ' Maria waits for the next storyteller.

'Sister Fox,' Dania adds. 'And she said, 'Who lives in this mitten?' '

Maria continues, ' 'Squeaky Mouse, Croaky Frog, and Hoppity Rabbit and there's no room for anyone else.' But Sister Fox decides to live there too and climbs over Hoppity Rabbit. The mitten stretches. And along comes . . . '

'Brother Wolf.' Katya betrays her knowledge of the story. 'And Brother Wolf asks, 'Who lives in this mitten?'

' 'Squeaky Mouse,' ' says Maria.

' 'Croaky Frog,' ' says Dania.

' 'Hoppity Rabbit,' ' says Sofia.

' 'And Sister Fox,' ' proclaims Katya.

'And there's no more room,' Maria whispers, their voices getting too loud. 'But Brother Wolf squishes in and the mitten stretches more. And along comes . . . '

'Growly Bear,' pipes up Ivan.

'And Growly Bear asks' — Maria drops her voice low and rumbly — ' 'Who lives in this mitten?' '

' 'Squeaky Mouse, Croaky Frog, Hoppity Rabbit, Sister Fox, and Brother Wolf. And there's no more room.' But Growly Bear crawls in and the mitten stretches.'

Maria pushes against the children, who squeeze in tighter. When she was a child, the story had a wild boar, but he has no place in Canada. The children giggle and yawn, forgetting what woke them in the first place. 'Then along comes Tiny Grasshopper. He asks, 'Who lives in this mitten?' '

' 'Squeaky Mouse, Croaky Frog, Hoppity Rabbit, Sister Fox, Brother Wolf, and Growly Bear. And there's no more room.' But the tiny grasshopper wiggles his way in under the bear's paw. But this time the mitten doesn't stretch; the seams split and the mitten bursts open.'

The children listen intently, knowing the story is almost over.

'All the animals go flying in every direction. They tumble and roll through the dirt, bumping their heads and tails. One by one they get up and dust themselves off and decide to find their own homes elsewhere.'

Maria's never been satisfied with that ending; she suspects it's been changed. She used to ask her mother how come the fox didn't eat the rabbit and the wolf didn't kill the bear, and the frog didn't eat the grasshopper, and the boy didn't come back with a gun and kill them all. Her mother would shake her head and sigh,

'That's the story.' Her own children have never questioned the fable's impossibilities. They want to believe. How long can she keep them believing? They bask in the afterglow of the story; their eyes are heavy again. Sleep is calling them back.

'What happened to the boy who lost his mitten?' Ivan murmurs.

'His mother made him a new one and told him to be more careful next time.' She can tell by Sofia's breathing that she has fallen asleep. She reaches across her nest of children, absorbing their warmth.

'So the coyote won't come into our house?' Katya ponders, half asleep. 'Because it has its own place to live?'

'That's right.' Maria yawns. 'It lives in the woods. Now go to sleep.' She knows she should get up and return to her own bed, but she wants to savour this moment. She has managed to keep them safe. Now that the letters have stopped, things will go back to the way they should be. The mitten has split open.

Katya is thinking about a frog, a mouse, a rabbit, a wolf, a fox, and a bear stuffed inside a mitten. Maybe the mouse is stuffed in the mitten's thumb and its long tail is tickling the belly of the frog whose webbed toes are stepping on the rabbit's ears. Maybe the wolf and the fox are hugging each other to make more room for the bear, whose big bum is poking out the end.

Katya squirms for more room in the crowded bed. She knows there was a coyote in her room.

But now that her bed is full, she knows that it won't be able to crawl in; Mama wouldn't let it.

★ ★ ★

Myron knows the mitten story. He mouths the words *I'm Growly Bear* on cue. That was always his part. He was awake long before Katya, the hair on his arms bristling with each howl. He could tell one of them was by the stone wall, racing back and forth. Maybe it could smell the blood.

Myron hasn't been able to check the snares in two weeks. He's been running a fever and has a cold in his chest. Maria won't let him outside. She has garlic bulbs under his pillow. Each night she rubs a mustard poultice on his chest and forces him to drink a tablespoon of wheat wine steeped with honey, fever root, and a raw egg. Twice she has heated the small glass domes and placed them on his body to draw out the sickness. Circular welts dot his chest and legs.

The first few days of his illness, he thought the coyotes were chasing him. He was lost in the snow and being hunted. No matter how fast he ran, he could hear the pack keeping pace behind him.

The coyotes started coming closer to the homesteads right after Myron's last trip to the snares with Ivan. Teodor says it's because the snow is too deep in the woods and the lake is frozen. They're running the trails looking for easy prey. But Myron knows that's not the reason.

344

He feels guilty that his father had to take on his chores. He's tried to force himself outside in the pre-dawn. But each time he takes down the rifle, his hands shake and he feels like he's going to throw up. It's the same feeling he had when he stepped between Teodor and Ivan. And when he held the gun on his uncle. And when he wished his father would die in the fire. And when he shot the rabbit. And when he doubted that there ever was a piece of paper. It's the same feeling he gets when he looks out the window, expecting to see a three-footed coyote. Everything that's happening is his fault. He took the coyote's paw.

With everyone asleep, he quietly gets out of bed. He slips his boots on, pulls his jacket over his nightshirt. If his father wakes, he'll tell him he's going to the outhouse. He inches toward the door. He looks up at the rifle hanging above the door frame, considers taking it, but doubts that he can retrieve it without his mother hearing. Sofia is snoring, masking his movements. He lifts the latch and slowly opens the door just wide enough to squeeze through.

Outside, the night feels dense, like a storm is coming. The crescent moon is filtered by a gauze of clouds. Thankfully, it is silent. The coyotes are gone. The cold seeps through his long underwear. It nips his ears. His lungs constrict. He tucks his hands in his coat pockets, wishing he had brought his mittens. He hurries around the side of the house, up to the outhouse, checking over his shoulder to make sure no one has noticed his absence. He searches the darkness, but there are no wild dogs in sight. He veers off the trodden path and heads behind the outhouse. The deep snow fills his boots and numbs his shins.

He scrambles uphill to the spruce tree with the two tops. Beneath it, a large boulder peeks through the snow. He stomps a path around it, excavating it from the drift and heaves aside the stone. Embedded in the snow is the foot. Hiding it had not absolved him of his crime. He had stolen from the wild. Myron extracts the paw. It leaves behind a perfect print.

He looks toward the woods crowning the lake. He's never gone there at night. It's about half a mile. He can turn back, forget about this piece of flesh. Let it rot into the ground come the spring. But he knows he can't. He took it. He has to return it. He has to make things right.

He heads toward the trees, running at first to keep warm, but the icy air cuts into his throat and his nostrils plug. He slows to a fast walk, checking behind him every few minutes to make sure he can still see the house. The tops of the trees sway. Gusts of snow spray over the drifts. The wind is from the north. Myron quickens his pace.

He can see the stark branches now; their gnarled limbs clatter in the breeze. He's entering the muskeg. He slows and comes to a stop twenty feet from the edge of the woods. He can see the frozen lake that could be mistaken for a field. Clouds of snow surge across its ridges, sweeping clear patches of glassy ice. The lake moans, protesting the weight bearing down on it.

The ice on the paw's foreleg melts in Myron's

grip. *Keep going,* he tells himself. He steps onto the crusted layer of glittering ice crystals. Each foot breaks through, grabs at his ankles, scrapes against his shins. He tries to walk quieter, lighter. But he can hear the rustle of his coat. They can hear him. They can smell him. His heart chokes in his throat. He remembers every story he's ever heard of boys disappearing in the woods. Tales of caution to keep him close to home when he was little. The frozen boy, the drowned boy, the lost boy, the boy who was turned into a tree, the boy eaten by wolves . . .

If the coyote is still alive, it will be in these woods; that's where its tracks headed. It might be inside a hollow trunk or in a burrow in the ground, nursing its wound. Animals instinctively retreat to someplace small and enclosed when they are injured. It holds them tight. It hides them. His father has seen animals with deep scars, missing ears and tails, twisted broken limbs, gouged eyes, and somehow they survived. Somehow they healed.

If it isn't alive, then its spirit is still trapped here. Myron is only a few feet away from the tangled stand of spruce and poplar. He could fling the paw into the dense underbrush and run, but it wouldn't be enough. It has to know that it was him, nobody else, that should be punished.

It is darker here beside the trees. The snow has drifted to the lee side of the trunks. An owl hoots indignantly that a trespasser is approaching. To his right, a branch snaps. The owl goes silent. The wind whistles softly through the branches.

Myron holds the paw up to the wilderness. An offering.

He bows his head and lowers his eyes to show his submission. He takes a step forward and then another, expecting the woods to explode any moment in a frenzy of teeth and claws. He climbs up the drift, and when he can no longer free his legs, he crawls. He drops his head lower. He pushes through the snow on his knees. *Forgive me. Forgive me.*

He reaches the crest and behind it sees a small windswept hollow, a carved ellipse haloing the trunks of two intertwined poplars. Katya calls them the loving trees. Myron reaches into the wilds and lays the paw at the base of the trees.

He holds his trembling hand out to the night and braces himself for his sacrifice. A hand for a hand.

A gust of wind wails through the woods, shaking loose a torrent of snow that pelts his hair, the back of his neck and shoulders. His legs cramp. His arm grows tired and sags. His wrist numbs. His fingers ache from the cold.

The wind subsides. The trees murmur softly. *Go*, they say. *Go*.

Myron retreats on hands and knees.

★ ★ ★

Two miles south, Stefan runs as though a pack of wild dogs are tearing at his heels. He claws his way over drifts. Icy snow cuts his hands. Snow clogs his boot tops. His cheeks and fingers freeze.

He runs from the money jangling in his pocket, he runs from the empty flask slapping against his ribs, he runs from the hardness between his legs.

He runs knowing it is the only good thing he has ever done.

'*Tch-tch-tch*,' Teodor calls the horse. It didn't greet him at the fence and now, inside the barn, he doesn't hear its welcoming snort. The wind whips through the rafters. Teodor wipes a drip from his nose. A shiver runs up his back, even his old leather coat can't keep out the north wind's chill this morning. The only creatures braving the wind are the crows. He noticed them at the edge of the woods. He's always hated their jubilant caws celebrating death. He checks the cow. Its teats are full and its stall hasn't been mucked out yet. Teodor proceeds cautiously. The horse lifts its head over the stall and nods a salute.

'What are you doing, old man?' Teodor asks. 'Is everything all right?' He rounds the corner of the stall. 'Why are you tied up?'

The horse whinnies. Teodor glances at the water and feed bucket. Both are full.

'Did someone give you breakfast already?' He pats its rump. A puff of dust plumes upward. 'You need a brushing.' He rubs his hand along its belly and up its neck. 'Move over, give me some room.' He thumps under its ribs. The horse leans in tighter against him. 'Move.' Teodor leans against the horse. It presses him against the boards.

Teodor sidles up to its head. 'What's this new game?' The horse blocks him with its nose. It turns its head so one large eye is looking right at him. 'Enough of this.' He slaps the horse's withers. It flinches but doesn't budge. He reaches over its back and presses against its side, in an attempt to trick it into leaning the other way. The horse pushes harder against him.

'You're going to move.' The horse tries to rub its head against Teodor's chest. 'No.' He wraps a piece of binder twine around the horse's nose. The horse rears its head, trying to free itself of the constraint. Teodor knows it hates being led this way. 'Move.' He tugs the horse's head sideways. It pulls back. 'Goddamn it.' Teodor steps toward the other side of the stall for better leverage. Lesya stands up from her crouched hiding position.

'What the hell are you doing there?' Teodor sputters, angry with himself for not listening to his animal. 'Why didn't you say something? Get out from there!'

Lesya meekly obeys. She steps out of the stall but doesn't run away. She stares at her feet, her face masked by her hair.

'Are you trying to get stepped on?' Teodor releases the makeshift halter, rubs the horse's nose, soothes its hurt feelings. He looks at his niece. He hasn't seen her in months. Each other's presence affirmed only through the exchange of baskets of eggs and loaves of bread. She looks thinner, her hair matted, her clothes in need of washing. He realizes that she has been waiting for him and immediately regrets yelling.

Teodor gives the horse the top of a smuggled carrot and pats its side. He walks out of the stall and stops a few feet from Lesya. He crouches low, brings himself to her size. He looks at the straw scattered at her feet, sticking to her stockings.

'Tell me,' Teodor asks as quiet as he can.

Lesya swallows. She speaks so softly Teodor barely hears. 'Tato's gone.'

He glances up at her hidden face; he can see a bruise on her cheek.

Teodor empties his voice of rage. 'Did he do that?'

Lesya shakes her head no. She whispers, 'Petro's gone too.'

★　★　★

Petro pulls his collar up higher around his neck. The constant north wind buffets him from behind, blasting him with ice-sharp snow scoured from the fields. He can stand the steady wind; it's the high gusts that threaten to knock him down. He hears them coming, a low rumble like a train far off in the distance. He stops as another gust whips around him and disappears in a cyclone of snow. His eyes water. He tries to blink away the endless white on white.

He pushes forward, following the dim recesses of his father's tracks. The footprints have become vague in the last hour, the crisp edges erased by the blowing snow. Drifts cut across his path, eradicating the trail for brief sections. Once he veered too far right and missed the track. Panicked, he retraced his steps, knowing his father couldn't just disappear. He ran in circles, criss-crossing and backtracking, almost ready to give up hope when he stumbled upon the trail, stretching toward the south, in a straight, unerring line. He looked back at his own erratic track, a wild careening scribble, and knew his father would be displeased by his untidiness. He stepped into his father's bootprint and vowed not to miss another step.

Petro knew something was wrong the moment he opened his eyes this morning. His father's flask wasn't on the table, his coat wasn't on the hook, his boots weren't under the stove, and Lesya hadn't got up to light the fire. He had jumped out of bed, not caring that his stone heart fell to the ground. He yanked his boots on over his new socks and ran outside, not stopping to grab his coat.

The moment he swung open the door, he was blinded by a blast of wind. He ran toward the outhouse, but could see the door swinging wildly open and shut. He raced to the barn, the wind whipping at his nightshirt, and swung open the heavy door. The horse and cow looked up at him suspiciously. He stood in the yard, looking up at the house on the hill, his skin prickling from the cold. He spun around, searching for any sign, any clue, and then he saw the remains of footprints leading toward the road.

Petro burst through the door and screamed at his mother, who was maddeningly still asleep. 'Where is he?' When she poked her head from under the covers, disoriented by the morning light and the screaming boy, he shook her. He dug his icy fingers into her flesh, wanting to hurt her. 'Where is he?'

She answered, 'Who?'

He roared as loud as he could: 'Tato, where is he?'

Lesya got out of bed and slammed the door shut. She was walking away from him when she said, 'He's gone.'

Mama sat up then. Lesya dragged her foot across the floor to the wood stove. Petro hated the sound of it scraping through the dirt.

She said, 'He left last night. He took our money and your ring, Mama. He didn't get your brush and mirror. He didn't find them.' Then she poked at the cold ash like it was any other day.

Mama shook her head, shaking away the words. 'When's he coming back?' she whimpered.

Lesya stood as tall as she could and said, 'Get some wood, Petro.' Like she was the one in charge.

His mother rambled on that he was coming back, that he wouldn't leave them, that he said he wouldn't leave. Then she came upon the idea that he had just gone for supplies. She tried to convince Petro that's where his father was. She ordered Lesya to make their father some breakfast. Something nice, because he'd be cold when he got home. She smoothed her hair and straightened her ratty nightgown to make herself more presentable. She wanted to make eggs and bacon. She told Petro to go to his aunt's to get more bacon. That's what she told him, even though she knew going there wasn't allowed.

His sister kept preparing the fire. She balled up a piece of brown paper and tossed it in the stove, then shoved in some twigs and struck a match. She crouched down and held the flame to the paper. It smoked, then flared. She closed the stove door and let the draft fan the flames. She said, 'He's not coming back.'

As she turned to get up, that's when Petro hit her. 'Don't you ever say that,' he snarled. The sound of his voice surprised him. He sounded like his father; not the pitch or tone, but the coldness, the disgust, the hatred . . . And the sound of his fist connecting with Lesya's cheek was sharp and hard, unlike the softness of flesh on flesh. The shock of contact was painless and strangely exhilarating.

He felt himself filling the room, every corner, every chink, felt himself growing large. He felt his strength in the fear and confusion in his sister's eyes. He felt it as she pulled back, averting her eyes and growing small. Hitting her made him feel like a man. They didn't try to stop him when he walked out the door.

Petro pulls his lopsided hat farther down over his ears, scrunches his fingers inside the ill-fitting mittens, and braces for another gust of wind. His father wouldn't leave him, not after he's worked so hard to prove that he's a good son. He's strong. He's obedient. His tato loves him. It's them Tato hates. A fat, lazy sow and a crippled mouse.

He'll find his father and tell him that he understands why he had to leave. That he wants to leave too. He'll work hard and make lots of money so they can buy the white house. Or they can hop the train and go somewhere else, to the city or all the way back to Ukraïna. He doesn't care where they live so long as they're together.

The rush of snow abates. The prints are mere impressions now. He looks up and the whiteness spills forever. There are no landmarks, no trees, no sun, only snow funnelling over drifts, reshaping the dunes. Tato wouldn't just leave him.

But Petro remembers being left before. Many times. He remembers standing at the edge of the road, waiting for Tato to come back. He remembers waking up in the middle of the night and finding him gone. He remembers never being told goodbye. He outruns those memories, his boots obliterating the remains of his father's trail.

He runs, not looking up, focused only on the fading depressions in the snow. He runs until the prairies are swept clean and there are no more footprints to follow. Panting, his legs knocking, his body shivering uncontrollably, Petro scours the horizon. He doesn't feel like a man any more, he doesn't feel strong or powerful, he feels small. Like he's seven years old.

He looks back and sees a shape lumbering toward him. A coyote? Too large. A man? His father? His father coming to get him. Petro almost cries with relief. How did his father get behind him? Maybe Petro got turned around and he's been walking in the wrong direction. He laughs at his own stupidity. He closes his eyes to the wind's onslaught. He is a boy made of ice. Snow blasts his face. The wind is from the north. His mind slowly churns through the facts: he is facing north. He didn't get turned around. Someone is following him. He opens his eyes.

The shape is white on the bottom and brown on top. It moves with a thrusting roll. It's an animal. A horse. A man. Teodor.

Petro turns and runs, letting the wind carry him. He leaps over the drifts. 'Tato!' he cries, hoping his father will hear him and save him. 'Tato!' He looks over his shoulder and Teodor is not far behind. The horse is bearing down on him, its nostrils wide, snorting steam, head high, ears back — it charges through the snow. Petro trips. He crawls his way back up and stumbles through a waist-deep drift.

Teodor reins in the horse and drops to a slow walk. He follows the boy, keeping ten feet back. He lets Petro walk.

In his mind, Petro is running. He's running faster than a horse. He's running to his father, who he can see on the horizon waiting for him. Petro has stopped shivering. He's not even cold. He is warm and nothing hurts inside him. He is inside the whiteness.

Teodor wraps Petro in a blanket and lifts him from the snow. He is surprised by how light the boy is and how far he walked before lying down. Cradling him, he hoists himself up on the horse, tucks Petro into his body, and pulls the blanket over his head.

White to black.

Anna sits at the table. She has pinned up her unbrushed hair and squeezed into an ill-fitting blouse. She has swept the floor and made the bed. The table is set for four. A stew simmers on the stove. She is facing the doorway. She has been holding this domestic pose for more than an hour. When the door opens, she stands and puts on her practised, most welcoming smile. A fury of wind rips into the room. Her mask crumbles at the sight of her brother. Petro hangs limp in his arms.

'Get more blankets and warm up some rocks,' he directs Lesya, who already has stones warming in the oven. She scrambles to retrieve them, burning her fingers as she wraps them in a scorched linen cloth.

Teodor lays Petro on the bed and unlaces his boots. He rubs his toes. 'Put them here.' His voice is calm and guiding. Lesya tucks the warming rocks under the covers at her brother's feet.

'He has to get out of these clothes.' He pulls off the boy's wet pants. 'Get his coat.' Lesya fumbles with the buttons. Her brother's face is grey. Teodor sits him up, and Petro falls forward like a rag doll. He peels off the boy's coat and shirt, exposing his nephew's scrawny chest and arms. Lesya throws a blanket around her brother's shoulders, embarrassed by his frailty. Embarrassed that he made her flinch. His coldness seeps through her dress.

Teodor tries to pull off his mittens, but Petro's

358

fingers curl, refusing to let go. Teodor slips two hot stones into each mittened palm, the hands loosen and wrap around the soothing round shape. He swaddles Petro in another blanket and gently lays him down.

Lesya piles him with quilts. Teodor pushes on the boy's cheeks. Blood colours the white flesh.

'He's going to be fine,' he reassures Lesya, who for the first time is looking him directly in the eyes. Her eyes are grey, blue, ancient. She searches for the truth. She tucks the covers in tighter, then limps to the stove and throws in another log.

Exhaustion and the cold overwhelm Teodor. His muscles ache and his toes throb. He smells the musty claustrophobia of this house's despair. He turns to his sister. She is sitting back at the table, facing the door, not looking toward her child.

Her matted hair sticks out on one side, pinned askew. The buttons on her blouse strain at her breasts. Her belly distends over her lap. He notices that she has rouged her cheeks and pinned a dried flower to her collar. Her hands and feet are swollen. Her toe pokes through a hole in her stocking.

How could this be his sister? His sister was fearless. She danced with her head held high, commanding everyone to look at her. He remembers a parade of boys tripping over themselves just to catch a smile. She could outrun them all. One by one they would pull back and admire her from afar — a wild horse they never wanted tamed. Anna looks at him

359

with broken eyes. 'He's coming back.'

Teodor looks away, unable to bear her need. 'Take care of your boy.' He turns to Lesya. 'Come by the house tomorrow, tell your aunt what you'll need.'

'He's coming back,' Anna insists.

Teodor doesn't bother answering. He gets up heavily and heads for the door. He wants to go home. He wants to feel Katya's arms around his neck, the softness of her cheek rubbing against his whiskers. He wants to answer Ivan's never-ending questions: *Where does the snow come from? Where do the worms go in the winter?* He wants to feel the calm of his eldest daughter. He wants to tease Sofia about her pincurls. He wants to watch Myron lumbering into manhood. He wants to hold his wife. He wants this to be over.

'Don't walk out on me!' Anna slams the table as she stands up.

Teodor stops at the door. He turns to her, weary from all the betrayals, all the disappointments, all the cowardice.

'What do you want me to say, Anna?' Teodor asks. 'You made your choice.'

It's his dismissal, his righteous condescension, his simple assessment of her life that infuriates Anna. This man who has never been left, who has never been used like a whore, who has never doubted that someone loved him, who has never had his insides torn apart giving birth to yet another hopeless life. What was her choice?

She had no choice the moment she was born. She would marry, she would bear children, she

360

would farm, she would be poor, she would sacrifice her desires for the good of her husband, her family, she would be obedient and selfless. That was all that was offered. That was her only choice. And she tried to choose well; she chose a life that would take her off the farm and into the city. She chose an officer. She made the best choice to save herself, and she ended up here.

She has become this bloated thing. Her nails are cracked; dirt has leached into her skin, staining the bottom of her feet, the back of her neck. Her teeth are yellow. Her vagina is loose and used. She is old. She is rotting. She needs Stefan to make it all stop. She needs Stefan to do what she can't. But she can't tell Teodor that. If she says it out loud, it will mean he is right.

'You did this!' she shrieks. 'He's gone because of you. You drove him away!' Her face flushes red, she hears the hysteria in her voice; pain tears through her abdomen. 'You came into our lives and took over!' She attacks him, needing to convince herself. 'You made him feel like he wasn't good enough. Like we were beggars on our own land.' The words tumble out, a torrent that can't be stopped. 'You're no better than he is. You're no better than any of us. You're a thief who washed himself clean. But underneath you're as dirty as everyone else.'

The words froth in her mouth. Teodor stares impassively at her, as though he's waiting for an animal to die. These are just the kicks and thrashings of a pig whose throat is already slit. Anna chokes back another contraction. She wants to stop. She wants Teodor to put his arms around her and she'll tell him everything. She'll tell him how afraid she is. She'll tell him everything that she's done. She'll ask him for absolution. She wants to be washed clean. But he's staring at her as if she's already ceased to exist.

'Why couldn't you just leave?' The words escape in a trickle, already regretted. The only question she wanted to ask, needed to ask, was 'Why?' That's all she needed answered. It's the only word welling inside her: 'Why?'

Teodor straightens his shoulders. Out of the corner of his eye he is aware of Lesya, chewing her fingernails, her foot splayed to the side, her eyes on him.

He answers with a chilling calm: 'Because it's my land. It's all I have and all I am. And no one will ever take it away.'

He walks up close to the table and leans in to Anna so Lesya won't hear. 'Why did he leave last time, Anna? And the time before that?' He can't hide his contempt. 'Look at you. Look what you've let him do.' She clutches the side of the table; the rouge on her cheeks has streaked down her face. 'You have a family to take care of,' he hisses. 'Think of them for a change.'

Anna slaps him hard across the face. Lesya cringes and braces for her uncle to hit back. But he doesn't. He steps away, the imprint of her mother's hand emblazoned on his cheek. He puts on his hat and gloves and walks out the door.

He goes to the barn, gathers up the tack, blankets, feed buckets, and a bag of oats, and loads it on the horse. He takes the reins and leads it across the field to its new home.

Anna remains standing at the table, her fingernails digging into the wood, until Teodor is well past the stone wall.

Then she tells Lesya her water has broken.

★　★　★

It is fading to night and it is only five in the afternoon. The wind has quelled to a low whisper. Water boils on the stove. The kerosene light flickers. Lesya dampens her mother's dry lips with a wet cloth. Anna is propped up in bed in a semi-sitting position, her knees bent, her thighs open. The contractions have been increasing steadily over the last twenty minutes. They are now no more than three or four minutes apart.

Lesya pleads again: 'Let me get help. Let me get Aunt Maria.' Her hand pressed on her mother's belly, she can feel that the baby has dropped low. 'I won't know what to do if something goes wrong. Please, Mama.'

Anna squeezes her daughter's hand as another contraction swells. 'No,' she blurts as her body writhes in pain. She pushes down on the bed, trying to get away from the spasm splitting her apart; her moan gives way to a scream. Petro covers his ears.

At first, he thinks it is a coyote howling. He wakes bathed in sweat, pinned under the weight of two quilts. He wrestles himself free, dazed by the darkness. It takes him a moment to realize that he is back in his own bed. He doesn't know if it is early night or deep morning. He doesn't know if he has dreamed the wind and his father leaving. He doesn't know if he is dreaming still.

He is naked, except for his mittens. He is holding two smooth stones. He wonders if the heart has split in two, but then he sees the heart stone on the floor. His father's coat isn't on the coat hook, and the flask is gone. Lesya looks at him as she runs to the stove for more hot water and he can see a bruise on her cheek. 'There's stew on the stove.' Then Petro knows he is awake, because his stomach growls.

He pulls on his long underwear and new socks that are bathed in the heat of the stove. He climbs down from bed and picks up the heart stone. Ice cold. Clutching it in his hand, he wanders to the roaring fire and looks inside the bubbling pot. The steaming smell of potatoes, onions, and salted beef obliterate any sounds his mother is making. He fills a bowl half full and carries it to the table. The broth slops at the sides. He sets down the stone, picks up a spoon, and shovels it in. Cramming his cheeks full, slurping it back, barely chewing. He burns his tongue and the roof of his mouth. He licks the bowl clean and wants more.

The next bowl he fills to the brim. He gorges until his belly grows round and soft. He watches his mother's face contort and twist, her mouth stretched wide. The muscles in her thighs shudder from the strain. He fetches the pot and scrapes it clean. He forces down the spoonfuls even though he is no longer hungry. He focuses on the sound of metal on metal, scratching away his mama's sobs.

He licks the spoon clean as she screams again. The pot is empty. Petro crawls back in bed and covers himself with the quilts. He peers through a tented peephole.

'Can you see it?' Anna pants, her face glistening with sweat. Her pelvis hinging apart.

Lesya has seen cows give birth, and cats. She saw her own brother spill out onto the dirt. She's never been queasy at the sight of blood. In a crisis, that's when Lesya is the calmest. Everything empties out of her. Her heart slows, her breathing shallows, her voice becomes flat and reassuring in its neutrality. Her eyes betray nothing. Her hands don't shake. Her body becomes a vessel for the wounded. *Give me your fear*.

Lesya looks between her mother's legs. The skin is pulled open wide, the top of a dome pushes against the crowning flesh like a perfect egg. She wipes away the mucus and blood. A raw yolk.

'I see it.' And then she realizes that soon she will have to catch the baby, bring it safely into this world, and that seems too much to expect from a ten-year-old girl.

'I see its head.' She sees her mother's back muscle twitch. 'Breathe now, Mama. Breathe. Here it comes.' The contraction hits.

'Now push.' Anna strains with all her might. 'Push.' A wave of pain slams into her. She is being cleaved in two. The head crests, the contraction subsides. Anna falls back.

365

'You're doing good, Mama. It's almost here. Just a little bit more.' Anna's body stiffens. 'Don't push yet. It's coming. It's coming.' Anna clings to her daughter's voice. 'Now.' The tide rips her away again.

'There's the shoulders.' Lesya cradles the head. She sees a fluff of wet, brown hair, small pink ears. She holds its shape in her hands, a perfect egg without the shell. 'You're almost done, Mama.'

Anna's eyes roll back in her head. White light explodes in the back of her mind. Her body disappears, electric. The baby's torso drops into Lesya's hands. Its soft head and loose neck flop back. Lesya grabs to support it with one hand, as the other grapples the slippery body sliding through her fingers.

'Now, Mama, now you have to push!' She can feel the baby's heart pounding against her hand through its thin, translucent skin. It flutters like a baby sparrow. Its arms are out, tiny fingers. She's never seen a baby so small; it fits in her two hands. It weighs nothing at all. The skin is blue tinged. The baby is still.

'Now, Mama, push!' The legs slip out. Two perfect legs and two perfect feet. Straight and perfect. The baby slides into her hands. 'It's a girl!'

She rolls it over; it lies limp in her hands. Its eyes closed. Its lips blue. She wipes the mucus from its face, unplugs its nose. It's going to die like the bird. She taps it on the back, massages its tiny ribs. She slaps it harder. Wake up! The baby chokes and coughs. A gasping inhale. Her lungs fill. Her skin flushes pink. Her mouth gulps, her face turns red, she exhales a squawking bawl.

Lesya wipes her baby sister clean and swaddles her in a clean blanket, leaving her perfect feet protruding. She bundles her in the rabbit-fur blanket. She's as small as a mouse, but as loud as a crow. 'It's a girl, Mama.'

'I don't want to see it.' Anna presses her eyes shut tight.

'You have to hold her, Mama.' She pushes aside her mother's protesting hands. She lays the baby on her mother's chest.

'Look at her, Mama.'

The baby squeals and fights its restraints.

'There's nothing wrong with this one, Mama.' She guides Anna's hand to the baby's head, leads her fingers over the face, down the chest wrapped in soft rabbit fur, to the exposed legs, then she lets go. She watches her mother's fingers hesitantly brush the skin, glide down the shins, barely touching, to the ankles, over the feet. Her hand embraces the toes.

Anna opens her eyes. The baby's face is scrunched up in protest, her eyes squeezed tight. She is so tiny. Yet she is fierce. Her mouth gulps silent wails. Anna is overwhelmed by a flood of familiarity, as if she has known this child forever. She knows her face, her smell. She knows everything about her. She is her. Anna's skin is splitting open, her heart cracking. She feels all people, all suffering, all hope, all loss, all rapture. She has never felt such exquisite pain. The baby is crying and she can taste the salt.

Her mother's face is radiant, almost beautiful, her hand cradling tiny feet. Lesya stands by, wondering when she should cut the umbilical cord.

Neither notices that Petro has gone outside. He is at the back of the house, rubbing his chest and arms with snow, numbing himself inside out, trying to get back to the place of whiteness — where he wasn't afraid.

★ ★ ★

Anna and the baby are asleep. Lesya has washed the linens, burned the bloody rags and afterbirth, tended the fire, and has just finished tearing a sheet into diapers. She checks the baby again. The only crib she could find was a soapbox, MRS. LEIDERMANN'S BLUEING SOLUTION. The baby is so small, she takes up half the length of the box and is lost in the folds of the rabbit-fur blanket. Her breathing seems shallow and congested, but she suckled ferociously before sobbing herself to sleep with her lips and tongue smacking for more. Lesya pulls the soft fur up under the baby's chin.

Petro is asleep too. He wouldn't tell her where he went and Lesya didn't push. She didn't want to know. They stood over the box together, looking in at the sleeping newborn. Lesya slid her little finger into the baby's hand. The baby gripped it tight, pulling it toward her mouth. Lesya pulled her hand away, not yet ready to give herself.

Petro didn't touch the baby. He didn't see a

baby. He saw a blind, bald, wrinkled, tail-less mouse gasping for air. 'It's not going to live.' He didn't say it to be cruel. It was just something he knew deep down inside himself; not to get attached. Lesya didn't contradict him. He wasn't sure if she had even heard him. She didn't speak to him at all. Even when he crawled back in bed, his muscles heavy with fatigue, his eyes already shutting — and called her name, she didn't come. He fell asleep clutching the heart stone for comfort, willing his tato to come home.

It's not that Lesya didn't hear her brother, or that she is angry, she just can't summon up the energy to care. She watches herself tidy up the house, plan tomorrow's meal, and assess what supplies need to be restocked. She watches her hands perform the tasks, efficient and assured, and is surprised by how small they are: a child's hands. Someone else's hands. She can't feel herself at all.

She puts on her coat and boots. Her twisted foot aches as she pulls the leather over her ankle. Lesya wrenches the boot on hard, jamming the deformed limb into the straight, rigid shape. She pulls her mittens on and limps outside to do her chores.

The night is blue and still. Drifts cling to the house, a new landscape sketched by the wind. The tops of the fence posts peek from shallow hollows. Barbed wire holds back walls of sheered snow. As she drags her foot over the uneven terrain, her thigh begins to quiver. It shudders down to her knee, gaining strength as it tremors into her foot. She stops and places her hand on her knee to quell the shake. As soon as she touches the leg, it quiets. Lesya steps forward and the quivering starts again, surging upward from her toes, rippling under her skin, flushing her heart with panic. She breathes deep, trying to remain calm.

Stop it, she orders. She steps down hard on her twisted foot, and a jab of pain mixes with the vibrating nerves. She runs to the coop, pulls aside the log pole, and ducks inside. She is greeted by the sweet smell of hay and feathers, tainted by the pungent stench of shit. Her foot rustles the straw. She crouches down, wraps her arms around her legs, but then the rest of her body begins to tremble.

The hens look at her quizzically, unaccustomed to night visits. Only Happiness bobs and coos, overjoyed by Lesya's surprise arrival. Its feet high-step, up and down, it bows its head and lifts its wings, dancing to music only it can hear. It is roosting in one of the other hen's nests. The displaced brood hen is perched nearby, clucking its indignation.

'What are you doing up there? Get down.' She swats Happiness off the nest. It jumps to the ground in a tornado of wings. It tries to hop on her. Lesya kicks it off. 'No.'

She wants to get the eggs and get out of there. She is so tired. She reaches into the nest; her fingers ooze into a thick, hot slime. Both eggs are broken. Happiness jumps up on the roost balancing on one foot, the other twisted backward. It softly pecks at Lesya's hand.

'Look what you've done.' The bird cocks its

head at the finger waving in front of its beak. 'Bad bird. Bad!'

Lesya scoops out the mire of yolk, shell, and straw and throws it on the floor. Happiness steps into the clean nest. Lesya shoves it aside.

'This isn't your nest. These aren't your eggs.' Happiness rubs its head against her arm and tries to worm its way back onto the roost.

'No! You think this is funny? You think it's funny if we starve?' The bird rubs against Lesya's arm. 'You think this is a game? You do nothing. You get fed, get taken care of . . . '

The chicken lifts its lame foot to Lesya, an offering. She grabs its claw, the bird tries to pull away, but Lesya holds on tight. 'Look how fat you are, eating all their food, stealing their eggs — you're supposed to make your own eggs! You're not even any good to breed. Look at you.' She holds its foot up. 'Look how ugly you are. Useless.'

The bird squawks, frightened by her intensity and her grip on its bad leg. Its wings flap in distress, its coos alarm into squawks.

'You think I'm always going to take care of you?' She shakes the bird, her own leg jittering uncontrollably. 'That you're always going to be safe?' The bird pecks her hand, drawing blood. 'You think you'd survive out there alone?'

She wrenches the bird upside down, gripping it by its crippled leg. She carries it outside. 'This is what it's like out here.' She swings it through the darkness. The bird flails and claws her arm; beats her with its wings. 'There's nowhere to hide. Nothing to protect you!' The bird cackles hysterically, its neck and head dangling inches from the ground.

Lesya marches to the woodpile. 'You have a job.' Her entire body quakes. 'You have a duty.' She grabs the axe. 'You don't get to live for free.' She holds the screeching hen down on the block and swings.

The headless bird teeters around in circles, falling onto its side, its wings flapping, its body tripping over its crooked foot.

Anna wakes to a small whimper. Lesya and Petro are fast asleep. A fire blazes in the stove. She hears the sound again. A soft cooing, like the wings of a bird trapped in the rafters. She looks around the room, sees the soapbox on the floor beside her bed. A nest. She wonders if Lesya has brought her chickens inside. She peers into the box and sees a rabbit squirming.

'Are you hurt?' Anna strokes its fur. Soft, white down.

'Poor little thing.' The rabbit calms to her touch.

'Don't be afraid.' She picks it up. Cradles it in her arms. 'Are you lost?' The rabbit has a child's face. Wide grey-blue eyes look up at her.

'You shouldn't have come here. It's not safe.' The little mouth sucks. Anna offers her a finger and the lips nurse strong and hard.

'Are you hungry?' she asks the rabbit-child. She opens the front of her blouse and lets the creature suckle her nipple. She looks at its feet. Its paws are hairless, the skin soft.

'How will you survive?' she asks the strange, magical creature. And she knows that something this beautiful cannot survive.

Its tiny fingers knead her breast. Anna pulls the fur skin over the top of its head. The baby squirms and mews.

'Shhh,' Anna coos. 'I'll take you home.'

Maria stares out the window into the night. She can't sleep again and this time it isn't the baby. The baby is quiet. She rocks slightly on the stiff-backed chair, massaging her stomach. Someday, she'll ask Teodor to build her a real rocker, so she can pull it outside on the stoop when the long summer nights return. She'll sit with her baby draped over her shoulder, pressed against her chest. Heart on heart. Rocking in rhythm with the frogs and crickets.

The chair creaks and Maria looks over her shoulder to see if she has woken Teodor. He doesn't stir. He returned home exhausted. Silent. He ate, rolled a cigarette, and crawled into bed, not even bothering to get undressed. When she prodded him as to where he'd been, he didn't answer. He told her: *Tomorrow. I'll tell you everything tomorrow.* He was asleep before the children.

Ever since this morning, she has had a bad feeling. It began when she saw two crows facing the house, their feathers ruffling in the gusts. They stood there so long she thought their feet had frozen to the ground, and when she opened the door they didn't fly away. They stared at her with black, glassy eyes. Not until Myron clapped his hands did they slowly lift and glide away, swooped up by the wind.

Then Teodor didn't come home. She tried to convince herself that he was waiting for the storm to blow out, or perhaps he and Anna were finally talking. When she knelt to pray for his safe return, a surging gust shook the house and the picture of the Virgin Mary knocked against the wall, decrying its sacrilegious use. When Teodor finally emerged from the windswept land, she didn't feel relief. If anything, her fear increased. Maybe it was just the storm setting her on edge.

Maria shivers, even though the fire is still burning strong. Her fingers worry against her wooden cross. And there weren't any rabbits today either. Myron checked this morning and at dusk. There haven't been any rabbits all week; perhaps the coyotes have driven them away. She'll have to start rationing the food better. It's been difficult to estimate how much they need to conserve to allow for Anna's needs. She worries that she hasn't been sending enough to her sister-in-law. She worries that she's been overcompensating and sending too much.

The bacon is already gone. They've used a pound of sausage and two pounds of roast. There's only enough flour to make three more batches of pyrohy, and there's three months of winter left. Self-pity wells in her throat; Maria prays it away, attributes her rawness to her pregnancy.

Anna's baby is due in two weeks. She's had no word from her. If something happens to the baby, she'll blame herself. She should have gone to Anna, disobeyed Teodor's decree. She needs someone with her. It's his brother-in-law that Teodor's at war with. Wars are always with men. The men fight and the women mourn. Tomorrow, she's going to see Anna and end this war. They'll talk as mothers, daughters, sisters.

They'll make peace for their families. This land is too big to be alone in.

It is well after midnight, the day is over, but still the bad feeling nags her. Everyone is asleep. They have food for tomorrow. The fire is burning. They have a house and a barn, and come next summer, she'll buy more chickens and hopefully a pig. She'll put the garden out front, facing south, so she can see it from her window. She'll get the boys to put up a fence to keep out the rabbits and deer . . . and the pig. She'll sit in her rocker and watch it grow. There will be a new child. Teodor will break another six acres, maybe eight, and with the harvest money they'll get a wagon and another horse. Next year everyone will have a new coat.

The chair creaks again. The even sounds of her family's breathing continue undisturbed. She worries too much. She has to learn to trust. Trust that her family will be taken care of. Trust that this is their home now. Maria leans forward in the chair. She cocks her ear, unsure if she has heard anything. She closes her eyes. She listens past the breath of her house, past the crackling of the fire, through the window's glass.

'Teodor?' Maria shakes him awake. 'I hear a rabbit crying.'

★ ★ ★

Having fallen asleep so early, Teodor now feels that it should be morning. But it must be only three or four o'clock. A million stars curtain the sky. Teodor finds Pivnichna zoria, the midnight

376

star. One of the guardian trinity, along with Rannia zoria, the morning star, and Vechirnia zoria, the evening star, that guard the chained dog from eating the little bear. If the chain ever breaks, the world will end. Teodor wonders if all the stars have names. He can't imagine anyone spending their entire lives looking up, mapping and categorizing all the seeds of light. He searches for recognizable shapes — the bear, the dog, the three leaps of the deer — but the star animals elude him.

He shifts the rifle from his shoulder to the cradle of his arm. He yawns, though he feels wide awake. The brisk cold fills his lungs. He pulls the warmth of his leather jacket closer and hunkers deeper into the sheepskin lining. He tried to convince Maria that she had imagined the sound, that it wasn't possible to hear anything that far away. But she wouldn't be dissuaded, even after he took her outside and they stood on the stoop and heard nothing at all. The more he pointed out the improbability, the more distressed she became until she was on the verge of tears. He told her he would check.

He still hasn't told her about Stefan or Petro. What will he tell her? That the son of a bitch is gone? For how long this time? Until next month, the spring, next harvest? He won't be back until winter is over. He's like a magpie chasing after shining bits of rubbish, feeding on the carcasses others fought and died for. Teodor spits. At least it's one less mouth to feed.

Maria will want to bring Anna to their place until the baby is born, but Teodor doesn't want her in the house. She signed the letters, even if she didn't write them. He stops and lights a cigarette. Inhales the strong tobacco. He exhales to the sky. Above him, northern lights flicker. Ivan says it's star people. Katya says it's God. Teodor doesn't know what it is. A reason to look up. He breathes in deep and the answer comes. It is freedom.

The word makes his throat tighten. *Free*. Of everything they did to him, it was the walls that nearly drove him mad. Not being able to see the sky. They tried to break him by breaking his body. Animals can be broken that way. They become husks of skin and bones. He saw it under Stalin. He saw it in prison, so many hollow, empty eyes. But some beaten animals become fiercer. Their eyes burn wild. They die before they submit. But still, they die. Staying alive requires remembering what it means to be alive. Still, he almost broke. It was the walls. When they left him alone. When he had nothing to fight; nothing to hate; nothing to defy. Five steps — wall, five steps — wall. They took away the sky.

But look at it now.

Shoosh, shoosh, shoosh. He smiles at the sound of his boots on the snow. He is not counting his steps. He loves being the only one walking through the night. The snow catching the moon's reflection casts a blue-white sheen. He doesn't feel small in this vastness. He feels as if he can expand as far and wide as he can see. He breathes deeper out here, walks taller. This is where they'll bury him. Under this unbroken sky.

He can see the outline of the stone wall, grey-white, slashing the night. The dividing line, his and hers. This stone wall will stand for a hundred years and a hundred more after that. Long after the buildings rot and the scrub grows wild. Someday someone will walk through this field and see the stones worn and pocked with time, sunken into the earth. They'll walk the line, run their hand over the rounded stones, and wonder, *Who put these here?* Maybe they'll pick up a rock and marvel at its weight. Try to imagine how long it took to build. Wonder, *Why is it here?*

Teodor chuckles. It was just a place to pile the rocks. He listens to his footsteps. Maybe, if he's honest with himself, he was marking a line, but he never thought he'd need it.

He sees the moon shadow of the first snare. Sixth rock in from the east end. The stiff wire loop propped tight against the base of the stone wall. Empty. No tracks mar the snow's crust. He shakes his head; he knew there'd be nothing here. The gun swings at his hip, loose and casual as a walking stick. One bullet in the chamber. One more in his pocket, as an afterthought. He runs his hand over the stones, plowing a cap of snow, following the line west. Now that Stefan is gone, Anna will do the right thing. In the spring, they'll go to the land office together and she'll sign it over in his name. That will be the end of it. If the weather breaks earlier, they'll go sooner. It's not right, them fighting.

They already left one world and one family behind. That's enough to lose. The day he left

Ukraïna, he shook his father's hand. As he walked away, they both waved a farmer's wave. A slight, friendly gesture — the universal code for *don't make a fuss, it's been good to see you, see you around.* Khlib i sil'. Bread and salt.

He doesn't even know if his father is still alive. There are no letters and no one from the village has made it to these parts. He can't remember his father's face or the colour of his eyes, but he remembers his hands. Gnarled and wrinkled, every cord and artery revealing the man. The short, thick nails, the moons ridged with dirt. The crooked left index finger, missing the tip and half a nail. The gouged scar on the left forefinger, beneath the first knuckle. The roughness of his callused palms. He remembers the strength of those hands, crushing his own, as they shook one last time. That was another world. Ten thousand miles away. Now the mile between him and Anna seems so much farther.

The second snare is empty. He is about to turn back when he hears a low grunt and sniff. He listens. Hears a snuffling. He steps closer to the wall and looks over. Not twenty feet on the other side are two coyotes, nosing the ground. They haven't heard or smelled him, too intent on rooting at something on the ground. Teodor pulls off his glove and slips his finger into the trigger. A decent coyote pelt is worth a dollar. He has two shots. He can get a clear bead on the larger one. Just behind the left ear. The shot will probably scare off the other one.

Teodor quietly, carefully raises the rifle and takes aim. The larger coyote paws at the snow. It sidesteps, exposing its flank but blocking a clean kill. Both dogs sniff curiously, timid. Teodor can see a dead rabbit at their feet. He steadies his arm, his eye. He has a clear shot on the smaller coyote. He cocks the trigger. The click is ear-splitting. The coyotes rear around, teeth bared. But they don't flee; they hunker their heads and close ranks. The larger one snarls a warning. Hackles ridge their backs and bristle around their necks. *Back off*, they warn. *This is ours.*

Teodor takes aim between the larger dog's eyes. It spits a fury of threats, its teeth gnashing with each snap. The smaller coyote grabs the rabbit and tries to drag it off, tearing the pelt. It grabs again, tugging at the weight. It hops backward, its right front leg slapping the air, a stump where there should be a foot.

Teodor takes a step forward, trying to get a better shot. The larger coyote whips around, grabs the carcass, and jerks it up, grasping for a better hold. The pelt slides off as if it's been skinned. Teodor sees a limb. His mind grapples with the shape. The hindquarters? The hare's leg? Pink, blue . . . a hand. Tiny, perfect fingers.

Teodor fires, not aiming. The shot explodes in the snow. He is screaming, lunging over the wall. The small female with the missing foot clamps down on the bundle and drags it over the snow. The large male charges after her, unhinges its jaw, and shovels the carcass to the back of its throat. They race for the woods. Teodor ratchets the bolt, emptying the spent shell. He fishes for the bullet in his pocket, jams it into the chamber.

He flounders through the snow, drops to his knees, takes aim, unable to steady his hands. Fires.

The crack of the gunshot ricochets across the prairies. The coyotes keep running, Teodor's howls chasing them relentlessly.

★   ★   ★

At the first shot, Maria is on her feet. She hears Teodor's shouts and she is racing for Myron's room. By the second shot, she has shaken him awake and is pulling on her coat. Her children file out of their rooms, frightened by their mother's flurry. Katya and Ivan are already sniffling. Myron pulls on his pants and sees that the rifle is gone. They can hear a coyote howling, howling. Katya starts to cry, wants her mama not to go. Maria yells at them to stay in the house and she is out the door, running across the field, not thinking what she will do when she gets there. Myron chases after her, his fingers fumbling to fasten his coat.

★   ★   ★

'Anna!' Teodor screams, hammering the door with the butt of the rifle. 'Open the door!' He kicks at the latch. The door shudders and heaves. 'Anna!'

Lesya and Petro jump awake, not recognizing the crazed voice screaming through the door. 'Let me in!' From the glow of the wood stove, Lesya sees her mother sitting at the table, dressed in her cloak, a puddle of melted snow at her feet, her hands clasping her stomach. The door sways on its hinges. 'Anna!'

The children cower in their bed. 'Mama?' Lesya cries. The door frame cracks. Petro jumps down from the bed and grabs a log to wield as a weapon. He shrinks into the corner. 'He's going to kill us,' he whispers.

Teodor tosses aside the rifle and batters the door with his fists. 'Open the door,' he sobs. 'Anna . . . ' He batters against the splintering wood, not feeling the pain. The wooden latch jumps, shimmying free with each pounding.

Lesya hobbles to her mother. Her bad foot folds under her ankle and she falls against the soapbox cradle. Empty. 'What have you done?'

The door crashes open and Teodor is across the room in two strides; he overturns the table separating him from his sister. Anna doesn't flinch.

He grabs her by the collar and drags her to her feet. 'Why?' He wants to kill her, he wants her to feel what he feels. He drives her against the back wall. 'Why?' She doesn't struggle, she looks beyond him, unafraid. Teodor slams his fist into the wall beside her head and they both know there is nothing more he can do. 'Why?' he begs.

'She died,' Anna says, her voice small and grieved.

Teodor doesn't believe her. He searches her eyes, knowing it can't be true. Her eyes are calm, peaceful. He looks to Lesya. Blue-grey eyes. Frozen eyes, cracked ice, dripping sorrow. *Tell me*. Lesya looks to the ground. She does the only thing she can. She nods.

Teodor exhales a broken keen, his head drops

to Anna's breast, and he clings to her mantle, sobbing like a child. Anna strokes his hair. His cries fill her empty belly. *She died,* she tells herself. *She died the moment she was conceived.*

'Don't cry,' she tells him, just like she told her. 'She's safe now.'

Teodor pulls away, not wanting to be touched by the same hands that laid a child in a snowbank. He would have buried her. He would have made a coffin. She. She. She. A girl. Nameless. He backs away, stammering, 'I'm sorry.' Sorry for the baby, sorry for the little boy hiding in the corner, sorry for the little girl with the crooked foot hiding behind her hair. Sorry that he will never speak to his sister again.

'Don't look at me like that,' Anna challenges his burning eyes. Accusing. Judging. Condemning. 'Don't look at me!' Teodor walks out the door, picks up the gun, and heads into the night.

Anna follows him to the door. 'She died!' The shrill words sound hollow and unconvincing. She chases after him. 'She died!' She wants him to understand. She wants him to see that they're all just ghosts. 'She was already dead!'

But he keeps walking, leaving only his footprints to betray he once existed. Anna stops chasing him, knowing he's never coming back.

'It's my land.' She hurls the words. 'I want you off my land!'

★   ★   ★

Maria and Myron meet Teodor coming up from Anna's on the far side of the stone wall. Maria throws herself around him. She clings to him, praising all that is holy that her husband is all right. Teodor gently loosens her arms.

'You shouldn't be out here,' he tells her.

'I heard the shots. I heard a coyote. Did you kill it? Did it get away?' *Talk to me.*

Teodor hands the rifle to Myron. 'You should be in bed. We should all be in bed.'

Teodor leads them home. *Tch-tch-tch.*

'Did you find the rabbit?' Maria persists.

He takes six steps before answering, 'There was no rabbit.'

He doesn't speak again until they are about to go inside the house. 'Go on in,' he tells Myron. 'I want to talk to your mother.'

He walks to the twin boulders and sits down on the seat of snow. He looks up at the sky. Maria takes a seat beside him.

The same stars are shining down. The dog is still chained; the little bear is safe. The air smells the same. The fields look the same. It should all be different, he thinks.

'There was no rabbit . . . ' Teodor begins.

★ ★ ★

Mama is crying in bed. Tato is speaking low. The fire is burning too hot. Katya swallows down another piece of Christ. The hard, dry dough sticks to the roof of her mouth. She gags. Pushes it back in. Its hardness clumps in her stomach. She chips off another piece and forces it in. She won't stop until she has eaten every bit of him.

The temperature hovers just below freezing. The sun has shone hard and insistent for the last three days. Blue endless sky, blinding white fields. The rabbits are running; birds descend, scavenging seed; mice scramble over and under drifts; cats pad across the banks, their ears tuned to what's under the snow. All the life that has been hiding scurries into the world with a heady exuberance, an insatiable lust, to gorge and stockpile. Chickadees herald winter's short reprieve. *Come out, come out,* they call. *We're alive. We're alive.*

Dania drapes the trees with bedding. White sheets, freshly laundered, stiffen with frost. She dresses the world with a kaleidoscope of blankets, quilts, pillowcases, and linens: soft blue, salmon, and yellow mingle with vivid orange and red. She suspends the woven flowers and embroidered stars, deer, rabbits, and wheat sheaves like pages from a storybook. A perfect, sunny world. She breathes in the lemon-scented soap. She will never forget this smell.

Myron has been splitting wood. The pile tumbles around him, large and sprawling. The frozen logs shatter effortlessly. His coat is folded neatly to the side. He needs only a sweater to fend off the chill. He doesn't think where to place the log or strike the axe; his mind and hands perform automatically. He dances with the wood and the blade in perfect rhythm. The handle, polished by his and his father's hands, is warm in his grip. He sets the log on its end. His arms stretch upward, his strength pours from him through the handle into the blade, slamming into the heart of the wood. The vibration drives down through the log, a clean line erupts, and one piece falls open into two. He will never forget this sensation.

Ivan gathers the wood and stacks it by the door. Three cords are already piled as high as he can reach. He likes fitting the logs together, stacking them like a puzzle to make the tightest fit. He piles them straight, then gradually slopes them back to bear the weight. He mixes soft wood with hard, large logs with small. Each log displays its rings, telling him its age, its type, whether it rained too much one year, or not at all, if it was healthy or sick. Special wood, like a clean, unblemished white birch or lodgepole pine, he sets aside in a separate pile. They look like ordinary sticks of wood, but inside are birds and spoons, crosses and horses, waiting for his father to carve them free. Tato says the wood shows him what's inside. Sometimes Ivan thinks he sees an eagle's beak, a horse's mane, a dog's head, a dragonfly, an old man's hand. He will always remember to look for what is hidden.

Sofia has shovelled proper paths leading from their door to the new barn, to the outhouse, to the twin boulders, and back around the house. The little roads curve and veer across the flatness, cutting through the snow. She walks the paths, loving the sound of her boots crunching on the hard-packed trail. Her skirt swishes daintily, untouched by the mess of snow. Her stockings are dry. Her gloved hands trail over the banks, as though she is a fine lady strolling through a garden of white lilies. She will never forget the sensation of a wet, sticky snowball spattering the back of her head or the sound of her little sister's gales of laughter as she chases her through the paths until they explode off the trails in a powdery cloud.

Katya will never forget how round and perfect the snowball was as it arced from her mitten, sailed through the air, and found its mark. A glorious accident, her first perfect throw. She will never forget the taste of the snow, its coldness slithering down her back, its softness as they tumble through it. How it sticks to their coats and stockings, hats and mitts, clumps in their hair, trickles down their collars. She'll never forget lying on their backs begging each other to stop. And the quietness of being held by the snow, as they closed their eyes to the sun. Their faces warm, their backs cold. Their fingers covertly rolling another snowball.

They are all trying to forget their father, who hasn't come outside the last three days. He is sitting in front of the window. Unmoving. Transfixed on a spot somewhere beyond them, down the hill, at the stone wall. He stood when Myron went to check the snares. He didn't sit again until he saw his son trudging back up the hill. Myron victoriously held up a rabbit for his father's approval, but Teodor was no longer watching.

Myron didn't question him about the coyote tracks on the other side of the wall, or his father's tracks, steady approaching the wall, then breaking into a full run, falling, then staggering down the hill to his sister's house. Or the rabbit-pelt blanket he remembers his mother making that he found trampled amid the tracks. Or the drag marks. He pushed the pelt under the snow with his toe and brushed away the tracks.

Maria and Teodor haven't spoken since that night. Too much was said that night. They can't find the words to start again. When she finally found the strength to enter the house, she stood in the middle of the room, unable to comfort her children. She knew the sight of them would release the tears and she would tell them everything. No child should know such things.

In the past three days, she has bottled two dozen jars of borshch and sauerkraut; rolled countless holubtsi, using up three of her soured cabbage heads and four cups of rice; baked buckwheat rolls; and braised a rabbit. Each meal is a grander feast. The children eat hesitantly, not asking for seconds, worried by their mother's sudden abandonment of restraint.

She doesn't let the children help. She doesn't look them in the eye. She doesn't hold them, or touch them. She consumes herself with her recipes, chopping and stirring, frying and baking. She empties her mind. She cooks from early morning to late at night. She washes the cast-iron pots and scours them in boiling water, unable to get them clean. Her hands are red and chapped. She hasn't prayed. She hasn't sent any baskets down the hill. She doesn't allow herself to think about them. She is out of milk and eggs. She crosses from her mind recipes that require milk and eggs and scrubs the pots harder.

Teodor sits with a stillness learned in prison. If he sits quiet enough, long enough, he can make himself disappear. Empty his mind, no more thoughts. He can become a rock, the dirt floor, a log, the snow. He can just exist and not feel.

He gets up, startling Maria, who steps aside not knowing which way to turn. He crosses to her side of the room, slides aside the picture, retrieves the jug, and pours himself a drink. He feels her eyes watching his hand. He hammers the drink back, lets it burn his mouth, sear his insides, clean his brain. It churns in his stomach, gags in his throat. He stoppers the jug, puts it back in the wall, returns to his chair, and waits for it to dull the ache.

He should get up and check the horse, cut the fence poles for the new paddock, clear another acre of bush, get ready for the spring, finish the barn, build a granary, sharpen the tools . . . there is so much he could do if he was still alive.

A snowball hits the window with a thud, splays wide and trickles down the pane. Teodor looks at the dissolving shape, trying to understand what has broken. Maria marches to the window, her mother instincts rearing up. They look outside and see a circus of snow children, laughing faces, ducking and running, dodging a snowball ambush. They see their children. Still innocent. Still alive.

Ivan pats another snowball in his mittened

hands, waves at them to come out, ducking too late to evade Myron's perfect aim.

Maria places her hand on Teodor's shoulder. It's time for them to go outside.

★ ★ ★

Lesya shovels the chicken shit from the coop. She doesn't speak to the two hens. She doesn't dally. She does her job, briskly and efficiently. She changes their water, tops up their feed, reaches under their warm, fat bodies, retrieves the eggs, and sets them in the pail. She looks at the empty roost. The straw has been brushed away, revealing the chipped, faded advertisement of the smiling chin and the hand holding a cake of soap. A hard white lump of dung mars the model's perfect teeth.

Lesya recognizes the soap. It's the same soap that Aunt Maria gave them. Half a bar, anyway. It's the soap her mother has been washing herself with. She's had two baths a day since that night. With each use, the bar of soap diminishes. The edges round and soften. Now it is the size and shape of a pale grey egg. Soon it will crack and break apart and there will be nothing inside.

Her mother has been cleaning everything. She's changed the bedding, swept the floor, scrubbed the table, washed all the dishes, mended clothes, and burned the ones that were stained. She's rearranged the shelves, folded and packed away the summer clothes. She's cleaned up everything except the soapbox sitting in the middle of the floor.

Lesya gathers up an armload of clean straw and spreads it over the roost. She forms a deep nest and sets the two eggs inside. *Happiness . . .* she calls.

Happiness . . . she sings, her voice chokes, knowing it won't come.

★ ★ ★

Petro stands on the edge of the road, looking across the field toward town. At first, he planned to make another attempt to find his tato, but his feet stopped when he reached the road. He took a few steps forward and couldn't go farther, like his ankles were shackled. A part of him afraid to leave, another part afraid to stay. What if he went searching and while he was gone his tato came back? What if they passed each other coming and going, going and coming? What if he veered too far east or too far west? They would never find each other. Petro kicks at the snow.

He remembers how far he walked the last time. The snow never ended. He never saw the town. His father wasn't following the road, maybe he wasn't going to town. Maybe Tato was looking at something else when he used to stand here. Petro scans the fields but sees just a grey curtain of clouds rolling in from the east.

If he goes, who would chop the wood? Not his mother. And Lesya isn't strong enough. He spits twice, like his father. The second spit sticks to his lip and dribbles down his chin. He wipes it away with the back of his mitten.

He misses Lesya the most. She doesn't talk

any more since her hen ran away. The same night the baby ran away. Petro wants to believe that his uncle stole the baby. He broke down the door and took it like he took the horse. But he knows the baby was gone before his uncle arrived. He saw his mama carrying it outside. Poor little mouse.

Petro thinks the hen was found by someone who knew it could dance. Now it's wearing a fancy dress and hat, performing for rich people in a travelling show. Maybe the baby is with it. The World's Largest Tailless Mouse and the Amazing Dancing Chicken. He looks across the field. He could go find Tato, the hen, and the baby, and bring them all home. Be a family, like the family on the hill. On their hill.

If Teodor was gone, like Tato said, everything would be better. Everything would be theirs. The wheat, the house, the money. They could live in the house on the hill and have their own rooms. There'd be nobody to make him feel the way his uncle made him feel the night the baby ran away. That same feeling when the teacher slaps his wrists with the switch for speaking Ukrainian. Or when the town boys laugh at his clothes, or the little blond girl refuses to sit beside him because she says he smells. It makes him want to cry. It makes him want to kill something.

If Teodor was gone, Tato would come back. He'd brush Mama's hair and make her laugh. Her hair would grow long and beautiful again. She'd dress up in fine clothes and Tato would be proud to be with such a lady. And Mama would tell Tato how much their boy had helped while he was gone. She'd show him the stack of wood that he cut all by himself. They'd ask to see his muscles and they'd notice how he's outgrown his pants. How his trouser hems dangle above his ankles. Lesya would talk again. She'd tell him stories and hold him until he fell asleep and her hen would dance on the foot of the bed. And the baby . . . the baby wouldn't cry.

Petro's first instinct is to run into the bush and hide when he sees the police car lumbering toward him, veering slowly through the wagon ruts, spewing black smoke from its tail, its engine growling. But he doesn't run. He stands there like he just happened to be walking down the road. He holds up his hand and waves them down, like old friends, just like his father.

The car rolls to a stop. Petro shifts his weight to his left foot and slides his hand deep into his pocket as the window lowers.

★ ★ ★

Ivan shifts the basket from one arm to the other. He leans backward, balancing the weight. Mama said he's not to talk to anyone. He's to set the basket on the stoop and leave. She waited until Tato and Myron were in the barn and she could hear them busy hammering. She sent Sofia and Katya to collect twigs for kindling and Dania for water. Then she told him the basket was for Lesya and Petro. She said it was their secret, he wasn't to mention it even to Tato or he wouldn't be allowed to go again.

Ivan is thrilled that he has been entrusted with

such a special job. He's worried, too; he's never had to keep a secret from Tato. Maybe he'll get to see Petro. A surge of excitement quickens his pace. He wants to show him his new mittens, and the mice holes in the snow, and the hollow tree you can sit inside, and the red berries that will make you sick, and the tree that tastes sweet when you peel back its bark. But then he remembers he's not allowed to talk to him.

He sucks solemnly on his last butterscotch candy. It coats his tongue but doesn't bring him any joy. Today it seems sticky and thick. Ivan glances up at the grey, swollen sky. A light wind is building from the northeast. Tato says it's going to snow. He's been watching the crows all morning. They are sitting in the fields, not moving. Tato says it's a sign of bad weather, when the birds are afraid of the sky.

Ivan looks down at the grey house, grey barn, grey posts. Even the smoke coming from the chimney is grey. His arms ache where the handle cuts into his forearms. He plops the basket on the snow; it's heavier now than when he left. He peeks under the cloth: jars of borshch and sauerkraut and half a loaf of bread. He grabs the handle and drags the basket behind him like a sled. He's almost halfway there. He can't see anyone outside. The thought that they can see him coming when he can't see them worries him.

What if they're still mad at him? It was his fault that Tato hit Uncle Stefan and Myron fired the gun, his fault that everybody is fighting. Maybe Mama's sending him to Petro's house because that's where he is going to have to live from now on and that's why it's a secret. It's his punishment for making everyone not allowed to talk. Maybe he can tell them he's sorry. But then he would have to speak.

Ivan heaves the basket onto the stone wall. He crawls over the rocks and jumps down on the other side. He hauls the basket over; it drops heavily to the ground. He is startled to find Petro sitting against the wall. His cousin glances at him, then looks away. Maybe this is part of the secret; Petro has been sent to meet him, but Mama said to put the basket on the stoop. She didn't say Petro would be waiting for him. Ivan slides the basket over the snow and sits beside his cousin.

He is glad to see that Petro is wearing his socks and mittens and hat. The boys stare out over the field dotted with crows. The bellies of the clouds are a threatening black. Ivan rolls the butterscotch over his tongue, glances at his cousin. He looks tired and sad. Ivan spits the candy into his mitten and offers it to Petro. Petro looks at the glistening, smooth buttery ball in Ivan's palm and reaches for it. The candy sticks to their mittens and for a moment they are attached, before it pulls away, stuck to Petro's mittened palm. Petro licks it, then puts it in his mouth. He sucks on it, rolling the sweet candy from cheek to cheek, his tongue smoothing away the woollen fuzz.

Ivan brushes away the snow and loosens a stone. He tosses it toward the crows. One lifts, then settles again. The others ignore the disruption. He finds another pebble. Stands up and takes aim. The rock skitters over the drifts and ricochets among the flock. The birds flutter upward, a jumble of wings and beaks, then land again. Ivan scratches at the snow and finds a flat, grey stone perfect for skipping. He hands it to Petro.

The boys scour the base of the wall, filling their hands with small rocks. Then, side by side, they fling their mittfuls. The stones hail down, peppering the crows. The birds screech and swirl upward. Some grab at the stones as if they were seed, catching them mid-air then letting them plummet. They circle between the snow and the clouds.

Ivan notices Petro reach into his pocket. He sees a sparkling glint of metal. A round, large coin . . . a quarter. Before he can ask him where he got it, Petro hurls the coin skyward.

Dania is in charge today. Maria and Teodor have gone to visit the Petrenkos. Old Man Petrenko is turning seventy today, which makes him the oldest man in the area. His son, Josyp, invited the entire congregation to celebrate. Rumour has it that he butchered a pig for the occasion. Maria was afraid they would get caught in the storm, but Teodor assured her it would be night before it reached them; besides, he wouldn't insult his neighbour by not making an appearance.

The children watched their parents get dressed for the event. Dania pressed her father's pants and shirt. She gave the black trousers an extra-crisp crease. Myron polished his father's boots, unable to hide all the cracks and ripples marring the leather. Teodor smeared his hair with pomade and allowed Ivan to do the same to his. Ivan pressed his shiny, wet-looking hair tight against his cheeks, then twirled the ends into cowlicks.

Maria wore her embroidered shirt with the red sash and her long grey woollen skirt. Sofia braided her mother's hair, then coiled it into two tight buns on either side of her head. Maria said she had never had such perfect braids. Katya buckled her mama's shoes and pulled her stockings up tight. She took her mama's belly in her hands and kissed the baby goodbye. Dania packed the two jars of chokecherry jam and the babka bread that Maria had made for the occasion. Two little dough birds perched on top of the braided loaf seemed about to take flight. Teodor winked and suggested taking some 'honey medicine' for Old Man Petrenko, but Maria vetoed the idea. She said they would be home before dinner.

The children watched as their father gave his hand to their mother and guided her onto the flatbed sled he had recently made. It was designed to haul logs, but today it would serve as their sleigh. He gallantly draped a blanket over Maria's legs and with a snap of the reins, the horse cantered away. The children sit quietly in the wake of their parents' happiness. Their absence somehow makes them feel closer. They can smell the soap they scrubbed their hands and faces with, the shoe polish and shaving cream. They notice the half a cigarette Teodor butted and Maria's apron draped over the chair, as though they were coming back at any moment. A thin dust of flour coats the corner of the table where she rolled the dough. The children don't feel the urge to test their new freedom; there is no giddy excitement to race outside and explore forbidden boundaries. They feel the need to stay close to home.

It is Katya who asks Sophia to tell them a story. Without much coaxing, she complies. She loves the English stories about poor servant girls, fairy godmothers, sleeping princesses, pumpkin chariots, and happy endings. English stories aren't about working hard, being good to animals, taking care of one another, and that the lazy get punished. English stories are about riches and gold and being more than you are.

Dania lets them sit on their parents' bed, close to the fire. Ivan and Katya curl up against the pillows. Katya takes Mama's side and Ivan Tato's. Katya eyes the wood stove, but all is calm since she started praying to the fire. She quickly recites the prayer in her head to keep it happy. *Our Father, who art in Fire, hallowed be Thy name, Thy kingdom come, Thy will be done on earth as it is in Fire. Give us our bread our daily bread and forgive us for trespassing.*

Myron, who pretends he's not interested in stories, takes down the gun to oil, even though he cleaned it two nights ago. And Dania, who should fetch water, decides to peel potatoes.

Sofia plays to her audience. Her eyes shine at the exciting parts, her voice drops low for suspense, her hands draw the scene. She walks around the room, transforming herself into the princess, the servant, the wicked stepmother. A spoon becomes a wand. A bowl a helmet. A broom a sword. She enchants them.

A knock on the door breaks the spell. Dania holds a potato in midair, half the peel dangling down. Sofia stands with her hand upraised about to turn a prince into a frog. Ivan and Katya lie still in the bed. They listen. Myron, who is closest to the window, looks out and sees two scarlet tunics. He ducks back down and jams the bolt into the gun. He waves Sofia over to the bed. Another knock.

'Open up,' a gruff voice orders. 'Police.'

Dania puts down the potato.

'No,' Myron whispers.

'Open it or we'll break it down,' the voice commands.

Dania silences Myron with a look. 'I'm coming.' She forgets the English words. She wipes her hands on her apron and releases the latch, opens the door a crack. The door fills with red and shining buttons. A man with a walrus moustache braces his hand against the door. The other man, shorter and younger, with sharper eyes, asks, 'Where's your father?'

'They no here. All gone,' Dania stammers, searching for the words.

The man with the walrus moustache cases the room, taking in the children huddled on the bed. They are thin, with the wide, sunken eyes of the malnourished. Their clothes are dingy. The shack smells musty and reeks of garlic and lye. A small boy with greased hair glances to the corner and quickly lowers his eyes. A young girl in a too-short skirt and stained blouse, with a bowl on her head and a spoon in her hand, stands as if in detention.

The moustached officer looks at his partner and deftly unfastens his holster. He rests his hand on the butt of his revolver. 'We need to look around. Step back from the door.'

Dania glances to Myron, who is squatting with the .22 across his lap. The moustached officer kicks open the door as he draws his weapon and swings around the corner.

'Drop it!' he yells, his gun trained on Myron's

chest, his eyes on the .22. Myron doesn't move.

'It's just a kid,' the other one calms. 'Put it down, if you don't want to lose it, boy.' Myron hesitates; the .22 hangs loose in his hand. He sees only the end of the police officer's barrel.

'Now!' barks the moustache man, his finger tight on the trigger.

'Put it down!' Dania orders. Myron lowers his eyes and lays the gun on the floor, careful not to spook the man.

'Get over there.' Moustache man waves his gun toward the bed. Myron moves slowly, not turning his back.

The younger officer checks the chamber. 'It's empty.' He leans the rifle against the wall.

'They back at supper. You come then.' Dania motions them to leave. 'No nothing here.'

The walrus officer holsters his gun. He walks to the bed and looks down at the children clinging to one another like a litter of mice. He goes directly to the picture of the Virgin Mary and stands before it. The children think he might be praying. He lifts the edge of the frame and slides it aside, exposing the niche. He reaches in and extracts the half-gallon jug, pulls the cork and takes a whiff. He stoppers the jug with his fingers and inverts it, touches his fingers to his lips. He nods to the other officer.

'Tell your father he has tonight to get his things in order. We'll be back in the morning for him.' And with that they are gone.

The children stare at the Virgin, unsure if they've just witnessed a miracle.

★   ★   ★

The snow started falling before dusk in large, wet, fluffy flakes. Already the trees and house are frosted in a thick, white coat. The wind has picked up quickly, driving the snow at a sharp, hard angle, slashing the north side of the buildings and trees, quickly erasing the indiscretion of their footprints.

One lamp flickers on the table, illuminating the solemn faces staring at their untouched plates. The potatoes cool, the ham congeals.

'Eat,' Maria commands.

Another year. That's what Mama said. Tato has to go away for another year.

The children force in a spoonful; it wads tasteless in their mouths. Katya spits her potatoes back out. Sofia sniffles inconsolably.

'That's enough,' Maria reprimands her. 'Wipe your nose.' Sofia drags her sleeve across her face.

Myron forces another forkful into his mouth; he chews on the stringy meat, unable to swallow. Ivan can't take his eyes off the Virgin. Her bleeding heart, her downcast eyes. *Liar*.

Teodor and Maria arrived home, their cheeks flush, their eyes laughing, brushing snow from each other's hair. As soon as Maria saw her children's faces, she knew something terrible had happened, felt it crush against her chest. Her eyes searched them out one by one, making sure they were all alive, fingers and toes attached. Nothing in the house seemed out of place. Yet everything was wrong. Dania sent the children outside.

Sitting on the stoop, the snow sticking to their eyelashes, grabbing at their hair and shoulders, the children sat as still and black as the crows in the field. They heard their father's voice roar, heard words they are never supposed to say, heard their mother's panicked voice trying to soothe, the mumble of reason, shouts tearing throats, 'Goddamned bitch, goddamned bitch . . . '

And their mama: 'You don't know it was her.'

'She's the only one who knew it was there! She saw it when I built it!' The words slurred in spit. Ripping through the walls.

The door swung open and they scattered to avoid their father's feet as he stormed to the barn. He is still there.

Myron was sent to fetch him for dinner. He found his father pacing back and forth from stall to stall, counting the steps. The horse was backed into a corner, spooked by Teodor's intensity.

'Tato?' Myron dared, his voice small. 'Dinner is ready.' Teodor didn't falter. He walked five paces and turned, his mind locked in its own cage.

'Tato,' Myron demanded, surprised by the anger in his voice. Teodor stopped, turned to him with eyes blazing. 'Are you coming back?'

He meant to say, *Are you coming in?*

Teodor looked at his eldest son, his arms and legs too long for his growing body. The pants hiked above his boots, his woollen coat strangling his shoulders. He saw the clenched jaw and frightened eyes. A man's eyes in a child's body. He saw the boy's chest rising and falling, his nostrils flaring, struggling to appear calm. He tried to imagine him completely grown. He would stand taller than him. Maybe his thick brown hair will grey prematurely, just on the sides. He will be long and lean. He will always walk with that loose gait of a man who feels every step of the earth beneath his feet. He will always prefer to be alone. He will always be a farmer. Dirt is his blood.

He looked to the horse, its ears back, its eyes wide, and when he reached for its nose, it thrust its head back, not trusting his touch. He looked up at the roof, to the logs' hewn marks, each one his mark. He heard the wind buffeting the walls and it pleased him that the walls were strong. He held his hand out to the horse again, his fingers open, an invitation. The horse eyed him suspiciously, smelled his hand. The same man. The animal rested its chin in his palm. Teodor brushed the long mane from its eyes. Nodded, as if answering the animal's question.

'You have to make sure to get him new shoes in the spring. Don't let the mud build up in his hooves.' He picked up the horse brush.

'I'll be in soon,' he told his son. 'I have to get ready.' Myron left him brushing the horse in long, slow sweeps as he whispered in its ear.

The family turns to the sound of Teodor's footsteps on the stoop, casually stomping off the snow. He enters, takes off his coat, and drapes it over the rifle propped against the wall. He sits down at the table, as though it is any other night. Maria hurries to retrieve his plate warming on the stove. He fills his spoon with steaming potatoes and takes a bite.

'Pass the butter,' he asks Sofia, her eyes red and swollen. 'Eat.' He proceeds to clean his plate. The family, one by one, takes a bite.

At bedtime, each child insists on a hug. He holds them longer and tighter. He tells Ivan to listen to his mother and learn from his brother. He tells him to look for a tree down at the dump that has the face of a fox hidden inside. He tells Katya that her dreams won't hurt her and when she's scared she should remember the snakes and how she drove them away. He tells Sofia to keep telling her stories and practising her English. He tells her that he thinks her curled ringlets are very pretty and that she shouldn't be afraid to show people who she really is. He tells Dania not to be afraid to dance and to hold her head high. He assures her that she will be a very good mother and that she shouldn't be afraid to leave. He shakes Myron's hand. He tells him: 'You'll know what you have to do.' He waves a farmer's goodbye.

After the lamp has been blown out and the children are sleeping restlessly, he and Maria lie in bed. He rubs her belly, breathes in her hair. She tells him: 'We'll be here, we'll be waiting. We'll be all right.'

When she can no longer convince herself, she proposes that they run, pack up what they can carry and leave now. Go south, where it's warmer and the land is flat and thick with rich, fertile soil. No stones. Or go east — leave this place, don't look back. The wind whistles over the house. They are trapped. Trapped in this godforsaken wasteland.

She swallows the bile in her throat, quells the urge to scream, to pound him with her fists, to blame him for tearing their family apart again. She doesn't want this to be what she remembers tonight. He'll only be gone a year. One year. That's nothing in the scheme of their whole lives. She holds him tight, memorizing his smell, the contour of his body, the size of his hands, the sound of his heartbeat.

Teodor stares out the window at the world lost in a blizzard, swallowing them alive.

★   ★   ★

Papa . . .

Teodor is awake. 'Shhh . . . ' He motions his son to be quiet, Mama is asleep.

'I have to pee.' Ivan rubs the sleep from his eyes. The house creaks from the force of the storm outside. Teodor slips from Maria's hold. He is still fully dressed.

He helps Ivan into his boots, doesn't bother to lace them. The half-asleep child rests his head on Teodor's shoulder. He helps Ivan into his coat.

'Where are you going?' Maria calls.

'I have to pee,' Ivan answers grumpily, not wanting to be awake.

'Go back to sleep,' Teodor gently assures his wife. She looks at him uncertainly, not knowing why she is nervous. Teodor attempts a smile. 'We'll be right back.' He takes Ivan's hand. He doesn't bother putting on his coat.

The snow is driving sideways. Ivan presses against his father's leg. They round the corner of the house and are lashed by the wind. They duck back behind the shelter of the building. 'How about here?' Teodor suggests.

Ivan hoists his nightshirt. Snowflakes tickle his ankles. Modestly, he turns his back to his father. He pees lazily. A hot, steady stream. Teodor looks the other way, into the white, driving fury. The trees bend and sway, groan under the crush of snow. The wind howls.

'I'm finished.' Ivan yawns.

Teodor rubs his head. 'Back to bed.'

He opens the door and takes off Ivan's boots, hangs up his coat. Ivan shuffles back to his room. 'Ivan . . . ' Teodor calls after him. But Ivan doesn't hear.

Teodor stands at the doorway, waits until he hears the creak of his son crawling back in bed. The house is dark, but with his eyes shut he can see every child, every log, the blanket on the wall, the washbasin, shelves laden with preserves . . . Maria. They are safe here. He picks his jacket up from the floor.

'Teodor?' Maria's voice wavers. She sees him as a shadow across the room.

'I have to check the horse.' He clutches his coat in front of him. 'It's bad out there.' He slips out the door.

Maria jumps from the bed and runs to the window. She sees him heading toward the barn, not putting on his jacket. Then the snow devours him and he is lost from her view.

★　★　★

Teodor unwraps the .22 from his jacket and puts on his coat. There are two bullets in his pocket. He loads one.

If you ask them what happened that night, Maria will say her husband said he was going to the barn to check the horse. She waited for him to come back and when he didn't, she went looking for him. The storm was at its peak, and she could barely open the barn door. When she saw he wasn't there, she ran back to the house and woke her eldest son. That's when she realized the .22 wasn't hanging over the door and that he must have taken it earlier and hidden it in the barn. Ask her if she knew where he was going and what he was going to do, and she will refuse to answer, saying only that he was a good man.

Myron will say that he was woken by his frantic mother, asking, 'Where's the gun?' He told her it was by the door, leaning against the wall. When she said it wasn't there and they had to find his father, he knew. He knew where his father was going and what he was going to do. If pressed to answer how he knew, he will reluctantly answer, 'My aunt turned him in.'

Myron will say that he tried to stop him. He ran as hard and fast as he could. But the wind was screaming and the snow was blinding and he couldn't find the stone wall. Everything was black and white. The snow kept swallowing him, pulling him down. He hollered, *Tato! Tato! Tato!* But his voice was drowned by the shrieking gale. And then he heard the shot. One shot. He couldn't tell from what direction. But he knew.

The girls didn't wake until first light. The fire had gone out and they were shivering in their bed. The house was quiet. They couldn't hear their tato stirring his coffee or smell his morning cigarette. They didn't hear their mama preparing breakfast or smell bread baking in the stove. They found her sitting at the window, staring out at the sorrowing prairies. When they asked her, 'What's wrong?' she told them to get on their knees and pray. Pray for their father. Pray for his soul.

Katya will say that she tried to pray, but the fire was out. She looked inside the stove and there were only ashes. Cold and grey. She will say the fire took her tato. It was only pretending not to be hungry.

Ivan didn't see a gun, he remembered going to pee. The wind tried to take him away. His tato held his hand and told him to go back to bed. He didn't say anything else.

Lesya will say she was asleep and there was a crack — like thunder. The window shattered and wind and snow shot into the house. Her mother, who was standing at the window, exhaled, looked down at her chest, and sank to the floor.

Petro will say he knew his uncle would come and kill them. He said that he'd be back to kill them all. No one will understand him when he says the crows took the quarter and that he can't take it back. He didn't mean to see the secret in the wall, but Ivan stole his hat. He didn't see Teodor, but he heard him crash through the window, a wild dog that tore out his mother's heart. He will ask over and over when his tato is coming to get him.

If Anna could tell you, she would say that she couldn't sleep because of the wailing storm. It sounded like a baby crying. She had the lamp burning because she didn't want to be alone in the dark. She doesn't know what made her look outside, maybe the snow hitting the window, like fingers tapping. She rubbed the ice from the pane and through the wind and snow's frenzied dance she thought she saw her brother.

He was standing in the storm, looking at her, and it scared her. She thought he was a ghost, a forerunner, and that something terrible had happened. But then she noticed the snow accumulating on his shoulders, on his hair, and drifting over his boots, and she knew that he was real. She lifted her hand to tell him to come in. Come in out of the storm.

The window cracked and the wind whistled through a perfect round hole in the glass. And she felt warmth spilling over her heart. When she looked down, blood was blossoming on her chest and her lungs were gurgling. And she had to sit down, because it was snowing inside and the wind was carrying her away. And the coyotes were howling.

Teodor would have said that he saw his sister come to the window. She looked at him and smiled. Smiled as if none of it mattered. He pulled the trigger. He didn't hear it fire. He didn't hear the children screaming. He saw red on her white shirt. He saw the question in her eyes. Like she didn't know why.

He saw her shudder and crumple.

★   ★   ★

When Teodor stops running, he is no longer a man. He has outrun himself. His legs quiver, muscles taut. His chest heaves. He pants wildly. He has followed the tracks of the others like him — into the woods, toward the water, under branches, into the deep smell of spruce, to the place of quiet. Here, the snow is packed down from their sleeping bodies. Smooth hollows. The storm roars around him, but he no longer hears the wind.

He takes off his leather jacket, his numb hands paw at the zipper, and he sheds the unfamiliar skin stinking of sweat and fear. He stares at the remains of the man and can't imagine it was ever him. He neatly folds the skin, crossing its arms over its chest. He places the man in the crook of two twisted trees. He removes his boots, clawing at the strings caked with snow and ice; he slips off his heavy feet. The soles are rough, the tops creased and scuffed. He tucks the shoelaces inside and places the feet side by side on top of the man.

He kneels down. He puts the gun under his chin and looks up.

He has never seen such

snow.

Spring

—⁂—

1939

The morning smells mud-green. Barn swallows dart in and out of the rafters. The horse stands patiently hitched to the cart, flicking away flies with its tail. The stove is lashed down. Bed frames dismantled. Blanket boxes, crammed with clothes and linen, are piled atop the inverted table. Chairs and benches are stacked. Two rolled mattresses are slung over the sides. A barrel holds a jumble of pots and dishes and the last few jars of borshch and sauerkraut. Tools, tack, rabbit pelts, and a deer hide are stuffed along the sideboards. The .22 is tucked under the bench.

Hidden deep within the everyday are their secret stashes. Nestled in a pail crammed with mittens and scarves is Ivan's WINCHESTER box containing a rabbit skull, a penny, a broken pocket watch, a wasp's nest, a rock shaped like an egg, and his father's pocketknife.

In the bottom of Katya's blanket box is a pressed wild rose, a carved wren whittled from birch, one lemon candy, and her tato's tobacco pouch, which holds a partially smoked, hand-rolled cigarette and a burned wooden match.

Between the pages of Sofia's English primer are two front-page newspaper clippings. *Woman Is Slain. Famed Dog to Assist Mounties in Search for Farmer as Sister Killed*. A half-page photo of a grinning German shepherd — 'Dale

417

of Cawsalta' — accompanies the story. The second reads: *Suicide Following Murder — Dual Tragedy in Land Ownership Dispute*. It is offset by a grainy photograph of a window and a moustached officer pointing to a single bullet hole.

In a coffee can, Dania has packed recipes jotted on brown paper wrapping — one in her father's hand, for *Wheat Wine* — a thimble carved from poplar, a half a skein of red wool, one dollar and seven cents she earned laundering hotel bedsheets, and a pair of her father's socks with the heels worn out. Wrapped in his handkerchief is a small handful of rich black earth.

Myron doesn't have a secret stash. His possessions are out in the open. His father's tools. Sharpened and oiled. The handles worn smooth. Each one marked with the initials T. M.

Between the folds of her linen, Maria has layered in seed packets, the picture of the Blessed Virgin, two wedding bands, a lock of Teodor's salt-and-pepper hair, and her carved cross. Her mother's Bible is there too, the pages loose in their binding. The cover page is scrawled with names and dates reaching back a hundred years. The most recent additions are written in Maria's careful, ornate hand.

Maria choma b. 1907 wife of Teodor Mykolayenko b. 1905.

Children:
Dania b. June 17, 1924

Myron b. August 31, 1925
Sofia b. May 4, 1927
Katya b. November 26, 1931
Ivan b. January 19, 1933
Maxim b. March 14, 1939

The last entry, written in loose, careless script with a wide pencil stub, reads:

Teodor Mykolayenko, died December 17, 1938, of the flu

Of the flu is heavier. The letters have been traced several times to make it true.

Marking the page is a black and white photograph taken six years ago by a travelling photographer. They are standing in front of a granary on their first farm. They couldn't afford the ten-cent fee, but Teodor traded three carved birds and two smokes.

They dressed in their best Canadian clothes and pretended there wasn't snow on the ground. It was the first time Myron wore a tie. He didn't tell his father that the knot was too tight. Ivan, still a baby, wouldn't stop squirming. Sofia cried, because her dress didn't fit and her hair had been cut short a few months earlier to get rid of the lice.

When Teodor crossed his legs to pose, that's when Maria learned that he had also traded his socks. The spring chill leached through their summer clothes as they sat unmoving. They looked into the black eye of the camera and held their breath until the photographer said, 'Breathe.'

It is their only photograph. Maria has studied the image a thousand times, searching his eyes. But there is no hint. No tell of what will come. In the moment between 'Breathe' and the children swarming the camera, Teodor turned to her. He was smiling. His eyes glistened. And she saw such pride.

Myron hoists Katya onto the cart. Sofia clambers over the wheels and perches herself on one of the lashed-down chairs. Dania, cradling Maxim, tucks in between the stovepipe and a blanket box. A month old, the baby is fast asleep, oblivious to the life he is leaving. A brown birthmark, like a pawprint, marks the top of his right hand. Ivan hops onto the backboard of the cart. He holds on to the twine lashing down their hill of belongings. His legs, too long for his trousers, dangle over the edge, exposing bare shins.

The children look to their mother.

Maria stands in the doorway of the empty house. She memorizes its smell, its shape, the way it looked when it was full of life. She notices how well built the frame is, how strong the timbers. She sees the clean, sharp lines etched by the hand planer, the sure, deep cuts of the saw and axe. This house would have stood a lifetime.

But this is not the time for goodbyes. Those have happened already. They happened when they took her and the children into the woods to identify the body. His face had been covered with a piece of burlap. The heels of his socks needed darning. The .22 still in his hands. Perched in the fork of two twisted trees, his coat neatly folded, boots resting on top.

She said goodbye when they carried her husband's frozen body into the house. He was curled up as though he were bowing. They laid him on the table. She washed him, put on a clean shirt. Waited for him to thaw to straighten his legs. He never fully uncurled. They buried him on his side in a wooden crate.

She said goodbye when the police, field agents, medical examiner, witnesses, and newspapermen streamed in and out of their house and Anna's for three consecutive days, as if they were no longer there.

She said goodbye as she watched from a distance as they buried Anna on newly consecrated land, on the edge of the north quarter. Half the town came to pay their respects to a woman they never met. They erected a solitary wooden cross, a name, dates, nothing more, paid for by Josyp Petrenko. They wrote her name in English. They spelled it wrong.

She said goodbye to Lesya and Petro as best she could. She went to the neighbours and pleaded through closed doors. She made the trek to town, ignored the stares and slurs. She got down on her knees, kissed the hem of the priest's robe. Told him that Lesya was a hard worker, a good girl who could clean and cook, and was blessed with a voice from heaven. She said Petro was strong and could keep the church stove burning. She pleaded with him not to let Children's Services take them, that they needed God's protection. But it was Anna's silver hairbrush and mirror that swayed the priest to take the girl. Not the boy.

It was Josyp Petrenko who offered to take Petro in as a farmhand. He also took the cow, Lesya's hens, and the store of seed grain. She watched from the other side of the stone wall as the children were taken away. Neither had a proper winter coat.

She even said goodbye to Stefan, though nobody knew where he was.

She said goodbye again when they refused to grant her the land in her husband's name and told her she would have to leave in the spring.

She said goodbye yesterday as she cleared away the thistle choking Teodor's unmarked grave, just outside of the cemetery's holy land, condemned even in death. Brother and sister still separated by a fence.

She has said a lifetime of goodbyes.

Maria props open the door with a large rock to let the souls wander in and out. *I give it back.*

She looks to her children, who are watching her, waiting for a sign that everything will be all right. Her low heels sink into the mud. She looks down over the field, past the matted thatches of winter grass and wildflower sprays of purple, white, and blue to the black tilled soil. Its furrows already softened and collapsing. Prairie fireweed beginning to heal its scorched wounds. Soon the wild grasses will reclaim the soil and all that will remain will be the stone wall. A pile of rocks that kept nothing in and nothing out. She looks no further.

She kneels down beside the stoop and for a moment the children think she is going to pray.

Instead, she takes hold of a large rock nestled against the riser and struggles to push it aside. Myron steps forward, uncertain whether he should offer to help.

The hem of his mother's long skirt wicks the dew from the grass. He can see wisps of grey, like fine threads woven through her dark hair, escaping the tight binding of her red khustyna. Her waist is larger, her arms fleshier. Her hands dry and chapped. Large, strong hands. The nails, short and chipped, permanently stained with earth. A pale indent brands her ring finger. The rock rolls away.

Maria looks to her children, watching impassively, no longer surprised by secrets. She scans the empty horizon, then pries away the barn board propped against the side of the stoop. She looks up at Myron. He crouches down and peers under the step. He looks to his mother. Her eyes betray nothing.

He drags out a bundle swathed in his mother's soiled blanket. Maria unwraps the faded woollen cloth, exposing a bulging burlap sack. She checks for mouse holes. No rot, no dampness. She unties the twine binding and opens the bag. The smell is dry and sweet. The seeds of grain are golden. For the first time since that night, she feels as though she might cry.

She stands brusquely. 'Put it up front with the .22.'

Maybe someday his mother will tell him how she covered her tracks following the tangle of men's bootprints into the moonless night and how still the horse stood at the stone wall as she went ahead. Maybe someday she'll tell him how slowly she unlatched the granary door. Or how quietly the bag slid across the snow as she dragged it, harnessed behind her. A low, soft scrape. Maybe someday he will be brave enough to ask if she was afraid. Maybe someday he will tell her that he followed her there and then they will talk like only a mother and son can.

Myron pushes back the too-long sleeves of his father's leather jacket, freeing his hands. His arms, all muscle and sinew, strain under the weight of the future. He hoists the bag on his shoulder and carries it to the cart.

Maria turns to Ivan, who is squirming to keep his bum from sliding off the narrow back edge. Soon he will need new pants. She places her hand on his chest to calm his sobbing heart. 'Hold on tight.'

She walks to the front of the cart, counting heads.

'My hotovi?' *Are we ready?*

The children nod their assent.

Myron picks up the reins to lead the horse. They watch their mother. The morning sun in their faces. Maria lifts the hem of her skirt and walks.

Myron rubs the horse's nose. His feet slide in his father's oversized boots. *Tch-tch-tch.* The cart lurches ahead.

The children sway to its roll, their eyes fixed on the greying house and the prairies unfolding between them.

Acknowledgements

I am indebted to many for the creation of this work:

Those who read my early, tentative scenes and drafts and responded with such enthusiasm: Carol Bruneau, Richard Cumyn, Gwen Davies, Stephen Kimber, Alice Kuipers and Daria Salamon.

The Writers' Federation of Nova Scotia Mentorship Program and the Sage Hill Writing Experience. Jane Buss who took me under her wing and was the first to cry. Sue Goyette for her mentorship and guiding light, who believed long before I dared to say the word 'novel.' Steven Galloway for challenging me not to look away when I was most afraid. Janice Kulyk Keefer for asking how. Heather Sangster and Olga Gardner Galvin, my copy editors, for making it better when I thought there was nothing more to find. Orysia Tracz for caring so deeply.

Though the characters and their stories are fictional, I tried to set their lives in a realistic framework anchored in historical fact. I could not have created their world without the Provincial Archives of Alberta, Alberta Justice Department, Government of Canada National Parole Board, and the Government of the Province of Alberta — Department of Lands and Mines.

I used photographs for inspiration and relied

on the incredible resources of virtual museums and photo galleries for my research: Glenbow Museum — Photographic Archives, The Great Depression of Canada, The American Experience Surviving the Dust Bowl, Alberta Depression Years, Saskatchewan's Heritage Multi-Media Gallery, Ukrainian Museum in New York City — Holodomor (The Great Famine) and the Holodomor Photographic Archives — Ukraine.

I learned from those who collected Ukrainian folklore, folktales and customs and shared them with those who had lost or forgotten them.

My family: Paul for the first spell check. Joanne for always being there. Shawn for all that he has taught me. Ron, Connie, and Christine for their blessing and sharing of all that is prairie. Uncle Marvin and Aunt Xan for family recipes. Baba whose stories I never had a chance to hear. Mom MacLeod for reading the characters as if they were alive. Mom Mitchell who never doubted. Dad where it all began.

Suzanne Brandreth, Sally Harding, Dean Cooke, and Mary Hu of The Cooke Agency for their unfailing quest to bring this book to the world. And especially Suzanne, who said yes.

My extraordinary trinity of editors who made it all shine and their creative teams who took such pride in every detail of their art. Nicole Winstanley of Penguin Canada for her passion, wisdom, and gentle, brilliant clarity. Arzu Tahsin of Weidenfeld & Nicolson, who asked for more light. Claire Wachtel, Jonathan Burnham, and Julia Novitch of Harper Collins US who trusted.

Nova Scotia Department of Tourism, Culture and Heritage — Culture Division for helping to keep food on the table and a roof over my head by investing in the writings of an East Coast Prairie girl.

Kino for teaching me the way of dogs.

And Alan

for everything.

We do hope that you have enjoyed reading
this large print book.

Did you know that all of our titles
are available for purchase?

We publish a wide range of high quality
large print books including:
Romances, Mysteries, Classics
General Fiction
Non Fiction and Westerns

Special interest titles available in
large print are:
The Little Oxford Dictionary
Music Book
Song Book
Hymn Book
Service Book

Also available from us courtesy of Oxford
University Press:
Young Readers' Dictionary
(large print edition)
Young Readers' Thesaurus
(large print edition)

For further information or a free
brochure, please contact us at:
Ulverscroft Large Print Books Ltd.,
The Green, Bradgate Road, Anstey,
Leicester, LE7 7FU, England.
Tel: (00 44) 0116 236 4325
Fax: (00 44) 0116 234 0205

THE BLASPHEMER

Nigel Farndale

On its way to the Galapagos Islands, a light aircraft crashes into the sea. Zoologist Daniel Kennedy is confronted with a stark Darwinian choice — should he save himself, or Nancy, the woman he loves? But how can one moment of betrayal ever be forgiven? And after he escapes the plane and swims for help, who is the elusive figure who guides him away from certain death? Back in London, Daniel thinks he finds the answer, and it is connected with what happened to his great-grandfather on the first horrific day of Passchendaele. But as the past collapses into the present, the fissures in his relationship with Nancy begin to show — until he's given a second chance to prove his courage and earn her forgiveness.

THE LONG SONG

Andrea Levy

Looking back to early 19th century Jamaica, this is a tale of the turbulent years of slavery and the early years of freedom that followed. July is a slave girl who lives upon a sugar plantation named Amity. She was there when the Baptist War raged in 1831, and she was also present when slavery was declared no more. From July's mama, Kitty, to her own son Thomas; from the people working the plantation land to the woman who owns it; July chronicles what befalls them all, and takes us on a journey through that time in the company of the people who lived it . . .

THE CONFESSIONS OF EDWARD DAY

Valerie Martin

In the seamy theatre world of 1970s New York, Edward Day is an ambitious young actor, whose life is altered forever by a weekend party on the New Jersey shore. He's saved from drowning by Guy Margate — a fellow actor with whom he shares an attraction to the beautiful Madeleine Delavergne. Forever after, in spooky and mordantly funny encounters, Edward is torn between his desire for Madeleine and indebtedness to Guy, his rival on stage and off. But as Edward moves closer to fulfilling Broadway dreams, Guy is driven to desperate measures. To the smell of grease paint and roar of audience applause the trio career towards a show-stopping finale.

A CHANGE IN ALTITUDE

Anita Shreve

'We're climbing Mount Kenya. Not this Saturday, but the next.' Patrick spoke of the climb without fanfare, as he might a party in two weeks' time. They were young, each twenty-eight. They had been in the country three months . . . When a British couple invites newly-wed Patrick and Margaret on a climbing expedition, they eagerly agree. But during their arduous ascent the unthinkable happens: in a reckless moment, an horrific accident occurs. In its aftermath, Margaret struggles to understand what took place on the mountain and how it has transformed her and her marriage, perhaps for ever.

THIS IS WHERE I LEAVE YOU

Jonathan Tropper

When Judd Foxman creeps into his house on his wife's birthday, he finds her in bed, having sex with his boss . . . Things get worse for Judd when the death of his father brings his entire family together for the first time in years. Conspicuously absent — Judd's wife, Jen, whose affair with his boss has become excruciatingly public. Judd joins his folks as they submit to their father's dying request: to spend seven days mourning together — in the same house — like a real family. As the week spins out of control, grudges resurface, secrets are revealed and old passions reawakened. Judd tries to make sense of the mess his life has become while trying not get sucked into the regressive dramas of his dysfunctional family . . .

THE CASTAWAYS

Elin Hilderbrand

From the outside, the close-knit circle of friends who call themselves 'the Castaways' share an idyllic lifestyle on Nantucket, blessed with money, children, beauty and love. But when Tess and Greg are killed in a tragic boating accident, it sends shockwaves through the rest of the group. As the friends grieve, the truth behind all their relationships gradually begins to emerge. And for the first time they are forced to ask the hardest of questions . . . Can you live without the person who made you whole? And how do you mourn for a secret lover and a relationship nobody knew existed?